Louise Fuller was once a tomb̶̶̶̶̶̶ always wanted to be the Princ̶̶̶̶̶ Now she enjoys creating heroines who aren't pretty push-overs but strong, believable women. Before writing for Mills & Boon she studied literature and philosophy at university, and then worked as a reporter on her local newspaper. She lives in Tunbridge Wells with her impossibly handsome husband Patrick and their six children.

Lorraine Hall is a part-time hermit and full-time writer. She was born with an old soul and her head in the clouds—which, it turns out, is the perfect combination for spending her days creating thunderous alpha heroes and the fierce, determined heroines who win their hearts. She lives in a potentially haunted house with her soulmate and a rumbustious band of hermits in training. When she's not writing romance, she's reading it.

DIAMOND DEMANDS

LOUISE FULLER

LORRAINE HALL

MILLS & BOON

First published in Great Britain 2024
by Mills & Boon, an imprint of HarperCollins*Publishers* Ltd,
1 London Bridge Street, London, SE1 9GF

www.harpercollins.co.uk

HarperCollins*Publishers*, Macken House, 39/40 Mayor Street Upper,
Dublin 1, D01 C9W8, Ireland

Diamond Demands © 2024 Harlequin Enterprises ULC

Reclaimed with a Ring © 2024 Louise Fuller

Italian's Stolen Wife © 2024 Lorraine Hall

ISBN: 978-0-263-32017-6

07/24

This book contains FSC™ certified paper
and other controlled sources to ensure responsible forest management.

For more information visit www.harpercollins.co.uk/green.

Printed and Bound in the UK using 100% Renewable Electricity
at CPI Group (UK) Ltd, Croydon, CR0 4YY

RECLAIMED WITH A RING

LOUISE FULLER

MILLS & BOON

CHAPTER ONE

DESPITE THE HEAT and the humidity there was a crowd of maybe fifty or sixty photographers waiting.

But not for him.

Trip Winslow tilted his face towards the tinted window of the limousine.

Nobody knew that he was coming. Incredibly, and despite the plethora of communication platforms available in the modern world, he had managed to stay incognito. All thanks to a phone call to Lazlo, the manager of the Diamond Club. It was Lazlo who had arranged the hot bath, wet shave, private jet, car and driver and security detail swiftly, quietly and with the same unshakeable calm that he did everything. It was what made him invaluable to the ten richest people in the world who made up the small, elite membership of the club.

But Trip's disappearance was still the story of the hour, the year, maybe even the decade. After all, how many times did one of the wealthiest people on the planet just vanish into thin air?

So he'd anticipated that the paparazzi and news teams would be here in New York. His blue gaze moved assessingly over the huddle of mostly men prowling the steps up to the iconic gleaming glass and steel Winslow Building.

And yet it still felt like an ambush.

A ripple of panic skimmed over his skin, and for a moment he was back in the jungle, his heart pounding as he watched different men inch towards where he was pressed against a tree, their eyes narrowed, guns high against their chests like in the video games he had played incessantly as a teenager.

Only these gunmen were real. So were their bullets.

'Do you want me to go round the back, Mr Winslow? Or I can call Security. Get an extra team out to block off the road.'

For a fraction of a second, he didn't respond to the driver's question, not least because even now, ten months after his father's death, he was still struggling to remember that he was 'that' Mr Winslow. For him, the title would always belong to his father, Henry Winslow II. Of course, Trip's older brother, Charlie, wouldn't have given it a second thought.

His shoulders stiffened. In many ways, he'd felt as though he hardly knew his brother. And now he never would because Charlie was dead. Killed three years ago in a plane crash along with their mother.

Which left Trip.

The spare. The runner-up who had won by default.

Not that he hadn't proven himself worthy of being CEO. But Charlie had always been destined to take over the business. Partly because he was twelve years older, but also because their father had raised him from birth to be his heir so that he looked and acted the part. Most important of all, Charlie was the type to defer to their father.

Unlike Trip.

He had been at odds with Henry Winslow II as far back as he could remember. Which probably explained why he had ended up being called Trip. That way, at least, his father could distance himself from the stubborn son who shared his name but rarely his opinions.

He glanced up, his gaze moving past the driver's inquiring eyes to meet his own in the rear-view mirror. They were the exact same blue as his father's. The only thing they had in common.

Like Charlie, his father was academically consistent, focused, disciplined, whereas he had oscillated between boredom and brilliance.

He had got into Harvard, like his father and Charlie, but had dropped out to set up a business that had failed in its first year. He'd learned from his mistakes though and his second venture was widely touted as a unicorn by the business media, reaching a billion-dollar valuation in its first year.

He had kept his stake and would probably have set up another business if his success hadn't caught the eye of his father. To his astonishment, Henry had reached out to him, invited him to take over the Far East division in Hong Kong.

His father hadn't gambled, had been notoriously risk averse, so Trip had known that he was being tested and that knowledge had given him a sense of purpose. He had effortlessly arrowed in on the failing areas of the business and each of those sectors had then outperformed themselves under his leadership.

His father had grudgingly admitted that he had done well, and, shortly before Charlie's death, Trip had been allowed to go to London to head up the European division. There, his strokes of creative genius had attracted the attention of the business press and given Winslow Inc its most profitable year on record. But it had never been enough as far as his father was concerned.

Because mistakes, failures, missteps had been unacceptable to Henry Winslow II. A decorated naval officer who had taken over his father's modest construction firm and turned it into the multinational conglomerate it was today. A private, committed family man whose one act of impulsiveness had led to a forty-two-year-long marriage that had ended only by his wife's tragic death.

Trip gritted his teeth. Except it turned out his father hadn't been that committed after all.

His spine tensed as he replayed the moment when he'd found the letters among his father's things. Letters from a woman named Kerry. Letters filled with unfiltered declarations of need and passion.

I am blind without you...being with you will restore my sight, my love...

The shock had sent Trip spinning off course to Ecuador, to the churning white waters of the Rio Upano, and from there into the rainforest and imprisonment at the hands of a passing drugs cartel.

He stared through the window, his gaze snagging on a couple weaving between the stationary cars. The tall grey-haired man was holding the hand of the woman beside him. His wife? Before Ecuador he would have made this assumption unthinkingly. Now, though, he could see only other possibilities.

His fingers clutched the upholstered armrest. Behind closed doors there had always been a distance between his parents so in some ways his father's infidelity should not have been that much of a surprise. But Henry Winslow II had led a note-perfect life, famously intolerant and unforgiving of failure in others, particularly in his youngest son. And yet, all along, he had been breaking the rules, lying, cheating, deceiving…

Was it any surprise Trip's world had tilted on its axis when he'd found out the truth?

'Mr Winslow?'

The driver's voice bumped into his thoughts and he dragged his gaze back to the photographers. Like all paparazzi, they looked hungry and determined. 'Let's go in the front.' He gestured to the car gliding to a halt in front of them. 'Security can handle them.'

It was the opposite of what his father would have done. Or maybe it wasn't. Having read those letters from his father's mistress, he wasn't sure he even knew who Henry Winslow II was any more.

As the driver opened the door, the heat hit him like a wall but he barely had time to register it before the photographers turned and saw him.

Their mouths collectively dropped open and there was a tiny suspension of air and noise as if the whole city were taken aback by his sudden appearance.

But then, it wasn't often someone came back from the dead.

'It's him,' he heard someone shout. 'It's Trip!'

And then, like fire ants sensing a juicy meal, they began swarming towards the car.

'Mr Winslow, is it true you were shot?'

'Did you lose your memory, Trip?'

'Were you hiding or lost?'

'Over here, over here, Mr Winslow—'

He was used to press attention, had grown up playing hide and seek with the paparazzi, but as the voice recorders and cameras rose like a wave he felt his heartbeat accelerate.

But the security detail was good and they held back the heaving, baying pack so he could make his way up the flight of steps into the office.

It was part of his father's world-conquering ethos that nature didn't intrude on the day-to-day running of his business. It didn't matter if New York was melting or buried under three feet of snow, the building was always the same unobtrusive, ambient temperature. And yet today the gleaming marble and wood panelled foyer felt somehow different. Cooler, familiar and yet altered in a way he couldn't quite put his finger on.

He felt different too. Which was no doubt why everyone was looking at him as if they'd seen a ghost. But then in a way they had.

'Mr Winslow.' The receptionist—Carole? Was that her name?—got to her feet, her eyes wide and stunned. Her colleague simply stared at him, slack-jawed.

'You're back. You're here—' Carole was blinking at him as if she had malfunctioned.

'Yes, I am.' He gave her a quick, dazzling smile that snapped off as he jerked his head towards the ceiling. 'Are they in?'

By 'they', he meant the C-suite and it was a rhetorical question. They were paid to be here, to manage the ship while he was away, so where else would they be?

'Yes, Mr Mason is holding an extraordinary meeting of the board this morning.'

'Good. Then let me go make sure it really is *extra*ordinary.'

He felt rather than saw her reach for the phone as he walked towards the lifts. But that was okay. It would give them time to roll out the red carpet. Hail, the conquering hero, he thought, stepping into the elevator.

As it rose upwards, he shivered. Was it him, or was the air in the building growing colder the higher they went? But that question stayed unanswered as the lift doors opened and Mason Cooper, Winslow's CFO and Trip's godfather, strode towards him, arms outstretched.

'Trip—'

He grunted as the older man pulled him into a bear hug. Mason was a firm believer in tough love and over the years he had often taken an unwilling Trip aside for pep talks. Trip felt a sudden urge to lean into the older man.

'I don't understand.' Mason was patting his shoulders and arms as if to prove to himself that Trip was not a figment of his imagination. 'How did you get here? How are you? What happened? Where have you been?'

'I can fill you in another time.' He clapped Mason on the back to stop the spate of questions that he had no intention of answering. 'It's a long and convoluted story and right now I just want things to get back to normal.' The trouble was he no longer knew what that was, Trip thought, his gaze snagging on his father's portrait as they walked past the boardroom.

'Of course you do.' Mason nodded. 'Let's go to your office.'

'It's okay, I know the way,' he said irritably as his CFO put a hand on his shoulder to guide him. 'I wasn't away that long.'

Mason lifted an eyebrow. 'I'd say five weeks alone in an Ecuadorian jungle is quite long enough.'

It had felt like five years, Trip thought. In places, the canopy of leaves had been so dense that night and day had often felt interchangeable, never-ending and he would have to stop moving or risk tripping over the treacherous, twisting branches and invisible dips in the forest floor.

And always there had been that pattering sound of water, dripping against the vegetation.

But that had been only a part of it. Some of the time, he would probably never know exactly how long for certain, there had been simply the absolute darkness of the blindfold and the ropes biting into his wrists.

He had never felt so alone, so helpless, not even when he was a child, and it started to become obvious to him that he experienced the world in a different way from the rest of his family.

But it was not in his nature to show weakness or reveal vulnerability, particularly here. Here, he was the boss, the man in charge. He was not just Mr Winslow, he was *the* Mr Winslow, and, now that he was back, he was going to make sure that that name was associated with him for ever, and not with his grandfather or father.

As he dropped down into the seat behind his desk, there was a knock at the door and Conrad Stiles, the chief operating officer, and Ron Maidman, the head of marketing, walked into the office, their feet faltering, faces freezing into masks of shock and disbelief as they saw him. He wasn't as close to them as he was Mason but they both shook his hand and clapped him on the shoulder.

'I can't believe you're really here.' Maidman was shaking his head. 'I thought I was hallucinating. What happened out there? Are you okay? Are you hurt?'

'Another time, Ron. Like I said to Mason, I just want to get back behind the wheel, so why don't you take a seat and talk me through what's been happening?'

Was it his imagination or did all their faces stiffen?

Mason nodded. 'Of course, of course. Obviously, in your absence, we had to make some decisions.'

Trip stared across the desk at the three men sitting opposite him. 'I'm sure you took care of everything,' he said softly. He couldn't quite keep the edge of bitterness out of his voice. His father might have formally named him his successor, but he'd made it clear that he expected his son to draw on the experience and expertise of his C-suite.

He'd been grateful for their advice and support in the immediate aftermath of his father's death, but things were different now. Okay, he'd been a little off his game at the start, but he'd been running the business for ten months without a hiccup.

'Now I'm back, and, in light of recent events, I want to make a few changes. You see, I had a lot of time to think in the jungle and I have a few ideas that I want to set in motion.'

Mason nodded. 'And obviously we will be more than happy to discuss that but right now you should be at home, resting. You've had a traumatic experience—'

'The doctor said I was fine, and I am,' he said impatiently. There was a bluebottle crashing against the glass, buzzing around the edges of the window frame as it tried to find an opening, and for a moment he stared at it, body tensing as he remembered his own equally frantic attempts to push through the towering vegetation.

'I don't want to rest. What I need is to get back to work.'

Conrad cleared his throat. 'And you will, but, as you pointed out, we need to bring you up to speed first. Clarify a few things. In light of recent events,' he added, his eyes meeting Trip's.

'Meaning?' Trip lounged back in his chair, trying to slow his heartbeat. The script he'd prepared in his head in the car was already starting to unravel.

'Trip—you've been missing for weeks. We didn't know where you were, if you were even alive—'

'You make it sound as though I planned for that to happen.' His eyes narrowed. 'I can promise you I didn't. I certainly didn't expect to cross paths with a cartel. Or be taken prisoner.'

'Is that what happened?' Mason looked shocked. 'My God, Trip, I don't know what to say—'

Trip gazed past him at the heat-soaked city skyline. That was just the start of it. But he didn't want to think about what followed. Not here, not now, not in front of these men. His breath caught in his chest. Not when he didn't know how he would react.

'Did they hurt you?'

'I'm fine.'

He stretched out his legs and pressed his spine against the leather upholstery. It wasn't a complete lie. He had been seen by a doctor in Ecuador shortly after he'd stumbled out of the jungle and, aside from a couple of nasty cuts and a mild case of dehydration, he was physically fine.

But he was sleeping badly, waking in darkness and sweat, cold with a fear that he could only shift by opening his eyes and getting out of bed so that he could feel the carpet beneath his feet. Because that was the only way he could convince himself that he had been dreaming.

'I'm glad to hear it.' Ron hesitated. 'We all are, obviously—' he gave Trip a nervous smile '—and we did everything we could to help find you from this end, but part of the problem was that we didn't know where you were.'

Trip frowned. 'I don't need permission to take a vacation, Ron. I'm the CEO.'

His head of marketing flushed and there was a small pause as the three older men glanced furtively at one another. 'Not permission, no, but it would have been helpful to know where you were,' Mason said after a moment.

Conrad frowned. 'We thought you were dead.'

Trip stared at him steadily, a ghost of a smile playing around his hard mouth. 'Sorry to disappoint.'

Mason shook his head. 'That's not fair, Trip—'

'No, what's not fair is you guys giving me a hard time for something that was out of my control. But it's in the past now and I'm here, so no harm, no foul.'

He was done explaining himself.

'No harm.' Mason was staring at him as if he'd grown an extra head. 'You were a prisoner of a drug cartel!'

'And I got away. Without a scratch.' That was true… ish but any detail would only serve to undermine his argument.

'And we're pleased to hear that.' Ron frowned. 'Unfortunately the business wasn't so lucky. The share prices plummeted—'

'I heard,' he cut across the older man. 'And now they've gone back up. Gone higher, in fact.'

Mason was shaking his head. 'That's not how your father did business. It's not how we do business.'

'There is no we,' he said coldly. 'This is *my* business. I'm the CEO.'

'But that can only stay true if you are the best person for the job,' Mason said, his eyes finding Trip's. 'The position of CEO is not allocated simply on the basis of surname or bloodline.'

'Is that right?' Trip said softly.

There was a long, pulsing silence. Finally, Mason cleared his throat. 'Look, Trip. Your father wanted you to take over the business, but he also gave us the option to intervene at our discretion.'

Yes, because he had never truly considered his youngest son as anything other than a spare, Trip thought, letting his gaze move across the distant skyline. He was too impulsive, too headstrong ever to see eye to eye with his father, but after Charlie's death Henry had had no alternative but to leave him the company.

Suddenly and fiercely, Trip wanted all three of them out of his office.

'You can't fire me.'

Mason gave him a small, stiff smile. 'You're not being fired, Trip. But we answer to the shareholders. As do you.'

Pushing back from his desk, Trip stood. 'Exactly, and in case you've forgotten I'm not just the CEO, I'm the majority shareholder.'

'Yes, you are.' The older man nodded. 'But as was explained to you when you took over, some of those shares are held in a trust of which we are the trustees. We have the power to use those shares to remove any CEO temporarily or permanently whose actions are damaging to the interests of the shareholders. And what happened in Ecuador...what could have happened...has raised issues. Shareholders like stability.'

Trip held his gaze. 'I do things my way. If they don't like it—'

'They don't, Trip. That's the point. They want to see that you are serious about running the business and, I'm afraid, currently your behaviour is not speaking to that.'

'My behaviour—?'

He felt a rush of fury. What about his father's behaviour? Had anyone held him to account for having a long-term mistress? As his eyes flicked across the other men's faces, he felt a slithering panic weave through his chest. Had his father confided in them? Did they know who

Kerry was? But he couldn't bring himself to ask. To ask the question would give the relationship a validity it didn't deserve.

'They—*we*—need a CEO who is stable and mature and focused.'

'I am all of those things— What?' The three men were shaking their heads. He gritted his teeth.

Mason sighed. 'You have the makings of a great business leader but you are impulsive, reckless even. Look at how you just went off to Ecuador on a whim—'

Not a whim, he thought, his chest clamping tight so that it was suddenly hard to breathe. It had been an imperative. He had felt as if he were suffocating in New York, smothered by the weight of his father's hypocrisy.

'And your private life is chaotic. Your friends make headlines for all the wrong reasons. Maybe if you had a steady girlfriend to anchor you…but according to the Internet you spend your free time running around the city bedding every woman you meet.'

His eyes narrowed. 'I'm not running around the city bedding every woman I meet. As a matter of fact, I'm engaged.'

The words were out of his mouth before he'd even realised what he was about to say and a stunned, fascinated silence spread across the room, blanketing all other sound. The other men looked, if anything, more shocked than before. As if it was easier to believe he had come back from the dead than that he was engaged.

Ron Maidman recovered first. '*Engaged!* To whom?'

Trip blinked. *Good question*, he thought.

Marriage had always been one of those things he thought about in an abstract way. It felt inevitable, in that most people tried it once so he imagined he would too. But the path there was hazy and uncharted. And besides, he had no real understanding of what marriage meant. His parents were often held up as an example of a happy, devoted couple, but that was just the public facade. In private their relationship had been more two people coexisting than sharing lives.

He felt the tractor-beam force of the other men's combined gaze and, setting his face back to blank, he reached for the name of the most stable, mature, focused woman he could think of. A name that would shut down his tormentors and give him back the upper hand.

'To Lily. Lily Dempsey.'

Now the astonishment in the room rose to such almost comic levels that he would have laughed. Except he didn't feel like laughing.

Lily Dempsey. With her Mona Lisa smile and cool, dismissive grey eyes.

She was the dictionary definition of stable, mature and focused. Pretty much an 'anchor' in human form.

Unfortunately, she also hated him.

To be fair, he wasn't her biggest fan either. Not for any specific reason. They just always seemed to clash, although that only happened when she acknowledged his existence. Often she seemed to look straight through him. And that was such a unique and uniquely irritating experience that he had found himself deliberately crossing her path, only to regret it when she spoke to him in the cool, withering tone that made it clear she found his charms skin-deep.

Which made the fact that they had been secretly sleeping together in the two months before he had gone to Ecuador not just incomprehensible but a mystery that was unsolvable.

It was just sex, of course. He'd never planned on taking it any further than that one night, but then they had bumped into one another at another charity event and it had been just the same. And it had kept happening and suddenly it had been happening for a month, then another.

And he still didn't understand why.

The phrase chalk and cheese could have been invented for them, but in bed they were like flames merging and curling around one another. His body tensed, groin hardening so that he had to blank his mind to the memory of her body wrapped around his.

'You're engaged to Lily Dempsey?'

He stared across the room at Mason's frowning face.

No, he thought.

'Yes,' he lied. 'We've been seeing each other for a couple of months, but she wanted to keep it on the down-low because of her father.'

That at least was true. Lily had been insistent that they keep the relationship quiet, presumably because she didn't want to cause any distracting noise around her father's career as a senator, and Trip hadn't cared one way or the other. There were very few people whose opinion mattered to him. Nor did he feel the need to explain himself to anyone.

Which was lucky, because he couldn't rationalise his attraction to Lily. It didn't make sense. They didn't make sense.

Which was why he'd ended things. Except that wasn't true either. The reason he'd ended it was because of those damned letters.

Reading through, he'd felt conned, duped, betrayed,

and he'd wanted to smash things. In that moment, there had been just too much overlap between the passion and secrecy of his father's affair and his heated, clandestine encounters with Lily, and he'd been angry and she'd been there and something had snapped inside him.

Ron got to his feet. 'Congratulations, Trip. That's wonderful news.'

He held out his hand, and Trip shook it mechanically.

'I'm so pleased for you,' Mason said quietly. 'Lily is a wonderful woman, and I know how much your father enjoyed working with her.'

'Congratulations.' Conrad joined the other two smiling men to take Trip's hand. 'But what are you doing here?' His smile stiffened. 'She does know you're back?'

No, not yet, he thought. Nor did she know they were engaged, but that wouldn't be a problem.

Would it?

He had a sudden, sharp flashback to their last meeting at her apartment. He hadn't quite known how she would react but, true to form, she had confounded him. 'It was just a fling,' she'd said. She wouldn't pine away if he never came back.

For some reason, ego probably, her words had stung more than they should, enough to echo inside his head during the weeks of his incarceration. Now he had to hope she would be so swept away by his sudden reappearance that she would be willing to agree to anything. After all, what woman wouldn't want to marry one of the ten richest men on the planet?

'Yes, of course. But she wanted me to come in, in person, to reassure you,' he said quickly, lying again.

'Which is why she's such an excellent choice.' Mason glanced over at the other two men, clearly pleased. 'But you've been through so much, Trip. What you need is some time and space to process everything that's happened and the best person to help you do that is Lily. You should be with her.'

He nodded slowly. 'You're right. I should. In fact, I might just head off there now.'

Not to process what had happened, he thought as he stalked past yet more astonished employees back towards the elevator. But because he needed to catch Lily and convince her to be his fiancée before she heard about their supposed engagement from a third party and blew the whole thing apart.

'So are you thinking a Kingston or an Empire swag?'

Gazing at the swatches of fabric, Lily Jane Dempsey frowned. She had no idea what she was thinking. Her current curtains were perfectly fine. Perfect, in fact, she thought, glancing over at the draping folds of cream silk. So why was she bothering to change them? Why was she here, talking about swag options with her mother's interior designer, Samantha?

Her hand moved to her throat, to the pulse beating against the smooth skin like a moth trapped in a jar, feeling, not her fingers, but his mouth.

Trip's mouth.

The same mouth that had kissed her to the edge of reason as she'd arched beneath him in the bedroom upstairs, and then told her that he was going to Ecuador.

He was the reason she had decided to change her curtains.

Because she couldn't change the past, couldn't take back the last words she'd spoken to him, and she had needed something to take her mind off the fact that he was gone and that she was partly responsible because she had told him to get out of her sight, to go to Ecuador and not come back.

And he hadn't. He had disappeared into the rainforest and, despite the various search teams that had been sent to look for him, he hadn't been found, and after five weeks he was not just missing but presumed dead.

Only it wasn't just guilt she felt. Part of her hated him for disappearing like that. Sometimes her fury made it impossible to sleep and then she would pace the apartment, imagining his return and feeling almost giddy with relief that he was alive.

Her hands clenched. But only because she would have a chance to kill him or at least slap his handsome face for being such a selfish, thoughtless idiot. Because that hurt—to think that she would never see those glittering blue eyes again. And when she thought about that, about a world where Trip didn't exist, she had to distract herself with work or by helping her mother on her various committees. Or by changing her curtains.

But it was hard to distract herself, because she had known Trip her whole life. They had grown up in the same social circles. Their parents had been on first-name terms.

Their relationship had been a little more frosty.

Or it had been when he'd actually noticed that she was there. Which he hadn't very often because he was all blue eyes and smooth golden skin and tawny-coloured hair falling across his forehead, and that smile, whereas she—

Her eyes moved to the mirror above the fireplace and she felt the familiar twinge of disappointment.

She'd often wondered why her parents had chosen to call her Lily first and Jane second. Lily conjured up flawless creamy petals and a seductive scent and she was neither flawless nor seductive. She was plain, like her middle name.

It wasn't a humblebrag. It was just the facts. Her hair was mousey and frizzy—although she had learned how to tame it now—her eyes were grey and she had a small bump on her nose that was absent from both her patrician-faced parents. Body wise, she was slim and her legs were long. Too long. Long enough to earn the nickname 'daddy-long-legs'.

She didn't light up a room as Trip did. Mostly she was invisible.

Then suddenly three months ago, without warning, without understanding why, they had ended up in bed. And it had been intoxicating and terrifying in equal measure, not least because it was pure happenstance.

If his father, Henry, hadn't set up the Alessandra Winslow Endowment for Music in memory of his wife, they might have simply remained as occasional sparring partners. But after Henry's death, Trip had reluctantly taken his father's place and suddenly he was there in her life, pulsing with heat and energy like a meteorite, lighting up the world, trailing a promise of something that she had never allowed herself to imagine because it didn't happen to women who looked like her.

She had let down her guard.

And there was no excuse. Not after what had happened the last time with Cameron, when her neediness and longing to be liked had blinded her to what was hiding in plain sight and ultimately put her brother in harm's way.

Then again, she was only human, and Trip Winslow was the most beautiful man she had ever known. In a crowded room and at a distance, the flawless symmetry of his features and blatant masculinity made him conspicuous. But up close his beauty was astonishing, mesmerising.

Nothing could have prepared her for how it felt to sit opposite him and just gaze and gaze. And every time his gaze had met hers, it had felt like a caress. And that had shocked her, scared her, angered her. How could you be so attracted to someone when you disliked them so much? It defied the laws of attraction.

Feeling Samantha's gaze on her face, she realised that she had no idea how much time had passed since the woman had asked her about her curtains, or how to reply.

'The Kingston,' she said quickly.

'I was hoping you'd say that.' Samantha gave her an approving smile. 'This room demands drama and a Kingston always adds that little va-va-voom. And what about the colour? Are you sure about switching from the blue to the green?' she asked casually.

Lily gritted her teeth. Her mother loved neutrals, but Lily had wanted a change from creams and whites, and blue, the right, flattering, timeless shade of blue, was Laura's compromise. But Lily liked the green and, for once, she was going to put her foot down.

'Absolutely,' she said firmly.

There was a quivering silence as Samantha held her gaze a moment too long and then the designer smiled stiffly and glanced down at her tablet. 'Now, I know we haven't discussed the bathroom blinds, but your mother did ask me to take a quick peek—'

It was another hour before Samantha left.

Flopping down on the sofa in a way that would have made her mother wince, Lily picked up one of the magazines from the coffee table and opened it at a random page, and then wished she hadn't as she glanced down to find Trip's out-of-this-world face staring up at her.

She felt a spasm of pain around her heart.

It had been weeks now since he'd gone missing. Five weeks and three days. There had been a lot of supposition about what had happened in Ecuador, but few facts had emerged from the rainforest. The one that had stuck in her mind was the discovery of the Jeep he'd been driving. Watching the news, she had stared at the bullet holes in the bonnet and doors, feeling devastated, then angry, then stricken with guilt.

The buzzer to her door sounded and she groaned softly. That would be her mother.

Laura Dempsey had been in charge of the original decor of the flat and Lily had fully expected her to be in charge of this revamp, but then her mother had called to say she had double-booked.

Lily had been slightly relieved, then felt guilty for feeling that way. Now she wondered why, because of course her mother would have 'asked' Samantha to call her the moment she left the apartment. No doubt the designer had let slip that Lily had chosen the green drapes, not the blue, and so here was Laura all ready to right the wrong—

Sighing, she made her way to the front door and jerked it open. 'I know you're better at all this than me, but I know what I w-want—'

She stuttered into silence. For a moment the apartment behind her seemed to fold in on itself as if some vast, invisible explosion had happened.

It wasn't her mother. It was Trip. Lean, muscular and as shockingly beautiful as ever, he leaned against the door frame, one thick, dark eyebrow arched, his astonishing mouth curved into a shape that made her heart relocate to her throat.

'Good to know,' he said in that familiar, deep Transatlantic drawl. 'Because so do I.'

CHAPTER TWO

LILY COULDN'T MOVE. She wanted to, but she felt winded and dizzy.

He was alive. *He was alive.*

She lifted her hand, wanting, needing to touch him, to prove that he was real, then pressed it against her throat, to where her pulse was pounding out of time.

'How? When?' Her voice was barely a breath. 'I thought you were—' Lost. Dead. Gone for ever. She couldn't say the words out loud.

He shrugged. 'Let's just say I got unavoidably delayed.'

When she didn't respond, his forehead creased infinitesimally and he fished out his phone and swiped across the screen.

She stared down at the picture. Trip was striding up the steps in front of the Winslow Building just as if it were any other day. Words jumped out at her from the accompanying story. Captive. Cartel. Escape.

Her mind was a bumper car, jolting back and forth and side to side as questions slammed into each other. 'Is this true?' she managed finally.

'It's a version of the truth. The kind that sells papers.'

It was too much, him being here. The force of him, being so alive and real, his body filling the doorway, broad-chested and taller than in her memory, those arresting blue eyes and lips that she knew could send ripples of heat rolling through her like wildfire. The shock of him and the chaotic emotions provoked by his presence filled her head, her chest. That was why she couldn't breathe, she told herself. Why her body felt as if it were coming apart at the seams, why she felt as if it belonged to someone else.

'Why are you here?' she said hoarsely.

'I wanted to see you. To let you know that I was back, in person. I didn't want you to hear it from the news.'

'Well, now I've heard—' Relief and other nameless feelings she couldn't, wouldn't acknowledge were swept away by an anger she had never felt before and she tried to shut the door but he wedged his foot in it as they did in old black and white films.

'What are you doing?' she snapped.

'We need to talk.'

'By "we" you mean you, because I have nothing to say to you.' She frowned. 'Oh, actually, yes, I do. It's goodbye.'

She pushed against the door, but he held it open easily.

'I'm happy to do the talking. Come on, Lily. I've just come back from the dead.' The curl to his mouth made her feel off balance. 'Surely you can give me five minutes.'

'Fine. You have five minutes and then you will leave.'

She let go of the door and he shrugged away from the frame and strolled past her.

Her breath was running wild in her chest.

Her eyes glanced over his superbly tailored and no doubt paralyzingly expensive dark suit and white shirt, over the scratches and his slightly too long hair that gave him the untamed air of a Hollywood action hero.

The stupidity of their mismatched relationship made her stomach clench.

'I must say you don't seem very pleased to see me,' he

said, stopping in the middle of the sitting room and turning to face her.

Her heart lurched. Pleased didn't exactly cover the vortex of emotions churning inside her.

'I'm glad you're safe.' She spoke to a point slightly above his left shoulder but her peripheral vision was greedily filling in the details so that she knew he was staring at her with those intensely blue eyes, and that his glossy brown hair was falling across his face.

'That's it?' He moved towards her and she had to dig her heels into the cream carpet to stop herself from stepping backwards. 'It's a little underwhelming, wouldn't you say?'

There was a mocking note in his voice and quite suddenly she was furious again. How could he joke about any of this?

'What were you expecting? A ticker-tape parade?' She spoke briskly. Oh, why had she agreed to let him in? She had prayed for him to be alive but now that he was, now that he was here, it was making her head spin.

'The mayor called on my way over here and offered, but I said no,' he said in that casual drawl that tugged at each of her nerve endings separately. 'I didn't want any fuss made. Not from him, anyway. But you...' He paused, his eyes locking with hers. 'I was hoping you might be a little more *expressive*. I mean, we were going out—'

It was a trick, a hook, and he was taunting her to take the bait. She knew that and yet she still couldn't stop her head from snapping round.

'We never went out.'

His eyes were clear and intensely blue. 'No, you're right. We always stayed in.'

The trap slammed shut. A prickling heat skated across her skin and she felt her body tighten. Everywhere. Her heart was pounding as if she were running hard, and that was what she should be doing. Running as fast and as far as she could from this beautiful, dangerous man.

He made her want things, and she knew all too well how wanting could make you lose sight of what mattered. She had done so before with Cameron and there had been horrific, far-reaching consequences. But it had been different with Trip. They weren't friends. They hadn't talked or gone out on dates. There had been no promises made, no expectations, and she had liked that he wasn't hers to lose. The fact that they had been using each other for sex was a kind of equality she'd found thrilling in some way.

And yet it had hurt more than it should when he'd ended things. And now that he was here, standing in front of her, it hurt to look at him, to remember what they'd had.

'To be honest what happened between us was so brief it kind of slipped my mind,' she said coolly.

He paused, just for a second. 'Then maybe it's time I jogged your memory.'

She felt suddenly unsteady on her feet, like a boxer on the ropes. Pressing her nails into her palms, she forced herself to hold his gaze. 'I'm not a fan of retrospectives. Personally, I find it better to live in the present.'

He was facing the window and in the sunlight through the glass his pupils were almost invisible, so that she felt as though she were drowning in the blue of his irises.

'I couldn't agree more,' he said softly. 'So here I am, ready to engage.'

She stared at him in confusion and felt a shiver of apprehension ripple down her spine. 'With what? You came to tell me you were back, and you have, so what else is there?'

'I told you. I want to talk.' There was a split second

of silence, and then he said softly, 'About you and me. About us.'

The word reverberated around the room as she shook her head. 'There is no us.' There were just darkness and bodies and warm breath and damp skin.

The sudden force of her heartbeat made her reach out and grip the back of an armchair.

'Not currently,' he said after a moment. 'But there could be. I want there to be.'

The bluntness of that statement made her feel hot inside, scalded almost. She felt her face grow warm and she knew that she was blushing.

'And why would you want that?' she said stiffly, hating him, but hating herself more for the shiver that ran over her skin.

He stared down at her, that mouth of his curving up. 'Because we have a connection.'

That was one word for it. For a moment she saw herself on the bed upstairs, breathless with wanting him, arms stretched out above her head, wrists in his hand, her body arching to meet his, tilting her hips up, driving herself against him. And his face above her, eyes dark and bright with a heat that seemed to pour straight into her.

'You're unbelievable.' She took an unsteady step backwards, anger blotting out the memory of their 'connection'. 'Seriously? Did you come all the way over here because you thought I might have sex with you? Because that isn't going to happen.' It shouldn't have happened before.

She knew it then. Knew that she was playing with fire. Although truthfully it had felt more as if she were dancing around the mouth of an active volcano, because even when he wasn't the focus of an international search and rescue, Trip made headlines. All those weeks playing hide and seek with the paparazzi had been part of the thrill of it, but if anyone had caught them, then what?

She shivered. And it would all be so much worse now.

Shaking her head, she met his gaze. 'Look, what we had worked for a few months, but it ended and frankly I'm done sneaking around like some grounded teenager. Next time I decide to see someone it will be out in the open, public. Real.'

'Real?' He frowned. 'You mean love?'

Did she? Like most people, she hoped love might happen one day. That someone would love and cherish and honour her. But given that the only time she'd imagined herself in love, she had been humiliated and deceived and made to feel like a fool, it was more an ideal right now than a likelihood.

It certainly wasn't going to happen with Trip. There were just too many differences between them. She had ignored that with Cameron and her brother was still paying the price.

Once bitten, twice shy.

Not bitten…mauled, she thought, throat tightening as she heard Cameron's voice. *Why would any man settle for you?*

Blanking her mind, she lifted her chin. 'Yes, I suppose so.'

Unsurprisingly Trip looked baffled, but then it seemed unlikely that love, the true, everlasting kind, the sort that involved promises to be kept and commitments to be honoured, the 'growing old and sick together' variety, came high on his agenda.

'Or something like it.' She felt suddenly self-conscious. Why was she even talking about love with Trip Winslow?

This was a man who had turned up on her doorstep hoping for an afternoon of sex without strings.

'Something like it,' he repeated slowly. 'And what would it look like, that something?'

'I don't know.' She glared at him. 'Does it matter?'

'It might. You see, in answer to your question, no, I didn't come all the way over here because I thought you might have sex with me.' He gave her a long, steady look, as if he was trying to see beneath her skin.

'I came here to ask you to marry me.'

If he'd asked her to fly to the moon with him, she couldn't have been more shocked. For a moment, she just stared at him, and then she gave a small, brittle laugh.

'You think I'm joking?' His eyes had narrowed.

'Yes, of course. Obviously.' Abruptly she sobered up. 'Although it's not a very funny joke.'

'It's not a joke at all. I want you to marry me.'

'Have you lost your mind?' She held up her hand as he opened his mouth to reply. 'You don't need to answer that. Clearly you have. Why else would you be asking me to be your wife?'

'Because I have a problem,' he said in that smooth way of his, all silk on the surface, but steel beneath. 'I want it to go away and I think you can help make that happen. Just in the short term.'

'By marrying you?' She met his gaze. 'Sorry to burst your bubble, but from where I'm standing that sounds more like a problem than a solution.'

For a moment he didn't answer. Instead, he leaned forward and picked up the swatch of blue silk that she'd been considering for the curtains.

'I like this colour,' he said softly. It was almost an exact match for his eyes, and she felt her face grow warm as he rubbed it between his fingers. Remembering the urgent press of his hands on her and the dark hunger in his eyes, she felt a sharp heat shoot through her and, terrified that he would see it on her face, she snatched the swatch from his hand.

'Well, I don't. I prefer the green, and stop pretending you care about my curtains. Or me. All we did was have sex—'

'We did.' His gaze dropped to where she could feel her pulse beating in her throat.

Ignoring the shiver of something hot and liquid trembling across her skin, Lily glared at him. 'Sex isn't a reason to get married. Thank you, but no, I don't want to marry you.'

There was a short silence and then he turned towards her, and she felt a current of awareness spill over her skin. She was over him in every way it was possible to be over a man. Unfortunately, her body didn't appear to have received that memo.

'I need this.'

His voice sounded taut. There was anger there but frustration too, and pain. 'You see, Winslow is my business. It's my name above the door. I'm the majority shareholder, but some of my shares are held in a trust and if the trustees think that the actions of the CEO are incompatible with or detrimental to the effective running of the business, then they can remove him or her.'

She gave a humourless laugh.

'You mean for some baffling reason they would have preferred that the man in charge hadn't got himself held prisoner by a drug cartel in an Ecuadorian rainforest?' She shook her head. 'How unreasonable of them.'

His gaze didn't flicker but she saw a dangerous glint

in his blue eyes. 'I went to Ecuador to go white water rafting.'

A pulse of anger beat across her skin. 'On some of the most dangerous rapids in the world, so you knew there was a possibility you might drown. You just hadn't factored in getting shot at or being held captive or getting lost in a rainforest.' She felt a stab of pain, imagining his beautiful eyes staring sightlessly up at the sky. How dared he risk his life for some stupid momentary thrill? Tears pricked behind her eyes, and she blinked them away, stonewalling the feeling as she watched his face harden.

'I don't have a death wish so, no, I wasn't thinking I might drown. I like the challenge, the purpose. There's a clarity in the moment—'

'In the moment?' She cut across him. 'And what about the aftermath? Everyone thought you were dead. Half the Ecuadorian police force was looking for you.'

He shrugged. 'It's their job.'

She raised an eyebrow. 'Yeah, I'm sure that's why they signed up for public service. To search for stupid "thrillionaires" who get themselves abducted.'

His eyes didn't leave hers as his jaw tightened, his expression hard and unforgiving and she saw the emotion smouldering there, the male pride and arrogance. 'I've already had one lecture this morning. I didn't come here for another.'

'That's a pity, because that's all you're getting from me,' she said crisply. 'But don't worry, I'm sure there are queues of women who will be more than willing to accept your proposal,' she said, keeping her eyes averted from the temptingly smooth, tanned skin of his arms. 'I don't even know why you asked me. You want a wife, and we barely managed a two-month one-night stand.'

His eyes rested on her face. 'I don't remember you complaining at the time. Moaning, gasping, crying out my name, sure…but not complaining.'

There was a hoarse softness in his voice that made her shiver, remembering the noises she'd made as she had come apart in his arms and against his mouth. It was suddenly difficult to breathe, much less speak.

She gritted her teeth. It wasn't fair of him to talk about the two of them in those moments. But then what did he know of fairness? He took his looks and charm, and wealth, for granted, assuming that they were his by right. He had never looked in the mirror and felt like an imposter or a let-down. Had never been surrounded by his peers and felt out of his depth.

Meeting his gaze, she shrugged. 'So I enjoyed having sex with you. That's all it was. I'm not going to take part in some charade of a marriage to get you out of a hole you dug yourself.'

He made a noise that was a mix of irritation and impatience. 'But it's not just my hole any more. It's our hole. Officially. In that it's in the open, public. Real. As far as they're concerned.'

They? The apprehension she had felt earlier was no longer a ripple but a huge, towering wave. 'Did you tell someone that you were going to come here and ask me to marry you?'

He shook his head.

'I didn't, no. It wouldn't have made sense. You see, I'd already told them we were engaged. That we were engaged before I left the States.' Now, he was shrugging off his jacket and rolling up his sleeves just like some husband in a sitcom.

'Look, believe me, I don't want to get married either,

but I'm not going to lose my business over one holiday from hell. I need to look as if I'm changing. That's why I need a wife. The trustees my father appointed are his peers. They have his values. They see marriage as a stabilising influence. They were putting pressure on me and I needed a name. But it had to be to the right woman. You know, someone reliable, sensible, unadventurous.'

She lifted her chin. 'And you thought of me? How flattering.' Curling her fingers into her palms, she stared at him, humiliated that was the only reason he had chosen her. Did he think, because she wasn't some leggy model type with bee-stung lips, that she didn't have feelings?

'And it did the trick. You should have seen their faces light up. They like you, Lily.'

He had it all worked out, she thought, wishing she had never opened the door and let him back into her home, into her life.

'I'm sure they do. It's you that's the problem.' Taking a jagged breath, she shook her head. 'But you're not my problem.' He had never been her anything, nor did she want him to be. Twisting her wrist, she tapped her watch. 'And you've had your five minutes. So I suggest you call up your trustees and tell them you made a mistake. That you spoke rashly. I'm sure they'll have no trouble believing you. You can see yourself out, can't you?'

Spinning away from him, she walked over to the far side of the room and flicked through one of the fabric books that Samantha had left behind. There was silence and she felt rather than saw him move. Her chest tightened with both relief and misery that he could find it so easy to walk away, but then he'd had practice.

She heard a rustling sound and, frowning, she turned and felt her stomach drop. Trip was lounging on the sofa, flicking through a magazine, his long legs stretched in front of him. Glancing up at her, he held it open.

'There was a good turnout that night, wasn't there? It's a nice photo too.'

For a moment she didn't respond, couldn't respond. She was too fazed by the picture. It had been taken the night of the auction when she had opened her tablet only to find that she hadn't uploaded her speech.

The same night that she and Trip had sex for the first time.

They were standing together, not touching, but she could remember how it had felt standing so close to him, his height, the curve of his muscles, the lightning snap of his eyes and that energy fizzing off his skin.

Her eyes fixed on the photograph. He looked like he always did. A masterclass in symmetry and flawless masculinity. Cool, confident, at ease with the cameras, whereas she…

Throat tightening, her gaze shifted to her own face.

She looked stiff and dazed. Partly because she was still reeling from the shock of Trip stepping up and giving a speech without any planning or preparation, but also because growing up with train-track braces had left her horribly self-conscious about smiling.

'It's just a photo.'

He was shaking his head. 'It's a story. The start of a fairy tale in New York.' His eyes on hers were as soft and intimate as a caress. 'A man and a woman who grew up in the same city, paths never quite crossing until, one day, fate pushes them together and they become lovers.'

Lovers. The word fizzed in her mouth and she felt heat break out on her skin. Trip wasn't the first man she'd had sex with, but he was her first lover.

Before him, she had understood the mechanics of sex and it had always been pleasant enough, only she hadn't been able to see why everyone made it into such a big deal.

Trip had made her see.

It had been revelatory. Sex with him had been wild, frantic. It had snatched her breath away. Left her reeling and hollowed out with a need she had never felt before. The more they'd touched and kissed and caressed, the more she'd wanted, and, like an addict, she'd lost touch with reality so that for the first time in her entire life she had felt beautiful, special.

But then he'd ended it.

Out of the blue. Just turned up, twitching with an anger she hadn't understood, still didn't understand, and he had ended it with her.

Folding her arms protectively in front of her body, she said coolly, 'Have you forgotten which way the door is?'

He let the magazine drop open onto the coffee table. 'Nice swerve, but I know you remember what we had. We could build on that.' His voice was a lazy drawl that played havoc with her nerve endings.

She gave him an icy glare. 'What I remember is you telling me that it had all gone on a little longer than you planned.' She could hear the bitterness in her voice, but she didn't care. All the pent-up confusion and anger and fear of the last few weeks seemed to have coalesced into one accusatory stream. 'What I remember is you standing in this room, itching to be gone.'

'And now I'm back.'

He got to his feet and she felt her body tense and soften at the same time as he walked towards her. She took a defensive step away from him, but he kept moving. Pressing the soles of her shoes into the rug, she held up a hand.

'Don't come any closer—'

'Because you don't trust yourself.' His teasing, dangerously sensuous mouth pulled into a smile that made her breath go shallow.

'Because you will regret it if you do,' she said stiffly.

The gleam in his eyes got more intense, and he took an infinitesimal step towards her.

'Why? Are you going to smother me with some swatches?'

He jerked the fabric in her hand and she should have just let go, but she didn't and he pulled her closer, drawing her in so hard and fast she had to push her hand against his chest to stop him. It was like fireworks exploding, sparking out from that point of contact, making her skin burn and heat race through her and she wanted to jerk her hand away, only that would make obvious the effect he was having on her, and she would rather set fire to herself than do that.

'Back off, Trip, or so help me I will call Security.'

'You mean Carlos?' He raised an eyebrow. 'I saw him on the way in, enjoying a hot dog and a frankly unfeasibly large portion of fries. No judgement. Next time I come over I'll give you a heads-up, that way he might have a chance of getting here before things get out of hand.'

A shiver spread down her spine. She knew exactly how out of hand things could get between her and Trip, and so did her body. Feeling her nipples harden, she let go of the swatch and took a step backwards, her heart racing.

'There won't be a next time,' she snapped. 'You can't seriously think I want to see you again, let alone marry you. Why would I? I don't need your money or your surname. In fact, I'm struggling to think of exactly what I would get out of your crackpot arrangement.'

She felt the ripple of that put-down spread outwards to the corners of the room, but Trip didn't react. He just stared at her, his blue gaze bright and hot and intent in a way that made her feel as if she were an animal in a trap.

'I suppose you'd get the same as you got before,' he said slowly.

There was a tense, electric moment she could feel everywhere.

She knew from the streak of colour touching his incredible cheekbones what he was talking about. Her body did too, because the air changed then. Or maybe it was the light. Whatever it was, she felt it snap taut, that quivering, electric thing between them that she'd been telling herself wasn't real.

Ignoring the heat flaring low in her pelvis, she stiffened her shoulders and met his gaze. 'That was then. This is now. Like I said earlier, I don't feel the same way as I did.'

She forced herself to hold his gaze as her lie ping-ponged round the room but all she was really aware of was the blue of his gaze washing over her like a wave, pulling her towards him and out into deeper, more dangerous water.

'Are you sure about that?'

Her belly clenched as he lifted his hand and smoothed her cheek, and the feel of his hand against her skin was so familiar and so irresistible that she stared up at him, mute and paralysed, incapable of convincing herself to do what was sensible and right, which would be to tell him to leave, to tell him that she was sure, could not be any surer.

But instead she said nothing. Did nothing even as he moved closer so that they were a breath apart now. His blue gaze was jewel bright on hers, striking against her skin like a match and she couldn't look away, couldn't bear to think that he would never look at her like that again.

She wanted to savour it. To let it linger on her tongue one last time, breathe in its intoxicating scent and let it roll through her like wildfire.

Maybe that was why she did nothing when he bent his head and fused his mouth to hers.

And just like that she forgot her anger and her outrage. She forgot that she was anything but a woman with needs. And as he curved his arm around her waist to pull her closer, she leaned into him, curling her fingers into the fabric of his shirt.

Oh, how she had missed this, missed him. She could feel herself melting, body softening and stirring at the same time with that same yearning need that only Trip had ever satisfied, and she wanted him so much, wanted him here, now...

As if he could read her mind or, more likely, her body, she felt his hand slide beneath the thin fabric of her blouse to find hot bare skin and her lips parted against his as his fingers stroked the swell of her breast, the nipple hardening.

It was like being on a merry-go-round, everything blurring into a shivering streak of vivid colour and hot, bright light.

She moaned softly against his mouth, and it was that sound that penetrated her brain. Suddenly she could hear Trip's voice inside her head.

'I don't remember you complaining at the time. Moaning, gasping, crying out my name, sure...but not complaining.'

And here she was again, moaning, lost in her desire and the muscle memory of those frantic, feverish months together as if he hadn't opened her up and carved out her heart while it was still beating.

She jerked her mouth away, pushing at his broad chest, and he stepped back unsteadily, releasing his grip, his blue eyes blazing with both frustration and a barely concealed triumph.

CHAPTER THREE

'WHATEVER YOU'RE ABOUT to say, don't,' Lily said hoarsely, trying to tamp down the flames crackling through her.

'Not even thank you?' His voice was mocking but there was a roughness there too, as if he was as thrown by this as she was. 'You're usually such a stickler for manners.'

She glared at him. 'Don't think this changes anything, because it doesn't.'

He started to laugh.

'I'd love to believe you, Lily, but out of the two of us you seem to be the one who doesn't know her own mind. What was it you said?' He screwed up his face as if he was trying to remember. 'Oh, yes. "I don't feel the same way as I did."'

She hated him then. But hated herself more for her lack of control, for still wanting him even at a moment like this.

Taking a breath, clinging to what was left of her pride, she met his gaze. 'Maybe I did respond to you. Because I'm human and seeing you alive made me feel things in the moment. That's all it was though, Trip, a moment. But marriage, that's about committing to someone. Sharing their life. I don't want to fake that just to help you rebrand your image. If and when I choose to get married, it's going to be to a man who understands what that entails. A man who understands me. A man who solves his own problems. Not makes them for other people. So, basically, not you.'

Heart thudding, she lifted her chin. 'You need to leave.'

He dropped back down onto the sofa once more, totally unperturbed by her words. 'And I will, but now that we're on the same page, why don't we go through our diaries? Get a date for the wedding.'

Same page? Had he not listened to a word she'd said? Clearly not.

She watched him stretch out his legs, hating him, hating the pulse of longing that still beat across her skin. He was so sure of himself. So sure of her, so sure that what had just happened was her acquiescing to his stupid plan instead of understanding that it was simply a muscle memory of that hunger they'd once shared.

Across the room, she could see the stairs that led up to her bedroom, the bedroom where Trip had stripped her naked on that very first night they'd spent together. He had stripped too with swift, expert precision, because he *would* be expert at getting naked with a woman. But she hadn't cared. She had been too busy staring at—no, drinking in—all those contoured muscles and the smooth, tanned skin and his erection, standing proud.

She had wanted him and wanted to give him everything in return in those feverish hours between dusk and dawn. But that wasn't a reason to marry him now.

Turning, she snatched up her bag. 'You're wrong,' she said with what felt like admirable calm, given that her body was still throbbing with the aftershocks of his mouth on hers. 'We're not on the same page. We're not even in the same book. And I will not be marrying you any time soon. Or ever, in fact.'

Her nerves were screaming. She'd spent the last six

weeks battling her emotions, riding a roller coaster of guilt and need and grief, and now she was in the middle of processing her shock and relief at his sudden reappearance. Not that he cared about any of that. He was too busy making demands, making assumptions.

He had the gall to smile then. 'You don't have a choice. I can't take back what I said. Besides, Mason has already texted me asking when we're going to make an announcement.'

She had to press her hands against her thighs to stop herself from slapping the complacent smile from his infuriatingly handsome face.

'For the last time, there's not going to be any announcement,' she said flatly. 'Now get out of my apartment or I will call Security.'

Her breathing jerked as his eyes locked with hers. 'Why are you making this into such a big deal? It's nothing in the scheme of things. A year maybe, tops. We'd have to do a handful of public appearances together.'

'Including a wedding. Our wedding. When we'd have to lie to our family and friends. I'm not going to do that. This is your mess, so you can sort it out. Anyway, I have plans so I'll be leaving the city. Tonight.'

He tipped back his head, back in control once again. 'What, and miss all the fun?—'

She glared at him. 'You and I have a very different idea of fun, Trip. Like I said, I leave this evening, and if you haven't spoken to these trustees and explained to them that we are not and never have been engaged by the time I touch down, then I will tell them myself.'

His eyes blazed but she was walking quickly and with purpose.

'Lily—'

He was moving now, coming after her, but she was already opening the front door. She caught a glimpse of his face, blue eyes narrowing in disbelief, and then she slammed the door, pushed the key in the lock and turned it with a rush of relief.

She couldn't be in the same room as him. Not for another second. In fact, she didn't want to be in the same city as him, the same continent even. Not when she could still feel the imprint of his mouth on hers and the burn of her own stupidity.

As she stepped into the sunlight outside, she felt a flicker of guilt at having locked him in. After all, he had only just escaped from a prison of sorts. But this was Tribeca, not Ecuador, and there was a spare key by the door. She just needed a head start and to prove that she was serious.

Even after he heard the turn of the key, it took Trip several seconds to realise what had happened.

Watching Lily lose her temper, he'd started to laugh. Because it was funny. She was so angry and outraged even though she had kissed him back.

But it had been a dumb thing to do, he knew that now.

Almost as dumb as kissing her.

He scowled. It was her fault. Lily had always been so uninhibited, so passionate, so responsive to him. Not today. Today her haughty froideur had put his teeth on edge and he'd wanted to throw her off balance.

But mostly he'd just wanted to kiss her.

That was all it had taken for him to lose control. He'd forgotten why he was there in her apartment. All that had mattered was her, making her his again.

Only then she had jerked her mouth from his and he'd

known from the storm in her eyes that she was furious at being proven wrong, which was no doubt why she had decided to punish him. Only by the time he'd realised that, she had already turned the key. And then he was locked in.

By the time he'd worked out what she had done he'd been too late to stop her. Even then, he'd assumed she was bluffing, that she'd wanted to have the last word, but, having called out her name a couple of times, he'd finally looked through the peephole and seen that she was gone, presumably on her way downstairs. A quick check of the street had proved that assumption correct and he'd watched, torn between disbelief and fury, as she'd looked up in the direction of the window and waved before climbing into a taxi.

Waved.

As if she didn't have a care in the world. But then she didn't. It wasn't her life, her future, that was being held in the balance.

Trip was back in his own apartment now, but by the time he'd realised Lily kept a spare key in a bowl next to the door he'd been stewing in her apartment for over an hour and a half.

He yanked open the drinks fridge, pulled out a beer, and started pacing back and forth across the huge loft space, oblivious to the dazzling view across Central Park.

He didn't like being on his own. His ADHD played a part in that. As a child he had been incapable of sitting still quietly, much to his father's irritation. Now that he was older, he had learned strategies—pacing, doodling, foot-tapping.

But there was so much going on in his head right now. He kept having flashbacks to the men in masks and his body was permanently tense with a dread he couldn't shift. And that was why this whole business with the shareholders was so unfair. Returning to New York, he had known that somebody would be holding the reins, but on his return he had assumed that he would simply take back what was rightfully his.

Only now he had the board and the shareholders on his back, and that was a real problem.

His mouth twisted. And his solution was currently planning to skip the country.

Picturing Lily's small, furious face, he winced as his shoulders tensed and he reached round to massage his back.

He opened his eyes and stared around the light, casually elegant apartment. It was his home. Had been his home for nearly seven years and yet he hadn't thought about it once while he was out there. He hadn't thought about anything much except staying alive.

And Lily Dempsey.

His fingers tightened around the bottle. He had no idea why she'd kept popping into his head. Perhaps it was the soft rainforest air that would slide over his skin at daybreak almost like one of her caresses. Or maybe it was darkness playing tricks on his mind.

It made it even more aggravating that she was refusing to play ball. Was, in fact, threatening to talk to the trustees.

Jaw tightening, he began to pace again. That wasn't going to happen. He wouldn't allow that to happen. He couldn't. One more mess-up and there was a real risk he could lose control of the business.

'One hundred and thirty years building a business into a household name and you throw it away for a few seconds of thrill-seeking.'

His feet faltered as his father's voice sounded inside his head and some of the beer spilled onto the polished concrete floor. He frowned down at it.

Henry Winslow II had forfeited any right to sit in judgement on him, he thought, jerking the bottle to his lips. In fact, none of this would have happened if his father had been the man he'd pretended to be. It was his lies, his deceit that had set this whole mess in motion. Without those letters he would never have accepted his friend Carter's invitation, never have ended up in a cartel hotspot.

But there was no point crying over spilt beer.

What mattered now was getting Lily to change her mind.

He felt his heart rate pick up. Outside, the sun was high above the tallest skyscrapers and the air would still be shimmering with heat.

Trip gritted his teeth. His skin was suddenly twitchy and taut. Nothing could compare to the heat of her kiss.

The effect Lily had on him was still as baffling to him today as it had been that first night. Before her, all his girlfriends had been of a type. Not through any conscious choice on his part.

But she was different.

Always slightly aloof, and serious and hard-working in a way that was unique among her more glamorous peers. Which was why it had been her name he'd plucked out of the air. She was the perfect woman to help him regain control of his business.

It was a pity, then, that she was so resistant to doing so.

He gritted his teeth.

It was all such a mess. He didn't want to get married, didn't want to have to make vows of eternal love and devotion, particularly now, after finding those letters. To do so felt wrong in so many ways.

Remembering the moment when he'd realised that the woman writing them was not his mother, he felt suddenly sick.

For a slice of a second, his mind was a flurry of thoughts, tumbling over one another, colliding, splitting apart, reforming, and he felt the same mishmash of anger and shock and pain. Because Henry wasn't perfect. He was a liar and a hypocrite and Trip was done trying to please his father, to be like his father.

Or he would be, once he had persuaded the trustees that he was the best man to run the company, and for that he needed Lily Dempsey.

But how could he persuade her?

Then again, maybe that wasn't the priority. He sat up straight. Right now, he just needed to stop her talking to the trustees. If he did that, then it would buy him some time and then he could concentrate on changing her mind.

'If and when I choose to get married, it's going to be to a man who...solves his own problems.'

Lily's voice echoed inside his head, and he got to his feet. If that was what she wanted, then that was what she was going to get. But first he needed to make a phone call.

The plane was waiting on the runway, sleek and pale grey like a gull at rest.

Lily stared at it, her throat tightening.

Her father, James, was a US senator. She was proud of him. Proud of his values and his work ethic. He was not just a charismatic speaker with catchy sound bites but a doer. Unfortunately, his job was also the reason she had been pushed into the spotlight at such a young age. It hadn't been all bad. She wasn't shy like her brother, Lucas, and when she was very young it had been exciting to be on stage at the end of a campaign with all the balloons and the cheering.

That had all changed when certain parts of the media and the unnamed, faceless trolls had decided that she was fair game. Except it hadn't been fair, and it hadn't felt like a game. Some of the things that had been said and written about her still had the power to make her chest fill with pain, and a shame that was in itself shaming.

She had tried to keep a low profile, and sometimes that worked. Other times, she was criticised for being aloof and stuck up. But mostly they had lost interest in her because she was single, fully clothed, and the only people she let get close to her were her family and tried-and-tested friends.

Except Trip.

And look at how that was working out for her.

Fleeing felt like too strong a word, but she was definitely escaping from New York, and fortunately her father's status as Secretary of State for Veteran Affairs meant she could just hop on a plane at short notice.

She was too frazzled to feel more than a pinch of guilt. She felt safe here.

Not that Trip scared her. But the idea of people thinking they were engaged was terrifying. Worse still was the prospect of anyone uncovering the truth. That Trip had needed a name, a wife to make him look like a changed man, and had thought of her because she was reliable, sensible, unadventurous.

That should have been enough for her to throw him out of her apartment.

Instead, she'd let him kiss her.

Not just let. She had kissed him back. And that scared her too. How easily she had softened beneath his mouth. How much she had wanted to be his again in that moment.

Three crew members, two women and one man, were waiting by the stairs to greet her. She smiled politely but none of their faces were familiar. Then again, it had been nearly eighteen months since she had taken the family jet anywhere.

It would be nice to be up in the air and out of reach of everybody, she thought, tossing her bag onto one of the cream leather seats and glancing round the cabin. Was it her imagination or did the cabin seem bigger than she remembered?

Had her father changed planes?

Truthfully, she had no idea, and she certainly wasn't going to ask any of the stewards and look like some Upper East Side princess. The pilot and co-pilot chose that moment to come and introduce themselves and then it was time to fasten her seat belt. She glanced at her watch. It was a quarter to eight now, so with the time difference she should arrive in London at—

'Good evening.'

It was a man's voice and she glanced up, smiling automatically, expecting to see the male steward. The smile froze on her lips.

Trip was standing there, one hand wrapped over the top of the seat beside her, his muscular body filling the aisle.

She stared at him, mute with shock, the memory of that feverish kiss in her apartment swelling up inside her, making her lips tingle as if it had only just happened.

He was the epitome of casual cool in a dark blue polo shirt, pale linen trousers and loafers, clothes that would have looked unremarkable on any other man. But this was

Trip. It didn't matter what he wore. Nothing could diminish that shockingly sensual, dangerously masculine aura that had its own gravitational pulling power. He was the physical embodiment of a risk worth taking.

Or so she'd thought. But not any more.

'This is where you say what a surprise and a pleasure it is to see me,' he said softly.

Her throat was suddenly dry and tight, and her hands felt shaky. But, lifting her chin, she met his gaze. 'But that would mean lying and you wouldn't want to make me a liar, would you, Trip?'

'Oh, there are worse things than lying.' His voice was all smooth and silk, but there was an edge to it that made her skin tighten with warning. 'Like leaving someone locked in your apartment.' She saw his jaw tighten, just a little. 'That was a mean trick, Lily.'

'You left me no choice. You wouldn't leave,' she snapped. 'And I didn't ask you to come to my apartment, any more than I asked you to come here. Don't sit—' she added but it was too late. Trip had dropped down into the seat beside her.

She glared at him.

'What do you think you're doing? Did you not get the message?'

He shrugged and, despite her shock and rising irritation, her eyes tracked the movement of his shoulder and arm muscles.

'I get so many emails,' he said, misunderstanding her on purpose. 'But I did hear on the grapevine that we were heading in the same direction and, as you know, I'm trying to be more responsible and measured, so taking one private jet instead of two seemed like a no-brainer.'

Lily blinked. Her mind was racing. How did he know

which direction she was heading? She hadn't told anyone that she was going to London except...

She felt her jaw tighten remembering how accommodating her mother had been earlier, letting her use the car and borrow the plane.

'Is that what you said to my mother?'

His blue eyes rested on her face and she saw that he looked neither remorseful nor guilty—or any of the other countless emotions he should be feeling for his behaviour, past and present. 'After you said you were leaving New York, I called her to get a few more details. Such a charming woman. Compassionate too. She's very concerned about you.' His gaze rested intently on her face. 'Apparently you haven't been yourself.'

A lump formed in her throat and for a moment she didn't trust herself to speak. How could her mother betray her like that?

Obviously she'd been devastated when she'd heard that Trip was missing, presumed dead. Equally obviously she was glad he was alive, because that was how any normal person would react.

But there were other emotions too.

Guilt, because up until the moment he'd disappeared she'd been wishing all kinds of ills would fall upon him. And fury. A dull, pounding fury that he should be so reckless, so thoughtless, so utterly solipsistic. So yes, she hadn't been herself.

'I was worried about you,' she said flatly. 'Everyone was.'

'Yeah, it's really upsetting when the stock market has a major wobble.' He stretched out his legs so that his thigh brushed against hers, not once but twice so that she knew it wasn't an accident. Gritting her teeth, she jerked her leg away.

'That's not why most people were worried. It's because they care about you.'

There was a small, prickling silence that made her skin sting. 'And were you one of those people? The ones that cared about me.'

She looked up, caught the glitter in his eyes and felt her cheeks start to burn even though she certainly shouldn't be feeling anything.

'Is that why you haven't been yourself?'

He shifted against the armrest but his gaze didn't move from her face, the slow burn of those astonishingly blue eyes of his tearing into her, seeing more than she wanted him to see.

Squaring her shoulders, she took a deep, fortifying breath. 'I'm not having this conversation with you, Trip. *No*, don't speak. I don't want to hear another word. I don't need to know what weaselly things you said to my mother so you could hitch a ride. You've had your fun and now you need to leave.'

'Can I speak now?' Trip sat back in his seat. 'Because I think you should know that isn't going to be possible. In fact, it's pretty much *im*possible given that I don't have wings or a parachute and we appear to have taken off.'

'What?'

Her head snapped round to the window and she stared through the glass in horror. Teterboro had disappeared. In its place was an endless, darkening blue sky.

She swallowed hard, then turned to face him. 'You did that on purpose. You knew the plane was taking off and you distracted me.'

He shrugged. 'I would have said something sooner, but you told me not to speak. I suppose we could ask the pilot to turn the plane around. It's a bit diva-ish, but if that's what you want to do. I'll let you do the talking—'

And say what? she thought savagely. Her head was starting to pound, and she wanted to scream. But it wouldn't alter things. There was no way she was going to ask the pilot to turn the plane around and Trip knew it.

She watched as he turned his head imperiously and one of the female stewards appeared at his elbow with almost comical speed. 'I'd like two glasses of champagne.'

'I don't want a glass of champagne,' she said through gritted teeth as the woman evaporated as swiftly as she'd appeared.

He raised one dark eyebrow. 'What's a celebration without champagne?'

She gave a small, brittle laugh. 'Strangely, having my flight hijacked by you doesn't feel like a reason to celebrate.' She was speaking calmly and precisely, as if that might change what was happening. But of course, it didn't.

'I was talking about our engagement,' he said, and his voice had a softness to it that made her shiver.

She felt her face get hot. 'We're not engaged.'

'And yet here we are. Together. Heading off into the sunset.' He glanced out of the window to where the sun was starting to slip beneath the horizon. 'It's almost as if fate is trying to tell you something. As if being "hijacked" by your fiancé is what you want. Only you don't want to admit it out loud,' he added, and, for a moment, she couldn't breathe properly.

She couldn't understand why she had thought there was more to Trip than met the eye. He was hiding in plain sight. A wealthy, powerful man who took what he wanted, when he wanted it, without any thought for the collateral damage he caused en route to satisfying his whims.

Unfastening her seat belt, she stood up. 'What I want is to be left alone.'

She snatched her bag and waited for him to move his legs, which he did with a measured slowness that made her fingers tremble. Ignoring him as best she could, she stalked down the cabin to a seat with a table beside it and spent the next hour pretending that Trip wasn't there.

But even though she was sitting with her back to him, it was impossible not to be aware of his presence. She was like the princess in that fairy tale, and he was the pea beneath all the mattresses. As she listened to him talking to the stewards, she knew exactly how he would be sitting. Not stiffly like her, with her spine digging into the seat, but lolling easily against the leather, his chin tilted upwards, limbs arranged with a kind of louche grace that inspired both envy and longing. What was more, she could picture the cabin crew crowded round him, hanging eagerly on his every word, wide-eyed like children watching a magician perform a series of elaborate tricks.

Steadying her breathing, she reclined her seat a fraction. As well as a headache, her neck was starting to hurt with the effort of not turning round and she felt a little queasy. As a child she'd suffered terribly from motion sickness, but nowadays it was rarely a problem unless she was tired or stressed.

Her lip curled. Thanks to Trip, she was both. Luckily, she had some pills with her so maybe she would take a couple and close her eyes…

She woke up with a start.

Her mouth felt dry and her eyes felt as if they were on back to front. Light was filling the cabin, not artificial light but daylight, and outside the sky was a dazzling blue. What time was it? She glanced at her watch and jerked upright, frowning. She had assumed that she had dozed off for a couple of hours, but it was morning.

'There she is. Hey, Greta Garbo. Have a nice sleep? I tried to wake you, but you were out for the count.'

As Trip sat down opposite her, she was still too woolly-headed to do anything more than answer truthfully.

'I get motion sick sometimes, so I took a couple of pills. As soon as we land, I'll be fine.'

As soon as we land.

The words echoed inside her head and she glanced out of the window, feeling that same quivering apprehension as she had back at the apartment just before Trip had told her he wanted to marry her. Looking down at her watch again, she frowned. 'Why are we still in the air? It only takes seven hours at most to reach London.'

'True.' Trip nodded.

'So why aren't we there?'

He smiled then. 'Probably because we're not going to London.'

'What do you mean?' His answer seemed to have sucked the breath from her lungs so that her voice sounded high and thin.

Now he studied her for a long, level moment. 'We're about an hour away from a private airstrip in Siena.'

'Siena?'

'It's in Italy. Near Florence.'

'I know where Siena is,' she snapped.

In the weeks since she had last seen him, his hair had grown longer, and he pushed it back from his face. But that wasn't why her heart began to beat faster.

'I don't understand. Was there a problem? Have they

had to divert the plane?' Except that didn't make any sense because Italy was further away than England.

'There's no problem.'

'Then they must have made a mistake.' She tried and failed to keep the edge of panic out of her voice. 'Why else would we be going to Italy?'

His blue gaze was bright and hot and satisfied. 'Because that's where I told the pilot to land,' he said softly.

CHAPTER FOUR

THERE WAS A slight bump that made the cabin shudder as the plane touched down and Trip was momentarily pressed back against the seat as the pilot reversed the engine thrust. Almost immediately, he heard the bark of the hydraulics balancing the steering and air pressure.

It had taken quite a few phone calls and several conversations during which he'd had to distort some of his motivations and intentions to get to this moment, but it had been worth it, Trip thought, gazing down at Lily's pale, stunned face.

'You did what?'

Her voice was frozen with shock or fury, he couldn't tell which. But then it didn't matter either way, he thought as he met her narrow-eyed gaze.

'I told the pilot to fly us to Italy.'

Glancing over at her, he saw that she was spluttering with fury, which in and of itself was immensely satisfying. He had never seen her lose control before.

His body tensed. At least not outside the bedroom.

He could still remember how stunned he'd been that first time they'd had sex.

He hadn't planned to.

They had gone for a drink at some bar with one of those huge screens showing some boxing match and nobody had even looked at them as they'd walked in. And perhaps it was that shared anonymity or maybe it was that she had looked to him to save her, but he'd forgotten that she was not his type, or that he even had a type, and they'd ended up back at her apartment, in her bed.

Eventually.

The first time they had barely got through the front door.

Before that evening, he'd thought he had her all figured out. But she had been a revelation. The sex had been a revelation. Tentative at first, then fast, urgent, clumsy almost, then hesitant again. Real, in other words, and all the more exciting for being so unscripted, so instinctive.

Watching her lose control like that had been the single most erotic experience of his life, but all he'd been to her was a pretty face.

'How dare you do that?'

He shook his head slowly. 'You deserved it—'

Her grey eyes were silver with fury. 'You're such a child,' she said after a quivering pause.

She wasn't used to losing her temper. He could tell by how she was holding herself and the tremor in her voice and he didn't like how it made him feel, knowing he was responsible. It stung that she thought he was acting out some petty vendetta.

Like so many people in his life, she had made the mistake of not taking him seriously. But now she did.

'It was your idea,' he said, making no attempt to soften his tone. 'You said you wanted to be with a man who can solve his own problems.'

She was looking at him as if he had sprouted horns.

'And you think this is the best way to do that? By playing some stupid trick?' she said in a withering tone. As if

he were extraordinarily stupid. 'Well, if you've quite finished your magic show I'm going to go and speak to the
pilot and ask him to fly me back to—'

But he was done with being scolded and made to feel
as if he were a fool.

'That's not gonna happen,' he said quietly. 'You see, this
is *my* plane, *my* crew and they are not going to be flying
you anywhere any time soon.'

Lily was still for a moment and he could see her fitting
his version of the facts against hers and testing it. Now,
she was shaking her head. 'No, this is my father's plane.
I asked my mother if I could borrow it—'

'You did. But then I spoke to your mother and I told
her that we had got engaged secretly several months ago
and that was why you'd been upset. Because you'd been
so worried about me, only you'd had to hide how you were
feeling.' He paused and his gaze narrowed on hers in a
way that made her breath go shallow. 'I explained that I
thought we needed time alone together. That you were
struggling to deal with everything that's happened but
were too stubborn to admit it.'

'That's not true—' The fury in her voice gave it a hus-
kiness he felt in all the wrong places, and he wanted to
touch her so badly he didn't even realise that he had lifted
his hand to touch her cheek.

'She was very sympathetic.'

Their eyes locked for one frozen second and then she
jerked her head away from his fingers, the movement ex-
posing the underside of her throat, the pulse beating there
at a rapid pace that matched his own.

'So it's not just the trustees who think we're engaged
now. Your parents do, too. In fact, your mother was all for
me taking you away. She said it would be like a pre-moon.'

He was needling her as much to see her draw herself up in outrage as for any other reason. And because he liked the flush of pink it brought her cheeks and the way it made her voice grow husky. She was the only woman he'd met who was as stubborn as he was, and even though her refusal to simply accept the inevitable was frustrating as hell right now, he found himself admiring her.

Catching sight of her narrowed gaze, he felt his heartbeat start to drum inside his head. She found him equally frustrating.

And he wondered if there was something wrong with him, that he should like it so much. Like getting under her skin.

Her chin jerked up and her voice was very quiet, very furious then. 'But it's not, because that would imply we're getting married and we absolutely are *not*.'

Settling back against the leather upholstery, he gave an exaggerated shrug, mostly so that he could see the pulse in her throat accelerate. 'I don't want to argue on our pre-moon, so, if it makes you happier, let's just call it a holiday.'

He watched her clench her fists, nails digging into the palms. 'It doesn't make me happy, and I don't want a holiday.'

'That's what people who need a holiday always say,' he murmured. 'It'll be good for you to step off the merry-go-round for a while, and the villa is a great place to relax and unwind. You can swim or sunbathe or go for a ride. Or if you want to go out there are some great restaurants in Siena, or we can take in an opera in Florence.' His eyes dropped to the pulse now beating frantically in her throat. 'Italy is a playground of the senses, so we could also just make our own entertainment—'

'I won't need entertaining because I won't be staying,' she said tightly.

Wrong, he thought, watching a spray of goosebumps spread along her bare arms. Now that she was here, there was no way he was letting Lily out of his sight until she had agreed to be his wife. Of that he was certain.

'That's what this is to you, isn't it?' Her eyes arrowed in on his face. 'Entertainment. Some kind of game. Well, it's not one I'm interested in playing. So I suggest you get *your* pilot back in here and tell him to take me back to New York.'

'That's not going to happen. And you're wrong, Lily. This isn't a game for me. It's my life. My business. My future. Which is why I released a statement announcing our engagement shortly before we left New York.' He held her gaze. 'Did you really think I'd just told your parents?'

'I don't believe you. You can't have done that—' Watching the colour drain from her face, he felt a pang of remorse. But what choice did he have? None of this was his choice. It was just the tail end of one careless decision.

'You left me no choice.'

He watched in silence as she scrolled down her phone with trembling hands. 'At least here…' he softened his voice '…you won't have to deal with the paparazzi.' She had never said as much, but he knew she had a fear and a distrust of the media, so in a way bringing her to Italy was an act of mercy.

'You have to change this. You have to call someone, tell them that you made a mistake. I can't marry you—'

The horror in her voice scraped against his masculine pride and he felt his temper flare.

'I'm not calling anyone. It's done, okay. The sooner you

accept that, the sooner we can both go back to living our lives. Separately.'

He didn't know what he expected to happen. He knew what he wanted to happen, which was that she would give in, capitulate to his not unreasonable demands and agree to marry him. He felt a twinge of guilt. Okay, maybe what he had trapped her into doing was a little unreasonable, but it wasn't as if he were asking her to do something that she hadn't done a version of before.

His body hardened with predictable speed as he pictured what that version looked like, as Lily folded her arms in front of her quivering body and glared at him.

'I'm not leaving this plane.'

'One way or another you will,' he said softly.

He watched the slow rise of colour on her cheeks. 'So now you're threatening me. This is turning into quite a day for you. And for me too, seeing all these new sides to your character.'

His jaw tightened. 'It wasn't a threat. More of a point of information.' He met her gaze. 'You see, as your host I have a duty of care—'

'Did you just say duty of care?' Her grey eyes grew saucer wide. 'You're abducting me, Trip.'

Later, he would wonder what had possessed him in that moment. Maybe it was the derision in her voice or the ice in her eyes or just the fact that she didn't seem to realise how much this mattered to him, but before he realised what he was doing, he had scooped her into his arms and was walking swiftly down the aisle.

'Put me down.'

She was twisting against him, but he was already moving down the staircase towards the SUV that was waiting on the runway. Without so much as blinking, the driver stepped forward and opened the door and Trip placed her into the back seat before following her smoothly.

'Have you lost your mind?' Face burning, Lily edged to the far side of the car. 'You've no right—no right—'

She reached for the door handle, but the SUV was moving now and she looked over at the driver, not because she was expecting him to leap to her defence, but expecting some kind of reaction, shock maybe, or horror.

But the driver's eyes were fixed calmly on the road as if he was used to his boss carrying women to his car like some caveman. Maybe he was. Maybe what she called an abduction was just an ordinary day to him.

'You couldn't stay on the plane.' His voice was taut. 'And you could just give in gracefully for once. This has been a very long day.'

The headache that had started on the flight was spreading now and she pressed a thumb against the pain building at the hairline.

'You're right. Frankly, I can't wait for it to end.'

'Such urgency,' he murmured. 'So some things haven't changed.'

Looking up, she caught the glint in his eyes and felt her belly backflip as heat suffused her face and body, skin prickling with anticipation and need and fear. Fear at how easily her body could betray her, and, despite there being so much more bad to choose from, how stubbornly it continued to remember the infinitesimal amount of good.

And she could remember it all too well.

Each time they had ended up in bed it was supposed to be the last time. But then she would catch sight of him at some function or at a restaurant and it would be all she could think about.

Like that night when she'd met up with some girlfriends at Piatto for dinner.

Trip had been there with his father and, though she hadn't gone over to talk to him, just knowing he was there had made the restaurant floor feel as if it were on an angle and she'd had to press her chair down into the floor to stop it sliding towards him.

He'd left the restaurant first, but he had been outside, waiting for her just as she had waited for him that first time. She felt her pulse fluttering, remembering the throb of the blood in her veins as they'd walked on opposite sides of the street, not looking at each other but so intensely aware of every step the other took that it had been as if they were joined by an invisible thread.

As they'd turned the corner, he had abruptly crossed the road and she had pulled him against her, the dark impatience in his eyes and the feel of his mouth on hers unleashing that hunger that shivered inside her, a hunger that she should have resisted because she knew the risks, particularly with a man like Trip.

But looking into his eyes, she had been sure he wasn't pretending. That he felt what she did.

Until he didn't, and then he'd ended it, and now he only wanted her because she was safe and dull. And because her parents believed in love, the head-over-heels kind that made you act like a fool and risk everything, and because they wanted her to be happy, they had accepted his lies.

They didn't know he was faking it.

But she did.

Shifting her body towards the car door, she stared helplessly into the fading light. So why did she still want to lean closer to him? To touch, explore, caress, kiss...

She felt flushed with the heat of it, and her voice was

scratchy when she replied. 'Everything's changed. Except you. You never change. Which is why you're in the mess you're in.'

The blue gleam of his gaze made her breath catch.

'You know what your problem is? It's all this thinking in absolutes. Everything. Always, never—it's exhausting. No wonder your parents think you need a break.'

Her shoulders were aching, muscles tensing from the effort of holding in the scream of frustration that was building inside her. Balling her hands, she inched closer to the door. 'If I'm exhausted it's because of you, because of this.'

She was lucky. She had a family she loved and who loved her. A job she adored. A small but close group of friends. A beautiful, spacious apartment and enough money to never have to think about money.

So why had she spent so much of her life living in the shadows?

Not all her life. Trip had been sunlight on her face, and she had basked in it greedily, gratefully, even though she knew that sunlight couldn't be trusted. That looking into it left you blinded and dazed so that you couldn't see what was right in front of you.

Like with Cameron.

He wasn't as traffic-stoppingly beautiful as Trip, but he was cool and edgy and popular and she had been flattered by his attention, intoxicated with the entirely new sensation of being one of the in crowd, so that it had only been later that she'd realised he couldn't be trusted.

By then the damage had been done. She had put her brother in harm's way, encouraging him to drive them all back to the city even though Cameron had told her weeks earlier that he didn't own a car. But it hadn't seemed important until she'd heard the police sirens.

She'd tried to explain, but the fact was the car had been stolen. By the time her father had arrived at the police station, Lucas couldn't stop shaking and he was crying too hard to answer questions. And the worst part had been that both her parents were so understanding.

No, actually the worst part had been Lucas going to the clinic in Geneva.

Her heart was beating in her throat.

It had taken a long time to forget the terror and misery of that night. But sometimes even now if they heard a police siren she would see Lucas' hands shake and his face stiffen with panic and she would want to cry. He had always been highly strung and shy and struggled with debilitating anxiety, but now he was reclusive.

As for her...

Over the years, all the sneering remarks about her appearance had left her cautious around people in general, and men in particular, but she had thought Cameron was different. That he had seen her inner beauty whereas, in fact, with one cool, assessing glance he had spotted the lonely girl who lived inside her who wanted someone to notice her. Talk to her. Think she was special.

The interior of the car shuddered in and out of focus as if she were sitting inside a snow globe and someone were shaking it. Her face felt hot with shame.

Which was why sleeping with Trip had been such a crazy thing to do. At least the risks she'd taken had not impacted anyone else. And nobody had been there to see how easy he'd found it to abandon her. As she remembered his haste to be gone, her breath felt ragged.

She felt his gaze on her face.

'And I don't have any problems,' she lied. 'Except you,' she added. 'You're my problem.'

'That's progress,' he said softly. 'Yesterday I wasn't your anything.'

He shifted against the leather upholstery and every single nerve ending in her body twitched in unison and it was so intense that she had to stop herself from pulling off her seat belt, throwing open the car door and leaping onto the road as they did in the movies.

She turned her face towards the window, seeing nothing, body taut with frustration, furious with herself for telling him what she was going to do and thereby giving him an opportunity to set this 'plan' in motion.

When he'd broken up with her, she had thought he was self-centred, arrogant and entitled, but this was a whole new level of impossible to process behaviour. He had lied to her parents, lied to her, tricked her into thinking she was on her way to London when all the time he was bringing her here.

Her gaze fixed on the distant hills with their patchwork fields of green and gold.

'Exactly where are you taking me?' she demanded, turning towards him.

'Villa Morandi. My father's villa. Mine now, I guess.' He seemed almost surprised, as if that thought had only just occurred to him, and there was an edge to his voice that hadn't been there before.

She had met Henry on a handful of occasions. Outwardly, Trip resembled his father in the broadest strokes. The height, the fine, straight nose and the blue eyes. But their personalities could not be more different. Henry had been all about planning and projections. He had been autocratic, disciplined and focused on the prize. Whereas Trip brought the energy and excitement into any room. He took chances—or risks, depending on your perspective.

But Trip was still his son, and for many boys, their father was a guide into manhood. Was that why he was acting like this? Because he had lost his polestar? She wanted to ask, to reach out and smooth that rigidity from his shoulders, but that would mean having to touch him and it would be beyond stupid of her to do that.

'And what would he think about you doing this?' She made her voice neutral, in the way she'd learned from watching her own father deal with political opponents and critics. 'I spent time with your father. He didn't act on impulses. He thought things through, and he left you in charge of his business so I'm guessing he wanted you to step up. To grow up and be a worthy successor. I'm certain he didn't expect you to marry someone against their will.'

He was watching her blandly, but now the light in his gaze sharpened in a way that made her breath go shallow and she knew she had landed a blow.

'Fine, so break up with me. Here, you can use my phone.' He tossed it across the seat. 'Make it official. Call your father. I should warn you, though, there's a fair amount of blood in the water, so the sharks are already circling. You tip in some chum, and it'll turn into a feeding frenzy real fast. Because it isn't just my image that's going to be affected by our splitting up.'

She stared at him, her heart beating out a drumroll of panic against her ribcage.

He was right. Headlines involving words like 'senator's daughter' and 'break-up' would make people sit up and take notice. Add in a photo of Trip looking louche and sexy stepping off a plane after his miraculous return from the dead and the story could run for days, weeks, months in the summer's slow news cycle.

It would be the ultimate clickbait.

Despite her attempts to stop it, a shiver ran down her spine as she imagined the trolling that would start the minute the story broke.

What fun they would have. Imagine, they would say, that Lily Dempsey thought she could enchant a man like Trip Winslow. Because it wouldn't matter what statement they put out, everyone would assume she'd been dumped. All the old pictures would be rolled out. The ones that made her want to curl into a ball beneath her duvet. No place had been beyond the intrusive reach of their lenses. No topic was taboo. Not her hair or dress sense. Not even her weight or the straightness of her teeth.

But she could cope with that, had been coping with it since she was nine years old and her father's career had apparently made her public property.

'But hey, you know that though, don't you?' Trip said then. 'You and your family know all about managing reputation and image. Why else would the world think your brother was learning musical composition at the Conservatoire in Paris three years ago, when in fact he was in Switzerland?'

Lily's eyes flew to his and everything inside her lurched as if the car had hit a pothole in the road. She knew she had gone white. Could feel the blood draining away. Nobody outside the family knew about Lucas' time in the clinic. Their father had driven him there himself.

'You don't know anything—'

He made an impatient sound. 'No, I don't. And neither do those photographers and reporters who are currently sleeping in their cars outside my apartment. But knowing things that other people don't know is how they make their living. Once they find a loose thread, they keep pulling on it until it unravels. Or snaps.'

There was a different note to his voice now. A kind of quiet firmness. Like a door closing that couldn't be opened from the inside.

Lily felt sick. Outside the sunlight was too bright to look into directly, but there were shadows beneath the trees and she could feel the darkness outside seeping towards her.

She had been thinking about herself.

Only it wouldn't just be her, it would be her family, too, who would be caught in the net. That was fine for her parents. Her father had chosen his career and her mother had chosen her father knowing who he was and where his ambitions lay, but Lucas...

Picturing her brother's face, she felt her ribs tighten.

He was the polar opposite of Trip. Shy, self-effacing, sensitive, not at all comfortable in his beautiful skin.

Not that Trip knew or cared about that. And in some ways, it was irrelevant now that their engagement was official. Trip had been the big news story for the last twenty-four hours, and the revelation that he and Lily were secretly engaged would be catnip to the press packs.

Picturing them jostling for position on the stoop outside her apartment, she shuddered. She hated being in the lime-light, but Trip had made that an inevitability. So, she had a choice, if you could call it that. Stay engaged and hope the media focused on the upcoming wedding and the bridal excesses of the Upper East Side. Or break up with Trip and wait for the sky to fall on her head. Because it would. And not just her head. The impact of ending things with someone so high profile would be impossible to contain.

Being caught in the wake of the media madness that would follow her 'dis-engagement' would be horrendous for Lucas, but if someone pulled on one of his loose threads...

Thanks to her last doomed decision to trust someone, he was still fragile, more so even than was usual.

She couldn't risk him unravelling again. Or worse.

There was a beat of silence, then another.

Clenching her hands so tightly that her nails dug into her palms, she lifted her chin. 'How long would I have to do it for? Be married to you, I mean.'

There was a short, pulsing silence.

'I hadn't really got that far. A year, I suppose. Maybe a little longer.' She had assumed Trip would be elated. This was, after all, his moment of triumph, but as his gaze moved from her face to her tightly closed fist, she could see a muscle working in his jaw. 'Does it really matter?'

No, not at all, she thought, turning towards the darkness, letting it swallow her up and blot out the panic in her chest and throat. If she could survive a day, she would survive any number and she *would* survive. She had to.

'What matters is that we broke the news of our engagement to suit our agenda. You see, there's a way to do these things. Announcing it when all this other stuff about my "return" is dominating the news means that people are going to concentrate on the positives. That's good for you too, Lily.'

Was it? She stared at him dully, not even caring that he so casually used 'we' and 'our' as if this were some carefully negotiated agreement instead of a unilateral ambush.

Because now she knew what mattered. Not her feelings. Not the trajectory of her life. But was that so surprising? She already knew there was a perceived association in most people's minds between being attractive and being important. Although they had started before she was a teenager, the years of being mocked and being made to feel inferior because her nose had a bump on it and her hair wasn't smooth and glossy were not some distant memory.

It hurt to have confirmation that Trip felt that way about her. To know that he had found it so easy to break up with her and just as easy to now manipulate her into this charade of a marriage.

She didn't know how long the rest of the journey took. It felt endless. Felt as if time had stopped and she was simply reliving the same moment over and over again. Finally, the car took a little twist to the left onto a road that led onto a drive edged with cypress trees.

And then she saw it.

Framed by the Tuscan countryside, the Villa Morandi looked like an enchanted palace from a fairy tale. Her heartbeat accelerated as the driver slowed the car, then turned off the engine and walked around to open her door. Stepping out onto the driveway, she gazed up mutely at the villa, her eyes moving appreciatively over the sun-faded walls and dark green shutters.

'What do you think?'

Trip's voice snapped her thoughts in two and she turned to face him. 'It's lovely,' she said truthfully. She had wanted to hate it, but it felt wrong to lie.

Wrong to lie? Her heart began to race again. What was wrong with her? Trip had not just lied to her, he had misled the trustees and manipulated her parents and was forcing her into a marriage of his convenience for which he had shown zero contrition. She needed to toughen up, and fast, or she was never going to survive this.

Lifting her chin, she gave the villa another cursory glance, then shrugged. 'But if you've seen one Italian villa, you've seen them all. I mean, they all look the same. Their owners do, too. Let's hope I don't get you mixed up with some other self-absorbed, manipulative billionaire.'

'That would complicate things.' His blue eyes glinted in the sunlight and she felt his gaze sweep over her. 'But given that we spent most of our time together naked, perhaps we should just take off all our clothes. That way there would be no confusion.'

There was no answer to that, and she turned away from the house.

Now that the shock of being there had faded a little, her senses felt as though they were being bombarded. A hot, dry breeze was caressing her skin and she could smell the earth and the grass and the cypress trees and, beyond the trees, she could hear...

Nothing.

Her body tingled. She was surrounded by silence, and she had a feeling she'd never had before. Of being far from civilisation, because she didn't need a map to know there was nothing for miles in every direction.

She shivered. There was nothing here except forced intimacy with the man standing beside her, and that thought made the darkness and the heat and the silence press in on her so that it was suddenly difficult to breathe.

A slight middle-aged woman with long, greying hair in a ponytail stepped forward to greet them with a smile on her face. 'Buongiorno, Signor Winslow, Signorina Dempsey,' she said. 'I hope you had a pleasant flight.'

'There was a little turbulence, wasn't there, darling?' Trip turned to her and gave her a smile that didn't reach his eyes. 'But nothing we couldn't handle.

'Lily, this is Valentina. She's the housekeeper and estate manager. Anything you need or want, start with her.

Except tonight.' He turned towards the older woman. 'Thanks, Valentina. I can take things from here.'

As they walked through the hall, Trip turned towards her. 'I'll let you get settled in and then we can have something to eat.'

Eat? How could he think about eating?

Lily stared at him blankly, suddenly light-headed. In the car, when she had agreed to marry him, it hadn't felt real. But now it did. It was actually happening, only this was just the beginning.

'I'm not hungry,' she said coolly. 'I want to lie down. And don't for one minute think that you'll be lying beside me.'

He raised an eyebrow but all he said was, 'I'll show you to your room.'

Heart pounding with misery and exhaustion, she followed him upstairs, her pulse accelerating wildly as he led her into a charming bedroom with a beautiful carved four-poster bed.

'This is where you're sleeping.'

She froze as he turned to face her. There was enough space between them to park a car and yet the taut, masculine power of his body was too close for comfort.

'There's a bathroom through there, and this is the dressing room.' As he stepped forward a light clicked on softly overhead and her eyes narrowed, not on Trip, but on a jacket hanging from the rail. She had one just like it—

Her breath caught in her throat as she stared at the other clothes that had been neatly folded and hung.

'Where did you get these?'

'Your mother had them sent over to my apartment before we left.'

Another betrayal. Wincing inwardly, and needing distance from his disturbingly piercing gaze, she backed out of the dressing room into the bedroom and walked towards the floor-to-ceiling picture window.

The drapes were open and she stared through the glass. Her eyes felt hot. It was strange to think that this was the same sun that she had watched set in New York yesterday afternoon. It seemed so much brighter, like a sun in a dream. Her fingers bit into the skin of her wrist. If only she could pinch herself awake from the nightmare that was engulfing her.

'You know it's not just me, Lily.'

Trip was standing behind her. She could see his reflection in the window, but she would have known he was there even if she'd been blindfolded. That thread again.

Their eyes met in the glass and she saw his pupils flare, felt it like a flicker of heat low in her belly, impossible to ignore, imperative to resist.

'Everyone wants this for us. You wanted it too. Wanted me.'

She felt something rough-edged scrape inside her and she wanted to back away, hide in the dressing room, but there would be no point. She couldn't hide from the truth, from that heat pulsing across her skin and the tightness inside her. And it was true. She had wanted him.

More than wanted him.

In those hours when they had been alone in her apartment he had been essential to her. Like air and water and sunlight. It had been beautiful too and even though she'd known it would end, could never be anything more than it was, it had been hers, and it had worked, the raw sensuality, that hunger, being wanted like that. Only now he was making the memory of it ugly.

'The idea of it, yes,' she said coolly, without bothering

to turn around. 'But most women have any number of romantic fantasies in their head and the trouble with fantasies is that they're always a bit of a let-down.'

For a moment he didn't reply, and then he reached into his pocket and pulled out a small, square box.

Her heart gave a little jerk as he opened it and she stared down at the huge marquise diamond surrounded by smaller sapphires. 'But this isn't a fantasy. It's a means to an end. We need to be engaged. Both of us. Which is why, from now on, you need to wear this.'

He held out the ring and as if hypnotised, she took it and slid it onto her fourth finger.

Trip was staring at her hand. 'Does it fit okay?'

She nodded and she wondered briefly how he knew what size to choose. 'It feels strange,' she said stiffly.

His gaze lifted to her face, the blue of his irises one shade darker than the stones in her ring.

'You'll get used to it.' He hesitated as if he had something else to say, but then he turned and she watched him walk away. He stopped at the door to remove the key and then he was shutting the door and she waited for the click of the lock, but she heard nothing.

Because he didn't need to lock her in. She wasn't going anywhere and he knew it, and it was all too easy to hate Trip then. Only hating him didn't change anything. He might have lied to her, tricked her, abducted her and blackmailed her. But she was still going to have to marry him.

CHAPTER FIVE

'WOULD YOU LIKE some more tea, *signorina*?'

Glancing up at Valentina, Lily shook her head. 'No, thank you. I only ever have one cup.'

She shifted position in her chair and returned her gaze to where it had been fixed for the last twenty minutes to a point about an inch to the left of Trip's maddeningly handsome face.

They were having breakfast outside beneath swathes of fragrant wisteria.

Beyond the formal gardens with their box hedging and parterres and half-hidden statuary was a rippling landscape of greens in every shade uninterrupted by anything man-made. Just paddocks of grazing horses, rows of olive trees and sloping fields of grape-covered vines and then finally the dark bosky hills that rolled up to meet the cloudless blue sky.

It was her first meal at the villa and the food was excellent, on a par with anything her parents' housekeeper, Marisa, produced back in New York. She was still a little too tense to fully enjoy her breakfast of delicately scrambled eggs with curling ribbons of crispy pancetta, but that wasn't Valentina's fault. She seemed like a nice person and she wasn't responsible for the actions of her capricious owner.

'The eggs were wonderful, by the way,' she said, glancing up at the housekeeper and smiling. 'And the bread. In fact, it was all delicious.'

Yesterday, probably because of the stress and the left-over effects of anti-nausea pills, she had fallen asleep and unintentionally missed lunch. Waking in the late afternoon, she had showered and changed clothes and, drawn to the miraculous view from her window, she had decided to leave the sanctuary of her room.

Only then had she caught sight of Trip wandering in the garden, looking irritatingly relaxed and handsome, talking on the phone, and she had felt so furious that she had picked up her own phone to call her mother and tell her the truth.

But, swiping right, she had been confronted by the screensaver of her family and, gazing down into her brother's sweet face, had felt her anger ooze away.

At some point, Trip had knocked on the door and called out her name softly and she had sat, muscles quivering, poised to dart into the bathroom, which at least had a key. He hadn't come in and she had spent the next few hours alternately hating him and trying to come up with some way to extricate herself without causing collateral damage to everyone she loved.

She failed.

Later, she had watched Valentina set a beautiful candlelit table with a mounting sense of dread as the reality of what she'd agreed to had set in. Maybe Trip had read her mind because it had been the housekeeper who'd knocked on her door that time. She'd opened it and explained that she had a migraine and would not be joining Mr Winslow for supper.

It had felt like a minor victory, albeit in a war she had

already conceded. But this morning, gazing out at the mist-covered hills, she had decided that she was done with hiding. She had spent so much of her life keeping her head down, trying not to be seen, not even for the things that she was good at, like her job.

And if anyone should be hiding away it was Trip. It was that thought that had propelled her downstairs and through the elegant sitting room with its marble-topped side tables and exquisite linen-covered sofas.

It was the right thing to do, she told herself. The warm, lemon-scented air was calming and, despite its elegance, the blush-pink house was a comforting backdrop. Hidden slightly by a hedge of paintbrush-tipped cypresses, a shimmering blue swimming pool glittered temptingly like a sapphire in the sunshine.

But the pool and the house were still overshadowed by the breathtaking beauty of its owner, she thought, watching through lowered lashes as Trip shifted back in his chair to squint up at the Tuscan sun that was partly to blame for that annoying but undeniable truth.

Given his behaviour, it should be hiding behind a cloud. Instead, the sun seemed determined to show Trip in his best light, illuminating the extraordinary sculpted angles and curves of his face like a master cinematographer.

Turning her face minutely away from the gravitational pull of his flawless features, she stared determinedly to where the horses, coats gleaming, were tossing their heads fretfully to dispel any curious flies. It looked exactly like—

'It looks like a painting, doesn't it?'

Trip's voice cut across her thoughts and, pulse stumbling, she turned towards him, jolted that he could read her mind. Not that it was the first time. Only then she had wanted him to. Now it didn't seem fair that he retained that power.

For Valentina's benefit, she gave an infinitesimal nod of her head. 'I suppose it does.' She had no intention of letting him know that he could see inside her head. Or of making this easy for him in any way.

He had thought she would, of course. Coming downstairs this morning, he had acted just as if they were here on holiday. As if this trip were something consensual, something they had discussed with excitement together, when in reality she had been pushed into a corner, trapped into a year-long charade against her will.

Not that Trip cared, she thought, glancing across the table to where he was lounging in the seat opposite her, handsome in pale chinos and a fine pale blue shirt. Now that he had got his own way he seemed to have completely forgotten what he had done to reach this point.

So maybe it was time to remind him.

As Valentina disappeared back into the house, Lily put down her cup.

'Just a point of information. I know you're not a details kind of guy, but if this is going to work, then you need to understand that there have to be some ground rules for our "arrangement". My rules.'

'You have rules for this?' That mouth of his curved into something that wasn't quite a smile, something that banged through her like falling scaffolding. 'And there was me thinking I was your first.'

Her temper flared.

'You think this is a joke? You've put me in an impossible position. That's why I've agreed to do this, Trip, and I will make the best of it. But the best version of this for me will be to spend as little time as possible with you.'

He studied her for a moment. 'You are aware that we're going to be married?'

There was that same slight curve pulling at his mouth as if her words didn't matter to him. But as he stretched out his legs there were different truths layered beneath his casual manner. She could see them in the slight narrowing of his eyes and the sudden elevation of tension in that mouth-watering body of his.

'I understand that we will have to spend time together in public, and when that happens, I will behave the way that couples do in a real relationship. You know, the kind where one party hasn't been coerced into the relationship by the other.'

He eyed her across the table. 'But our way is so much more stimulating, don't you think?'

She ignored him. 'I will make conversation and smile but, just so we're clear, that doesn't mean that I want to.' And she wasn't going to let him forget it. 'I don't want anything from you, except my freedom. Unfortunately, you've made me a co-conspirator to your lies, but that doesn't mean I have to lie when we're alone. So I won't be making small talk with you when we're on our own. It's bad enough that I'm going to have to play-act in public. I won't do it in private.'

Private. The word jangled inside her head, made her think of low lighting and locked doors, and her stomach cartwheeled, nipples tightening as every single cell in her body quivered into a state of such heightened awareness that just meeting his gaze made her feel dizzy.

'Nor are there going to be any "benefits" between us,' she said stiffly, trying to sound like the opposite of the woman who had melted against him less than forty-eight hours ago.

'Benefits?'

The skin on her face felt suddenly too tight. 'You know, intimacies,' she said quickly, ignoring the pulse of heat that beat up over her throat and face as her brain unhelpfully suggested the range of acts that word might include.

Steadying her breathing, she pushed back her seat. 'And now that we both know where we stand, I'm going to—'

'What about kissing?' He frowned. 'What's the rule about that?'

'What?' Lily tensed all the way through.

'Kissing?' he repeated, his eyes finding hers. 'Does that count as intimate?'

'Of course it does,' she said quickly.

'Then I'm confused,' he said, mildly enough but there was a gleam in those blue eyes of his that she felt everywhere. 'Because the other day when we kissed at your apartment, we were one hundred per cent on our own.'

That shimmering thread between them pulled taut as she realised too late that she had stepped into a trap of her own making. There was no answer to that. Or none that she was willing to share with Trip, here in the beautiful Italian sunshine.

At the time she had been lost in the moment and the press of his mouth on hers and the scent of his skin.

It was only afterwards that she had attempted to rationalise her behaviour as something that had needed to be done. So not rational, but understandable. Because she had hated how it had ended before, with her telling him that she didn't care what he did or where he went. Or even if he came back.

Kissing had felt right, and the rightness of it and the fierceness of it had taken her breath away, and all of it, all her anger and hostility, had melted away and there had just been heat and need and truth.

Only now there was nothing but lies.

'There will be no kissing at all,' she hissed, getting to her feet. 'If we have to look like a couple, we can hold hands.'

'And why would we have to do that?' His gaze was so blue, so deep, she felt as though she were drowning. 'Just for information purposes, of course,' he called after her as she stalked back into the house.

She stayed upstairs until lunchtime. When Valentina knocked on the door to tell her the meal was ready she was tempted to pretend she had another migraine, but she couldn't do that every single time Trip annoyed her. Clutching a novel in front of her like a shield, she followed the housekeeper downstairs.

Lunch was light but just as delicious as breakfast. As one of the maids arrived to clear the table, she was fully intending to retreat to her room to read. Trip had other ideas.

'We'll take coffee by the pool. It's cooler down there. More private,' he added, reaching out to take her hand, no doubt in retaliation for her words at breakfast. She had no option but to let him, but as soon as Valentina had deposited their coffee onto one of the tables by the sunloungers she snatched her hand away again.

Of course, she didn't need to worry. Trip needed constant stimulation and within five minutes he had disappeared back into the villa.

Tipping her head back, she gazed up at the cloudless blue sky and then quickly looked back down again. It was too much like looking into Trip's eyes. Reaching down, she picked up her book and opened it. A light breeze was moving in from the mountains and, liking the feel of it against her skin, she half closed her eyes.

That was better…

'So what would be the next step?'

Her eyes snapped open and she stared across the rectangle of glittering blue water. Trip was back, a satellite phone pressed against his smooth dark head, sunlight dancing across his face as if it were delighted to see him.

Oh, and he had changed into black swim shorts. *Great.*

She stared at him, dry-mouthed, conscious suddenly that she was not quite controlling her reaction, but thankfully he was walking away from her, pacing back and forth along the length of the pool, moving with that familiar mesmerising athletic grace. Judging by the tension in his shoulders, it was a business call, although she didn't really care one way or another. Nothing about Trip was of any interest to her.

Liar, she thought, a beat of heat looping down to her stomach and back up to her throat as she tried not to stare at his semi-naked body.

She hadn't forgotten how gorgeous he was, but it was still a shock to be within spitting distance of all that bare, golden skin and curving muscle.

Not that she wanted to spit. She wanted to press her lips against his chest and follow the trail of fine dark hairs with her tongue to where they disappeared beneath the waistband of his trunks. Then go lower still to where the hairs thickened, and keep licking until they were both panting and mindless with hunger.

Her throat was so dry now it hurt to swallow and she could feel the back of the chair pressing against her spine. Just for a moment, she allowed her gaze to rest on the ripple of muscle but then it was too much.

Gripping the book tighter, she ducked her head and stared blindly at the words, seeing nothing, reading nothing, her body twitching restlessly against the lounger.

Trip was still pacing, but now he stopped so that he was in profile to her, the outline of his body silhouetted crisply against the blue of the sky, taut, lean, undeniably male. It was no surprise to her and yet she felt the shock of it curl through her body as hot colour flooded her cheeks when he glanced over and found her watching him.

'I have to go,' he said softly.

Jerking her gaze away, she stared back down at the lines of type, her heart bumping against her ribs as he came closer.

There was a slight creak as he sat down. She could see his body out of the corner of her eye, but it was his scent that was playing havoc with her nerve endings.

'What are you doing?' Her fingers fumbled against the book and she had to flatten herself against the cushions as he suddenly got to his feet and leaned over her.

'Calm down.' His eyes narrowed on her face. 'I'm not going to jump you.'

'You did before.' She swallowed, hard, remembering the heat, the fire, the devastating rush of need, her own unthinking impatience to walk through the flames with him. 'And then you tricked me into flying here with you and you've done nothing but threaten and bully and manipulate me ever since, so you'll forgive me if I'm a little hazy about your intentions.'

He held up his hands as if he were the one being threatened.

'I was just moving the parasol.' He gestured up towards the bleached-out sun high above them. 'So that you don't get burned.' His blue eyes rested on the blouse and pants she was wearing. 'Although you might actually die of heat-stroke before that happens. Are you not hot?'

Lily smiled thinly.

Thanks to her mother, she was, because, aside from the jacket she had recognised, Laura had packed the kind of clothes that would be suitable for a romantic holiday à deux. Which was, of course, what her mother thought this was.

She gritted her teeth. Only she didn't want to wear some conspicuously new and humiliating unworn skimpy bikini or semi-transparent dress in front of Trip any more than she wanted to make small talk with him. Which was why she was dressed in the same clothes that she had worn on the plane. Because, despite the heat of the day, she needed her armour.

'I'm fine, thank you,' she said stiffly.

Trip stared down at her for a moment, his blue gaze momentarily hotter than the sun, and then he shrugged. 'Suit yourself.'

She held his gaze. 'Nothing about this situation suits me, Trip, as you very well know.'

She half expected him to respond but he was already turning towards the pool, and she watched with a mix of fury and envy as he dived into the water. It was the kind of dive that barely made a ripple on the glassy surface, which had to be a first for him, she thought, her heart still beating out of time from that last interaction.

Partly it was the fact that he was one of the richest men in the world, partly it was his extraordinary looks, but there was more to Trip than just the obvious. He had an energy, a presence that changed the atmosphere around him, making it shimmer and ripple like the air above roads in a heatwave. She had seen first-hand how he could cause a kind of seismic ripple to the structure of any building he was in. Even when his muscular outline was distorted by the water, there was something that kept pulling your gaze towards him. Anticipation, maybe, for the moment when he would emerge, godlike, from the water.

As if on cue, he did just that, pulling himself up onto the tiled edge of the pool with effortless grace. Her pulse ticced in her throat as he smoothed back his wet hair, sending water trickling down the hard planes and angles of his back and shoulders.

It was impossible to look away, excruciating to keep looking.

So move, she told herself, but Trip was already walking towards her and then he was sitting beside her, stretching out one long muscular leg and tilting his head up to the sun.

'Ah, here's Valentina,' he said softly, and before she had a chance to react he had taken her hand and lifted it to his mouth.

The housekeeper had brought out a jug of freshly squeezed peach juice and, pressing her lips together in a tight smile, Lily sat fuming while Trip dragged out the conversation on purpose by asking Valentina which peaches she had used. And the whole time, he caressed the back of Lily's hand with his thumb in a way that made her feel restless and light-headed.

Finally, Valentina left and Lily jerked her hand free of his grip and got shakily to her feet.

He glanced up at her, frowning. 'What are you doing?'

'I'm going indoors.'

'For real?' His face was expressionless, but she could hear the frustration in his voice. 'Why? Because I held your hand? I'm following your rules. Maybe you should too, Lily, because you need this to work as much as I do. If it doesn't, I think life is going to be real hard for you and everyone you care about, so stop fighting me and stop fighting yourself, because this is happening.'

He was right on both counts, she thought as she headed back into the house for the second time that day. But knowing that didn't make it any easier to live with.

Staring after her, Trip felt his hands curl into fists. Yesterday had been a challenging but ultimately satisfying day. Obviously Lily had been furious with him and it had taken longer than he'd thought for her to stop fighting him. But then he'd mentioned Lucas and she had acquiesced with a speed that had confused him.

And unsettled him.

Picking up the jug of peach juice, he poured himself a glass and drank it swiftly. Normally, he found the familiar sweetness calming but now it sat in his stomach like a lump of ice.

He knew Lily's younger brother. Not well, but enough to know that he was shy and sensitive and probably not equipped to handle the modern media machine. Nor did he know for sure what Lucas had been doing in Zurich, and to be truthful he probably would have never given it a second thought. But then he'd realised that the Dempseys had lied about Lucas' whereabouts.

There had been no need to join the dots for him to work out why. Among his set there was only one reason people lied about being in Zurich. It was because they were in rehab.

He hadn't ever planned on using it as leverage, but then Lily wouldn't give in and he'd been getting impatient. And working and living with Henry Winslow II had taught him that if you found a crack, you pushed on it to see what, if anything, broke.

And Lily had capitulated.

But as victories went, it had been less than satisfying. She had looked small and fragile, just like that time at the auction, and, watching her face grow pale, he hadn't liked how it made him feel. It wasn't who he was, whatever she might think. He was impulsive, occasionally thoughtless, sometimes arrogant, but he didn't lie or cheat or bully or blackmail or do any of the other things she had accused him of doing.

And he didn't want to hurt Lily. In part that was one of the reasons he'd decided to bring her to Italy.

Because something had happened to him in Ecuador. It might be a cliché but staring down the barrel of a gun had rewired him in some way. All those weeks of feeling vulnerable and alone had made him understand that he could rely only on himself. That he needed to be ruthless. Single-minded. Selfish even.

And then there were the letters. Lily had been the first person he'd seen after reading them and shock had made him colder, and crueller, than he should have been. More like the man he couldn't not love, but resented and hated. Knowing that had angered him, and he'd felt guilty too for taking it out on Lily, but in the moment it had been easier to blame her for making him feel so out of control.

He'd done the same thing earlier today, his guilt at dragging her into all of this colliding with his frustration at her continuing and pointless refusal to accept the new status quo, and so he'd lashed out at her with the kind of ultimatum Henry had specialised in. And he hated being like his father.

Tilting back his head, he stared into the sun until ev-

erything turned white and he was forced to blink. If only
he could blank out those pages, unsee those lines of cur-
sive script, but he couldn't.

It was what he'd hoped would happen in Ecuador. But
the blindfold and then the silence and claustrophobic
gloom of the jungle had simply made everything inside
his head sharper and louder. He'd thought he was going to
lose his mind. Only one thing had kept him going: Lily.

He had dreamed about her constantly, often with such
clarity that when he'd woken he'd half expected to find her
by his side. And when, finally, he'd escaped his captors
it had been her eyes that had been like silver stars guid-
ing him onwards whenever he couldn't see the night sky
through the rainforest canopy.

His shoulders tensed.

Obviously, he hadn't been himself in those days and
weeks in the jungle, but in some ways it made sense for
him to have imagined Lily. After all, he had ended up in
her apartment every night for months, right up until he'd
left for Ecuador.

No doubt that was also why hers had been the first name
to pop into his head when he'd been squaring up to Mason
and the other trustees.

Not that he was planning on explaining any of this to
Lily. He didn't need to.

She hadn't come quietly or easily, but she was here now,
with her rules and that tilt of her chin. And her uncanny
ability to find the cracks in his armour.

Remembering how she had thrown his father's name at
him like some verbal gauntlet, he gritted his teeth.

'And what would he think about you doing this?' Lily
had asked. *'He wanted you to step up. To grow up.'*

The answer to that question made him get to his feet

abruptly, because it wasn't Lily's voice inside his head, but Henry's, and his chest clenched, tightening hard, tightening around an emptiness that was as familiar as it was painful. He swayed forward. His brain felt as if it were short-circuiting and his hands moved automatically to his face, but it would take more than tapping to quiet his mind. He turned and began to walk swiftly away from the house.

Rereading the same paragraph for the umpteenth time, Lily looked up from her book and sighed. She was sitting on the window seat in her room and it was in many ways the perfect spot to read. Light but not bright, comfy enough to relax but not to doze off. But she couldn't concentrate. All she could think about was what Trip had said to her earlier.

He was right. She did need this to work. No doubt, news of their engagement would leak out if it hadn't already, and it didn't matter that she hated everything about the situation. There was more at stake than her ego. Her throat tightened. Only it was turning out to be so much harder than she had ever imagined.

Her fingers twitched, and she made a fist, trying to banish the memory of how it had felt when Trip had taken her hand out by the pool. She knew that it had been for Valentina's benefit, oh, and to prove a point, but why then could she still feel the imprint of his touch? Why did it still burn now, sharp and hot like the lick of a flame?

Why then did it make her want more heat? More touch, just more…

Needing to distract herself, she stared through the window at the view. She had been to Rome only once with her parents and she had loved all the art and architecture and the buzz of the moped and the oven-hot streets. But this was the other side to Italy. Lush, rural, so quiet you could hear your heart beating. It was like looking at a painting. Or perhaps the backdrop to a play or a ballet. But there were no dancers waiting nervously in the wings, just horses, heads low as they grazed the lush green grass.

She put down her book.

Her family were sailors. Her dad had a yacht and they spent their summers around Martha's Vineyard, taking the boat out all the way to the Bahamas and back. She liked horses but they were large and unpredictable, so mostly she was happy to look at them from a distance.

But maybe that was something else that was going to have to change too if she was ever going to take a look around her home for the next few days—weeks?—because there seemed to be an awful lot of them.

As if to prove that point, she heard a whinny from nearby and, leaning forward a fraction, she narrowed her gaze in the direction of the sound.

She was more than a little scared of horses, but perhaps if she could get past her fear then everything else would seem easy in comparison. At the very least it would stop her thinking about Trip. First, though, she was going to change clothes. She was just too hot and she couldn't keep wearing the same things day after day.

Having changed into a light gingham print dress with puffed sleeves, which was no doubt her mother's idea of what to wear for some imaginary picnic in the country, she slipped on her sandals and made her way downstairs.

It was easy to find the stables, although only the two-part doors with their hay rails gave any hint that they were for horses, not humans. They shared the same stucco walls and pantiled roof as the main house and were easily the most opulent-looking stables she had ever seen. But there were no horses.

And then she heard it again, the same noise as before, only softer, more of a nickering sound than a whinny. It was coming from a slightly larger building next door, some kind of barn by the looks of it.

The door was shut but it opened easily and she slipped inside, glancing up, momentarily transfixed by the dust motes spiralling lazily down from the ceiling.

And then she saw him.

Trip was standing next to a beautiful chestnut-coloured horse. Given that he was standing in a barn, she would have expected him to be wearing chinos or jeans, but he was still wearing his swim shorts. His one concession to the equestrian setting was that he no longer had bare feet. Instead he was wearing some of those short riding boots.

At first she thought he was on the phone. His head was lowered slightly and one hand was pressing against the side of his face, but then he moved and she saw that it was empty. He seemed to be just standing there. No, not just standing, she thought, her gaze resting on the rise and fall of his chest. He was concentrating.

Abruptly, the horse shook his head and took a couple of steps forward and she saw Trip frown, adjust his breathing, then follow the horse.

Her own breath was trapped in her throat. What was he doing?

Now, Trip was bowing his head again, closing his eyes and for a moment nothing happened and then the horse turned and gently nuzzled his shoulders, and she had a sudden, strong feeling that she was intruding.

Without turning, she took a step backwards and collided with something hard and metallic. A shovel—

'Ouch!'

'Lily?'

The horse made an accusatory whickering sound, but it was Trip's voice that made her legs momentarily weave beneath her, then freeze.

Trip had turned and was walking towards her. In the soft, smothered light of the barn his beauty transcended any words she could muster.

'Are you okay?' He was squinting but she felt his gaze like a searchlight. Behind him, the horse was walking over to tug at a net of hay.

'I'm fine.' She cleared her throat. 'I heard the horses, so I thought I'd come and have a look at them.' Remembering how Trip had followed it around, she said, 'Is it okay?'

'Acrux?' He turned to where the horse was pulling at the hay. 'He's good.' She couldn't see his face but there was something odd about his voice. A hesitancy, almost as if it was a struggle to speak.

'He's beautiful.'

Another hesitation but the tension in his voice dropped a notch. 'And he's smart. People think horses are just dumb animals, but they're not.'

'Is that why you chose him? His intelligence?'

His face softened. 'I didn't choose him. I bred him, raised him from a foal.'

That surprised her. That he could have that focus and perseverance. Something of what she was thinking must have shown on her face, because his mouth curved up at one corner. 'You don't believe me.'

'Well, it does seem a little out of character,' she admitted. But then it wasn't the first time he'd caught her off guard. Her body stiffened as she remembered the moment when she'd realised that she'd forgotten to upload her speech.

'I never thanked you,' she said slowly. 'For what you

did that night at the auction. Stepping in and just giving a speech like that, it was really impressive. I don't know what I would have done if you hadn't been there, so thank you for that.'

There was a short, slightly startled silence.

'What made you think of that?' he said finally.

She shrugged. 'I don't know. Just you being different from how I thought. From how you were when we had lunch that first time.'

He laughed then, a real laugh, not a mocking one, and she couldn't stop her eyes from moving towards the sound. It made her feel as if her limbs were filling with a golden light that poured straight from the sun.

'Yeah, well, that wasn't my finest hour.' His eyes moved to find hers. 'You were pretty impressive though. Seriously bossy, but impressive. I can remember being astonished that you were so young.'

'To be fair, I'd been working on it for some time.'

He shook his head. 'Which is why it was so impressive. It didn't feel like you were phoning it in. You made it feel fresh, exciting. Even though you hated me,' he added.

She felt herself blushing. 'I didn't hate you. Well, maybe I did, a bit, but you were late. And hungover. And distracted.' Her mouth twitched. 'But when I took away your phone, you had a lot of good ideas.'

His eyes were clear and steady on her face. 'We were a good team. And you did thank me that night,' he added softly and there were no words to describe how the softness in his voice made her feel.

Maybe that was why she forgot for a moment why she was there in Italy. Why it suddenly felt as if it were just two people, talking normally, a couple almost. Instead of what they were, which was actors rehearsing their lines for the opening night.

She took a breath. 'I don't know how to do this, Trip,' she said quietly.

His face stilled then and for a fraction of a second, the doubt and nervousness she was feeling was visible in his eyes. And then it was gone. 'You're overthinking it. We're both in the public eye, Lily. Which means having to play a part sometimes, putting on a mask.'

She felt a jolt of surprise. She didn't just wear a mask in public, she wore full body armour. It was the only way she could do the job she loved, be the daughter she wanted to be. But she was surprised that Trip felt that way.

'Remember how we stood up at that auction together.' He was impatient again now. 'It'll be just the same as that.'

Except it wouldn't be, she thought. At home, with her family, her close friends, she was herself, but here with Trip, she wouldn't be able to relax. She couldn't risk letting her guard down and something happening, as it had at her apartment.

'No, it's not. You have live-in staff on site. That means I'll have to be in character almost all of the time.'

His face hardened. 'What do you want me to say, Lily? Life's not fair.'

Lily stared at him, her throat tightening. She didn't need Trip to tell her that it was dog eat dog out there. She knew life wasn't fair.

'Okay, maybe that's the wrong word—'

It was. Expecting her to fake what had once been real was not just unfair, it was unkind.

He cut across her. 'I don't know why you're making it into such a big deal. It's not as if I'm asking you to do something you weren't already willing to do.'

Her heart contracted.

'Yes, you are. We were having sex. In private. Now you're asking me to be your fiancée, your cheerleader, your guarantor. In public.'

He stared at her, his mouth curving upwards into a shape that was more sneer than smile. She felt her heart thud too hard inside her chest. 'But I'm not asking you, am I?' Now his face was dark with impatience. 'Look, Lily, you know how the world works. People love a story. All we have to do is make them believe it. And you're a very smart woman, so I don't think that's going to be a problem. Particularly as you have an incentive. We both do.'

She drew a rough breath. 'I don't like that word.'

'Which one? Story? Incentive?'

'We,' she said tersely. 'There is you and there is me. We implies consent and intimacy, neither of which are present in this current arrangement.'

His gaze narrowed, mouth curving mockingly. 'You mean current as in this particular moment, because not long ago we were kissing, and it was definitely consensual—'

She could feel the buttons of her dress burning into her skin. The air around them was growing thicker. It was making her breathing go messy and her brain felt fuzzy.

'That was—'

'What?' He raised an eyebrow. 'A bad idea? A mistake?' He took a step forward and she felt the tension between them snap tight as his eyes fixed on where she could feel her nipples pushing against the checked cotton.

'You're lying to me, you're lying to yourself. You wanted me, Lily, you still do. I don't know why you won't admit it—'

He was standing so close she could see the smattering of freckles along his cheekbones, the faint shadow of stubble on his jawline. Too close. But she didn't need to be that close to feel the truth of his words and even though she didn't want them to, they did something to her, made her remember how it felt to see him aroused, to know that she had the power to arouse him.

And right now that felt like the only power she had left.

'So let's have sex.' She took a step forwards, hands on hips as if she were a prizefighter throwing down a challenge. 'Let's do it. Here. Now. Let's have sex here in this barn.'

He looked taken aback in about five different ways, and after so many weeks of feeling conflicted and helpless that felt good.

'What? You said it yourself. I want you, you want me. It's just bodies, and it's not as if we can have sex with anyone else. It might as well be here as anywhere else.'

She reached for him, her fingers clumsy against his shirt, pulling him closer, and she felt him tense, his hands moving to her hips, steadying her, stopping her—

'What are you doing?' His voice was hoarse but he wasn't pushing her away and she could feel him against her stomach, the hardness of him making her shudder inside and arch against him.

As if he weren't the man she had tried to run from. The man who was blackmailing her, as if she were just heat and need.

'Lily, no, not like this—'

It was the gentleness in his voice that made her stumble backwards and she stared up at him, her face burning, and she knew that she was crying. She didn't feel powerful any more. She had wanted to punish him, to make him hurt as he was hurting her, and she knew only one way to do that, because sex was when she had felt his equal.

Not any more.

She was just a tool, a means to an end.

'If not like this, then how?'

Her face was wet, but she didn't brush the tears away, instead she crossed her arms. 'Like before maybe? Is that how you want it to be? Because that can't happen. Not ever.' Her voice was shaking now. 'Do you think because I'm not beautiful like you that I don't have feelings? That I don't care that—'

She pressed her hand against her mouth. She had said too much. So much more than she wanted him to know.

He looked stunned, his eyes wide and bluer than she had ever seen them.

'Lily—'

But she was already moving, stumbling through the door and out into the sunlight and then she was running, running from the pain in her heart and the pity in his eyes.

CHAPTER SIX

LEANING BACK IN the chair, Trip gazed up at the sky and breathed in deeply. It was another perfect day.

The sun was shining hard but there was a light breeze, just enough to make the heat bearable. He tilted the glass in his hand to his mouth. This wine was perfect, too. Cool, bright and energetic with apricot and peach flavours.

Finally, everything was going according to plan.

He glanced across the table to where Lily should have been sitting.

Lily was cooperating. But only in the same way that a soldier accepted being a prisoner of war. Outwardly passive while privately counting down until the day of their release.

Somehow she had managed to eat breakfast and then lunch without saying more than ten words to him in total, before evaporating without any explanation or excuse. It was annoying as hell, doubly so because he could hardly force her to talk to him so the chances of things being any different at dinner seemed slim at best.

Because Lily didn't want to talk to him. Didn't want to look at him. Didn't want to be around him. Which was why he was drinking alone—always a good look—and she was presumably holed up in her bedroom, no doubt hating him with every fibre of her being.

His shoulders stiffened as he remembered that moment out in the barn when he'd realised she was crying.

Because of him.

He gazed up into the sun, deliberately letting the white light fill his head so that it would block out the image of Lily's face and an ache that was stretching from one temple to the other. But that only made things worse because now he could hear her voice.

Not ever.

The phrase batted back and forth inside his head and his fingers moved automatically to tap the union valley point in the webbing between his thumb and finger.

He still didn't understand what had happened in the barn.

That she had even been there at all had thrown him off balance. She wasn't supposed to have been. In fact, he had only been there because the tension between them was turning to chaos beneath his skin.

A shiver ran across the bare skin of his arm. Turning to find her watching him with Acrux, he'd never felt more vulnerable, more exposed. Aside from his immediate family and the various therapists he'd seen over the years, nobody knew that he had ADHD. Not officially anyway. His teachers had suspected, his friends joked about it, but Henry had always refused to have him labelled. The family name must be protected at all costs.

Remembering how he'd used to catch his father watching him sometimes, Trip felt his spine tense.

He'd lost count of the number of times he'd been told that coping mechanisms could and should involve family members, and maybe if his mother had been less wrapped up in her own affairs then it might have been different. She might have recognised and praised his ingenuity and energy and his ability to talk to anyone. Perhaps if Charlie had been closer in age and not so scared of displeasing Henry, they might have been friends and his brother could have helped him navigate those confusing early years.

But the Winslows were not a family. They were four individuals who shared a surname, some DNA and a portfolio of prime real estate.

He was ten when, finally, he'd been diagnosed and initially it had been a relief to know why he was different from other people, particularly the father he admired but with whom he so often clashed. The downside was that his father had made it his mission to 'fix' him and his relief had evaporated and he'd started to feel like a lab rat. There had been countless assessments, medication tried and abandoned, counselling sessions, techniques to master, some of which helped some of the time. But it wasn't until one of the therapists had suggested equine-assisted psychotherapy that he'd found a way to make sense of the chaos inside his head.

And because his dad was Henry Winslow II, he hadn't just sent him to an accredited therapist. Wherever it was possible, his homes around the globe had been equipped with stables and the all-important horses to fill them. On the face of it, his father had gone above and beyond what any parent could reasonably be expected to do.

But it had always felt like just another double-edged sword in their complicated, combative relationship. Because despite the progress Trip had made, it had never been enough.

Not even when he had proven that he was more than capable of running the business, more capable than Charlie in many ways because out of the two of them he was the one who had taken risks. He had gone out on his own without his father's blessing or guidance. And yes, he had failed initially, but for him failure was part of innovating. He anticipated it, accepted it. His goal was always to fail better right up until the moment he succeeded.

And he had succeeded. Above and beyond what Henry had at the same age.

But still his father had made him wait, had held back anointing him as his successor, and, via those old men back at the office, he was still holding him to account even though he had no right because Henry had not been the perfect man he'd claimed to be.

His eyes moved to where Acrux was standing beneath one of the chestnut trees that stippled the curving green landscape. Discovering his father's hypocrisy was just one of the reasons why he was struggling to stop his thoughts from stampeding like a herd of wild horses.

He felt the skin on his face tighten.

What he hadn't fully acknowledged until yesterday was how much Lily was struggling too.

Reluctantly he returned to that scene in the barn, those grey eyes of hers resting on his face. Curious, but soft too. As if she understood him. As if she had crept beneath the barriers he'd built between himself and the world.

He couldn't remember anyone looking at him like that. Not even his mother. Alessandra Winslow had been too lost in her own thoughts to have ever really focused on his.

Maybe that was why he'd been caught off guard. Why what had happened next had been so shocking that he'd forgotten his frustration and his anger, that dark consuming fury that he couldn't seem to shift so that it felt as though he'd been furious for almost his whole life. Since before he'd found those letters in his father's things.

He felt his chest tighten. He wasn't a total moron. He

knew that there was grief mixed up in that terrible fury. But knowing that hadn't done much to soothe the fury, or staunch the pain, the ache of losing his father, not once, but twice, because that was what it had felt like finding those letters. Reading those impassioned words from Henry's mistress had made him question everything he'd thought he knew about the man who'd raised him.

It had been like an oil spill inside his chest, spreading slowly, coating everything in toxic, impenetrable darkness. And he didn't know what to do with all of those feelings.

But then gazing into Lily's eyes in the barn yesterday, he'd felt the world steady. And something had changed. All the anger and frustration had just disappeared and he'd found himself relaxing. It had seemed so easy, just talking, and then she'd smiled and he hadn't been able to breathe because it had never been like that with anyone.

Only then she'd told him that she didn't know how to do this. As if, to her, being there with him in that sun-soaked barn was an effort.

And even though he was used to being made to feel like an unwanted complication, it had stung. More than stung. Her words had pierced like a blade. His hands balled. He didn't understand or like this feeling of needing her to like him. It made him conflicted and outgunned because to feel anything other than simple lust was so alien. And pointless too because in his family emotions had rarely been expressed. Even his father's disappointment had been carefully tempered.

But there was no one there for him to rail against and that was a different kind of pain, but, in the moment, he had wanted to hurt Lily, so he had pushed her to admit her desire.

He sucked in a breath, body tensing as he pictured Lily

in that dress with the sunlight behind her, revealing what lay beneath the checked cotton. That she hadn't known what she was revealing had made it even more erotic.

But she had felt it. Felt the shift in the air, felt that quivering, electric thread between them pull taut so that when she'd reached out and touched his chest it hadn't surprised him. What had surprised him, shocked him, was what she'd said and the way she had said it. Talking about sex as if it was just something functional, a nuts-and-bolts need to be screwed tight with a wrench.

Which it was, he told himself irritably. And he had wanted to respond, wanted to press his mouth against hers and his hand against that maddening indent in the small of her back, wanted to fuse her body with his. Only then he had realised she was crying.

Because of him.

He had stopped it, and then she had changed again, pushing him away, her face small and pale and breakable as if he were a stranger, a threat...

And that wasn't fair because, surely, she knew he would never hurt her. Had in fact been trying to do the right thing.

Only now she was acting as if he was the one who had started it. As if being his wife were some kind of life sentence. He got to his feet abruptly and walked swiftly back into the house and up the stairs. Her door was shut, and for a few half seconds he stared at the bland, knotted wood as if that were her answer and then he knocked.

Silence.

He knocked again, more irritably this time because that was who he was, how he was. But there was still no answer, and his anger reared up, full-blooded and unthinking, and he twisted the handle and opened the door.

'Why the hell do you have to—?'

He stopped. The bedroom was empty. Frowning, he checked the bathroom and the dressing room. Both empty. Heart pounding against his ribs, he stared wildly around the room, his head filling with static and then his gaze narrowed on the window.

Through the glass, he could see a figure in shorts and some kind of top moving determinedly through the grass, and then the land curved away and she disappeared.

Trip felt his pulse accelerate. Was she running or hiding? No matter, he would find her. Not that he'd ever even pursued a woman before.

But then he'd never wanted to.

Lily was walking fast.

Back in her bedroom she had tried reading but every time she'd focused on the page, her mind would turn blank and, before she could stop herself, she'd be right back where she'd started in the barn with the tiled roof, making a fool of herself.

It had been enough to get her moving quietly through her bedroom door and down the stairs. A glimpse of Trip out on the terrace, wine glass in hard, soaking up the sunshine as if nothing were wrong, had sent her spinning away from the villa and across the green grass like a bowling ball.

She had no idea where she was going but just being on the move made her feel calmer. There were horses grazing on the left-hand side of the paddock so she kept to the right, kept moving.

It was her phone that finally stopped her in her tracks.

'Lily?' Her father's voice was so familiar and yet it was still a shock to hear him.

'Daddy.'

'Do you have time to talk? I know Mom told you how happy we are, but I just wanted to congratulate you in person.' He paused. 'Although you're probably still fuming with us, aren't you? I know you must be because I know how independent you are, but Mom and I just wanted you to have some time with Trip. Private time. That's why you didn't tell us about the engagement, wasn't it? Because you hate the drama that goes hand in hand with being my daughter. But you could have told us, you know,' he added gently. 'We would have kept your secret.'

Her fingers tightened around the phone. What she hated was having to lie to her parents. To know that she had made them liars too. 'Of course I'm not angry. And it wasn't your drama I was worried about.' That at least was true.

Her father laughed.

'He certainly knows how to make an entrance. Looks the part, too. In fact I heard yesterday that somebody wants to make a film of what happened to him. Probably be quite the blockbuster. Your mother would certainly go and see it. She's quite taken with him. I was too, although I was a little surprised. I always thought you'd choose some penniless artist.'

He was trying to make a joke but Lily's chest squeezed tight. That her father imagined she had a choice of potential husbands was almost as heartbreaking as his unquestioning acceptance that Trip had chosen her.

'We did connect through art,' she said quickly. That was true too, although their connection had been very different from their current situation.

'You don't need to explain, darling girl. We're just delighted that you've found someone you love. But I hope he knows how lucky he is, and he is lucky, Lily.'

Suddenly she could hardly breathe, much less speak. Misery was swelling in her throat. Her parents were so partisan, so blind to her imperfections. They would be heartbroken if they ever found out that Trip had picked her to be his wife solely on the basis that she was the woman least likely to spook the shareholders.

'He does, Daddy.' She cleared her throat. 'I should probably be going—'

'Of course, darling. Now you have fun. Mom sends her love, and Lucas does too.'

Lucas.

As she hung up, she stared down at her brother's sweet face. He was the real reason she was here. The reason she was going to go through with this sham marriage for however long it took. Lucas needed to be left alone. She couldn't take back the past, take back the part she'd played, but she could play her part now.

And there were worse places on the planet to be stuck in limbo, Lily thought as she gazed down at the Tuscan countryside. It felt both epic and lost in time, and, truthfully, if she had come here under any other circumstances she would have been enchanted.

And if this were real. If Trip had really proposed...

If. The shortest, cruellest word in the English language, she thought, body swaying forward in the soft sunlight. She was the stupidest of fools to let herself get caught up in this charade. Because that was what this was. Wasn't it?

For him, yes. But for her...

It was hard being here with him, hard to hate him when he was so close. Harder still when he looked at her as if he wanted to know what she was thinking. Wanted to know her.

But not have sex with her.

She'd been humbled before but what had happened in the barn had been the single most embarrassing thing to happen in her entire life. She could still feel the red blotching her skin. It wasn't just that Trip had rejected her, she had made it slap-in-the-face clear that she knew he would never have proposed to her for real, and that it hurt.

She hadn't wanted to wait around to see the pity in the eyes. She didn't need to. She'd seen it enough times in the past.

The first time she'd realised that she was the ugly duckling in a ballet of swans was when she was seven years old. It had been her mother's thirtieth birthday. Her father had secretly arranged to have a family portrait painted and she and Lucas had been very excited to be in on the surprise. It had been a huge success, one of those memories that families talked about for years afterwards.

But her memory of the moment was different from everyone else's. Staring at the perfectly rendered versions of all of their faces, she had suddenly realised she wasn't beautiful. It had been like a thundercloud breaking over her head.

She'd never raised the subject of her otherness. She hadn't known how because her parents had never treated her differently or made her feel less loved, less valued.

But other people did.

Some did it snidely. Others more openly. She had learned to deflect, to ignore, to not draw attention to herself, to keep her head down. Which had some positives. She had outperformed all her peers at school, and then in college, and after a few years overseeing her parents' charitable trust she had started her own philanthropic advice platform. Her success hadn't completely stopped the trolls, but she'd been busy doing something she loved.

And then she'd met Trip.

Her eyes stung. There must be something wrong with her. After what had happened with Cameron, she should have kept her distance. There was no need to get involved with another handsome, outwardly charming but inwardly self-serving man. Once bitten, twice shy. Or, in her case, spiky.

But Trip had smoothed out all those prickling insecurities.

He had made her feel hungry, lithe and bright with a need that transformed her from flesh and bones into quicksilver.

He had made her beautiful.

But in many ways sex made you as blind and foolish as love did. That was what she hadn't realised before. On the contrary, she had congratulated herself for keeping things contained with Trip in a way she hadn't managed with Cameron.

Because people like her didn't end up with men like Trip. Not in real life. This sham marriage was all that was on offer.

In New York, the sun always felt harsh but here she liked the soft lick of heat and the tease of the breeze. She stood for a few moments, breathing deeply, letting the light play across her face and then she took a step forward between the leaf-covered branches, and touched the cluster of dark purple grapes. They felt firm and warm. But, of course, what really mattered was how they tasted, and, tongue tingling, she pulled one loose and lifted it to her mouth…

A shadow fell across her. A bird? No, it was bigger than a bird, and she turned to glare at the cloud that had dared to spoil this most perfect of moments.

She gazed up, hand frozen mid-air, the foliage around her suddenly watery at the edges, her vision shuddering just as if she really were suffering from the migraine she had been pretending to have.

It wasn't a cloud. It was the beautiful chestnut horse she had seen in the barn yesterday. Acrux—was that his name?

Yesterday, she had thought he looked like a rocking horse, but he seemed a lot bigger this time. Probably because he was standing closer to her. Or maybe it was because Trip was sitting on his back, his broad shoulders blocking out the sunlight.

'Try some if you want, but you might be disappointed,' he said, shifting forward slightly on the horse's back so that his face suddenly slammed into focus, all dazzling blue eyes and glossy brown hair and that body, solid and humming with that energy that instantly made everything around him feel hyperreal.

'The berries are smaller than with table grapes and the skins are much thicker so there's a much higher ratio of skin to pulp. So you can eat them, but you have to chew a lot and then spit out the skins and the seeds.'

That he was riding without a saddle or bridle was mind-boggling enough to a non-rider like her, but now she watched, muted by a slideshow of emotions, some contradictory, each more intense than the last, as he dismounted, dropping to the grass with the same smooth grace with which he did everything physical. He removed the rope from the horse's neck and gathered it in one hand.

'We do grow some grapes for the table over here.' As he started to walk away, the horse followed him and, after a moment, she followed too.

'These are Italia Muscat. They mostly grow in Puglia commercially, but my father always likes…' He paused, his eyes leaving hers briefly to scan back to the villa. 'He always *liked* to have table grapes, so when he bought the estate they started growing this variety, too, just for the family. I think they taste like wine before it's bottled.'

She felt her nerve ending twitch as he held out a small bunch of golden-skinned grapes. 'Don't worry. They're seedless so you won't end up in the underworld for half the year,' he added as she hesitated.

Her eyes jolted up to meet his. Trip knew about Persephone and the pomegranates?

'Are you comparing yourself to a Greek god now?'

That smile. The one she knew by heart.

'Just try one. Please,' he said softly, but there was a tension beneath the softness.

She was still working to breathe but now she glanced up at him, caught off balance by the hook in his voice. It wasn't an olive branch or even a pomegranate, but it was a peace offering…or an attempt at one. And the strangeness of that, of Trip Winslow following her here to broker peace, allowed her to take the grape from his hand and bite into it.

It was sweet and the flesh melted in her mouth so that she had to press her hand beneath her lips to catch the juice.

'Good?' Watching her nod, he seemed to relax a little.

He ate a couple and then held out his hand to Acrux.

She frowned. 'I didn't know horses ate grapes.'

'They love them, which is why I don't normally bring him up here.' His eyes found hers. 'But needs must.'

Needs. The word quivered between them and his gaze felt heavy and hot, like the earth beneath her feet.

The sky felt as if it were pressing down on her head and yet something in his eyes made her feel as if she were being lifted. But that was the trouble with Trip—he made her feel two often contradictory things at once.

She cleared her throat.

'How much wine do you produce here?' It was just something to say. She didn't much care, nor did she expect him to know the answer, but he replied immediately. 'Around five hundred cases. We're what you might call a micro-winery, but we've won awards for our *rosato*. According to Stefano, the vineyard manager, we have high hopes for this year's crop. He dropped by this morning. Apparently, they're days away from harvesting, so you'll get to see it, which is lucky. Although I'm guessing you probably don't feel lucky,' he added after a moment or two.

She stared up at him, her heartbeat jamming her throat.

'It's just I didn't think about that until yesterday. When you got upset.' He frowned. 'And I know that you hate me right now, but I didn't have a choice. You see, I was never a contender.' She could see that his anger was back—no, not anger, she thought a moment later. It was frustration and pain too. He was wrapped in it.

She waited, watched him regain control.

'It was always going to be Charlie and then suddenly it was me and I knew a lot of people had their doubts, but I knew I could make the business work harder, smoother, leaner. Just better. And I did, but then I went to Ecuador and when I got back everyone was freaking out and I had to do something because I couldn't lose control of the company. I couldn't prove them right. Not after everything that I'd—'

He broke off, his gaze scanning across the vines, and she knew from the slight rigidity in his shoulders that he was no longer in Tuscany, but back in Ecuador. Her own body tensed as her brain tried to imagine what it must have been like to face violence and death alone. And if she hadn't been here, he would still be alone, she thought with a jolt.

'I don't hate you,' she said at last. Because she didn't. 'But you do stupid things sometimes.'

Thinking back to that moment when the police car had appeared from nowhere and Lucas' pale, frightened eyes had met hers in the rear-view mirror, she cleared her throat. 'Everyone does. And the reason I'm here is because you were right. There will be other, better times for us to break up. Any point, really, when the world isn't fixated on your return from the jungle.'

Trip was gazing down at her in silence and there was something about the expression on his beautiful face, almost as if he hated hearing her say that. Which made absolutely no sense.

Now he was nodding. 'That's true,' he said after a moment. 'But what's also true is that I'm only here because of you. You're the reason I got out of that jungle alive.'

Trip felt his chest tighten. Lily was staring at him, a small, puzzled furrow between her eyebrows. Her hair was tied neatly at the nape of her neck and she was wearing shorts and a cropped white blouse that seemed to hide everything and yet still hint at what lay beneath in a way that both confused and excited him.

'I don't understand.'

Watching her frown, he felt his hands ball into fists.

He hadn't either. He still didn't, which was why he hadn't told anyone what had happened, what he had seen, why he had planned on never telling anyone. But he found that he wanted to tell Lily.

The memory of it was suddenly clearer and more real

than the vines and the earth. 'The guy who was in charge of tying me up drank—I could smell the alcohol on him—and one evening I realised I could get my hands free. I waited until they fell asleep and then I took off the blindfold and I managed to get away.'

He could still remember the fear that one of them would wake or, worse, shoot him. His heart had felt hot and slippery in his chest and he'd had that same feeling of being in a game so that even though it had been the most intense situation he'd ever been in, it had also felt as if it were happening to someone else.

'How did you know which way to go?' Lily's grey eyes were light like summer storm clouds and, suddenly and overwhelmingly so that it winded him, he wanted to bury himself in their softness.

'I didn't,' he said simply. 'I was just making it up as I went along. One day, I was trying to climb up to the top of this ridge when everything just collapsed under me. That was when I lost my water bottle.'

The memory rolled over him like a cool mist, barely there but still enough to chill him to the bone.

'Everything got a bit harder after that.' Catching sight of her pale, stunned face, he forced his mouth to curve at one corner. 'I was so thirsty and I drank from this pool. I don't know what was in the water but afterwards I could hardly walk. I was shivering so much I kept biting my tongue.'

Backed up against a tree, skin burning, canopy closing in on him, he had offered up a prayer in desperation.

'That's when I saw you. You were wearing a cream dress like the one you wore to that lunch meeting the first time we met, and you held out your hand to me—'

He felt his fingers tighten around the rope in his hand. Even then, he'd known he was hallucinating, that Lily was in New York. But he had still reached out for her hand, stumbling forward, heart slowing with relief as her fingers had closed around his and suddenly he had been blinking into the sunlight.

After so many days of near darkness and delirium, he'd thought he was still hallucinating so that for a moment he hadn't even realised that there were people moving towards him. All he'd cared about was Lily and he'd called out her name but, as the dark foliage had fallen away from him and his eyes had adjusted, she'd disappeared, breaking apart into petals.

He blinked away the image. 'That's how I found the village. Because of you. You were there with me—'

She was gazing up at him, an expression on her face that he didn't understand but that turned his heart into a pinwheel beneath his ribs, and he reached out and touched her cheek, grazing his fingers against the skin.

'I didn't mean to make you cry,' he said hoarsely. 'And I didn't not want you yesterday.'

Did that even make sense? Did it matter if it didn't? It was just words, a collection of sounds that were just a step up from the babbling of a child. It didn't come close to what he meant, to what he was feeling. But there was something taking shape between them, something tentative and precious and fragile, and he was scared that if he tried again, he would get it wrong and that newly formed shimmering thing would burst like a bubble.

Maybe Lily felt the same way because instead of replying she swayed slightly, the movement making her lean into the curve of his hand, and he felt his body react instantly. Hungrily.

Her chin jerked up and round towards the rumble of an engine and he followed the direction of her gaze to where a tractor was cresting the brow of the hill. He swore inwardly as Lily stepped back into the shadow of the vines and the air opened up between them.

'It's just Maurizio. He works here,' he said, unnecessarily, because why else would Maurizio be driving a tractor across his land? But he wasn't thinking straight. Correction: he wasn't thinking at all. His mind was just heat and hunger.

Maurizio must have spotted him, because the tractor came to a stop and suddenly it was silent. Trip watched him climb down from the cab. Maurizio had worked on the estate since he'd left school and was now well past retirement, but after his wife's death he had been so lost, so in need of occupation, that Trip had kept him on.

He turned to Lily to explain all of that but she was moving between the vines in that delicate, precise way of hers. At the dark fringe of woods edging the field, he watched as the trees seemed to move apart a little to receive her and then, in the blink of an eye, she was gone.

Something between loss and panic spiralled up inside him but it took another five minutes before he could extricate himself from the old man. By then Lily had long since disappeared. But he had to look for her.

And he knew he would find her. He could feel every single cell in his body, each breath and beat of his heart arrowing in on her location.

It was cool and light and green in the woods. Heart pounding, he followed one of the twisty paths, picking the wider one when it split in two, only to backtrack a moment later to take the one that was more overgrown. And that was when he saw her.

Lily was standing in the middle of the path, her grey eyes wide in the half-light crisscrossing her face, a flush of pink highlighting her cheekbones.

His pulse jumped. They had looked into each other's eyes a hundred times or more over the last few days but there was something different this time, an intensity, an anticipation that made his mouth dry and his stomach tremble.

It was the single most erotic moment in his life. And he hadn't even touched her.

In the distance he could hear the quiet rumble of the tractor, but here in the woods there was nothing but the sound of insects and his breath rising and falling in time to the pulse beating in her throat.

'You waited for me,' he said hoarsely.

Her gaze fixed on his face. 'You came to find me.'

For a moment, neither of them spoke. He felt as though they were underwater, that he was holding his breath. He could hardly bear to move in case he was hallucinating and then she held out her hand and he walked swiftly towards her. As his fingers found hers, she pulled him away from the path, through the undergrowth into a shaded clearing dotted with tiny yellow and blue flowers.

The air was different now, warm and still and shimmering with light and shadow and the static hiss of anticipation.

His heart stopped beating as she stopped and turned and they stared at one another, palms still pressed together.

'Are you going to tie me up?'

It was as if she'd slapped him. He stared at her, his pulse raging. 'What?'

She gestured wordlessly to the rope still coiled around his other hand.

'Is that what you want me to do?' he said hoarsely.

Her pupils flared. 'Yes. But first I want you to kiss me.'

The rope slithered to the grass at his feet as, breathing unsteadily, he leaned forward to cup her chin and his mouth found hers. They kissed, tasting one another, pushing back and forth, each time a little deeper until she pulled back and turned her head to touch her lips to his hand.

'I want you, Lily.'

He found the band at the base of her neck and he pulled it loose, weaving his fingers through her hair.

'And I want you—'

She leaned into him, grazing her body against his, her mouth maddeningly light now against his mouth and then, as his hands reached for her, she pushed him backwards.

'Watch me undress.'

She kicked off her sandals and began to unbutton her blouse, slowly, deliberately slowly, and he watched, his body pulsing with a hunger that seemed to magnify his heartbeat so that he could feel his pulse throbbing through him.

Suddenly losing patience, he pulled her closer, yanking the blouse apart, tearing the fabric as he tugged it away from her arms. She wasn't wearing a bra and he cupped her breasts in his hands, body hardening as she gasped, and then he lowered his mouth to lick the soft skin there, teasing her nipples until they stood proud from her body.

She pushed him back. 'I said, watch me.' Behind her, the trees shivered in the dappled light as she unbuttoned her shorts and let them slide down her legs to pool around her bare feet.

Now she was wearing only a pair of pale peach-coloured panties.

For a moment he thought he might black out and then, toeing off his shoes, he grabbed her wrist and pulled her closer.

'Now undress me,' he said.

Shaking inside, he let Lily pull his shirt over his head and run her hands over his chest, his stomach, sliding her fingers beneath the waistband of his trousers. He felt her tug down on the zip, grunting as she freed him, and then his body turned to iron as she dropped to her knees and took him in her mouth. His breath shuddered in his throat, and he reached down to slide his hand through her hair. Shock waves of desire were rippling over his skin and he jerked his hips backwards.

'Not like that. Not this time.'

Pushing his trousers and boxer shorts down, he knelt in front of her and, running his hands over her breasts and waist and legs, explored every curve, every inch of skin until finally he slid his fingers inside her. She moaned against his mouth and the sound was gasoline to the fire of his hunger and he tore off her panties, shuddering as she wrapped her legs around his kneeling body and lifted herself against him.

He pushed up and into her, and groaned. She was so slick and hot.

'Lily—' He breathed out her name as she pulled him closer, her hand a small, splayed encouragement at his hip, and now he was pushing into her, moving rhythmically, his breath ragged against her throat as she arched against him and he tensed, thrusting upwards, the grip of her muscles sending him over the edge, his climax colliding against hers like a runaway train hitting the buffers.

CHAPTER SEVEN

LILY PRESSED HER head against Trip's muscular chest, her body shattering around him as his hips jerked against her, each movement breaking her into ever tinier fragments. His hand was tight in her hair and she breathed him in like oxygen.

She had tried to forget how good it was between them, tried to tell herself that she had misremembered the storm of their passion. But she had been lying. Trip was the only man who had ever made her feel so helpless and hungry all at once. His was the only touch that could wrap her in a blaze of desire, turn her inside out and dissolve her into a creature of pure, endless need. A woman, no less.

It had been just like that first time. Like every time in between, and maybe it would always be like this with them. With each of them scraped raw, dazed and aching, shivering with the aftershocks of their encounter and that head-spinning need and longing that stormed through their limbs until it exploded into a firestorm that blinded and burned everything in its path.

But they stayed safe, bodies fused in a painless white heat.

'Lily—' She felt his fingers move and then he was tipping her face up to his, his blue eyes hot and fierce like the centre of a flame. Her legs were still wrapped around his waist and it was then, gazing down at the place where their bodies were pressed together, that she realised that he was still kneeling, his other hand supporting the weight of her so casually that it made her tremble inside.

'I didn't check. Are you…?'

'Yes. I'm on the pill.'

Something shifted in his face, beneath the surface of the skin, too quick to capture, but he didn't make any attempt to break their embrace and she didn't either. She just wanted to stay there for ever, splintered into a thousand pieces, with his hardness clenched deep inside her, and his heart raging next to hers.

It took a while for her muscles to relax, for her to take a normal breath and even then he still held her close. Finally, he shifted his weight, lifting her up and letting her legs drop from around his waist and laying her down on the warm grass. She watched in quiet wonder as he moved to lie down beside her.

A breeze was lifting the leaves high up the trees and she gazed up at the fluttering sunlight as Trip caressed the palm of her hand, his face relaxed, at peace, whereas she—

It had taken only a few minutes but the events of moments earlier were starting to fill her head, each frame tossing up one question after another.

Her eyes moved across the clearing. In this circle of quivering pines and oak saplings it felt as if the world outside were gone, had become a shimmering desert. All that remained was this tiny oasis.

And she had taken his hand and led him here.

What had she been thinking?

Nothing.

She hadn't been thinking, just feeling. Her need to touch Trip, to press up against the familiar curve of his shoulder and the solid warmth of his arms, had spread white and blinding across her mind, blotting out both common sense and any thought of self-preservation.

And she still wasn't thinking about her own well-being now. How could she after everything Trip had been through?

Her fingers moved to touch a long thin scar on his leg and, now that she was looking, she could see more scratches, grazes and discoloured skin beneath his tan.

The creases around his eyes made her heart contract. He was never more beautiful than when he smiled, and the thought of him being hunted, hurt, shot or worse made her feel panicked. She reached up and clasped his face in her hands and pressed a desperate kiss to his mouth, needing to feel his breath, his heartbeat, to prove that he was real.

He kissed her back, his hand moving, his touch firm, compelling, sliding slowly up to cup her breast, palms grazing her already taut nipple, shaping her ribs, her waist, her hips.

She pulled him closer, her breath suddenly staccato in her throat as he lowered his body onto hers and she felt the press of his erection, hard and as thick as her wrist. Helplessly she arched up against him, opening her legs wider, and then he slid inside her and she moaned softly, her pulse frantic against his skin, meeting each thrust of his hips with one of her own until there was nothing but heat and need and their quickening breath.

The sun was starting its downward descent when they finally headed back to the villa. Valentina was in the kitchen, preparing the evening meal. She turned towards Lily and smiled warmly.

'Did you have a nice afternoon?'

Lily nodded. 'We did. We…' She hesitated, dry-mouthed as the events of the afternoon unfurled in front of her eyes in all their naked, unfiltered glory so that she could almost feel Trip's hands on her belly and waist, his fingers light against her hips and between her thighs. She was hardly going to share that version of events with the housekeeper, but she was a terrible liar, particularly when put on the spot like this.

'We—'

'Yes, we did.' Trip cut across her smoothly. 'I showed Lily around the vineyards and then we went for a walk in the woods. To cool off,' he added, his eyes finding Lily's. The slide of blue heat across her skin made her shake inside.

'Do you think she guessed?' Lily asked as they made their way upstairs. 'That we weren't—I mean, that we were—'

Trip's eyebrows pulled together a fraction. 'What? That we were having al fresco sex?' Shaking his head, he reached out and picked some grass seeds from her hair. 'I'm going to go with no. But even if she did, so what? We're engaged. We're allowed to have sex.'

They had reached her bedroom now and he followed her through the door quite naturally, almost as if they were the couple they were pretending to be.

And could be for real?

The romantic part of her that she had always suppressed, or, rather, smothered after the mess she had made with Cameron, unfurled a little and she felt the world rearrange itself into a place of possibilities. In this new world, Trip would tell her that they no longer needed to pretend that they were engaged. That a year wasn't long enough because he wanted to spend the rest of his life with her.

Abruptly Trip leaned forward and wrapped his hand around her head and kissed her hard.

He straightened then, his fingers still tangled in her hair. 'You worry too much. Do you want to take a shower before we eat? Because I'd be happy to join you—'

'No—' She shook her head, the word rushing out to cover how her body had stiffened at his suggestion. Her body was still rippling from his touch. The last thing she needed was to be up close and personal with a naked Trip rubbing soap over her.

'I'll have one later. But I might just go and sort out my hair.'

'Why?' She felt another seismic shimmer ripple across the room as he dropped down onto the bed and stretched out his legs. 'I like it like that.' That remark, or maybe the slow, assessing gaze that accompanied it, followed the suggestion about sharing a shower to press against a point low down in her pelvis.

'It'll get all knotty if I don't brush it through,' she said quickly. 'I can meet you downstairs.'

Inside the bathroom Lily closed the door and leaned against the wood. If only she could go downstairs and climb into the refrigerator, let the chilled air cool the smouldering flame Trip had lit inside her. Because that was the trouble when you played with matches in a heatwave—you started a fire and there was no water to put it out.

Pushing away from the door, she walked over to the sink, giving the mirror a perfunctory glance as she leaned forward to switch on the tap.

She felt the skin on her back prickle.

As she gazed at her reflection, her cheeks grew hot. It had taken a long time but, after they had finally broken apart that last time, Trip had helped her get dressed. But his mouth had kept finding hers so that she hadn't really been paying much attention and now she saw that, not only were some of the buttons on her top in the wrong holes, but others had simply disappeared.

The heat in her cheeks intensified as she remembered Trip ripping open her blouse.

In that moment she had simply wanted him. Even afterwards as they had lain with their bodies overlapping, she hadn't thought of what came next. Neither, she was sure, had Trip. But for him, the past, their past, was not so very different from this new arrangement. What was it he'd said?

'We're engaged. We're allowed to have sex.'

And they had. And she had loved every febrile second of it. Only this 'engagement' wasn't real. It was a pretence, so sex was superfluous.

Then again, a year was a long time for a man like Trip not to have sex, she thought dully. She felt oddly fragile then, and exhausted.

But then it was a lot, connecting with him like that, not just physically, but hearing him talk about what had happened in Ecuador. Before, with her anger buffering them, it had been easy to hold back other feelings. Confusing, contradictory feelings that were as reckless as Trip's decision to visit a smuggling route used by drug cartels.

Only out there in the woods, something had changed.

Or maybe *she* had changed. She didn't know if it was the sex or because she understood now how close she had come to losing Trip for ever, but her anger was starting to lose shape, to crack and crumble, and other emotions were starting to seep through.

This engagement couldn't work, *she* couldn't make it

work if she let Trip get under her skin. She couldn't change what had happened but that didn't mean it had to happen again.

Even if she wanted it to.

Her fingers pressed against the cool porcelain of the sink.

And she did want that.

She might be lying to the rest of the world, but she couldn't lie to herself, and when he'd leaned over a few moments ago and fitted his mouth to hers, the desire to keep kissing him, to touch his face and press her hand against where she knew his body would be hardening, had been nearly impossible to resist.

And the intensity of that struggle proved to her that she had to stay within the lines because that was the trouble with sex. You had to be intimate, and intimacy combined with hormones fed into that biological need all humans had to be held and touched. But this arrangement was already complicated enough. Casually, carelessly introducing another layer of complexity for something as transitory and self-indulgent as sex had bad idea stamped all over it.

His hand moving against her cheek, the potent blue of his gaze holding her still, captive as his body sank deeper into her in the dappled light...

She blanked her mind.

It didn't matter that it had felt so right and so real and so perfect with Trip, her judgement was flawed. Cam had taught her that, then Trip had hammered it home and she was still living with the collateral damage from both of those miscalculations.

Staring at her reflection head-on, she rebuttoned her top correctly and smoothed her hair back into another low ponytail and, then taking a deep breath, she opened the bathroom door.

Her pulse skipped a beat.

Trip was still lying on the bed. The book she had been trying to read for days now lay open in his lap.

'Ms Lily Jane Dempsey. BA Amherst, MBA Oxon.' Trip shifted against the pillows. 'You have a lot of letters after your name.'

It was then that she realised he was holding out her invitation to the scholarship reunion dinner she had been using as a bookmark.

'You have them too.' He had been to Harvard.

'True.' She saw something flash across his eyes, too fast to catch, like a fish darting away from an unseen predator in an ocean of blue.

'So did you have fun?' His eyes were clear and blue and fixed on her face as if he cared, which seemed unlikely but today was turning out to be a day where little, if anything, made sense and so she simply shook her head.

'I didn't go. I had a lot on at work,' she lied.

His gaze held hers, jaw tightening infinitesimally. 'And that's the only reason you didn't go? Because of work?'

No, it wasn't. The dinner had taken place the weekend after he'd come and ended things with her and, for days after he'd left her, her body had felt tired and achy as if she'd had flu. But there was no reason to share that with Trip now. No reason to ever share it with him.

'Not completely. I was worried about you.'

'But you wanted to go—'

She nodded. 'I had a great time in England and I made friends there. I don't often get a chance to catch up with them so, yes, I would have gone.'

'Is that why you were going to London? You wanted a trip down memory lane?'

What she had wanted was to get away from him, this man sprawled on her bed, before he could take the wild rapture of their time together and turn it into something ugly. Before he made it so that all she could remember was that he had named her as his fiancée because he thought her dull and sensible enough to reassure his jittery shareholders.

'You mean, the other day when you tricked me into coming here?' She watched that mouth of his flex into something not quite a smile.

'In part. But it's also because England isn't New York. London can be tricky but in Oxford it's not that hard to have a normal life.'

'You mean, no press?'

In short, yes. No press meant no photos, which meant no humiliation, no jeering headlines, no mocking memes.

She shrugged. 'To an outsider, all students look pretty much the same so it's easier to be anonymous.'

'Easier?' He frowned.

'People think they can say things. Because of my father.' She could feel his gaze, curious but a little baffled because, of course, what did he know about being belittled or deemed inferior? 'And I know that how they talk about me, what they say, is because they're angry, and that anger kind of spills out. But sometimes it's hard—'

It had been bliss. For the first time in as long as she could remember she had fitted in seamlessly. And she had loved it. Loved the old stone buildings. The book-lined libraries. The seriousness of it all. She had felt accepted, felt safe.

It was one of the reasons why returning to the US fifteen months later had been such a shock. Suddenly she'd been back in the spotlight for all the wrong reasons. The brutality of it had left her winded, then angry, and angry people were vulnerable to manipulation. Which was why she hadn't seen Cameron Carson for the danger he was. Why she needed to remember how that felt and not let herself get lost in a pair of blue eyes. She couldn't be trusted. More importantly, he couldn't either.

Suddenly she felt close to tears as she made a different, more painful journey down memory lane, back to when she had found Lucas on the floor of his bedroom, the pill bottle beside him. It was her fault that had happened. Blinded by her own neediness, she had placed her trust in someone who was a literal walking, talking red flag.

And this neediness she was feeling now meant that she couldn't trust herself, trust her judgement. In fact, it was a reason to do the polar opposite of what she wanted to do. So there would be no more giving into that hunger that had stormed the barricades of her common sense and self-preservation out there in the woods.

And she would tell Trip that.

But it would be easier to have that conversation when he wasn't lying on her bed as if he were her fiancé for real, rather than an ex she'd had sex with for reasons that frankly had made sense only in the heat of the moment.

Needing space from that thought, from him, she glanced down at her watch.

'Is that the time? We should go down for supper. It's past seven.'

Glancing across the table, Trip licked the spoon clean and rested it in his bowl. Something was different, he thought, his gaze leapfrogging from Lily's shuttered grey eyes to the pulse beating out a staccato rhythm at the base of her throat.

'Was everything okay?'

Valentina had come to clear the table.

'It was delicious. I wonder if I might be able to have the recipe. *Bunet* is my father's favourite dessert.'

Watching Lily smile up at the housekeeper, he felt an unfamiliar pang of envy, both for that smile and the way her eyes softened when she mentioned her father. It was the same, he noticed, whenever any of her family called or texted. Her face, her voice would alter because, despite the part they had played in getting her here, her love for them was clearly unconditional. And they loved her, too, and he felt uncomfortable at having so casually exploited that love.

Uncomfortable too with that hunted look on her face when she talked about people saying things about her, presumably on the Internet. He had no idea what mud they could throw at Lily. She was smart and hard-working and loyal and brave and passionate. Not that she was perfect, he told himself, feeling his body twitch in response to just how passionate Lily could be. She was stubborn and snippy too. But still, he didn't like knowing that she had been picked on in that way.

'Prendiamo il caffè in salotto, per favore,' he said quietly to Valentina, then, pushing back his chair, he turned to Lily. 'Shall we?' It was a question but also an assumption and he took a step back to allow her to pass.

It was four hours since she had taken his hand and led him into that clearing and his body was still flushed with post-orgasm dopamine so that it had taken a little while for him to register it, but at some point between then and her walking out of the bathroom, something had changed.

She had changed.

At first, he'd thought it was just her blouse. She had done up the remaining buttons in their correct order, which was a pity. How Lily looked after sex was one of the things that gave him the greatest pleasure. Ever since that first time, he had loved knowing that he was responsible for her hair tumbling loose over her shoulder. Loved, too, the contrast with how prim and poised she normally looked.

But there was more going on than a few adjustments to her blouse.

On the way back to the villa she had got quieter, and, even though they had been holding hands, he had been able to feel her retreating from him so that every time he'd glanced over at her, she had been a little more out of reach. And now she was so distant and distracted it felt as if she were behind glass.

His eyes rested on the faint red marks on her bare shoulder where, earlier that day, his stubble had scraped against her skin.

And it didn't take a genius to work out what was on her mind.

She looked up at him then, her grey eyes resting on his face then moving past his shoulder as if it hurt her to look at him.

Which was ridiculous, he thought, with a flicker of irritation, given that her body had been fused to his for most of the afternoon.

'Is everything okay?'

'Everything's fine. I think I caught the sun earlier.'

He glanced over at her pale face, his chest tightening. Now she wasn't just holding back, she was lying. And it didn't make any sense that he should mind. This whole arrangement was a web of lies, but that was hard for him too, although he doubted that she'd believe that.

Somewhere in his head he could hear his mother's voice as she made up yet another excuse.

Of course, she had plenty of practice, he thought, his eyes moving past Lily's face to the classical acoustic piano at the other end of the room. His father had often been late or he would change his plans at the last minute. Nothing was sacred. Not anniversaries or school sports day or birthdays.

There were so many to choose from but one in particular stood out. He and his mother had flown to Italy for Spring Break. It had been the weekend of his father's birthday, but Charlie had been studying for his exams and had stayed on at grad school to revise, and Henry Sr had been due to join them but then, inevitably, he had called to say that he would be delayed.

Trip felt his gaze drift back through the house, seeing his eleven-year-old self. He had been out riding all afternoon and come back hungry, and feeling guilty because he had left his mother on her own. But the house had been so quiet that for a moment he'd thought it was empty.

And then he'd heard it. A tiny catch of breath, like a gasp.

She had been sitting at the piano in this very room and at first he had thought she was singing softly to herself as she had sometimes when it had just been the two of them. Then he'd realised she was crying. Which had been the other, more likely option. But no child wanted to find their mother weeping.

Not that his mother had seemed to realise that. Her face had stiffened but it had been several moments before her hand had risen like a brushstroke to wipe away the tears.

'Everything's fine. It's this melody, it always makes me weep.'

His childish self had accepted her explanation. But then six weeks ago he'd found the letters and the first one he'd picked up had made it clear that his father had been with his mistress that night. Had chosen to be with her instead of his family.

He felt the shock of it reverberate through him as if it had only just happened. For so long he had chased the perfection his father had demanded. But all the time Henry had been presenting a perfect front, he had been lying, cheating, deceiving. And constantly calling his youngest son to account.

The memory of his father's cool, excoriating gaze made his spine stiffen. Or maybe it was that he felt like a hypocrite for getting so out of shape with Lily for lying to him when he'd made her an unwitting and unwilling accomplice to his lies.

His jaw tightened. But her lying to him was different from the two of them deceiving other people. Her lies were personal, and it hurt because, confusingly and without precedence, he found that he cared about what she thought of him.

'Why don't you just say it? Whatever it is that you want to say but aren't.'

His voice was harsh, too harsh. He knew that even before Lily's eyes pulled back to his.

As Lily's forehead creased, he made an impatient sound. 'I'm disappointed, Lily. It's not like you to play dumb. In either sense of the word.'

There wasn't a flicker of reaction on her small, pale face but, as a silence settled between them, her cool grey eyes fixed on his and he saw the truth. She was angry.

'Okay,' she said at last. 'You want to talk about what happened earlier? I don't regret it—'

He shifted back against the cushion, his heartbeat suddenly and unaccountably running wild beneath his ribs because he didn't want to hear the end of her sentence. Didn't want to hear her tell him that it was a mistake. Or worse, imply that he was a mistake.

'That's lucky.' He cut her off. 'Because it's a little late for regrets.'

She blinked as if she were momentarily blinded by the blindingly obvious then. 'But it shouldn't happen again.'

Not happen again? He stared up at her, seeing that moment in the clearing when he'd let the rope drop to his feet, feeling the pulse in her throat leap towards him, each beat, separate and vivid like the first heavy drops of rain from a thundercloud.

'Any particular reason why not?'

'You know why,' she said after a moment, as if she'd needed a breath or two before she could speak. There was another sliver of silence and then she frowned. 'It's not what I want.'

'Not what you want?' He held her gaze, not seeing her as she was now, pale and stiff and hostile, but as she had been earlier, arching against him beneath the quivering leaves. 'And what do you want me to say to that? Other than I don't believe you.'

Her eyes darkened and a flicker of lightning split the irises. 'I don't want you to say anything. I want you to listen. For once.'

The 'for once' scraped against his skin like a blunt blade.

'I am listening, and you're lying.'

She was shaking her head now. 'Just because someone says something you don't like doesn't mean it's a lie, Trip.' Her jaw jammed out at an angle that made him want to lean in and fit his mouth to hers, and prove her wrong.

'My liking or not liking what you're saying is irrelevant to its veracity, Lily.'

He got to his feet at the same time as she did and now they were inches apart, close enough that he could see her chest rising and falling. See a brightness in her eyes that she wouldn't share with him.

'In other words, you don't care what I want, but then I knew that anyway.' There was a second of silence. 'So what happens now? Are you going to try and manipulate me into thinking your way is the only way?'

He clenched his teeth. 'What the hell are you talking about? Is that who you think I am?' The thought angered and appalled him. Maybe it did her, because her chin jerked up.

'No, I don't but—'

'So why are we arguing about this?'

'Because you make assumptions. Back in New York you assumed I'd just go along with what you wanted, what you needed, never mind what I felt, and then when that didn't work you brought me here and assumed I'd give in. And now you're assuming that because we had sex, it's going to happen again.'

He held her gaze.

'I was assuming it would happen again because we both enjoyed it. Or are you going to lie about that too?'

That caught her off balance. She swayed a little as if she was going to fall into his arms but then her body stiffened.

'No, I'm not going to lie about that.'

There was a shake to her voice that made the air hiss at the edge of the room. 'I did enjoy it, and I know it felt like it did before and if we had sex again, it would probably feel the same way. But it's not the same. None of this is real. Acting like we can just pick up where we left off will just complicate things, and it's not fair of you to assume that can happen. Because it can't. Because back then we were honest about what we wanted, and I don't want to take that truth and mix it up with all these lies.'

'It's not all lies—' he protested.

'You're not that man that I waited for after the auction, and I can't pretend you're him—'

He tried to set his face to blank as he had done so many times in the past, but it felt as though he were dissolving. But why should he be surprised? Even before he'd lost his whole family, there had been nothing solid in his life. Not as Lily had. No core of love and understanding and acceptance. The nearest he'd got to it was Mason Cooper, who had at least sat him down and talked to him.

But Lily had listened. Talking to her earlier about what had happened in the jungle, he had felt as if he could tell her anything, felt as if she cared, so that just for a moment he'd forgotten that this was supposed to be a charade for the shareholders.

He had to clear his throat to speak. 'It gets easier with practice.' His mouth twisted into an approximation of a smile. 'You know, all my life I've been the runner-up, but this is the first time I've come second to myself.'

Lily watched him turn and walk away, her head still trying to make sense of the expression that had skidded across his face. Not anger this time, but pain, and a kind of exhaustion.

The room felt cold all of a sudden. Her heart was beating crazily fast, as if she had been sprinting for a finish line, and she had in a way. Only now the prize-winner's medal looked cheap and tarnished.

What had he meant, saying he was always the runner-up? It made no sense. Trip had everything. Looks, charm, brains, money...

And yet there had been an emptiness to his voice that was as baffling as his words. She glanced furtively across the room towards him. A lock of hair had fallen half into his eyes and he blew it away in a gesture that was so un-selfconscious and familiar that she had to look away. It would be so easy to give into temptation, and Trip was the definition of temptation. But she had been tempted before by another not quite so beautiful or charming man and look at how that had ended.

Not with any attempt to explain his behaviour, she thought, replaying Trip's words from earlier.

On legs that shook slightly, she walked over to where he was sitting on the piano stool, his fingers splayed above the polished ivory keys.

Her heart was beating with clumsy little jerks.

'I didn't know you could play,' she said quietly as he raised his head.

'I can play a bit. Charlie was the musical one. I think he could have been a professional, but he was already lined up to take over the business.' There was that same depth of loss to his voice and she shivered, imagining a world without a brother. How close she had come to that happening.

'He seemed kind.'

Charlie Winslow had lacked the precision-cut features and seductive, curling mouth that made Trip shift the gravity in any room, but she could still remember him and she wondered what kind of hole his death had left in his younger brother's life.

'You never said you knew him.'

'I didn't know him. But I dropped my ice cream once at a polo match and he went and bought me another one.'

Trip nodded slowly as if picturing the scene. 'He was a good son. A good guy, I think,' he added. 'We weren't close. He was much older than me.' A catch of breath lifted his chest and she felt her ribs squeeze around her heart.

'It was supposed to be him running the business.' His gaze dropped to his hands. 'I'm just the understudy. Or that's how my father saw me.'

The air in the room seemed to gather and tense. She stared at him uncertainly. 'You were running the Far East division of one of the biggest corporations in the world,' she said finally. 'That's hardly being an understudy.'

Trip turned his head. There was that same exhaustion on his face as before, but now it was tinged with a self-mockery that pulled at her. 'My father liked that my company was touted as a unicorn, so he invited me into the family business. But we never really saw eye to eye. I found his management style too constrictive and cautious.' He reached out and pressed two keys down together to make a jarring, discordant sound. 'And, well… I wasn't exactly what he had in mind for a son.'

Was that true? She realised she and Henry had discussed his wife a couple of times and he had mentioned Charlie in passing, but he had never once mentioned his younger son.

Trip had turned away and had begun to play the opening bars of an aria she recognised. He was wrong, she thought, gazing at his profile. He could play, and more than a bit. And he must be wrong about his father, too, but she couldn't think of a way to say that without sounding either patronising or dismissive.

'You don't believe me.' He straightened then, blue eyes narrowing on her face.

She shook her head. 'It's not that I don't believe you. I just don't understand why you would think that.'

'Join the queue,' he said with a smile that contradicted the edge to his voice. 'Nobody understands anything I think or do. My incomprehensibility is part of who I am. You see, I have letters after my name too—'

Was he talking academically? 'I know.' She frowned. 'You went to Harvard—'

'I never got my degree. I didn't finish. I dropped out.' That note in his voice was one she had heard so many times before—mocking, careless, with a shadow underneath that made his face seem older, wary and weary.

He took a long breath and she watched his profile tighten. 'My letters aren't like yours. Or Charlie's. And my father hated it because he couldn't change them, and because he couldn't change them, he ignored them.'

There was a taut, humming silence.

'What letters?' she said quietly.

He hesitated then, and for so long that she thought he had unilaterally ended the conversation but then, finally, almost imperceptibly, his shoulders shifted.

'ADHD. I'm sure you've heard of it.'

She felt as if he'd slapped her across the face. 'I—I didn't know—' But how? How could she not have known? She felt confused and ashamed.

'Outside the family and a couple of therapists nobody does officially. My father didn't want me to have a label. But I didn't need one anyway. He made it clear that I wasn't ever going to be good enough.'

The ache in his voice made her feel as though she were turning to stone. She had been so sure before that she knew who Trip was. Had readily accepted, in fact, that he was like Cameron. A beautiful, but unscrupulous, self-serving charmer. It was why she had kept her distance, kept it strictly physical. But this man was more than a pretty face. He had been hurt, badly, been judged and found wanting, and she understood how that felt. Only it was worse for Trip because her critics were strangers. His were people who should have loved him unconditionally.

Her chest was so tight now it was hard to breathe. She knew how hard it was to trust, how hard it must have been for him to talk about himself. But he had trusted her.

Glancing up at him, she saw that the last rays of sun were flooding through the window, blazing so brightly that he seemed to be losing shape, and she felt a rush of panic that he would dissolve into the light just as he had disappeared into the darkness of the rainforest.

'When did you get diagnosed?'

'When I was about ten, but I think my mom suspected way before that. My teachers, too. But my dad didn't want to hear it, and besides, he had Charlie, and Charlie was always first and top.'

His mouth twisted into a shape that made her breath catch in her throat.

'You know, I think it killed him that we shared a name. It's probably why I was always "Trip". And because, deep down, I think he thought it suited me. He was always so precise, so absolute and I was impulsive, reckless, a risk-taker so sometimes I'd trip or stumble.'

She reached out and covered his fingers with her hand. 'We all stumble sometimes.' And sometimes you ran into the spears and arrows willingly, stupidly, selfishly, she thought, remembering Cameron's sly smile. 'And when you set your mind on something, you make it happen.'

He raised an eyebrow. 'You mean like abducting my ex?'

Her fingers tightened around his. 'Actually, I was thinking about your company. Nobody builds a unicorn business by luck. You need expertise, drive, optimism, an understanding of the customer and the market.' She hesitated. 'And I'm not your ex. You're stuck with me, remember?'

'I wanted to be, remember?' he said, his gaze moving over her in that way he had that made everything inside her feel sweet and slow-moving.

She bit her lip. 'Are you on medication?'

'Not any more. I was when I was younger, but some of my symptoms stopped when I got older and some of them I manage with coping strategies and therapy.'

'Like tapping?'

He nodded. 'Tapping and CBT.' Turning her hand over, he stared down at it as if he was making up his mind about something. 'And natural lifemanship. That's where you work with horses to regulate your body's energy. I'd always ridden and one of my therapists mentioned it to my mother. I tried it and it really clicked with me.'

So that was what she had seen in the barn.

'How does it work?' she asked.

'It helps develop your understanding of non-verbal cues. You see, horses are highly selective about who they trust so you have to learn how to control the chaos inside. That helps you deal with what you see as the chaos around you.'

She could see him standing, head bowed, trying to steady his breathing. 'Is that why Acrux walked away from you?'

He nodded slowly. 'After we argued, I was spinning out. Angry with you. Angry with myself too. He could feel it…' His voice trailed off and she could feel his regret pulling at her like a tide. 'I'm sorry, Lily, for making this your problem. For making assumptions and for lying to you. And your parents.'

He was apologising? Staring down at him, she felt that same quiver of petals opening in spring sunshine. Trip had hurt and manipulated her and the closeness of his behaviour to Cameron's had struck a still raw nerve. But they were not the same. She knew that now.

'I was angry with you too.'

'You had every right to be. You still do.' He made a small, tense gesture with his other hand. 'I've messed everything up. I thought it would be easy, but I don't know how to do this either. But I do know I can't do it on my own.'

'You're not on your own. We're in this together,' she said, suddenly fierce.

His blue eyes locked with hers and she stared up at him, mesmerised, thrilled almost by the expression on his beautiful face, as if they really were together.

'I think you mean that.'

'I do,' she said, and it was hard to hear her voice over the clattering of her heart.

He touched her cheek near the hairline. 'You were right earlier. About me. I did make assumptions. About what would happen. Because I'm used to people falling in line with my wishes. But also because I wanted you. Always. Right from that lunch meeting when you gave me such a hard time.

'I know I've hurt you, and I regret that more than anything, but I can't regret bringing you here, Lily.'

The softness in his voice made her name sound like a poem and she wanted to bury her face in the crook of his neck.

'I can't regret being with you, being inside you, because

it's real. What happened in that wood was real. And what we have together is the simplest, realest part of me.'

It was too much of a risk to tell him she felt the same way. It would be an act of wanton recklessness and she opened her mouth to tell him that nothing had changed. That what happened in the wood should never happen again. But she couldn't somehow. It was as if something had changed between them. It wasn't only the sex. It wasn't even his apology.

It was him. And she didn't want to think about what that meant. She just didn't want to lie to him.

'For me, too,' she whispered, and his pupils flared, and when he slid his hand along her cheek she leaned into it and then he was pulling her against him and his mouth found hers and he took, and took and kept taking as the light turned to darkness around them.

CHAPTER EIGHT

'*GRAZIE*, VALENTINA. I've got it from here.'

Smiling easily at the housekeeper, Trip closed the door. He deposited the tray on the chest of drawers and then picked up the remote control and watched the curtains slide apart fractionally.

It was morning, and outside it was looking as though it was going to be another perfect day of clear blue sky and bright sunlight, made all the more perfect because Lily was in his bed, her long hair fanned out against the pillow, her eyelashes fluttering in her sleep.

He gazed down at her small oval face.

He still couldn't quite believe that she was here. But when, finally, they had stopped kissing, she had taken his hand and led him through the house and up the stairs as if it were something they did every night. On the top step, she had turned to him, her pupils flaring as he'd stared down at her, and without speaking, without needing to speak, he had scooped her into his arms and carried her to his room.

Not to sleep. His body tensed, remembering the splay of her limbs against the white linen and the curve of her throat arching beneath his lips.

It had felt like a miracle so that he had been buzzing, but in a good way. All the tension and obstacles of the last few weeks dissolving into the certainty of their desire, so that, waking this morning, he had felt smooth and ironed out in the way that only sex with Lily could make him feel.

But that had all come later.

Before, while he had still been reeling from that feverish encounter beneath the trees, she had told him that what had happened in the woods was a one-off, not quite a mistake but a misstep, and it had punched a hollow in his chest, just like when he had found those letters. There was that same feeling of powerlessness and panic, and he'd had to walk away. Only he hadn't got as far as Ecuador this time.

And it wasn't a phantom Lily who had come to find him.

His chest felt tight or full, as if something were pushing against the ribs.

She was real, and this time when she'd taken his hand, she had led him out of the jungle inside his head, where instead of twisted tree roots and slippery rain-soaked ground there had been dark, tangled memories bookended by that expression on his father's face.

He still wasn't entirely sure why he had opened up to her. Or why it hadn't been the sky-falling-in-on-his-head moment that he had imagined it would be, because somehow, despite everything he had done to her, Lily had made it easy for him to talk about himself, about the diagnosis that he had kept hidden for so many years.

She had listened in that careful way of hers and asked some questions, but she hadn't tried to make out ADHD was a superpower or that it was something that needed fixing.

She had simply accepted it. Accepted him.

Chosen him.

An unfamiliar feeling pulsed across his skin, vivid,

blazing gold and, suddenly needing to reassure himself that she still felt that way, he reached out to stroke her face. She shifted in her sleep, eyes blinking open, and he felt his body tense, nervous suddenly that the sunlight beating through the window would break the spell that had brought her to his bed. But then she gave him a small, sleepy smile.

'Hi.'

'Hey,' he said softly as she looked up at him. 'I hope you're hungry. I had Valentina bring up some breakfast.'

The pastries were delicious, buttery and still warm from the oven and Lily ate appreciatively and with an appetite that surprised her. For weeks now it had been a struggle to eat anything, but all those knots in her stomach had simply disappeared.

Trip seemed easier too. There was still that pulsing energy humming beneath the golden skin, but the edginess that had seemed to cling to him like a shadow was gone.

And it wasn't just that release of tension that followed sex.

It was as if something deep inside him had shifted, unlocked, opened. But then he had opened up to her, she thought, remembering last night's revelation. She glanced over to where he was lounging on his side, his head propped up on his elbow, one finger chasing flakes of laminated pastry around his plate.

Not that she saw Trip as in any way defined by his ADHD. It would take so much more than four little letters to sum up the man in front of her. But it made sense of that fizzing energy and force that seemed to radiate from him. And there were other things too that were probably explained by the neurological make-up of his brain, like his impulsiveness and those sudden bursts of intense focus.

It was a part of who he was, like Lucas' ability to hear music inside his head, and she could no more imagine Trip being any other way than she could envision the ordeal he'd had in the jungle.

And what had she done? Nothing. Not a thing. She had sat and stared at the news bulletins. But it was as though her head had been filled with mist. Everything had been muffled, except her own voice inside her head telling Trip that she wouldn't care if he never came back from Ecuador.

Those words had haunted her for weeks.

'I shouldn't have said what I said when you left. About not bothering to come back. I never wanted that, but you hurt me and I wanted to hurt you. So I said things that weren't true.'

'You said a lot of things that were true too.' Now he stretched out a hand and took hold of her wrist. 'I was selfish that day, and thoughtless and I hurt you and I hate that I did that. I wish more than anything that I hadn't done it—'

He meant the way he'd ended things, she told herself quickly, not *that* he'd ended things. Although it would be so tempting to think that was what he wished when his eyes were holding her captive and there was no distance between them any more.

'I wish I could change things, change the past—'

She could hear the regret in his voice, and another note she couldn't quite put her finger on. But she understood only too well the anguish of remorse and wishing to have done things differently.

'Not all the past,' she said quietly.

Her skin tingled as he looked at her for another long moment. 'You're a good person, Lily.'

She glanced past him to the clock by the bed. It was Tuesday morning in New York. The second Tuesday of the month. Lucas would be talking to his therapist. Picturing him, scrunched up in a chair, she felt the crushing weight of her guilt. She wasn't a good person at all, but, unlike Trip, her failings were not in the public domain because her father had used his influence to make the mess she had made shrink to the point where the consequences of her actions amounted to little more than a talking-to.

'Too good for me,' Trip continued. 'And I know I messed up your plans, so I'd like to make it up to you.'

'And how are you planning on doing that?'

Her abdomen tensed as he leaned forward and kissed her shoulder.

'I have an idea. But I'm open to suggestions.' She heard the smile in his voice and when he lifted his face, she saw that his eyes were bright with a heat that she could feel inside.

'Let me hear your idea first,' she said quickly, shivering as he bent his head and kissed the side of her throat.

'I thought I might take you to England.'

'England?' His mouth was moving lower and she was finding it increasingly difficult to form sentences.

'We could fly there today. You could show me around Oxford. I know how much you wanted to go, and I want to take you. Would you let me do that, Lily? Would you let me do what I want?'

He was sliding down the bed and now she felt his warm breath above the cluster of curls between her thighs.

'Yes,' she said hoarsely, and then he was parting her

legs and she arched against his mouth and she couldn't speak, couldn't think because her mind was nothing but heat and hunger.

They arrived in Oxford the following morning.

After the open hills of Tuscany, the city felt hot and airless.

'I forgot how many tourists there are in the summer,' Lily said, gazing out of the window of the car at the people crowding on the pavement.

'We'll fit right in, then.' Trip pushed back his fringe and pulled a ball cap onto his head. 'We have a map too.'

She laughed as he produced it with a magician's flourish. 'I don't need a map. I lived here for over a year.'

'I know but it's part of our disguise.' He gave her one of those megawatt smiles then and she felt her heart contract. It would take more than a map and a ball cap to make Trip disappear into the crowd.

'*Our* disguise?'

'You have a cap too.'

The blue of his eyes was glossy and sharp and she was touched by how much thought he'd given to their visit. 'Did Lazlo get these?'

That smile.

Trip was a member of the Diamond Club, and Lazlo, the club's concierge, had quietly and efficiently arranged everything, including conjuring up a private jet, a car complete with driver and security detail, and a discreet, fully staffed home for the entirety of their stay. But then it was probably a work of moments for the man who had got Trip out of Ecuador and back to New York without so much as one news story breaking.

'There's nothing he can't get hold of. That's why he was

the first person I called in Ecuador when I got to the village. He had a car there within an hour. But that's kind of the point of the club. Their concierge service doesn't just do your laundry, it can facilitate things. Legally, of course. Well, mostly,' he added, and she felt her skin tighten as his smile reached his eyes. 'Ah, we're here.'

'Is this it?' Lily gazed up at the honey stone, three-storey town house. 'I cycled past here every day on my way to college. I used to wonder who lived here.'

'We do.' Trip nudged her out of the car. 'For the next few days anyway.'

The house was cool and elegant inside, but it was the views across the sun-soaked city that excited her most. If she stood on tiptoe she could just see Magdalen Tower.

'Is it okay?'

'It's perfect.'

Trip was standing behind her now. 'So, what do you want to do first?'

Her pulse gave a twitch.

'This,' she said softly and, turning, she leaned in and kissed his mouth, her body turning to flame as he pulled her closer.

It was early afternoon before they finally left the house. A sudden short downpour had emptied the streets and left the city gleaming in the returning sunlight. They wandered slowly, enjoying the languid heat and their lack of purpose, moving closer to one another as other tourists gradually emerged from shops and cafes to join them.

'Impressive,' Trip said, turning on the spot. 'So this is your old college. We should get a photo.'

'No, honestly, we don't need to—' she protested, but

it was too late. Trip was already pulling her against him and holding up his phone.

With an effort, she tried to paste a smile onto her face. Over the years, and thanks to the numerous staged family photos required by a US senator, she had learned how to pose for the cameras, but she still found it hard not to stiffen. And even harder not to snatch the phone out of his hand, because photos were so unforgiving, and selfies were the most brutal of all. There was no softening at the edges. Every flaw was there in close-up.

And he would see it, and then she would see his pity…

She grabbed the phone.

'Hey—' Trip turned towards her, laughing, thinking she was messing around, and then his smile fell away, his eyes narrowing, and she knew that her face must be as tense and panicky as she felt. He hesitated, then took her hand, the one not holding his phone, and it was only when he began to gently open her fingers that she realised her fists were clenched.

'What is it?' And then when she didn't reply. 'It's just me taking a photo. What's the worst that could happen?'

She stared at him, her pulse jerking in her throat.

'It doesn't matter. I want to go back to the house—'

She felt light-headed, the misery in her chest suffocating her, but then she felt his arm slide around her waist, warm and solid, and he was steering her away from the crowds, leading her quietly and calmly across cobblestones into a park, where everything was quiet and green like the woods in Tuscany where he had come to find her, to hold her against him.

As he sat down beside her on a bench, some of the tension inside her started to soften. A light breeze lifted her hair and that helped calm her too. Or maybe it was the way Trip was holding her hand as if he were the one who needed steadying.

'I'm sorry I upset you. Again—'

'You didn't.'

'But something did,' he persisted. 'When I was taking that selfie.'

Trip watched her hands ball into fists. Up until that moment, it had been a near flawless day, effortless in a way he had never imagined any relationship could be, and Lily had been happy and relaxed in a way that he had never seen before.

And then she wasn't.

He gritted his teeth. There had been so many days like this in the past when everything would be going well and then he would go too far. Take one risk too many. Forget to put on the brakes.

Except he hadn't done anything this time. It was Lily who had changed the mood. *Killed* the mood.

And he still wasn't sure why it had happened. One moment he had been leaning into her in the warm sunshine, feeling the light press of her body against his and thinking, Isn't this easy? The next she was demanding to go back to the house, her eyes shuttered, her body taut like an archer's bow.

'Maybe if you told me what it was, I could help—'

'You can't. You wouldn't understand.'

Her body tensed as it had before, almost as if she was bracing herself against some unseen threat.

'I might, and, even if I don't, I can still listen. Like you did.' Her face softened a fraction but then she shook her head.

'You wouldn't understand because you look like you. And I—I look like this.' Her hand moved to cover the slight bump on her nose.

He stared at her in confusion. 'Like what?'

'Like this.' Her voice turned sharp and she typed something into his phone and then held it out with a hand that shook slightly and he stared down at the screen, his brain jamming in shock and disgust as he read the headlines that accompanied photos of Lily as a child, then an adolescent, right through to almost present day. A few were the right side of jokey. Others were cruel. Some were just barbaric.

No wonder she hated having her photo taken. His anger was heavy and jagged beneath his ribs.

'Did your dad not stop these?'

'He did.' He heard the protective flare in her voice. 'He tried. But it's difficult. If you go after them, they just make out it was supposed to be a joke. And if you do get an apology, it just gives them a chance to resay or repost it all over again. It's just better to ignore them and not give them any oxygen. That's why there are fewer photos of me now. Because I'm careful.'

He felt sick. In other words, she kept a purposefully low profile. And he had dragged her into the spotlight.

'Look, Lily, these people are inhuman. That's why they're called trolls. You can't believe that normal people see you like this.'

'You did,' she said quietly. 'That first time we had lunch, you couldn't have made it any clearer that it was under duress.'

Was that what she had thought? His gaze moved from her high cheekbones down to her soft mouth and up to the bump on her nose. Her profile was not 'classically' beautiful, but she was a very beautiful woman. How could she not see that?

'I was hungover and you were snippy with me, so I was snippy back.'

'You only met me because you had to. You would never go out to lunch with someone who looks like me ordinarily,' she countered.

'How could I? All the women I know look exactly the same.' Her face made it clear that he had simply proved her point. 'Not naturally. They've had fillers and "tweakments" and surgery. But just because you haven't, it doesn't mean these photos are an accurate representation of who you are.'

'How are they not accurate? They're not some AI-generated content. They're me.'

Shaking his head, he pocketed the phone and took hold of her hands. 'They're moments in time. It's not who you are.'

The shape of her mouth made his heart feel as if it were being squeezed in a vice.

'Is this where you tell me beauty is only skin-deep? Or in the eye of the beholder? Or that real beauty comes from within? That what matters is that I'm a good person?'

'That does matter. And you are a good person.'

'No, I'm not.' She pulled her hands free and as she wrapped her arms around her stomach, it seemed to transform her from hostile to vulnerable. 'I'm not. It's just that nobody knows.'

He stared at her in confusion. 'Then tell me,' he said finally. Because he wanted to know. To prove her wrong. To take that haunted look off her face.

Silence.

His throat was tight and aching. Silence was his nemesis. He had got better at managing it, mostly by tapping, but he was too scared that one tiny movement would send her spiralling away from him for ever. Or perhaps he had already lost her, he thought, gazing at her still, tense body.

'His name was Cameron.'

His shoulders stiffened. It was just a name but the way she said it made him want to seek him out and erase him from the face of the earth.

'Do I know him?'

She shook her head. 'I doubt it. We met when I came back from Oxford.' Her mouth twisted and she was silent for a moment. 'Sometimes I think if I'd never come here, it wouldn't have happened. I got complacent. I had such a wonderful time just being me that I started to believe I was okay. You know? Acceptable. But then I went back to the States and I realised I wasn't.'

'What happened?'

'I went to this fundraiser with my dad and I wore this dress and I thought I looked nice. Not incredible, just not—'

There was a tiny shake in her voice and he reached out and pulled her arm away from her waist, his hands seeking hers.

'Did he say something?' he said softly.

She heard the edge to his voice. 'Yes, but not in the way you're thinking.'

He felt his jaw tense. 'What did he do?'

'He was nice to me.' Her fingers tightened around his. 'I'd seen him around but we'd never talked, but I was sitting in this coffee shop a few days after the fundraiser, hiding really—' She gave him a small, bleak smile. 'He came over and told me that I was his hero. Then he sent this incredibly cutting message to this woman who'd posted a comment about my hair. Nobody had ever done that before. I was flattered.'

She took a deep breath. 'That was kind of our first date. We started seeing each other and then one Saturday he invited me and Lucas to this party at the Colvilles' house upstate.'

He nodded. He knew the house. Knew Ward Colville and his brother from school.

'At first it was fine. It was fun. Everyone was drinking and I did too, but I knew I had to get back because I had a breakfast meeting with a client. Only Cameron was too drunk to drive. We all were, except Lucas. I knew he didn't want to drive but I asked him anyway.'

He heard her swallow.

'Cameron put the music on real loud and he was singing and I forgot about Lucas because it felt like I was in a film. Only then suddenly there was this police car. And I wasn't worried because I knew Lucas hadn't been drinking. But what I didn't know was that Cameron had stolen the car Lucas was driving.'

Her hand moved to her face.

'Lucas was arrested.' The pain in her voice made his heart squeeze tight. 'We all got taken to the station. It was awful.'

'Why didn't I know about this?'

'My dad made it go away.' She hesitated. 'And it was about the time your mother and Charlie—'

He thought back to the days and weeks, the months after the accident. The whole world could have been on fire and he wouldn't have noticed.

'And Lucas?'

She bit her lip. 'He's not a lawbreaker. He was devastated. He wouldn't leave the house. He stopped composing and then one day I came back from work and he was lying on the floor in his bedroom and I couldn't wake him up.'

A tear ran down her cheek and he felt something wrench apart inside him. In answer to his earlier question, *this* was the worst that could happen. 'I'm so sorry, Lily.' He slid his arm around her waist and pulled her against him.

'Afterwards, he said it was an accident. He hadn't been sleeping well since the arrest and he was so anxious all the time. He told my mom and dad that he just wanted to stop all the noise in his head.'

He knew that feeling. When he was a child, it had been excruciating. At its worst, it had made sleeping, even sitting still, a torment.

'But my parents wanted to be sure. That's why they sent him to Switzerland. To the Galen.'

'It's a great clinic.' Pulling her closer, he kissed the top of her head. 'Carter's brother did rehab there. That's how I knew about Lucas. Carter asked me to go with him to collect his brother and I saw Lucas walk past a window just for a moment. I don't think I would even have noticed him, but he was holding a violin.'

Her face twisted.

'It was my fault. I knew Cameron was trouble. He was always telling lies. Stupid lies. Like once he left a restaurant without paying. He said it was a mistake, but he liked the danger. And I liked that he liked me because he was cool and good-looking and he validated me, made me feel beautiful. So I didn't care that he was dangerous. Because I'm shallow and selfish and not a good person.'

'Not true. You made a mistake and, sure, you have flaws, but you're only here with me because you care so much about Lucas. Because you know he struggles. But those struggles are part of him, *not* because of you or something you did. You're a good person. Better than good. Better than anyone I know, and, yes, that does make you beautiful. But so does this.' He touched the bump on her nose. 'And this.' He ran his finger along the curve of her jaw. 'And this.' Her eyes widened as he stroked a loose curl away from her cheek.

She had clearly wanted to believe him, but it was harder than people thought to let go of the bad things, the things people said or did and how they made you feel. That would mean hoping things could be better and hope was a dangerous thing and his throat thickened as she covered her face with a shaking hand. Finally, in a small, bruised voice, she said, 'You know, when we left the police station, I thought Cameron would apologise, but he didn't. I was angry with him and upset. I asked him how he could do something like that to me. And he laughed. He said that it was never serious. That he had "standards."'

The tears she had been holding back spilled over her cheeks now and, watching her attempts to control them, Trip pulled her close and held her close for a long time, letting her cry, pushing back against the hot burn of anger rising in his chest, wishing he had more than words to make her believe what he was saying.

Finally, her sobs subsided and she breathed out shakily. 'I'm sorry—'

'No, I'm sorry.' Ignoring her attempts to hide her face, he tilted up her chin. 'Listen to me, Lily. You were right, earlier. I wouldn't have asked you out to lunch, but not because I think you're not up to my standard. You were always so cool and aloof. I thought I wasn't up to yours. I thought—'

* * *

He fell silent, and, looking up at him, she felt her chest tighten. He looked taut and unhappy, as he had that time when he'd sat at the piano in Tuscany. Only back then there had been an edge to him, a challenge, as if he'd been testing her with the truth.

Now he looked tired, as if he was shouldering some huge unseen weight, and she thought about everything she'd had to keep to herself and carry alone. How hard it had been. How alone she had felt. But Trip had helped ease that burden. She had told him the truth, every ugly detail, and he had said she was beautiful. Made her feel beautiful.

'Thought what?' she said quietly. His fingers tightened infinitesimally so that she could feel his pulse beating against hers.

'I thought I would never be good enough. For anyone. But mostly for him. My father.'

There was another silence, and she made herself wait because she couldn't lead him where he needed to go. She could only hold his hand as tightly as he had held hers.

'But then I found these letters, and I was going to burn them. But they don't feel like they're mine to burn. I mean, he kept them for a reason.' He cleared his throat. 'You see, they're from a woman. Her name is Kerry. She was his mistress.'

Lily stared at him in shock. That couldn't be true. Theirs was a small, insular world but she hadn't heard so much as a whisper of scandal in relation to Henry and Alessandra Winslow's marriage.

'Was it serious?'

Trip shrugged. 'It went on for more than a decade, so, yeah, I guess it probably was. From the dates, I think they started seeing each other shortly after I was born.'

'When did you find the letters?' She hesitated. 'Was it before he…?'

He shook his head. His eyes were hard and flat. 'It was the day before I went to Ecuador.' He took a breath. 'It was why I went to Ecuador.'

The day he'd broken up with her. She could still remember it as if it had just happened. He had been angry, distant, spoiling for a fight and desperate to leave. And yet, in the end, she'd been the one to push him out of the door, too angry and hurt at the time to register the contradiction in his behaviour.

It was all too easy to imagine how he'd felt. Foremost shock, that sense of unreality and then the feeling of stupidity at not seeing what was right in front of you.

She felt Trip's eyes on her face. 'You know, the craziest part was that all I wanted to do was tell you. That's why I came to your apartment. But then when I saw you, I couldn't do it. I couldn't say the words out loud because I had this stupid, irrational need to protect him.'

'Not stupid or irrational. He was your father.'

'He was.' He was shaking his head as if to deny that fact. 'But sometimes, a lot of the time, he felt like an opponent. And he was always the reigning champion and I was the underdog and nothing I did could change that. And I spent all my life trying to be his equal, to be worthy—'

The ache in his voice bruised her skin.

'And then it turns out he wasn't this perfect, unattainable being. He was just a man with flaws and weaknesses. And I was so angry with him for lying to me, to my mother, to everyone. For making me feel irrelevant and not good enough.' His eyes were suddenly very blue. 'For dying.'

'Oh, Trip.' She slid both her arms around him, feeling

his pain. Because it wasn't the trustees or the shareholders he wanted to impress, it was his father.

He pressed the heel of his hand against his forehead. 'Only I took it out on you because he wasn't there, and then I ran away because I knew if I stayed I'd do something stupid.' His mouth twisted. 'So I left and it happened anyway, because my head wasn't in the game. And the whole time I was there I kept imagining that look on his face. And then you'd pop into my head and it would disappear. I think that's why I kept thinking about you in Ecuador. You were a match for him.'

'You were too. That's why you clashed. Why Winslow's profits have gone up twenty per cent since you took over.'

'Until I got myself kidnapped.' The skin across his cheeks was taut. 'I proved him right.'

'You proved him wrong too. Multiple times.'

'But it was never enough.'

'I disagree. I think your father was old-fashioned enough to think that the oldest son should inherit, but I also know that he wouldn't have let his business be run by someone who wasn't good enough. You don't have to prove anything because he had proof. He chose you, not because he loved you, but because you are the best man for the job.'

Reaching out, he tucked her hair behind her ear. 'You know that, do you?' he said softly.

'I met your dad, remember? I worked with him. He had standards.' She paused and he knew that she was thinking about what that bastard Cameron had said to her at the police station, but then she gave him a small, tight smile. 'High standards, and he wasn't sentimental.'

'Not in the slightest.' His eyes fixed on hers and there was an expression on his face that made her scalp prickle.

'And what about you? Am I the best man for you?'

'Yes, you're the best man for me.' The only man. Her heart twitched and, panicking at the truth and stupidity of that thought, she rolled her eyes and quickly added, 'Or you'll do for now anyway.'

He smiled a little.

'Is that right?' He stared at her steadily. 'I thought you weren't going to do this.'

'Do what?'

'Talk. Hold my hand. Offer me a shoulder to cry on. Give me the best version of yourself.' He reached out to touch her cheek, his thumb tracing the line of her mouth. 'What changed your mind?'

Her heart was racing, mind turning over his words, over and over, not because she didn't know the answer, but because she did. He had changed her mind. Changed her. Changed everything. Rearranged the world into a place of possibility, filled it with light and laughter and love.

She felt dizzy, drunk, but she wasn't drunk. She was in love. Helplessly, frantically, impossibly in love with Trip.

'Oxford,' she managed. 'Being here made me realise that we're in this together.'

It was the truth, part of it anyway. But there would be other, better times to say more. Better than now when the torrent of emotions stampeding through her were making it hard to sit upright.

His eyes were very blue.

'We are. And I meant what I said before. I wasn't expecting what happened between us to happen, but the truth is that I've never wanted any woman like I wanted you. Like I want you, now, all the time and not in spite of the fact that you're different from those other women, but *because* you're different.

'You are beautiful, Lily, and I don't mean on the inside. I think you're sexy as hell and where you see flaws, I see authenticity. Because a diamond with a flaw is more beautiful than some perfect manufactured gemstone. That's me trying to be poetic, just so you know.'

She smiled. 'It's a pity the shareholders aren't here.'

'I don't care about the shareholders.' He frowned as if he was surprised to find that was true. 'I care about you. You're with me now, and I'm going to keep you safe. I won't let anyone get close enough to hurt you. I promise.'

It wasn't love but it was enough for now.

CHAPTER NINE

THE SUNLIGHT WAS weaker here in England than Italy, Lily thought as she sat down in front of the dressing-table mirror. But it was still bright enough to make sunblock necessary. Glancing over her shoulder, she massaged the cream into her back. She could, of course, just wait for Trip, but the last time she had asked for his help they had spent the rest of the day in bed.

Desire curled inside her at the memory and her gaze moved to the bathroom where Trip was showering. But it wasn't desire that had pushed them into each other's arms on that park bench.

Something had changed. It wasn't just sex any more. It felt like a relationship. He had told her he cared about her, that he would keep her safe. Nothing had ever meant more to her than knowing Trip had her back.

It had been one of the hardest things she had ever done, showing him those photos of herself. Her heart had been racing, hands shaking. She had never told anyone how it had made her feel. Never wanted to. Had been too scared to, because then they might see her in that way and be repulsed by her 'ugliness'.

But when Trip had taken her hand it had all come pouring out of her and he hadn't looked at her in disgust. And just as momentous had been Trip's confession to her. His father's infidelity had been shocking, but more shocking still, more devastating to her, was finally understanding the full extent of his insecurities in relation to Henry. How he had protected himself by pushing back against his father's indifference and disappointment, presenting an image of himself as cool and emotionally indifferent. She knew now that he was not that man. Not with her, anyway.

Maybe that was why she had felt a peace that was deeper than she had ever known.

As long as she didn't think about the future, she still felt at peace now. Some of the time anyway, she thought, her breath catching as Trip strolled back into the bedroom with a fluid grace that made it impossible to look away.

'So, what do you want to do today?'

'You choose.'

'I was hoping you'd say that.' He grinned. 'Let's go for a punt.' His gaze flicked over her bare back. 'But first…' Her pulse jerked as his warm hand slid over her shoulder. 'You missed a bit here.'

'Is that right?'

'I wouldn't lie to you,' he said softly, tracing a lazy, sensual path down to the swell of her bottom. 'Not about anything.'

His eyes met hers in the mirror and she stared back at him dizzily.

Before yesterday, she would have told herself it was just words, but she could see the truth written across his face—no, not written, she corrected herself. It was deeper than that. As if it were cut into him like letters into stone.

And the strange thing was that in the past she had hated to be looked at. But here in Oxford, she liked it when Trip looked at her in that fierce, focused, incisive way of his that told her he liked what he saw. Maybe that was why being here felt as if she were in a dream, she thought, but then he leaned down and his mouth found hers and she had no thoughts for anything but him and as her hunger flared, white and brighter than any sun, she reached for the towel around his waist, reached for him.

Punting was a good choice, she thought, two hours later as they took turns to push the flat-bottomed boat through the rippling waters of the Cherwell. Away from the centre, it was quiet and cool on the river. Now, as she lay back against the cushions, gazing up at the sky, it was easy to feel outside time, adrift.

And Trip was great company. Smart, funny, curious and he had that incredible energy and excitement. But it was when he talked about his plans for the business that she started to realise that he was a lot more than just a pretty face. A whole lot more.

Another punt was gliding into view now. Not a couple but a group of women taking photos of each other. She felt an instant flutter of panic as they glanced over at Trip but then her gaze snagged on the magazine one of the women was holding. On the cover, next to a photo of some soap star who'd split from her husband, was the same photo Trip had shown her back in New York, the one from the auction. No doubt because it was one of the few in existence of the two of them together.

So far.

'Hey...' Trip turned towards her, and she felt her stomach swoop upwards by the curving uptilt of his mouth. 'Where'd you go?'

'Nowhere,' she lied, watching as the women disappeared. 'I was just thinking about how different it is here from New York.'

'Are you missing it?' There was an edge to his voice that hadn't been there before.

No, she thought, but as she opened her mouth to reply there was a crash and the punt shuddered sideways. Gripping the sides, she looked over her shoulder to where another punt occupied by a couple had rear-ended them.

'Sorry.' The man was getting to his feet, grimacing. 'That was my fault,' he said in that clipped, English accent, his cheeks flushed pink. 'I wasn't looking where I was going.'

'It's fine.' Trip smiled easily. 'Really. No harm, no foul.' To Lily, he murmured, 'Don't worry, we've got this,' his hand squeezing hers.

The woman in the punt was smiling and crying a little. 'He just proposed.' She held out her hand and the small diamond solitaire winked in the sunlight. 'And I said yes,' she added unnecessarily.

'Congratulations!' Trip turned to Lily and there was a glitter of excitement in his eyes that made her pulse hum with happiness. 'We actually got engaged earlier this month, didn't we, darling?'

'Oh, congratulations.' The woman leant forward, smiling at Lily. 'Can I see your ring?'

Beside her, Lily felt Trip shift his weight as he reached to take her hand. He was smiling too, but as she stared down at the glittering band on her finger, she felt a lump form in her throat. The jewels in her ring trumped the other woman's in size and worth, but they felt cheap and gaudy in comparison. Because of course they were not a declaration of love. Her ring was simply an expensive but impersonal prop selected by Trip, or more likely Lazlo, to persuade the world that their engagement was real.

And it wasn't that she didn't know that to be the case,

but seeing this couple, feeling their love and hope and excitement, was a crushing reminder that her relationship with Trip was a sham.

She shivered as the sun momentarily disappeared behind a cloud. She couldn't let herself think about that now. 'I love the shape of yours,' she said quickly, ignoring the ache in her chest.

'It's beautiful,' Trip added smoothly. 'But I'm sure you've got better things to do than talk to us. Congratulations again—'

As the couple moved off downstream he met her gaze.

Reaching out, he touched her cheek lightly. 'You know, I don't know why you were ever worried about getting people to believe in us. For a moment there, even I believed you. And the shareholders are going to believe you too.' He smiled then, one of those miraculous smiles that made the earth tilt on its axis. But for once it was hard to smile back.

And that was what mattered, she thought, over the dark ache in her heart. She knew if she sat there, leaning into Trip's warmth, living the lie, she might shatter.

'We should be getting back.'

The punt wobbled alarmingly as she jerked to her feet, and she would have lost her balance if Trip hadn't grabbed her wrist.

'Don't.' She shook him off. 'What's the point of being in disguise if you're going to draw attention to us?'

Grabbing the pole, he steadied the punt calmly. 'Be fair, Lily. You're the one who nearly capsized us.'

He was right.

And the stupid thing was that she didn't care about anyone noticing them. Didn't even care about the paparazzi. Had never cared less, in fact. Her eyes snagged on the dazzling diamond and sapphires on her finger and everything inside her rolled sideways as if she herself were about to capsize. Yesterday, and this morning, she had felt so close to him, so safe, so known. And she had thought she knew *him*. Had thought that things had shifted, changed in some intangible but fundamental way—

'Lily—'

The gentleness in his voice was so unexpected that she was suddenly close to tears. 'Don't do that. Don't say my name,' she said shakily.

The sun had slipped behind a cloud so that his eyes looked like bruises. Watching his face stiffen, she wished she could turn back time to when it was just the two of them in this fantasy he'd created.

She sat down, turning her face away from him. It didn't matter that he had brought her to her safe place, or that he had shown her the man beneath the teasing smile and the careless manner. The beautiful, bright day was ruined. Their lies had sent the sun scurrying behind the clouds.

Quite suddenly she wished she had fallen into the river and sunk to the mud at the bottom, where there was no sunlight and Trip's smile would be a blurred, indistinct memory.

They made their way back to the house in silence, but as soon as they were inside the bedroom, Trip rounded on her.

'What is going on? Lily, what's the matter? You can't just give me the silent treatment. Talk to me.'

Trip's flawless face was creased into a frown that was a shock after days of light and laughter.

'You didn't propose,' she said quietly.

His frown deepened, his frustration palpable now beneath his confusion. 'Because it would have felt weird. It wasn't that kind of engagement. But that doesn't suddenly mean something just because we met some couple on a punt who did the whole down on bended knee schtick.'

A couple who were in love, she thought dully. A couple who weren't performing a part.

His expression shifted, softened. 'Look, I'm sorry I didn't propose.' He took a step closer, reaching for her hand. His handsome face so familiar, so necessary now, and it would be so easy to just accept his apology.

'But you have a ring and if you want we can post some pictures to show it off. And I can get Lazlo to send over some venue ideas for the ceremony.'

It was like waking from a dream. He was talking to her as if she were a colleague or a client. It jarred, unfairly so, because Trip hadn't romanced her into this relationship. For him, their engagement was a pragmatic, spur-of-the-moment solution to a business dilemma. There was never any need for him to personalize his love, because he didn't love her.

But in her newly loved-up state, she had let herself forget that he had needed a wife, needed her to improve his image.

Or had she chosen to ignore it? She pressed her hand against her chest to quell the queasiness that question provoked. Because she had done that once before with appalling consequences.

Better to face it head-on.

'It doesn't matter now,' she said slowly.

His eyes narrowed on her face. 'What do you mean?'

She flinched inwardly, but continued. 'In Italy you said that there was an agenda, a right time to announce our engagement. I think this would be the perfect time to announce our separation.'

He was looking at her as if she were an imposter. Someone playing the part of Lily Dempsey. 'I don't understand. Why are you talking about separating? We haven't even picked a date for the wedding. Look, it's going to be fine, Lily. Everyone is going to love you and when they see us together they won't suspect a thing. They'll all think we're madly in love—'

For a few seconds she remembered how he had comforted her while she'd cried. How tightly he had held her hand as he'd told her about his father's affair. She thought she would throw up if she asked the question, but she wasn't going to make the same mistake twice.

'But we're not, are we?' She took a deep breath. 'Or, rather, you're not.'

Heart hammering against her ribs, she waited, watching as he ran a hand across his face. Hiding his eyes, she thought, her stomach lurching as she saw the implication of her words hit home. He looked stunned, and even before he started to speak, she knew that her feelings were not and would never be returned.

And it hurt. It hurt so badly she wanted to curl into a ball around the ache in her chest. She felt small and foolish, as she had so many times in her life.

He was shaking his head. 'I don't—I'm not—'

His stumbling, uncharacteristic inarticulateness told her everything she needed to know.

She felt as if she were slipping underwater. 'Of course.' Her nails bit into the palms of her hands. Just hours earlier she had felt cocooned and needed at the heart of his life, but she wasn't in his heart. He didn't want a real relationship and she couldn't be in this fake one. Couldn't be this diminished version of herself, not even for Trip. 'Can I leave it to you to make a statement? You know how to explain things.'

He moved to stand by the window and she took a step closer to the door, both of them moving like actors blocking a performance. Because that was what they were. That was all they could ever be, and accepting that gave her the willpower to stay strong.

'If that's what you want.' His voice was flat, distant.

It wasn't, but she didn't want to just be a solution to a problem.

'What I want is to be loved. What I want is to truly share my life with someone, not pretend to share it with someone just to please a bunch of shareholders I've never met. And I suppose I should thank you, because you made me realise I deserve better than this. I deserve more. I deserve someone who loves me.'

'You do,' he said hoarsely. 'Look, Lily—'

She cut across him. That he had so easily given in, given her up was like a spear lancing her heart. But she couldn't stand here and listen to him tell her that he was fond of her. 'All I ask is that you hold off making any announcement about us until after I've told my family.'

'Will Lucas be okay?'

Lucas. Without him, she would never have agreed to this engagement. But she couldn't use him to stay with Trip now, couldn't use love in that way. And oddly, Trip had made her see that she didn't need to feel responsible for her brother. She would protect him, but her family was strong and they would stand together. As for herself, no troll could inflict pain that would match that of staying with Trip and knowing that it would never be real.

There was a sharp beat of silence and then he nodded. She took a deep breath. 'I'll just get my things—'

She held her breath, hoping, praying that he would stop

her, stop this from happening. But after a few beats of silence he said stiffly, 'I'll get Lazlo to organise a jet.'

'You don't need to do that.'

He glanced towards the window. 'I want to. In fact, I insist on it. The main airports are probably under siege by the paps and I said I'd keep you safe.'

His matter-of-fact tone made her flinch inside. The last time he had spoken those words, his voice had been soft and tender. Now it was as if he were sitting in his office, dictating a letter to his PA.

But then this had always been about business for him, she thought, her pulse pounding hard in her head. Keeping control of Winslow. He had never promised love.

'I'll wait downstairs. Come and find me when you're ready to leave.'

Her legs felt as though they were no longer solid beneath her. It was unimaginable to be without him, but it would be worse, so much worse to marry him and then have to wait for it to end.

'Thank you.' Clenching her fists to stop her hands shaking, she lifted her chin. 'Goodbye, Trip. I hope it all works out for you—'

He didn't look at her. Just continued to stare at the window and then abruptly he turned and walked away. She watched his back, willing him to turn around and come striding back to her. She pictured him pulling her in his arms and telling her that he needed her in his life for ever.

But this wasn't a fairy tale, so instead he kept walking and she kept standing there, her heart breaking, shattering inside her ribs.

CHAPTER TEN

LEANING FORWARD TO rest his elbows against the kitchen counter, Trip stared blankly at his laptop screen. It was good news, the best in fact. Winslow had just signed a deal with the world's biggest fitness tracker. It was his project and it had sent share prices soaring. His email was clogged with congratulatory messages from trustees and shareholders. He had no need of a wife to improve his image.

But there was nobody to share the moment.

His chest felt as if it had been hollowed out with a spoon. He was alone.

Not officially. Not publicly. Not yet.

That would happen tomorrow. If he could find the right words.

It was two hours since he'd walked out of their bedroom, and it felt like a lifetime, but he could hardly rush her. So he was giving her space even though he still couldn't believe that it had ended this way. That it had ended at all.

It made no sense for her to react as she had. Everything had been going perfectly. There had been a smoothness to every second that he knew logically was beyond her control and yet her being there seemed to give everything a tensile certainty. But, at some point between stepping on and off the punt, it had all fallen apart.

Don't say my name.

That was what she'd said to him, and it had been a shock, like a physical blow, because he knew how it felt to hear her say his name and he'd thought she felt the same. Only her voice had had that snap of some last thread fraying, as if she'd grown tired of pretending.

And that had hurt, so he'd done what he always did when something pushed him away. He'd pushed back.

He could still see the expression on her face, that mix of shock and hurt, and he knew that was on him. But Lily had caught him off balance talking about separating and then suddenly...

The floor tilted beneath his feet as if he were suffering from vertigo. It was the same feeling as before when she'd told him she loved him in so many words. When she had stripped herself bare of all her protective layers. He knew what it must have cost her to do so, and he had done nothing. Said nothing. Nothing coherent anyway. He had just stood there, watching her try to hold herself together.

His hands clenched into fists and he slammed them against the counter, welcoming the sting of pain because it took the edge off the ache tearing through his chest and splitting his heart.

But what was he supposed to say? Their 'engagement' was never about love. Hell, he wasn't sure he even knew what love was. He understood the concept, but in his family love was expressed primarily through material support. There was financial security on an unimaginable scale but affection, emotional support and that intuitive understanding were absent.

Right up until he'd tricked Lily onto that plane.

She had fought with him, challenged him, comforted him, and been at his side during one of the hardest periods of his entire life. But he hadn't been prepared for her loving him.

Or for how much he loved her.

And that was when he realised why he was hurting so much. Why he felt sick and split and broken and empty. He loved Lily.

Wanted her, needed her, loved her with an intensity that matched the surge of blood beating from his heart.

Turning, he walked swiftly through the house. The door to the bedroom was open and he strode in, his heart hammering in his throat.

'Lily, I—'

He stopped. The bedroom was silent and empty. So was the bathroom. So were all the other rooms in the house and the garden. He checked and double-checked, retracing his steps, panic swelling inside him but no amount of searching could change the facts.

Lily was gone. His gaze snagged on something bright and glittering on the bedside table. But she had left the ring.

It was starting to rain. Tugging her jacket around her shoulders, Lily glanced dully up at the clouds, then crossed the street.

She had taken the red-eye from Heathrow to JFK. Nobody had given her a second glance. The steward had come by with the trolley but the effort of choosing, of talking, had overwhelmed her. Instead, she had turned towards the window and wrapped her arms around her waist to stop her from disintegrating and, surprisingly, she had fallen asleep instantly and slept until the early morning light seeped through the window to press against her eyelids.

Waking, she had remembered all of it and her misery

had been caustic. In some horrible parody of her flight to Italy, she hadn't wanted to leave the plane. But she couldn't stay there for ever, and finally she had got to her feet and made her way down the aisle.

She'd had a momentary wobble as she'd walked through the terminal. It had felt so final, so absolute. The taxi ride back to the city had been a welcome diversion but she'd made the driver drop her off a few streets from her apartment. She'd wanted to set the pace for herself. Not just be driven up and deposited on the pavement.

And it was okay, walking through the quiet, familiar streets with her keys clutched in her hand like a talisman. Just putting one step in front of the other gave her something to focus on, and with each step she was one step closer to home. One step closer to the life she needed to start living now.

As she turned the corner, her feet faltered as she spotted a group of young women weaving their way along the pavement towards her. But they were drunk and, frankly, she was past feeling worried about anyone recognising her. Past feeling anything.

The memory of Trip walking out of the room without so much as a backwards glance made her chest feel as if it were a gaping wound. That love could hurt so much was astonishing, but she couldn't undo what had been done, and she wouldn't even if it were an option.

She couldn't let herself think about that now. It would fade in time, become bearable. And in the meantime she had a career she loved, a family she loved even more, and friends to distract her.

She had reached her street and, picturing her small, cosy apartment, she felt a rush of relief and gratitude. She would be safe there. She could heal and then she would face the world.

'It's her—'

'Lily—'

Glancing up, Lily felt her breath stall. Men with cameras and microphones were uncurling themselves from car seats, staggering to their feet, their eyes hard and flat as they started to run towards her.

Her feet froze and for a moment everything went into slow motion as she stared at them, panic swelling inside her. If she hadn't been so distracted she might have noticed them, been more prepared, but she wasn't prepared at all and, before she even had time to think of a Plan B, she found herself surrounded by a pack of paparazzi and reporters shouting questions.

Somewhere beyond the jostling men she heard the roar of an engine and the screech of brakes. Then footsteps, heavy, urgent. There were more of them.

'No comment,' she said, holding one hand in front of her face, trying to block out their lenses and their questions as she looked for an exit. But there were too many of them. They were like a dark cloud smothering her.

She blinked into a sudden glare of light. But it wasn't the flash of a camera, it was sunlight. Breathing out shakily, she saw Trip shouldering his way through the pack. His blue eyes were blazing with a fury that made most of the paparazzi step backwards. Behind him a team of men in dark suits and even darker glasses were creating a human barricade in front of the remaining reporters.

'Are you okay?' Trip was by her side, the blaze of anger softening as he stared down at her.

'What are you doing here?'

'I promised to keep you safe,' he said, his shoulders rising and falling on a deep breath and, reaching down, he scooped her into his arms and carried her and didn't stop until they were inside her apartment.

'You can put me down now,' she said stiffly. 'And then you can let yourself back out.'

Trip let go of her and she walked quickly away.

'I'm sorry I upset you. Again.'

He stared over to where she was looking at her phone, or pretending to look at her phone. There was a tension to her bowed head that made him think that she was seeing nothing on the screen. That her whole body was arrowed in on his position in the room.

'I didn't mean to. I didn't want to. I never want to upset you.'

The stiffness in her shoulders moved to her spine but she didn't respond and, for a fraction of a second, he almost turned and left. But then he thought about how she had stayed with him after they'd argued, how she had let him talk. Listened. Comforted him. And so he tried again, because he had to. Because this time he couldn't leave. He didn't want to.

'And I didn't take you to Oxford so that people would see us together,' he said quietly. 'I wouldn't do that—'

Her shoulders were still rigid but her eyes floated over to his. 'No, because tricking people, pushing your own agenda—that's not your way of doing things, is it?'

The tiredness in her voice pierced him. It made her sound so much older than twenty-eight, and yet younger too. Like a frightened child. He took a breath.

'It was, before. Back in New York. I felt trapped and I was angry and I didn't think about what you wanted. I was only thinking about myself. But that's why I asked you to come with me to Oxford. Because I know you loved being there and I thought it would make you happy.'

Her eyes found his. 'I was happy.'

Was. Past tense. He felt the rush of fear and panic that had swamped him as he walked back downstairs from the empty bedroom, that same sense of being trapped inside a shrinking tomb. 'Why did you leave? I thought you were upstairs, but you were gone. And you didn't take the plane.'

'You don't get to tell me what to do.' Lily wrapped her arms in front of her chest like a shield, walling herself off, shutting him out.

'You could have been hurt.'

'I already have been,' she said slowly. 'I think we're done here, Trip.'

'I'm not finished.' He looked at her impatiently. She was as stubborn as she was beautiful.

'Well, I am. I have nothing to say to you, Trip,' she managed to say, 'and you said everything you needed to say yesterday—'

'But that's just it. I didn't.' Trip stared at her. His heart was still beating out of time from seeing her surrounded by reporters like a deer cornered by hounds. 'I didn't know what I thought. One minute you were saying all this stuff about wanting to separate and the next you were saying you loved me.'

'That was yesterday.'

'Lily, please.'

The tightness in his voice made everything inside her roll sideways like a capsizing boat. But this was what Trip did. He rushed headlong in where angels feared to tread. To Ecuador or into a pack of baying paparazzi.

'What? I know you. I know how you think. How you

react, how you overreact because that's who you are. It's what you do, it's what you did before. Only instead of going to Ecuador, you turn up with a bunch of bodyguards and make out that it's because of a promise you're keeping.'

'I did make you a promise. And yes, you're right, this is what I do, but I'm not that person any more, Lily. You changed me. You made me look at myself, look at the person I was.'

He took a step closer. 'I've been so angry for so long. Angry with myself, but mostly angry with my father. When I found those letters I didn't deal with how it made me feel, I just ran away. You made me realise that I needed to deal with that anger. Or I'd ruin the future.'

'You don't need to worry about that. I saw the headlines. Congratulations. I'm sure the shareholders are more than happy for you to run the business now.'

'I'm not talking about Winslow, Lily.' The fierceness in his voice made her flinch. 'I'm talking about our future.'

'We don't have a future.' Her chest squeezed tight. 'I told you, I'm not going to marry a man who doesn't love me.'

'No, you're not. You're going to marry a man who's madly, helplessly, completely and utterly in love with you.' His voice was choked with tears. 'Because I love you, Lily Dempsey. I love you, and I need you in my life, not just in my heart, but by my side.'

She watched in astonishment as he dropped to one knee and took her hands in his.

'So will you be my wife? Will you marry me?'

'You're proposing.'

Trip nodded. 'Say yes, please.'

'Yes,' she said softly, her tears falling freely now because they were tears of happiness, and then he was pulling her down and his mouth was on hers. They kissed hungrily, kissed until the pain of parting was forgotten.

'You know nobody will know the difference,' Lily said shakily, searching his face, seeing the love there, feeling it radiating through his body to hers.

His hands slid down over her body, holding her steady, steadying himself. 'We will,' he said softly. 'We'll know. And I wanted, I *want*, to give you a new ring to show you how different it is for me now. But I didn't want to rush into anything. And I don't have to. Not when we have forever together.'

And he pulled her against him, breathing in her scent, the scent of this woman who was everything he needed in the world.

* * * * *

ITALIAN'S
STOLEN WIFE

LORRAINE HALL

MILLS & BOON

For Caitlin, writing partner extraordinaire.

CHAPTER ONE

Francesca Campo sat in the beautiful suite of Valentino Bonaparte's estate and studied herself in the ornate gilt mirror. She looked perfect. Not a dark hair out of place, not a speck of makeup smudged. The white bridal gown had been made just for her and would look flattering at every angle.

Francesca would accept nothing else. This moment was the culmination of years of hard work. *Desperate, imperative* work. In a few short hours, she would be Francesca Bonaparte.

And she would be *free.*

She was on the cusp of getting everything she'd spent the past four years planning. Escape from her father. *Certain* it was a better situation than the one she'd grown up in. She'd made sure of it.

Maybe Vale was a little…uptight. Aloof. But they understood each other. She had done her due diligence in selecting him. So, Vale would give her everything she needed. Freedom, above all else. Safety, on this beautiful, ancestral tidal island off the coast of Italy. Her father couldn't—and more importantly *wouldn't*—reach her here.

As long as today went off without a hitch. Anxiety

twisted in her gut, but this was normal. Every day, really. She'd spent her entire life walking on eggshells around a volatile, violent father whose money made him, essentially, invincible. She had been the pawn he'd moved around the world of his making, molded into perfect, obedient submission—or so he thought.

But he'd had no idea that instead he'd built the kind of person who would one day design her own escape. And no one would ever believe her capable of such pragmatic, single-minded ruthlessness because everyone only saw the flawless image her father had crafted.

Which made her plan perfect.

In the press, she was goodness personified. A veritable *saint* of an heiress to Bertini Campo's impressive fortune. No one had ever been able to find a single flaw—her father had beaten those out of her long ago—and she wouldn't start with flaws on the most important day of her life.

Even now, after so much hard work, it was difficult to believe she'd made it. In the beginning, Francesca had assumed she would have to pretend to fall madly in love with Vale Bonaparte. Fluff his ego and play to his pride and continue to portray the image of exemplary, obedient bride material.

But this had not been the case. Over her months of trying to woo him without letting him *realize* she was trying to do so, she had soon learned that Vale had no interest in passion or romance.

He was looking for a sure deal, and, fortunately, so was she. They understood each other, would help one another, and that was *that*.

She gave herself one last look in the mirror, took a

deep, careful breath and counted as she let it out. Then she fixed on her best, sweet, innocent smile that she would flash at all the guests. Every last onlooker.

No cameras. No one outside the carefully curated guest list. Vale had insisted, and she, being the good, obedient *perfect* fiancée, had agreed. Of course, she wouldn't have minded a *few* pictures. Deep down, she would have rather liked a grand, rollicking party to celebrate her freedom.

But she'd long ago locked up those "deep down" impulses. Besides, this very small, very private wedding was a nice reprieve considering her father usually insisted on every camera he could wield his power over to follow her about, forever growing her reputation as the perfect heiress.

Forever holding her prisoner.

Angelic enough to be acceptable, charitable enough to not be considered vapid. She'd gone to university, proven her intellect so that even whispers of her father buying her grades were laughed off. But she also dressed modestly, smiled, never argued, and made everyone in her orbit feel listened to.

She knew how to wrap *anyone* around her finger, and all the biting her tongue, pretending she was someone else, perfecting a mask that sometimes made her feel dead inside...well, it was all paying off.

She moved to the arched window that looked down over the entrance. The day was sunny and warm beyond her window, and guests were filing in. It was almost here. She was *almost* free.

She saw a woman with a scarf wrapped around part of her face, an odd choice in the warmth of the afternoon.

Francesca studied her, something about the woman's half-hidden profile so familiar.

From this distance, Francesca almost ignored it, but then the woman tilted her head just to look around, and Francesca had the image of many, *many* pictures.

This was no ordinary guest. This was *Princess* Carliz del las Sosegadas. And she was *not* on the guest list.

Francesca felt her chest get tight with panic. Vale's ex-lover, princess or no, could *not* ruin this for her. She whirled away from the window. She had to do damage control. To make a big deal about the woman's appearance—as though she had been thoughtfully and graciously invited.

As though they were all the best of friends. So the press could not twist it into something that might cause a problem. So this woman could *not* interrupt her very necessary wedding.

In retrospect, this moment should have been Francesca's first clue that she did not wield *quite* the control she thought she did.

She reached for her mobile to call her assistant but didn't finish the move because she heard the door to the room squeak open. As she had been insistent that she wanted to be alone to have some private, *prayerful* contemplation before the ceremony, she assumed this interruption would be her father—who was still under the impression marrying Vale had been *his* idea, *his* boon, *his, his, his*.

Gritting her teeth, she took a breath and fixed the smile of servitude on her face and turned to face him. The last time, she promised herself, she'd ever have to pretend. She would get rid of him and then—

Except it wasn't her father. It was not anyone she knew. At least personally. She'd seen this man's face splashed across a dozen magazines and gossip sites. She had heard stories of him from *everyone* around her—except Vale, who was *very* careful to mention his wild, impetuous, illegitimate half brother as little as possible.

They looked so very much alike. Thick dark hair, broad shoulders, arrestingly handsome features and olive skin. They could have been twins, really, except for the eyes. Vale's were blue. This man's were brown.

And perhaps that *smile*. Which spoke of a wildness and danger that if Vale had, he kept hidden well under wraps.

"Ciao," he offered, very carefully closing the door behind him. Aristide wore an impeccable tuxedo that couldn't be all that much different than Vale's groom attire. And yet, where Vale would look ruthlessly styled, perfect from every angle just like her, Aristide Bonaparte somehow gave off the aura of casual insolence. His dark hair wasn't mussed but seemed to hint that a woman's fingers had been trailing through it not all that long ago. His posture was straight, his shoulders broad, and still he gave the impression of a man who could care less about what went on around him.

Because in his world, everything revolved around *him*.

It was strangely dizzying, all these suggestions that weren't the reality of the man who stood before her. For a moment, she forgot about her very pressing business of a princess crashing her wedding.

"Hello," Francesca replied carefully. When he said nothing, she remembered herself. Smiled. Lowered her gaze to unassuming timidity. "You are Aristide, are you not? Vale's brother."

"I am Valentino's half brother, yes."

He didn't offer anything else. Francesca tamped down her frustration—he was ruining her timetable. She needed to get *her* version of the Princess's arrival out before anyone else did. Still, she kept her smile in place and decided to treat this like a meeting. Smile. Shake hands. Ask questions. Feign interest and get to the bottom of why he was here. She held out her hand. "I am Francesca. It is so good to mee—"

He took her outstretched hand, but he did not shake it. He simply held it, turned it slightly to the right and then the left, as if to watch her jewelry sparkle in the light. Something about the move, the contact, the size of his hand made it somehow impossible to finish her sentence.

Slowly, he moved his gaze from her hand, and up to her eyes. The impact of all that swirling dark—knowing and arrogant, with a hint of humor she had definitely never seen in Vale—felt like a detonation.

"Yes, I am very well aware of who you are, *cara*."

His smile felt like some kind of lethal blow. Francesca could not understand why it should make her feel breathless and devastated.

But she had spent her life in such a state. So she kept her smile in place and waited patiently for him to explain his appearance. Even if her heart seemed to clatter around in her chest like it was no longer tethered. A strange sensation indeed.

"I am afraid there has been a change of plans today," he said at last, his low voice a sleek menace.

Francesca kept her sweet smile in place, her hand relaxed in his grip, her posture perfect. She was an expert at playing her role. Even as panic began to drum its familiar beat through her bloodstream. "Oh?" she said, as if she was interested in everything he had to say.

No one would change her plans. *No one.* She narrowly resisted curling her free fingers into a fist.

"You will be marrying me instead."

Francesca prided herself on being the kind of woman who could roll with the punches—after all she'd been dealt plenty of the literal kind. She held her mask up no matter the circumstances, but her mouth dropped open at that. "I'm sorry...what?" She jerked her hand away before she thought the action through to put a positive spin on it.

But why be positive to a man who was clearly *insane*.

"Vale has made a solid choice in such an upstanding character as yourself. So upstanding, I simply must have you for myself."

For himself? She shook her head, taking a step back away from him and then another. "That is *not* the plan, and...it's ludicrous." So ludicrous that... "Is this some kind of prank? I regret to inform you, a wedding day is *not* the day to try and pull one." She already had unwelcome royalty to deal with.

Aristide shrugged. "No prank. I am known for the ludicrous, of course. But you will be my bride, Francesca. We will leave at once and we will be married before the day is through. You can make that easy, of course."

She barked out a laugh. Not her usual dainty one either. She breathed in through her nose, reminding herself that she was *this* close to escape. She would not be thwarted now. "I don't understand what this is, but as *this* wedding is almost upon us, I think I shall see my plans and promises through." She smiled. "Thank you," she added.

But he did not look put in his place or swayed in any

way. The curve of his mouth stayed arrogant and know-ing. His eyes trailing over her like she was a possession he was determining the value of.

His possession.

It should disgust her, but she was too thrown off by all these unexpected things to really dissect the strange feeling that spiraled through her.

"You misunderstand me. You will either come with me to *our* wedding, or I will stop your wedding to Valentino in *other* ways, and from everything I've seen of you, *angioletta*, that would be a catastrophe. So, shall we go?"

Aristide Bonaparte had a few expectations of how this would go. The most likely reaction would be dramatics, of course, but everything he'd discovered about Franc-esca Campo in the past forty-eight hours since he'd de-cided she would be *his* bride, instead of his half brother's, pointed to a woman who did not do dramatics. Ever.

She was a bit of a tabloid favorite—for all the oppo-site reasons he was. Her father trotted her about from glittering event to posh dinner, creating an image of the perfect heiress. Full of goodness, warmth, and a heart of gold. Any man would be lucky to have her, and so it made the most sense that the great, honorable Valentino Bonparate would win her.

Aristide, on the other hand, was known as a *playboy* who cared for nothing and no one but his own pleasures and whims. No one would celebrate their union.

At first.

Aristide doubted he or Francesca were as bad or as good as the press made them out to be. The great thing about his plan was it didn't matter. The fact Vale was going to marry this woman only proved that even if she was not *privately* everything she made herself out to be, publicly she would be everything Aristide needed.

You could never have the kind of reputation your brother has built.

Aristide wanted to sneer at the memory of his detestable father's dismissive words—delivered via messenger, because that was the only way his father deigned to communicate with him these days. Aristide didn't mind living down to a low expectation—as long as he could take it even lower, but there was one man he *always* wanted to prove wrong.

So, he would.

Besides, it would be a fun little challenge to completely rebuild his public persona—as everyone said he couldn't—while feeling the satisfaction of embarrassing Vale, the betrayer.

A man had to find enjoyment where he could, and Aristide *always* found his.

Francesca had stopped backing away from him, stopped shaking her head. She was staring at him with wide eyes.

He would give all the stories and gossip about her one thing. She *was* beautiful, in an unearthly sort of way. Like she didn't quite belong in this world. But he did not think it was some *inner goodness* everyone else attributed it to. She was not a saint from a better world. Not an *angel*.

No, there was too much calculation going on behind those dark eyes. Because she didn't reach for her phone, and she didn't make a run for it as he'd half expected she might. No, she stood there. Regal and considering.

Instead of, say, screaming.

"How would you ruin my wedding to your brother?"

Interesting that the question was not *why*. But that was neither here nor there. "So many options, but I think the best is to wait for the priest to offer the crowd a chance to object, and to choose that moment to claim that you cannot marry my brother when you have been spending your nights with me."

Once again, the woman's mouth dropped open before she seemed to get ahold of herself. "What a ridiculous lie. Why would Vale believe that? Why would *anyone*? I've never even *met* you!"

Clearly, Francesca Campo did not know his brother all that well. "It does not need to be true for Valentino to believe it of me. Regardless of anything he might feel about you, he's quite determined to believe the worst of me. Always. So, as you can see, it is in your best interest to come along." He held out his arm. He had planned and timed this perfectly, but he didn't have time for extensive conversations on the matter until he got her into his car.

"You want me to go with you," she said, very calmly. She even brought her hands in front of her and clasped them, as though she were conducting a meeting. "Marry you, instead of your brother, immediately?"

"Yes."

"And… You live on the island as well, yes?"

He very nearly frowned. He'd expected some…upset. Some tears, even if he knew she'd have to come with him after that threat. But this was all very…calm. "Yes." The island had been split nearly in two, between him and his brother. His estate was on the opposite side of the island, the *good* side, he liked to tell Valentino the rare moments they were in each other's presence.

Usually only at the Diamond Club they both belonged to—exclusively for the richest people in the world. Aristide smiled to himself. His brother still wasn't over the fact Aristide had gotten himself an invitation. And *loved* to appear when he knew Valentino would be there. Just to twist the knife.

"And after we were married, we would live here?" his future bride asked with clear eyes and a speculative expression.

"Indeed. Some even say *my* estate is much more livable than Valentino's mausoleum." He smiled at her.

She did not smile back.

"It is quite well known that you are…not selective, shall we say, with your romantic exploits. Why would you want to marry at all?"

"The years have weighed on me," he lied. Easily. "I want to rehabilitate myself, start a new leaf, and what better start than the perfect wife?" It was *told* that this woman was quite intelligent, but if she believed this story, clearly people were wrong.

Her expression didn't change. "Yes, stolen brides and threats are known to be a great start for a character change." Her delivery was so dry it nearly took him a moment to understand her true meaning.

He was tempted to laugh. "My, my, *cara*. Do I sense a flicker of a personality underneath all that polish?"

Her eyes cooled, but she didn't jump to the bait. "What about a contract?"

There was something downright *mercenary* about her. It was quite surprising, and Aristide didn't care one way or another if he *enjoyed* his chosen bride, but it would be nice to know she wasn't *quite* the wet blanket the press and his brother had painted her as. "I have drawn one up that is almost identical to the one you were to sign with my brother. With my name instead, of course."

"How did you have access to the contract we drew up?"

He shrugged. "Dastardly means, naturally."

She sighed as if she was vaguely irritated with him. A bit like his mother did when he was purposefully baiting her. "So, we will just go. Now? And be married…?" she asked, still so unreadable, steady dark eyes studying him as though he were a complex math equation she would no doubt figure out if given the right tools.

It was unnerving, and not at all what he'd expected.

But this had always been where Aristide excelled. His name did not mean *the best* for nothing.

"Immediately," he supplied.

Yet again, he braced himself for some kind of reaction. Tears. Despair. Anger. Fear. Maybe even demands.

But this woman simply nodded a regal chin. "Very well."

This was not what he expected. He raised an eyebrow. "That easily?"

"You threatened to ruin this wedding either way, if you recall." Inexplicably she looked behind her, out the window that looked down over where guests were entering. Then her gaze returned to him, dark and direct. "I know enough of your character to know you have ample means to accomplish this. Is capitulating to a threat *easy* or is it the intelligent course of action?"

No, she was not quite what anyone had made her out to be. *Fascinating.* "You didn't even try to get around it."

She waved this away as she walked over to her vanity table and picked up a mobile and a small purse that matched the white of her bridal gown. She fixed him with a gaze that had a strange ribbon of unease move through him, like he was getting in over his head.

When that was as ludicrous as she accused this turn of events of being.

She lifted her chin. "I am determined to be married today, and the identity of the groom is rather immaterial if the contractual terms remain identical. You have just as much money as Vale, you have just as much land on this island. The two of you are basically interchangeable to me if the contract is indeed the same. I need a groom. I don't need a scandal."

He frowned at that. That was *his* line. It suited his purposes that she be this amenable, though he was baffled what the perfect, honorable Valentino was doing marrying a woman who felt her groom was *immaterial* and *interchangeable*.

"I assure you, nothing about my brother and I are the same."

She studied him, like she could see through his every thought. Ridiculous. "If you wish to think so, I won't argue with you."

"Excellent. I prefer a wife who doesn't argue."

Her expression went even more bland, sweet, *innocent*. "Of course," she said, and there was no reason not to believe she was exactly that unassuming.

He was surprised to find he did not believe the image she presented. At *all*.

But it did not matter. He would get what he wanted.

Always.

CHAPTER TWO

ARISTIDE DID NOT *sneak* her away from Vale's estate, precisely. He just seemed to know where to go in the long,
complex hallways where they ran into no people. Then
out a side kind of servant entrance and into the bright
sunny afternoon on the other side of the estate, opposite
to where the wedding was taking place.

Francesca was very well aware she had options. She
could have run to find Vale. She could have used her
mobile to call for reinforcements. Maybe it would have
created a bit of a scandal for the brothers to essentially
fight over her, but she had little doubt she could still ensure a wedding to Vale by the end of the day.

Maybe, just maybe, if the Princess had not shown up,
Francesca would have done just that, but something about
the alluring, *interesting* beauty felt like the only true
threat to Francesca's arrangement with Vale. Not just
today, but the entire future of their marriage.

She couldn't risk Princess Carliz being a ghost that
threatened her freedom. So she'd take this *ludicrous*
course of action, as long as it got her what she wanted.
The end result was all that mattered. Not how she got
there.

As she'd noted, Aristide was not known for his long-term *relationships*. There would likely be scandal attached to him, but the kind of scandal she could no doubt weather if it kept her out of her father's orbit. Not the kind of scandal that would end her freedom if Vale truly *did* love Carliz and would end up leaving her for the beautiful princess.

Sometimes, you had to pick your poison based on what effects you could survive.

Aristide led her to a sleek sports car and opened the passenger door for her. She didn't hesitate to slide into her seat, to arrange herself gracefully, smoothing out the skirt of her dress as he moved into the driver's side.

"Will there be guests at our wedding? A photographer?" she asked as he pulled out of the long, winding drive.

They both pretended they didn't see a suited man— likely security—trying to wave them down.

"No. Our love could not wait for such accoutrement, naturally."

She wanted to laugh, but she kept her expression mild. Until the contract was signed, she had to play this very carefully. Aristide was not as…contained as Vale. He was known for whims and wildness, even if he wanted a reputation redo, and perhaps Francesca could hope to be more of herself in private once the ink was dry.

But the ink had to be dry first.

Besides, Aristide hit the gas pedal as though the very hounds of hell were on their heels and took the curves at a breakneck speed that had Francesca looking for *something* to grab on to. In the end, she could only brace herself against the door and hope she did not end up dying in a fiery crash in the wrong brother's car.

Now, *that* would be a story for the press.

She wanted to laugh again. What a dizzying and irresponsible way to travel.

Why did it feel like freedom?

None of this was what she'd planned, but then, what had ever gone according to her exact plans? She could make this one work. She *would* make this one work.

Aristide had a completely different reputation than Vale, but it was still one that might be enough of a threat to her father to keep him far away. And then there was the contract.

"Did you read the contract when you stole it to replicate it with your name?" she asked him, watching as the landscape passed by at dizzying speeds.

Aristide's gaze slid to her briefly, then back to the road, where he took another curve hard and sharp. "Naturally."

"So you know what will be required of you if you marry me?"

"Protection from your father—both in location and monetarily. An interesting choice of terms, *angioletta*."

The press had been calling her that since she'd been a little girl. She worked hard not to scowl. "I don't care for that nickname."

"But everyone loves to portray you as just that. A little angel."

"Then I suppose I should call you *piccolo diavolo*." She didn't wince, though she wanted to. She needed to hold her tongue. *Until the ink is dry.* It had been her motto to get to this day, and now it would be her mantra to get through this unexpected turn of events.

"Calling me a devil does not bother me in the least,

but I would hesitate to characterize anything about me as *little*."

His smile was so self-satisfied it was nearly contagious. This was all nearly *funny*, really, but he took a hill too fast and her stomach flipped into her throat and then back down again.

She needed to focus on what he thought of the contract responsibilities, not finding his ridiculousness *amusing*. But she needed to find a smart way to negotiate. This might have been the easier course of action, but until the marriage certificate was signed and filed, this was perilous.

She had to behave as though every step was *imperative*.

They drove down the coastline of the island. She had not paid much attention to Vale's family beyond what he'd mentioned of it. He *never* mentioned Aristide if he could help it. And she had certainly never pressed. Especially after she'd had tea with Vale and his odious father.

It seemed best to be involved as little as possible in the Bonaparte soap opera, and she also knew enough not to step on toes.

She knew Vale and Aristide did not get along, did not agree on perhaps *anything*, and Vale considered Aristide an embarrassment. And an enemy, there on the other half of *his* island, *his* rightful inheritance—according to him.

For a moment, she felt a pang of guilt for leaving Vale in the lurch. Perhaps she should have fought harder against his enemy.

But in the end, Vale was a rich, powerful man. He could withstand losing her. Besides, he had a princess there, no doubt just for him.

Francesca could not withstand losing her chance at freedom.

"I will need to look through the contract before we marry, of course," Francesca said. "Just to ensure it *is* the same."

"Naturally, though I can assure you I have no need to change anything. A perfect bride on paper, a good reputation, this is all I'm after. I will pay your father off and never allow him on the island."

She let out a careful breath. That was all that was needed. She could weather everything else if he did that alone. But…if Aristide was expecting *rehabilitation* as payment…

"Do you really think stealing your brother's bride is going to rehabilitate a terrible reputation you've spent your entire adult life exacerbating?"

"If *you*, *angioletta*, fell in love with a man such as me, enough to throw Vale aside and marry me, surely there must be some good in me."

"Ah, so we are meant to pretend we're in love, rather than the truth." She could do that. She'd been pretending her whole life. It was just strange that for the first time in so long, the pretense felt more like a new weight than the old one she was used to carrying.

"What would you prefer, considering you find the identity of your groom *immaterial*?"

"I didn't say I didn't prefer it. I'm just trying to understand the layout of this arrangement as I cannot believe that a man such as yourself believes much in monogamy. Respectability. Love."

"No, I do not believe in love, *cara*. But I cannot imagine a woman who considers her groom *immaterial* thinks much of it either."

"No. I don't." Love was a fairy tale for people who could afford one. Probably a *princess*. Perhaps with some years of security under her belt she might wish for such things, but for now, there was only escape.

"Relax, Francesca, we will give each other exactly what we need."

"And what is it you think I need?"

"Based on that contract and your lack of concern about the identity of your groom? I think you need escape. Any way you can get it. I think you want freedom, and I can give this to you easily. Happily, in fact, as your freedom harms me in no way at all."

"And what is it you need?" she asked, studying his profile as he drove recklessly. Like he had no cares, but if he wanted to become respectable, he would need to find a way to care about that.

"Simply the foundation on which to rebuild my reputation. Sainted wives are a great foundation."

What a depressing thought. She was so very tired of being other men's *foundations*. But that heavy cloud of *what have I gotten myself into* lifted as a large, sprawling, what could only be termed *castle* came into view beyond his profile.

"Welcome home, *angioletta*," he murmured.

Something like excitement fluttered through her at the sight. It was... It was... "It is certainly not a mausoleum." Not that she thought Vale's estate was as grim as Aristide had been making it out to be, but there *was* a difference. Vale's was all stark, ancient, *ordered* beauty. Respectability seemed layered into every brick.

This was...chaos. Spirals and color. The ocean somehow more dramatic in the background because of the lack of order. Like it could win, any day, and all this... what have you would be swept away.

It was...thrilling.

"A masterpiece, isn't it?" he said, with no humility whatsoever. "Come. Let us promise to love one another for eternity."

Francesca's beauty was something else in the light of dusk and candlelight. She *looked* like an angel, standing there across from him in the little chapel-like room. It was not a *religious* room, per se, but he was a man who liked the superficial beauty of the church without the heft of threats of punishment and hell.

He had built this estate, piece by piece, to whatever whim had struck him at the time. So it was only what *he* liked. Only what *he* cared to be surrounded by. He had learned early that to care what other people wanted never ended well for him.

So he drowned himself in his own wants and lived a much happier life than his brother, who lived as if constantly housed in a prison of the Bonaparte name.

Perhaps, on occasion, he purposefully chose what he knew Vale would hate. Like the naked mermaid weather vane undulating on top of one of the tall, twisting spires. Valentino would consider it crass, embarrassing, a black mark on the Bonaparte name.

Good.

Francesca had not displayed the reaction he had expected when they'd initially arrived. He'd expected that having been intended for his brother, she might share Vale's disgust for the chaos of it all.

Instead of vague disapproval, or poor attempts to hide it, she had looked up in *awe*. As though she quite enjoyed what she saw. Like she'd just been taken to a fairy-tale castle where dreams might come true.

This had pleased him. He'd enjoyed watching her take it all in. He'd enjoyed watching the way her smile softened her beautiful face, and *life* had sparkled in her dark eyes.

There was *something* of interest under that outer shell of perfection. Perhaps he was not sentencing himself to years of boredom if she could find some pleasure in the ridiculousness of his choices.

Then she had insisted upon poring over the marriage contract. She had read every word, every punctuation mark, *three* times. She had asked question after question until he'd felt as if they were in a boardroom and his eyes might cross from the banality of it all.

But he'd seen what was under her fastidiousness. A determination to get exactly what she wanted out of this union. To *ensure* it. So calculating and exacting. Admittedly, the world's perfect angel being a bit mercenary had been…arousing.

The current image of her, bathed in soft light, wrapped in bridal white, while the officiant yammered on about love and duty, was not *less* arousing. Like there might be as many different fascinating facets to his bride as there were to the big, unwieldy diamond now on her finger.

A problem, because no doubt his Francesca was as virginal as they came—even if she wasn't everything the world thought she was. Wife or not, he didn't have any designs on preying on some sheltered innocent.

He preferred everyone know exactly what they were getting themselves into. He preferred having very careful lines that he did not allow anyone—himself included—to cross.

Of course, he would have to behave himself to begin to rehabilitate his reputation. There couldn't be even a whiff of an affair—and if there was anything he'd learned from his brother, it was that a man didn't have to act on his passions and whims for people to determine what might have happened with a beautiful and fascinating woman—the only kind Aristide preferred.

So Aristide would have to submit himself to *some* sort of celibacy to keep his lines intact. What a pity.

Perhaps he had not thought this plan fully through, but that had never been his strong suit. He was a man who acted and dealt with whatever consequences befell him. His brother had once accused him of only *ever* reacting, and perhaps in that one way Vale had been right.

Aristide felt there was nothing wrong with it. These were his consequences, and he would find a way around them. One way or another.

"I do," Francesca said very solemnly, bringing Aristide back to the ceremony at hand. He listened to the officiant recite the same promises he'd already outlined for Francesca. Then gave his own grave *I do*.

As the officiant announced them as married in front of precisely two witnesses—Aristide's assistant and his driver—Aristide allowed himself the satisfaction of knowing he'd done what he'd set out to do.

Stolen his brother's bride.

A coup indeed.

"You may kiss your bride, Signor Bonaparte."

Aristide had kissed many a woman in his day—and not *only* with the express purpose of talking them into bed. But he had never kissed *his* wife before. What a strange first to feel suddenly uncomfortable with.

But Aristide didn't *do* uncomfortable.

Francesca tipped her chin up, met him with that steady, dark gaze. She had taken this all in stride, with only a short moment or two of surprise back at Valentino's. He found he wanted to see that *true* reaction back on her face, instead of all these pretends she wore so effectively.

And Aristide did not know how to get through to this woman, but he knew how to get through to *women*.

He reached out, gripped her lifted chin between his thumb and forefinger, drawing her closer, while the remaining fingers brushed featherlight across her neck.

Her breath shuddered out, her eyes were wide on his. Not quite the prepossessed mercenary he'd seen before. Not the sweet, timid mask she wore so well—or some sign of her well-guarded virginity. No, there was something else entirely in that reaction.

That unease he'd first felt at Vale's was back, curling around deep inside him. A gut feeling that she might be more than he'd bargained for. A consequence, rather than the answer to his challenges.

Then she smiled, demure and sweet, and he *knew* she would be a problem.

A problem he was now contractually obligated to solve. But first, kiss. As had often happened in his life, he found himself struck with the urge to upend something. In this case, the serene, blank look on her face.

He had *meant* to remain fully hands off. A marriage in name only. Lines not crossed. And it would be that.

After this.

He lowered his mouth to hers, still holding her chin, pausing right there. Taking in the details of that beautiful face that he'd seen in print so many times, but never flesh and blood, never up close and personal.

The aristocratic nose, the heart-shaped face aiding in all the talk of *angels*. A little ring of hazel around the inner edge of wide eyes. The hint of gold in her left eye only.

And he waited, *waited* until he felt her breath hitch, just enough, to swoop in and finally close that minuscule distance between them. He wasn't sure what to expect, exactly, but that was half the fun of a kiss.

But he could not characterize this as *fun*, the gentle softness of her lips, the hesitant give of her body. The way she smelled of the wild oleander that permeated this island—like she belonged here when only his cursed bloodline truly belonged on this island of acrimony and pain.

It was a twist to the gut, a strange bolt of electricity, as though God himself was striking down this union. Devil to angel. *Cursed.*

He pulled back, not sure what…any of that was. He had kissed women before where the chemistry did not quite live up to what he preferred. He had kissed women perfectly pleasantly and blazed through passion often.

But he had never felt any of…that. Nor been left with this uneasy sort of…foreboding in response to a simple kiss.

She looked up at him, and he could not *read* her, there hidden behind whatever masks she wore.

He had thought this would be so straightforward. Steal Valentino's boring, sainted bride. Well, stealing Vale's toys had never gone quite according to plan, so why would he think it different now?

He dropped her chin. Smiled just as blandly as she and waited for the officiant to dismiss them. Once he did, Aristide took her by the arm and led her out of the room.

"Come, I will show you to your suite. Once the dust has settled over at Valentino's, we shall have your things brought over here. In the meantime, I am sure we can supply you with whatever you need."

"Dust." She blew out a breath. "I suppose I should feel some guilt for that."

"But you don't?"

"Vale will survive," she said with a firm nod. "And now, so will I."

"So dramatic, *angioletta*."

She did not respond to that. Just marched on next to him as he led her through the maze of hallways, curving stairwells. This place made no real architectural sense, which was why Aristide loved it. The island might be cursed, but this was his antidote.

This was where he could be whatever he damn well pleased, without concern about what anyone else thought or needed. A hard-won lesson he now embodied full throttle.

Much like the architecture, the woman next to him didn't make the sense he thought she had either. But they had time yet. He would puzzle her out. She was just a person like any other. He would understand, and all would be as he wanted it to be.

Always.

He led her to what would be her suite of rooms. For appearances, they connected to his own, but there was plenty of space for the two of them to exist as apart as they wished as the years wore on.

He tried not to think in *years*.

He opened the door to the main part of the suite. "Through here, you will find your bedroom and private bath. You will—"

But it was clear she wasn't listening to him. She certainly wasn't following him to the other rooms. She walked straight to the door that led out to the balcony that looked down over the beach. She didn't stop until she reached the edge, curling her hands around the railing and looking down at the crashing waves.

He followed her out into the balmy night. Darkness had fallen, but the lights of his estate—always bright and blazing *at* his brother—illuminated her gaze as it tracked across the coastline, the glittering moon and stars. Her expression began to soften, her full lips slowly curving into a smile. A *real* smile that threatened to outshine the moon itself.

Then she turned to him, a brightness in her that was all new. All…alarming.

"Might I have some champagne? Perhaps some cake. I feel like celebrating." And she *looked* like a celebration. She couldn't seem to keep the grin off her face. Her eyes were sparkling and a joyous energy pumped from her.

"Celebrating your marriage to a stranger?"

"I have lived under the thumb of my father for twenty-four years. And now I am finally free. *That* is cause for celebration. Whatever the means, whatever the cost, I am finally free." She shook her head vaguely, as if she couldn't quite believe it, and looked back out at the ocean.

"You do realize that some become adults and obtain jobs and leave their parents' thumbs with no dramatic marriages required?"

She stiffened, some of that unbridled joy leaving her face. Everything in her expression smoothed out, until she looked like...anyone. There was nothing special about this woman if he believed this facade she could shroud herself with.

But that she could was fascinating enough.

"I had not considered that." She clasped those hands so tight it pointed at something more than the lifeless words. "I was raised to believe marriage was my only option, of course, so that is the option I took." She smiled blandly up at him, her eyes devoid of anything.

But what she said was not true. It wasn't that he could read the lie on her. It was more her insistence that the contractual terms protect her from her father, combined with this freedom she wanted to celebrate, that had him wondering what went on at the Campo estate in Rome.

"Perhaps we could set aside these pretends and speak the truth. After all, we are husband and wife." And because he could not *quite* resist being himself, he grinned. "We must share all kinds of things now."

CHAPTER THREE

FRANCESCA REMINDED HERSELF that this was all part of the plan. That she had gotten exactly what she wanted, even if the groom was different. Even if he now spoke of *truths* and…*sharing* things.

Perhaps it was not as sturdy as the agreement she and Vale had made, but she had a contract. A signed contract. A signed marriage license. She was free. She was safe.

What did truths matter? Perhaps this was *better*. Even if Aristide wanted to use her reputation to salvage his own, she couldn't make his *worse*. There wasn't nearly as much pressure here as there would have been as Vale's wife, and there wouldn't be constant comparisons to one very beautiful and interesting princess.

There *would* be speculation, raised eyebrows, and perhaps concern. For her. But she did not have to be as perfect as she'd always been—because she would always look better than Aristide.

Besides, truths laced with omissions were not *lies*. They were self-protection. So she gave him a watercolor version of the truth.

"You have a rather awful father of your own, based on everything I've experienced with Vale. Surely you can imagine how a rich and powerful man might keep his daughter exactly where he wants her. A job? Who would hire me knowing Bertini Campo would sweep in and make their lives hell if they did? Perhaps I should have run away. With what? Stolen money? That he would track down, easily enough. Nothing? He also would have tracked me down, or the press would have. Believe me, I tried every means of escape I could, but they were all thwarted. Except the one thing he wanted for me. All I had to do was ensure *I* was in charge of the groom and make him think it was his idea."

"Won't he be upset with this turn of events as you were, in fact, not in charge of the groom?"

Francesca smiled sweetly. "You are a Bonaparte, are you not? The contract is the same. My father still gets everything he wants. This will keep him happy and far away." She refused to think otherwise. "Surely you have some supply of alcohol and sweets in this castle of debauchery? I would like to celebrate," she said. She wanted to get drunk. She wanted to eat an entire cake. All things she'd never been allowed to do.

She was *free*, and she damn well wanted to celebrate getting everything she'd planned.

"I prefer other kinds of debauchery, *angioletta*."

She might be virginal, but she had heard more than her fair share of sexual innuendo in the course of growing up. She understood his meaning, all too well. Though it left a strange trail of warmth through her, not the usual nausea.

Her father never minded his oily friends *saying* inappropriate things, *looking* at her in inappropriate ways. He had, in fact, encouraged it. As long as no one got handsy. Her precious virginity was a selling point in the great amassing of *more*, but that didn't mean he'd protect her from being harassed in other ways.

No doubt Aristide, famous for his trail of women, would expect his own version of *more*. She hadn't... thought that part of the groom switch through, had she?

Well, she'd just keep brazening through these unexpected detours. As she always had before.

"Vale and I had an agreement when it came to...sharing things," she said quite forcefully.

Aristide raised a dark, aristocratic eyebrow. "Please tell me how you planned to share my brother's bed," he said, so dryly she might have cracked a smile if she was not so uncomfortable. "I can think of nothing I'd like to hear more about."

"Your sarcasm is not quite the weapon you think it is."

"And your reputation is not quite the one *you* think it is."

"You stole me for my reputation."

"Yes. I did. Though *stole* feels a *bit* dramatic, don't you think?" He held up a hand, a kind of "hold that thought" gesture, and then he disappeared inside. He was only gone a few moments before he returned with a bottle of champagne in a bucket of ice, and two glasses. He placed them on a small patio table in the corner. Then went about the process of opening the bottle—all dramatic movements capped by the popping of the cork. It made her jump.

She reminded herself to relax. She had gotten away from the hell of her childhood. Maybe this wouldn't be heaven, but it would be *better*.

Aristide poured two flutes of champagne. She had meant champagne for *herself*. She had meant celebrating *alone*. Still, she accepted the glass when he handed it to her and did not invite him to leave.

Much as she kind of wanted to.

He held up his glass. "To a mutually beneficial union."

Mutually being the operative word, she thought to herself before clinking her glass to his. She took a long, deep drink, trying to let the celebratory bubbles ease some of the coils of anxiety inside of her.

She was so happy to be free, and she wanted that to be enough, but this man across from her was making things…complicated.

He studied her with dark eyes as he sipped his champagne at half the pace of her. When he finally spoke, it was probably the most serious she'd yet to hear him. "There are no photographers here, Francesca. No businessmen I make deals with, gossips who spread stories about me. My staff is loyal and know their worth here is more than any story they could sell. Here, in *my* castle, it is simply you and me."

How she wanted that to be true. To simply be *her*. For once. For *once*. To follow her own whims, her own desires. It was hard to believe she'd actually get that, but…here was a man who did that. All the time. No matter the backlash.

Perhaps…perhaps she could learn something from him. She lifted her glass, drained it and held it out for him to refill.

He obliged, but not without commentary.

"There is no rush."

"I think I'd like to get very drunk. I've never been drunk."

"Never?"

She shook her head. "Never been allowed even a full glass of champagne. Or more than one piece of cake on any given day. There was a woman employed by my father whose entire job it was to count my calories once I reached fifteen." She likely shouldn't have told him that, but she was free.

Free.

She could tell all the truths about her upbringing as she liked. She wouldn't go public with them, of course, but she didn't have to hide them from her *husband.*

She wanted to laugh at the absolute ridiculousness of that word, of this situation.

"What other *never*s are you looking to rid yourself of?" Aristide asked as he refilled her now drained glass.

She immediately took a sip from it. She liked the frothiness of it. The way it all seemed to go immediately to her head and make her feel less tethered to *everything* that weighed her down. She hadn't eaten today—too nervous, too determined to see everything through—so that likely added to the effect of it all. She could really use that whole cake right about now, but she decided to consider his question instead as she sipped from her glass.

She studied him. Maybe it was the alcohol. Maybe it was being in the desperate situation she found herself. She knew better than to show her vulnerable underbelly, so she started with the superficial.

"I want to learn how to bake."

He waved it away as though it were nothing. "Easily done. I'll set you up with Maurizio first thing in the morning. He is world-renowned in the kitchen, and if he cannot teach you what you wish to know, he will find someone who does."

She blinked. She hadn't thought so far ahead as to actually…getting the things she'd always wanted. She had only wanted the possibility. She had only wanted the space to breathe. To be...safe.

But learning to bake was *easily* done, according to Aristide. She swallowed against the emotion rising in her throat.

"I want to sleep in. I've never had a pet. I always wanted a dog. Something big and ridiculous. The more hair, the less brains, the better." It was all too...much. She felt like crying suddenly. Just collapsing into a heap and sobbing her heart out.

But she would never do that in front of him. Or anyone else, for that matter. Champagne or no.

So she just kept listing things. "And...never, *ever* see another piece of gym equipment."

"I don't mind a good workout now and then, so of course I have a gym on the property, but you may avoid it all you wish. *I* prefer to get my physical exertion out elsewhere anyhow."

Another innuendo. She could let it go. Smile and nod like she usually did before extricating herself from an uncomfortable situation. But he was just so *casual* about the whole thing. He wasn't watching for her reaction. He wasn't playing some weird power game. She thought these lazy little comments were just...the kind of thing he was so used to saying he didn't even consider the true meaning.

Perhaps it was that realization. Perhaps it was the champagne. Perhaps it was this strange turn of events and a break with reality, but she looked him right in the eye and said her next sentence very, very clearly.

"I do *not* want to sleep with you." Which brought strange images to mind. Like that kiss back in the unique and beautiful room they'd been married in. The way his hand had felt on her face, the warmth that had pooled inside her, lower than it should. That strange shuddering thing that cascaded through her.

She had kissed—if you could even call it that—Vale once or twice for the demure photo op and there had never been any of *that*.

But Aristide did not get all puffed up and angry. He only smiled. "I didn't ask."

"I may be a virgin, but it is not in my experience that men do a lot of *asking*."

Something changed in his gaze just then. All that lazy indulgence sharpening ever so slightly, but the smile did not falter. "I'm a great believer in consent. And begging, naturally."

Begging. Her frank and brief discussion with Vale on the matter of marital relations when they'd been drawing up their contract had definitely not discussed consent or *begging*.

Francesca had no smart comeback, no quick quip. So she simply stood there, and finished off yet another glass of champagne. All while Aristide stood—a good distance away on the balcony—*watching* her.

When he finally finished his one glass, he set it down on the table. And moved over to her. She held her breath, wondering if he'd touch her face again. Wondering if... something was about to happen. Her heart clamored in her chest, but she did not back away. And it wasn't her usual obedient mask that kept her rooted to the spot.

She didn't *want* to back away from the height and breadth of him, the heat of him.

What did that mean?

But he didn't touch her. "You are a fascinating creature, *angioletta*. Perhaps this entire endeavor will be more fun than I originally planned."

She didn't know what she was having. Not fun, per se. But this was...different. Liberating, maybe. Fun sounded... fun, though. "I don't think I've ever had any fun."

"Well, then we shall start tomorrow."

Aristide did not sleep well, but he did not allow himself to dwell on the *why*s.

He was an expert at denial.

He did not dwell on the way Francesca had smiled, or the look on her face when she spoke of some *woman*, hired by her father, counting her calories. Or how seriously she'd told him men did not do a lot of asking.

Her experiences up to this moment were immaterial. Whatever had happened before had no bearing on now.

He had a plan to enact.

This first week as husband and wife would be fairly quiet. To give the illusion of a cozy honeymoon at home. Then they would begin the real campaign. Events. Charity. And most of all convincing the entire world they were desperately in love.

What better story could there be than a debased playboy turning his life around for a perfect angel? Once he convinced them of it, everyone would *love* the story. Alone, he could never outshine Vale's perceived goodness, but with Francesca by his side?

He would have everything. And his father could go to hell.

Cheered by that thought, he went about preparing their morning. She'd said she wished to sleep in, so he had the staff prepare a brunch rather than a breakfast, to be set up outside once there were stirrings from Francesca's quarters.

When he was informed Francesca would arrive shortly, he made his way to the outdoor setup. It was already warm and sunny. Aristide had always loved the heat and shine of summer. The perfect backdrop for excess, he liked to think.

When his bride arrived on the sprawling, ornate patio, she was dressed in something bright and flowy—a swimsuit cover-up, if he had to guess by the brevity of the skirt. She looked around—at the statues of mythical creatures that lined the stairs leading down to the beach, the waves, the sun in the distance, the table of food.

But not at him.

"Good morning," she greeted, studying the layout of food quite seriously.

"Good morning, my wife. Join me for brunch."

She did not sit down. "Vera said the best time for a swim would be now," she said, speaking of the staff member he'd assigned to take care of Francesca.

"She is right, but you should eat something first after your first night of champagne debauchery."

"Vera supplied aspirin."

"Which you shouldn't have on an empty stomach. Sit. Eat."

She eyed the table with a mix of avarice and distrust. "How could two people possibly eat all this?"

"Two people who aren't counting calories but are instead enjoying their honeymoon, *angioletta*."

Still, she did not meet his gaze. She settled herself into the seat across from him, and sat there, looking around like she couldn't possibly know where to begin.

So he decided to aid her. He got up and took her plate from its spot in front of her and then began to pile it up with buttered bread with jam, a *sfogliatelle*, an assortment of cheeses and figs, wedges of caprese cake and a spinach frittata. He poured her both juice and coffee and placed it all in front of her before returning to his seat.

"If I eat all of this before I swim, I fear I will simply sink."

Aristide shrugged. "Eat what you wish. Take a swim break and return. We are on our honeymoon, *cara*, we may laze about however we wish."

She inhaled through her nose, then gave a little nod like she was accepting orders to march into battle. She lifted her silverware, and only hesitated a moment before she spoke again.

"Have you heard…" She trailed off, placing a bite of frittata in her mouth, but he knew what she had wanted to ask even if she did not finish.

"You have access to all the same news outlets as I do, Francesca. If you wish to know what befell your jilted groom, you can look it up yourself."

"Yes, but you're his family. I thought perhaps you might know…"

"Trust that if it involves my 'family' I do not know any more than the next person. This is by design—theirs, and I have no need to change it."

"Don't you care what damage you might have done?"

"Damage?" Aristide snorted out a laugh. "Did I interrupt your grand love match, Francesca? I know I did not, because I know my brother. For all the ways he does not make sense to me, I'm pretty sure you both knew you were making a business deal. Nothing more. Therefore, whatever *damage* results, is something he'll no doubt slither his way out of as he always does."

She shook her head, pondering the pastry on her plate. Finally, *finally*, she lifted her gaze to his. All dark eyes. Still unreadable, but there was something soft in her expression.

He didn't care for it one bit.

"Why do you and Vale hate each other so much?" she asked. Gently enough to poke at his temper.

"Surely my brother made sure to paint me the dastardly villain in all his stories of me."

"He went through great effort to never discuss you at all."

Aristide scowled at that. It shouldn't *surprise* him, and yet it felt like age-old dagger lodged into his back. "It is all very complicated, and very simple. He *thinks* I betrayed him with the truth. I *know* he betrayed me with his reaction to it." Aristide studied the mug of coffee, then set it aside as his stomach curled into a hard knot that often accompanied thinking too much of what had happened between him and Vale. "Perhaps we are both right."

"How did he betray you?"

Aristide considered the truth, and the lie he liked to trot out. He didn't mind the lie, liked playing it up for the right audience, but for some odd reason it felt wrong to lie to Francesca's interested gaze.

"We were quite close growing up, when he thought I was the lowly housekeeper's son and not his competition. When I discovered the identity of my father and informed him we were not just friends but brothers, I rather thought our connection was the only good thing to come out of something so terrible. He did not agree."

"That doesn't make much sense. Why would it matter whether you were related or not? You had no say in your existence."

Aristide shrugged, plucking a piece of cheese off his plate and studying it. Instead of taking a bite, he set it back down, not sure why he couldn't stomach the thought.

"It did not make much sense to me then, no. Part of the problem, I suppose. But as we have grown it has become clear that it was fine enough to be my friend when he thought me beneath him, but to think we might be the same made such a relationship difficult for his precious ego."

"Perhaps you are missing some piece to the story."

He met her gaze across the table. "I did not think you were in love with my brother."

She didn't bristle. She rolled her eyes, which for some reason eased some of the tension inside of him. "I'm not. But he was nothing but kind to me. And so have you been, so far. Aside from the whole stealing me away, I suppose. Not that I put up a true fight."

"I have never been accused of being *kind*, Francesca."

She gestured at the table. "But you have been."

"If supplying you with food on our honeymoon is a kindness, it will be quite easy to convince you I am the kindest man alive from here on out."

"Well, that would certainly help in redeeming your reputation. As would supplying me with a swimsuit with *any* modesty at all."

"If the clothes supplied are not the right fit—"

"It is not the *size* that is the issue, and as much as I have always been curious about skinny-dipping, it would not be…"

She had clearly not meant to say that, as she trailed off

and blinked. Immediately snapping her mouth shut and looking vaguely embarrassed.

He liked that this woman of so many facets might have been comfortable enough to let a truth slip out without thinking it through.

"It is a private beach, *angioletta*. You may swim in as much or as little covering as you wish. Be my guest."

"Honestly, Aristide. If I should do *any* skinny-dipping, it would not be with *you* in attendance."

He liked the way she said his name. All haughty and clipped, like a scolding schoolteacher. Even as her cheeks turned a pretty shade of pink.

He grinned at her. "Ah. Pity."

She shook her head, but there was a curve of amusement to her lush mouth as she stood. "I am going to swim," she announced grandly, like she was waiting for him to argue with her. When he didn't, she started to walk toward the stairs that led down to the beach. She looked back over her shoulder at him. Once. "You may join me, but I am *not* taking off my bathing suit," she stated—not that he'd asked. But she was smiling, like it was a joke.

The same feeling from the chapel swept over him. This swirling, soaring feeling that could only mean bad things were on the way. It could only be *dread*, even if it ribboned with a lightness that seemed created by her and her alone.

Aristide tracked her progress to the beach. He considered joining her, as he quite enjoyed a morning swim in the surf himself, but then she drew the cover-up off her.

There was no doubt she was beautiful. The wedding gown she'd worn yesterday had not *hidden* her body, per se. He'd been able to see the outline of her curves, the slender slope of her elegant shoulders, the flare of her hips. There were no surprises in the swimsuit—which was hardly *immodest*. Yes, it was two pieces, but the swath of olive skin visible between the dark fabric was hardly obscene.

It was that something in her expression had changed as she stepped into the calm, waving surf. All that calculation, all that *fake*, washed away. It was the joy he'd seen last night on her face when she spoke of freedom, but now it seemed deeper, as she stood out there on her own in the water.

It was something about the *glow* of her. Like that dress had made her a statue, and this was the soul beneath it. She walked deeper and deeper in, turning to face him.

Her smile was like the sun itself. And then she flung herself backward and disappeared beneath the surface, only to appear again, hair wet and flowing behind her, reminding him of the foolish mermaid that he would see atop the spire behind him if he turned to look.

But he did not. Nor did he follow his initial thought to go down to the beach and swim with her. No, if he was determined to keep his hands off his virginal wife—and he *was*—it would be best if he stayed right where he was.

Someone cleared their throat behind him. It was some effort to take his gaze off Francesca as she dove and re-surfaced over and over again. When he did finally turn, one of his staff members stood there with an envelope.

Aristide did not smirk, though he wanted to. Ah, finally, a response to his actions. Something to focus on besides his surprising new wife. But when he took the envelope and opened it, it was not his brother's stationery or harsh penmanship as he'd expected.

It was a short and to-the-point missive from father dearest.

You will come to my estate and discuss this at once.

Aristide crumpled up the piece of paper, wished for a fire so he could dramatically toss it in. He didn't care for the fact he'd been so certain he'd receive *something* from Valentino. Some reaction. Some…explosion. Something that might actually afford them the chance to clash.

It grated that he'd not considered his father might *also* have a response.

"Ignore it," Aristide told his messenger. "Ignore everything from Signor Bonaparte. I have made it clear to him I have nothing to say unless he can be bothered to show his face here." And that was one thing Milo Bonaparte refused to do. So it was easy to be as no-contact with his father as he liked at any given time.

Besides, as much as he was turning his reputation around to spite his father, that was not the attention he *really* wanted. He had long since given up on Milo Bonaparte, but there was another Bonaparte he couldn't quite seem to leave be.

Before Luca could fully withdraw, Aristide held up a hand. "Wait. Has anyone from Vale's estate brought over Francesca's things?"

"Not yet."

"Send a missive, just like this one but on my own stationery. Short and to the point, requesting Francesca's things be returned to her before the end of the day." If there was anything that might get under Valentino's steel armor, it would be something that *appeared* to be from their father but was from him instead.

Aristide smiled to himself and went back to watching his bride swim.

CHAPTER FOUR

FRANCESCA HAD ALWAYS loved to swim, but like all the things she'd loved that she'd managed to get her father's approval on, it had come with strings.

She couldn't just *play* in the water. She'd had to train like an Olympic swimmer, no matter that competition was *beneath* a woman of her important standing. Laps and correct form and instructors watching her every move. Timing her. Urging her to do better and be better. All for...nothing, really. She'd never understood it, but she'd borne it to get the thing she wanted.

But this was *more*. Here, she simply allowed herself to...play. Like a child. And the simplicity of it, the joy of it, caused tears to form in her eyes. And since she was essentially alone, she let them fall, then be washed away to sea.

She knew Aristide watched her, though she did not know why, but he was not close enough to see tears track down her face. He would not be able to tell them from the droplets of water. So she just let herself *feel*. Cry. Fall into the surf and pretend to drown, only to claw her way back up again and live.

Live.

It was like a baptism. A new life. Hope and joy. So big and bright she was almost afraid to believe it was true.

But the week went on just like that. All the things she'd packed for her new life as Vale's wife had appeared the second day, and other than some dark mutterings from Aristide about his brother, there seemed to be no real fallout from being *stolen away*. She hadn't heard from her father, from Vale angry with her, from anyone. There were stories, of course, but they all seemed to focus on Aristide and why he might have done such a thing.

She slept in, swam every morning—usually as Aristide watched from a distance. She ate luxurious meals, not at all concerned about calories or fat content, and spoke with her husband about anything and everything.

It was a struggle, though not a painful or unwanted one. Just… She had always been a quick study of people. Learned how to maneuver them to whatever suited the moment. It had been necessary when living under her father's iron fist.

But even with days under her belt, she did not know how to handle Aristide. He was an enigma. Not quite matching his reputation—which didn't surprise her as she knew she didn't match hers. But she couldn't quite figure out what the disparity was.

He acted as though nothing bothered him, just as his reputation suggested. He made lazy innuendos, but never pressed. Never *asked*. He was the epitome of respectability and kindness underneath that facade of reprobate.

It was the kindness, she supposed, that she allowed herself to trust—slowly. Because she knew that kindness could not be *truly* faked. Meanness or true motives had always shown through. She knew he was kind to her not because he *cared* in any way, but because there was no reason to be *unkind* in these moments.

And she had precious little of that in her life.

Slowly, very slowly, she allowed herself to be...herself, instead of the outer shell her father had crafted. Always testing the waters, always careful not to show too much too quickly. But Aristide never seemed surprised or horrified by who she really was or what she really wanted.

She supposed this was one of the positives to marrying a man who, allegedly, had no morals or concerns.

Maurizio taught her how to bake. They'd started simple. Cookies. A cake. It was exhilarating, creating something delicious, though not always pretty, from simple ingredients.

"I did this one all on my own," she announced, perhaps more excited than she had a right to be over something as simple and humble as her *very* rustic *schiacciata alla fiorentina*. It was their fourth night, and Aristide sat out on the porch they often retired to with a drink. She brought out her cake with perhaps too much fanfare, but Aristide had yet to make her feel foolish for enthusiasm.

She sat the pan down on the table, cut a piece and placed it on a waiting plate. She walked over and took the seat next to him. She didn't know what possessed her, but she used the fork to section of a piece and then held it out to him.

"You get the first bite."

His mouth quirked up, all charming amusement. But he dutifully leaned forward and took the bite she offered. Their gazes held as he took the fork into his mouth.

It was like a jolt of electricity, a reminder of the way her body had reacted on their wedding day, except this time they weren't touching. And still that buzz of electricity moved over her skin, tightening and tingling all the way down deep into her core.

Francesca had no real experience with desire. She wasn't even sure she would have recognized the disorienting swirling if she hadn't read *some* romance novels—hidden from her father, of course.

But this felt like all of those descriptors. Wild and untamable. Alluring *and* alarming. Until she realized he'd taken the bite, so there was no reason to still be holding the fork up.

She dropped it to the plate like it had scorched her, when the only thing that had was this strange new heat he created inside of her.

"A feat, *angioletta*," he offered, and if she was not mistaken his voice was more gruff than usual. "I shall have two pieces."

She wanted to *giggle*, which was the most ridiculous thing. But it gave her an excuse to move. To serve him said two pieces, and then she went ahead and took two for herself. She settled into her chair, trying to resist the urge to study him as he ate.

It was such a strange thing, having spent some time with Vale, who had been...not harsh, exactly. But very... contained. There had been a stillness about him. A stillness she had recognized as the one she tried to project to the world around her.

Aristides was all energy. All action. He had this outer appearance of laziness, but there was such movement in him. Such...*reaction*, and it created this reaction in her too.

And not just that sparkling heat, but something else.

He…sparkled, really. In conversation, in dinners where there were just the two of them. Even in silences such as now as he ate her cake. *Two* pieces.

He made her feel…

Well, she supposed that was it. Here in this strange world of his castle on his side of the island, she was just allowed to *be her*, for the first time *ever*. And there were a cascade of feelings that came from simply that.

Perhaps Aristide did not really *care* about her, nor did she expect him to. Perhaps he was wild in his personal life, reckless in business—though thus far it had only worked out for him. But he had never once been cruel to her or any of his staff. He had never once pressed her about *begging*, though she oftentimes felt his gaze hot and intent, like a brand itself.

It was like discovering a…friend.

"All those books you requested should be here tomorrow," he said over dinner the following night as the week came to a close.

Because he'd encouraged her to order practically a *library* full of books after she'd mentioned the types of fiction her father had never let her read—one of the few things she'd been able to successfully sneak under his nose, but not enough to truly satisfy her.

"Wonderful, but I suppose next week won't be quite as leisurely with lots of reading time."

"No, we must do some travel. Emerge from our love cocoon."

Francesca wrinkled her nose. "What a hideous term."

He chuckled. "And yet, this is what the stories I so very carefully plant will say. Never fear, it will not be all balls and dinners. You will have reading and swimming and baking time and whatever else here and there as time allows. You are not to be treated as a prisoner just yet."

She watched as he ate his dinner. Every move was languid, as if he had no care in the world. But he had plans, and no matter how different they might be, he surely had things he hadn't done because of who he was.

"What about you?"

"What *about* me?"

"Is there anything you've always wanted or wanted to do that you haven't been able to?" She sipped the wine, still even after nearly a week of this amazed that she could have as much or as little as she liked. She wanted to somehow offer Aristide the same.

Perhaps even some of that *same* reaction she felt from him.

Aristide raised those acrobatic eyebrows of his at her across the candlelit table. "What gives you the impression I have ever been under anyone's thumb?"

Francesca rolled her eyes, then took a moment to revel in the freedom of letting her face do whatever she pleased. "Surely there was something you haven't been able to do that appeals to you. Hot-air balloon rides? Climbing Mount Everest? One of those dreadful races where you spend days going from terrible climate to terrible climate on foot? An African safari?"

"I assure you, Francesca, if I have wanted to do it, I have done it."

"Except rebuild your reputation." Which she could definitely do for him. She could be an *expert* at that. Maybe this entire week had been a ruse to gain her loyalty. But that thought did not bother her. It was simply a ruse that worked, if so.

"Precisely. And on that note, the real work must begin. Up first, we will attend Ludovica Gallo's ball in Rome."

She was tempted to make another face, and then, reminded herself she could make whatever faces she liked. She stuck her tongue out at the invitation Aristide slid her way.

He chuckled. "My sentiments exactly. Signora Gallo is a mean old beast, but she wields a lot of power among the gossips of our world. We must go to her ball and convince her we're madly in love."

"She always tells me I am too skinny. I think it is the only flaw she can find with me. It will likely be quite exciting for her to believe I could do something so foolish as to fall madly in love with you."

"Excellent. We want attention. Maybe even speculation to start, but over the course of the next few months we will build the image of the perfect couple. You have reformed me with your love and so on."

Love. He brought that word up a lot for someone who didn't believe in it, but she supposed that was the angle. The fairy tale. The sainted good girl reforming the careless rake.

But *love*, or whatever went on between any man and woman that got the whispers going, would require more than going to balls on each other's arm. It would need more than their ability to have a pleasant conversation with one another. It would require…something more.

She did not think Vale had been gallivanting around with Princess Carliz behind her back, but he didn't *need* to, because people liked to whisper about the way they *looked* at each other, the way they couldn't be in the same room together. A chemistry *everyone* could feel, regardless of whether Vale and Carliz had acted on it at all. People were drawn to the *drama* of it all.

When it came to Aristide and Francesca, well, she supposed he *did* watch her, with intent eyes, any time they were together. And she might not know a *thing* about being kissed, but even knowing next to nothing about the real person inside of Aristide's many masks, she had been affected by their lone kiss at the altar.

Maybe it was foolish to think there was any kind of *attraction* in a kiss, in a look over a bite of cake. Maybe he was acting, and it was all about his plans.

But she didn't think so. Because he kept a very careful distance, even with his ever-present innuendos flung her way. And while she wasn't sure how she felt about closing that distance he kept, they would need to if his plan was going to work.

"You know, to convince other people we're in love, we'll have to exist in the same orbit," she said.

"Are we not doing exactly that right now?"

"Every meal you sit an almost entire length of table away from me. At the ball, we will be on each other's arm. We will have to sit next to one another. Likely we'll have to dance together. I have seen the pictures of many a model, actress, socialite et cetera draped across your arm. There is not an entire expanse of space between you and them when you walk into a ballroom."

"Is this not the respectability we are in search of? I was not under the impression that saints went about groping one another in public."

It was such a ridiculous image, she laughed in spite of herself. "Love and respectability are two different things entirely. We must accomplish the image of both." Deciding to take matters into her own hands now that she had an objective, she stood. She dragged her chair down the length of the table and set it next to his before retaking her seat.

Aristide raised an eyebrow at her. "And what exactly will sitting elbow to elbow this evening for our meal do?"

"It's called practice, Aristide. One must practice to get good at anything. We will need some work at portraying the image of a couple in love. And the lessons must begin now if we are meant to be successful at Signora Gallo's."

"I have never been much of a believer in lessons, practice, or anything else that sounded like *work*."

She made a considering noise, because that could hardly be true when he'd amassed his own fortune independent of his father's, but she was beginning to figure him out. He was more complicated than most—she'd certainly never spent more than a day or two puzzling out a member of the opposite sex—but there were telltale signs anyone gave off. When they were being serious, when they were putting up a mask, pretending to be what everyone else saw.

She would know. And she would maneuver him accordingly until she fully understood who he was underneath all that.

So she did not argue with him, even though she knew he had not spoken a full truth. "Unfortunately, if your plan is to work, you will have to put forth an effort in all those things. You married me for a reason, did you not? Trust that while my father controlled every aspect of my being that he could, *I* quickly learned how to make everyone including him think exactly what I wanted them to think about me. We can do the same for you, but you will have to take instruction. And you will have to practice."

"I do not care for these stories of your father's overbearing control." He said it in the same dark way he often talked about his own father. Something fluttered in her chest, but she ignored it.

It had never mattered what anyone else thought of her father or his behavior. It only mattered that she was free of it now. "Join the club. He will likely be there. A ball in Rome? He won't miss it." She tried not to dwell on that, on seeing him again, on all the pretend that lay in front of her after this week of fantasy life. Just her. Just the ocean. Just her husband she didn't fully know enjoying a cake she'd made.

Instead, she focused on her mission. She was free now, so what did her father matter? He could not take her home after and keep food from her, use his fists on her, rage and throw things at her.

No. That was over. And in order to ensure it, she had to make sure Aristide knew how to pretend they were in love for everyone to see.

"Now, when we are sitting at the grand dinner table, next to each other just like this, how will you sit?"

"Like a man eating his dinner, Francesca," he said, gesturing at himself. Leaned back in his chair, one hand cradling a glass of wine, the other draped leisurely across his leg.

But there was something in his posture, ever so slightly leaning *away* from her. Rather than in. The thing about her station in life, being in her father's iron control, was that she'd spent a lot of time observing people. Deciding whom to mimic, whom not to be like. Watching conversations to suss out what people were really thinking or feeling so she could behave accordingly.

She might not know anyone personally who was desperately in love, but she had watched strangers lean into it and desperately try to lean out of it. And Aristide himself certainly knew how to portray a man in lust if not love. They would have to use that.

"If I was your real date, a sparkling jewel with a generous bosom spilling out of her dress like its own buffet, where would your hands be? Your eyes?"

His mouth curved in the way that had her stomach doing strange little somersaults, a feeling she had been chasing more and more with every passing day.

"Ah, you know my type so well. You must have been paying attention."

She ignored him, and the fact that her bosom certainly wouldn't be classified a *buffet*. "Your gaze would drift over her, and even if you had the control to keep that gaze from taking in the sights, you would look at *her*. You would touch her. Lightly. On the arm, the shoulder. You would lean in to whisper something in her ear. Correct?"

"Yes. That is what I *would* have done, as a single man trying to talk a woman into my bed. Not as a man who already has a bedfellow as we're trying to portray."

She shook her head. "It's the same thought process, you only alter it a little. You would still lean in, but perhaps instead of the neckline of whatever I was wearing, you would gaze into my eyes. You would lean into whisper something funny, and I would laugh, of course, gazing lovingly back. You would—as though you weren't fully thinking the motion through—reach out and touch the ring you gave me as if to reassure yourself our union is real, and not just dreams come true."

"My, you have given this some thought."

"No, I know how to set a scene, through and through. I know how to get people to believe the image. I have spent a *lifetime* learning optics. Now, let us see if you can accomplish this." She settled into her chair in her picture-perfect posture that she hadn't had to trot out in almost a week. She pretended she was wearing a heavy gown and jewels instead of a fresh face and a light sundress.

He studied her, eyes narrowed subtly. "You do that well, *angioletta*."

"What?"

"Put on the mantle of someone else."

"That's how I survived as long as I did. You will need to do the same if you wish to change years of debauchery into a beacon of goodness. Now, go on. Show me what you can do."

It took another few seconds before he lost that studying look. He didn't move, but he gave the impression of a more...*intent* than languid posture. Then he sat up a little, putting down his wineglass, and as his hand returned to his lap it brushed against hers on the way.

Electricity seemed to fission out from the contact—brief, almost nonexistent, and still her skin felt prickled with some kind of...heat. Instead of leaning back in his seat, his whole body angled toward her and he moved elegantly and seamlessly so that his mouth was at her ear.

"If you were not my wife, I think the whispers should be quite scandalous."

That was all he said, and still, her breath caught a little in her throat. Just the touch of his breath against her ear *felt* scandalous. Who needed words? Certainly not Aristide Bonaparte.

"But as you *are* my sainted wife, an angel among mere

mortals, I suppose I will not mention that I would happily partake in any *buffet* you might offer."

Words and thoughts tangled in her mind for a moment. But this was…a party trick. He saw her as that stupid angel moniker. He wanted her reputation, not her. And those little innuendos meant nothing except to…shock her, she supposed. Set her back a little, because he *did* seem to want distance.

No matter what his eyes said.

She turned to meet his gaze, hooded and mysterious. As much as she thought she understood why he did things, said things, behaved a certain way, she knew there was an entire mystery under all of that of who he really was.

And she knew it would never be her purview to know it.

"The goal is not to shock me," she managed to say, sounding prim and disapproving. "The goal is to make me laugh. *Demurely.*"

"Ah. I may need you to furnish some *comedic* talking points that aren't shocking, then."

"I will do just that," she returned. She should leave it at that. Every rational part of her brain told her to leave it at that.

But there was some other part of her that had bloomed here. The one free to dive into the things she was interested in, curious about. There was no one here to tell her to be perfect, above reproach.

"Now you will show me how you can dance."

He leaned back in his chair on a sigh. "*Cara*, please. You must know I can dance."

"But can you dance with me? Can you make it look as

though I am the great love of your life who has changed all your heedless ways?" She raised an eyebrow at him, all challenge. "I will remind you this is *your* plan. I'd be quite happy to never leave this castle and let everyone think you've locked me in a tower for good."

His expression went grim, irritated, but eventually he must have realized she was right, because he carefully stood and held out his hand. She took it and allowed him to help her to her feet, then a few steps away from the table to a corner of the dining room that could act as a makeshift ballroom.

When he stopped, he took her other hand as well, then adopted a position that might start a dance.

If they were brother and sister. He held her—at arm's distance—with enough space between them that an entire other person could fit right there.

"Aristide. You cannot be serious."

"Am I supposed to ravish you in front of an audience?" he demanded, clearly annoyed.

She shook her head. "You would not have your hands anywhere…untoward, but you would hold me close. Not as though there were some holy spirit between us for chastity's sake."

This got a laugh out of him, which made her smile in return.

Until he pulled her close.

It made breathing easily hard. It made everything inside of her seem to tangle into disparate parts and she did not know immediately how to proceed. He still held one hand of hers in his, but his other arm had come around her so she felt it, warm and large, on the small of her back.

He was so much bigger than her—tall and broad—

like a glacier looming over her tiny boat. She thought this should feel oppressive, but it made her want to lean in. To find some shelter.

What a strange thought.

"Is this better?" Aristide asked, his voice so low it seemed to reverberate against every inch of her exposed skin. It shivered through her, and she was glad she'd decided to practice this, because she would learn how to...brace herself for this. This...physical reaction to her handsome husband.

And she would *not* let him see. She would not let her voice be hoarse. She would not let all these strange sensations show on her face. She had a feeling that would be... dangerous. So she met his gaze and spoke very clearly. "Yes. Much."

She tried to step forward, to begin the dance even though they had no music. It was a pantomime, after all. But he did not move with her. When she looked up at him with confusion, his mouth was curved in that ironic smile that made her wonder things about his mouth that she had no business imagining. Married or not.

"You follow *my* lead, *angioletta*."

"In dancing, yes, but in love, you must follow mine."

"All I know of love, so called, is that it blinds a person to everything sensible," he said darkly, moving her in a rhythmic circle. "Every other person, every need of their own. It is a...parasite, really."

"That is quite dire."

"Have you witnessed love?"

"Not intimately, I suppose." She did not allow herself to consider intimacy as her body moved in time with his. "I cannot imagine my mother loved my monster of a father, but she died before I can remember, so I could hardly say for certain. I've never believed it in the cards for me, so I haven't given it much thought, but we must consider it if we are to mimic it."

"Mimic what is essentially a parasite?"

She pulled away enough to look up at him. "I think the first step would be to not call love a parasite."

"Perhaps."

"Why... Why a parasite?"

Aristide shrugged. "All I have ever seen is it eat away at a person. My mother, for instance, loves and had an affair with a married man—who was cruel to all parties, I might add. And yet, she works there still. As his *housekeeper*. I have offered, time and time again, her own house, her own *life*, but she toils after a man who still pays her as the *help*. She calls this love."

"Maybe she is simply wrong?"

"I thought you did not believe in fairy tales, Francesca."

"I don't, but it was always nice to think they might be reachable for other people. Perhaps Vale will get his princess and all will work out well there."

"That would not bother you?" He quirked an eyebrow.

"I'd like to see *someone* in this situation happy."

"You may pursue whatever kind of happy you like, Francesca. Love is certainly not the only happiness out there."

"You are right." And he *was*. And he held her close enough that to all and sundry it would look as though they cared for one another. Just a whisper of a distance that spoke to the idea they'd rather close it, but that was between the two of them—not anyone who watched.

It was perfect, and she had the strangest coiling sensation inside of her. An odd kind of grief. Like they would fake this for years and years to come and it would never be real. Nothing would ever truly be real for her. Because whatever she was deep inside, whatever she felt was wrong and needed twisting into a better version.

She closed her eyes against such old, foolish thoughts she had hoped she'd banished when she'd decided to find a way out. Because other people got to like what they liked, feel what they felt, be who they were. She was not special in any particularly bad or good way. She was only herself, just like everyone else.

But it was strange and alarming to realize her great plans for escape and find that being on her own would still be so *lonely*.

Aristide stopped abruptly. "There. A dinner demonstration. A dance." He released her completely, stepped away. And didn't quite look down at her when he spoke. "People will no doubt be fooled by our performance. Are you happy?"

But she wasn't. She should feel some satisfaction. She'd taught him something, or he'd at least pretended that she had.

But she wanted to lean into him, to cry on his shoulder, and that was clearly *not* okay.

CHAPTER FIVE

RESTRAINT HAD NEVER been a word in Aristide's vocabulary. He liked excess. Going after what he wanted when he wanted. There were lines he didn't cross, of course, but he was almost never in a position to test those lines, because he didn't put himself in those positions.

Francesca was testing *everything*. He'd never once felt twisted up over *pretending* to be anything he pretended to be. He loved a mask, playing a role, but pretending to be her besotted husband twisted something sharp and ugly inside of him.

Especially when she looked as if she might *cry*, and he'd felt her tremble in his arms. Not because she was overcome with lust—he knew what that looked like, felt like. There was something deeper going on inside that woman.

He wanted nothing to do with it.

There were *lines*, and she wasn't meant to be of any interest to him. She was meant to serve a purpose, and he did not mix purpose and pleasure. She would be what he wanted, so he could get what he wanted, and in return he would reward her with all he could. Freedom and all that.

Not *interest*.

So he'd put her neatly aside. Physically, anyway. The

past week seemed to take residence in his mind like some kind of fever. The triumphant smile when she'd revealed the cake she made with no help, that moment when their gazes had met. Held. The strange mix of joy and grief that crossed her face when she threw herself into the surf over and over again most mornings.

It was like watching someone being born. Realizing some great potential. She seemed to be sprouting before him like some sort of beautiful bloom. Like the pretty oleander that dotted the island—picturesque and fragrant.

And poisonous.

Because it felt like there were barbs sticking their sharp and tiny points into his chest. Every interaction with her felt like he was walking a dangerous tightrope. When she was only ever meant to be a means to an end.

And he did not touch his means to an end. He was not his father. Would never be.

So, the following day, he reminded himself of her real place in his life. He made all the arrangements to fly to Rome for a few days, followed by a trip to Milan, then Nice and Paris. He told his assistant to accept any and all invitations that came their way, as once they appeared at one event likely more invitations would follow.

They'd had their honeymoon, and now it was time to work.

He did not know why he expected Francesca to balk at this, to argue with him. But he found himself somewhat… shocked when she agreed easily to everything. Quickly packed her things so they could drive to the mainland before the tide swept in, then got on the airplane that would take them to Rome with nothing but pleasant smiles and a clear attempt to get to know all his staff by name.

She was in as much "business" mode as he, and he did not know why that left him feeling *edgy.*

They flew to Rome, her curled up in a seat reading one of her new novels, enthralled and completely unaware of *him.*

While he brooded. *At* her. He hated brooding. He wanted to act, but he didn't know *how*, because the only action he seemed to *want* at the moment was touching her.

A line he'd promised himself he wouldn't cross. He'd never taken anyone else's promises seriously, but if there was one thing he prided himself on, it was keeping his promises to *himself.* To behave in keeping with the personal tenets he'd developed for himself, *by* himself.

It did not matter if anyone else saw it, believed it, or agreed with it. If he followed his own inner compass, that was all that mattered to him. No matter what rules of respectability, society, man-made laws, et cetera, he bent.

It had always been easy enough.

How dare this woman *test* him.

When they landed, he watched as all that relaxed enjoyment slowly drained off Francesca's face. This was where she'd grown up, and she clearly had no fondness for it.

He understood that all too well. Her expression perfectly mirrored how he felt any time he forced himself to visit with his mother at the estate of his youth on the peninsula of the island.

It made him want to offer Francesca some kind of... comfort. Reassurance. These were impulses he'd long since refused to indulge himself in, as offering solace and reassurance to the people he loved most had only ever exploded in his face. He could not imagine what offering them to someone who was a business partner at *best* would do.

He said nothing the entire trip from airport to hotel. He checked them in and took her up to a beautiful *honeymoon* suite in a beautiful luxury hotel in the middle of Rome.

Where he very carefully made certain their luggage was placed in separate bedrooms. A silent and clear message to her. Of what, he wasn't certain. Even less certain when she said nothing about it, or how it might look to the staff around them. She'd simply walked to her bedroom door and turned a sweet smile at him.

"Good night, Aristide," she had said, pleasantly.

"Good night, *angioletta*," he had replied. Irritably.

And he had spent the evening, once again, not sleeping. Then he'd gotten up early the next day and gone into the city center to do business. He had left word with his staff that he would not return until it was time to pick Francesca up to attend the ball and to let Francesca do as she pleased for the day.

At the ball, he would *lean in* to whisper in her ear at dinner. He would dance with her as if she were the only thing he could ever imagine laying his eyes or hands on. Because she was not *wrong* about any of that.

And maybe once it was all over, and he saw the response from the crowd he was playacting for, whatever frustrating discomfort dogging him would fade.

But when he returned to the hotel, to find her dressed and ready to go, all his plans simply...evaporated.

She wore a deep purple gown, form-fitting and regal, with hints of sparkle about the bust. Her hair was swept up in one of those intricate twists, and her makeup seemed to make her eyes larger, her lips plumper. Diamonds dangled at her ears to match the ludicrous one on her finger that he'd put there. She *sparkled* like a gem, and he suddenly felt like some kind of maniacal wizard who wanted to hoard all that magic to himself.

This was not what he'd expected. *She* had yet to be anything he'd expected. He was not sure he'd *ever* seen a picture of her with her shoulders bared, and maybe he had spent the past week watching her in much less, watching her swim, watching *her*, and he had not expected island Francesca to translate into the Francesca who was meant to give him respectability.

She looked like… Well, not the angel she had been presented as for long. Not some sultry she-devil, either. Just a beautiful, alluring, desirable woman. And still it threw him off his axis. Because he'd expected boring respectability. The elegant angel to save his fall from grace.

And here she was, looking a temptation. One that slid along his body like the whisper of a lie, hardening what it shouldn't, softening what it shouldn't.

He cleared his throat. Travel on the plane must have given him a touch of congestion this evening. "This getup is not quite what I had in mind for a ball to reinvent my reputation, Francesca."

She blinked. Once. Something crossing her expression that he might have called startled, and a little hurt, if he was cataloging her expressions. But the flicker melted away into that cool pragmatism.

"No. But I got to thinking as I shopped. I could wear the overly virginal gowns my father insisted upon, or I could dress to please myself. I thought, given the circumstances, it made more sense to choose a gown that pleased me. That might match *you*."

The words, and callback to her father's control, were a bit of a careful, polite *slap*, and he hated that it landed. Especially when she met him with that demure blankness that had been her go-to in the beginning, and he hadn't seen much of it the past few days. Like she'd begun to trust him.

When he couldn't possibly let her do that, knowing what happened when he allowed himself to think anyone saw any *goodness* in him.

"We do not want to match *me*, I assure you. *Me* is the problem. The point here in public is respectability. Was I not clear?"

She didn't move. He wasn't even sure she breathed. She didn't flinch or slump or look away. There were no flickers of hurt in her eyes. She held his gaze, cool and detached. When she spoke, her voice matched it.

"Is my dress not respectable?"

It was. He tried to be rational enough to accept that it was. It covered more than many he'd seen in glittering ballrooms and galas. But there was something about *her* in it, for all to see, that made it very difficult to hold on to the rational part of his brain.

When he didn't respond, she continued. "Do you wish to pick out a dress for me? Tell me how to wear my hair? What lipstick color is appropriate for a woman of my station. Would you like to ration out my meals?"

"No," he bit out, irritated that she would use her father's controlling behavior against him. Worse, make him *feel* low and slimy when he wouldn't have thought that possible.

Because he didn't mind being low and slimy when it suited, but *she* made it feel *wrong*. "I trust your judgment of course." Which was both an outright lie and said only to placate her so he could get away from this *feeling*.

"The thing is, I gave this considerable thought," she continued, still so damn dull if not for the sparkle of her dress. "No one is going to believe you were immediately turned into a saint by the likes of me. It has to be more… gradual. And I think we'll both have to bend toward the other a little to get our point across."

"They will think I defiled you. *Ruined* you, the sainted angel of Italy. A demon drags down another paragon." Which did not matter to him in the slightest. If he cared at all what people thought of him, he would have lived his life like Valentino. But there was a line he now had to walk. And it wasn't so much *caring* what people thought of him, it was crafting it himself.

And she was… She looked… This wasn't going how he had planned it, and he did not know why she was making things so damn difficult.

She shook her head. "Some may say that at first, you are correct. But dressing as though I am locked into some kind of chastity belt isn't going to change that if you're on my arm. We must make it look as though we've changed each other. For the better. I think that is the kind of story that will carry more weight, that will be more successful for you in the long run. But regardless, one ball will not magically transform your reputation after stealing your brother's bride. The only way to soften that truth is with a story of love. As we had already agreed, if you recall."

He did not know why it infuriated him when she spoke like that. Of stories and optics and what other people needed to believe. Like she had chosen *him*. Like she was in charge of helping *him*. Like this was all *her* doing.

When he had stolen her. Simple as that. She was supposed to be doing what *he* wanted, following his plans. Not making *better* ones that made too much sense. Not making this feel like a partnership when he never allowed those to take root.

"Shall we go?" she asked, all feigned brightness. "Or did you want to make a fashionably late entrance slightly...mussed."

Mussed. Such a prissy word. And he had to remind himself, no matter how she behaved, how she tempted, she *was* sheltered. Perhaps her father had been a controlling bastard, but that only proved Aristide's point.

She was out of her depth, and she was making him feel like *he* was. So he decided to return the favor. He leaned close, until her eyelids fluttered and her inhale was sharp. He waited for her to back away, but she didn't.

Which shouldn't be arousing. Shouldn't make him momentarily forget his purpose. He shook it away, that iron backbone of hers. The flush that spread over her cheeks even as she met his gaze with cool, dark eyes.

He leaned in close, so his lips were *almost* on hers. "Would you *like* me to muss you, Francesca?"

She met his gaze, steady and searching, and he realized he'd miscalculated when she didn't blush, didn't look away. Simply angled her chin, almost closer to this near-kiss, then dropped her gaze to his mouth.

"I think I would not mind finding out what that would be like, actually." Then she brought her eyes back up at him. And *smiled*.

For a moment, his brain was utterly blank. Nothing but

the rush of blood, the tightening of his body, an alarming, deep-seated need that threatened to drown him where he stood.

So he said nothing, and she said nothing. They simply stood, too close, their breath mingling in the small space between them. The feeling of it slithered through him. That poison again. Weakening what he'd decided on, weakening what he knew he must do.

Keep her in the neat little box of *business* partner. Sex could be stringless fun with the right party, but this was not the situation to introduce nakedness, body to body. Not when everything he planned rested on her ability to pretend to be his perfect bride and lend him the respectability he *would* prove to the world he had.

Whether he did or not.

They would help each other, but they would *not* blur lines. This was the only right thing he knew.

So he drew his best weapon—cruel words and disdain—and used it. "I do not waste my time with senseless virgins who will likely get far too attached and have to be explained to how things between a man and woman work."

She blinked again, that one *harmed* blink, as if by simply closing her eyes for a second she could make anything that hit a sore spot disappear by the force of her eyelashes.

"Perhaps *I* do not waste my time with playboys who think they're invincible and throw little tantrums when they feel as if their power or control has been tested," she said in an even voice, mimicking his disdainful tone far too easily it seemed.

"Tantrums?" He laughed, low and bitter, shocked clean

through that she would turn his barb around on him. That it would *land*.

Perhaps he should have been better prepared. In *all* of this.

"Tantrums don't have to be loud, Aristide," she said, like a scolding nanny. "Sometimes withdrawing is a tantrum all its own." She ducked out from where he'd all but caged her at the wall. "I think it's best if we're on time. One of those ways that I have oh-so-helpfully worn off on you that people might notice and comment upon." She grabbed a little bag that matched her dress but sparkled more.

She straightened her shoulders, met his gaze. All business. All certainty.

All *mask*.

He wanted to peel it away from her. Here and now. Layer by layer. Until she looked like she had after he'd kissed her at their wedding. Shaken and confused and out of her depth.

Exactly like he felt.

But as much as he'd built a reputation for himself as carefree and wild, he was not careless when it came to people. It was why he continued to get invitations, why he succeeded in business. Why people *liked* him, in *spite* of his reputation. In *spite* of his wildness.

Perhaps his mother claimed it was some kind of coping mechanism—coping with what, he didn't have a clue. Perhaps Valentino had—during one of their rare in-person arguments—accused him of keeping everyone at a distance with his vapid personality, as if Vale had any room to talk.

But Aristide understood himself and the world and

people around him, because how could he not? He had built himself into all this, and you didn't succeed while drowning in denial. He understood himself quite well.

He could be the laconic playboy all he wanted, but he did not *harm* anyone who was perceived to be "below" him because he would never allow himself to be the kind of monster his father was.

Francesca *was* beneath him—in experience, in understanding—so he would keep his hands to himself and pretend the night away as her besotted *fake* husband.

Temptation be damned.

CHAPTER SIX

THEY DID NOT speak on the way to the ball. Francesca thought it was best for a wide variety of reasons.

She felt too close to tears. Not because of what he'd said. She didn't mind a few mean comments said in the heat of the moment, especially if she could return the favor without a backhand to the face.

Strange how even an argument felt like freedom when there was no threat of physical violence tied to it.

What bothered her was not the argument, though. It was that she'd let her guard down. She'd been so thrilled to pick out her own dress, to look the way she wanted to look and *like* the outcome. She'd been excited enough, lulled by the past week enough to believe Aristide *easy*. That he would go along with her at all turns. That he would give her that indulgent smile and compliment her on her choices.

But he was a man, and she should have known better. Moods were perilous things and his had changed last night. She should have known it would continue to threaten like a storm until it broke.

She would just have to get to know him better. Then she would predict his moods better. Then she would say the right thing to ensure they didn't have any more little blowups.

And you'll be right back where you started.

Except Aristide had gotten angry—though she still didn't understand why—and he'd yet to so much as grab her. She was not in physical danger here. He had given her that much. So she could learn how to…sail his tricky waters without feeling like she used to.

That was how she'd gotten this far in life with *everything*. It wouldn't stop now. She didn't have to forget herself, hide herself, be someone else to figure out how to deal with him. She could find *balance*.

That was the promise of a life without violence.

What was clear from his little outburst was that there was something that held him back from acting on any of his little innuendos, even when she offered. She did not know what it would be, but she would seek to get around it.

Because even angry at him, even hurt by his precarious mood, she wanted to know what it would be like to be swept away in the heat that swamped her any time Aristide was close. She wanted *all* the freedoms she could get.

Once she understood him better, she would.

The car came to a stop and she waited until Aristide came to her side and offered a hand to help her out of the car. She could already hear the low murmur of voices of people who were clearly recognizing him and anticipating the fact he'd brought his stolen bride.

He smiled down at her and camera flashes went off from outside the car. But she did know enough about him now to recognize *some* of the looks in his eyes. This one was blank, with absolutely no warmth behind it.

She slid her hand into his, warm to her chilled, and allowed him to pull her out into the evening. His smile dimmed a little at her hand, and he wrapped his hand fully around hers as if to warm it.

She tried to think of a time that anyone had ever tried to warm any part of her, particularly if they were irritated with her. And she was quite certain it had never once happened.

She blew out a breath as he drew her into the fray. She had to focus not on him right now, but on the situation. She was an old pro at acting and presenting exactly what she wanted to project.

But no one had ever been holding her hand while she had to project anything. Even the events she'd attended with Vale hadn't included hand-holding. But she liked to think she'd learned something from being his fiancée while the press kept beating the Princess Carliz drum.

It didn't matter what the reality was. It mattered what the *story* was.

She and Aristide were a story.

She just wished she felt the same sort of distance from Aristide that she had felt with Vale. They were both handsome, powerful men. Who looked quite a lot alike, in fact, so Francesca didn't quite understand why it *felt* different. Only that it did. For her, anyway. She wasn't sure what Aristide felt. Some attraction...maybe. But there was a simmering anger or frustration that went along with it that she did not understand.

"Perhaps, like usual, you are simply not good enough."

She rolled her shoulders, willing her father's voice away. She would damn well be good enough. She would turn around Aristide's reputation quickly and easily. And he would *have* to be impressed by it. And her. Maybe then... He would act on what arced between them.

Aristide led her straight to Signora Gallo and greeted her with an enthusiasm she knew was forced, and the skeptical look on Signora Gallo's face told Francesca the older woman knew it too.

The signora looked over at her, gave her an up-and-down perusal. Then sniffed. "Well, marriage agrees with you, I suppose."

Which was a far cry from her usual greeting of feigned politeness: *Do you even eat, dear?*

The signora's gaze turned to Aristide. "Not quite sure how you pulled off such a thing, or why, when everyone knows you've never kept an eye from wandering."

Aristide kept that smile on his face. All charm and ease. *A lie*, she wanted to hiss at him just to see how he might react.

"That was all before I met *mio angioletta*. Why would my eye wander from a prize such as this?" He looked over at her, and Francesca wondered if anyone else noted that wry twist to his smile. "Who puts up with my wicked ways and encourages me to be better."

"And I assume you encourage her to be worse."

"Not worse," Francesca corrected gently. "Aristide allows me to be myself. It's…irresistible."

The older woman studied Francesca for a long-drawn-out moment. "That is a gift," she said carefully, almost reverently. But then her smile sharpened. "If it's true."

"That was the difference between my brother and me, naturally," Aristide's said, and Francesca wanted to groan. Because he should *not* bring up Vale if they wanted the stories to rehabilitate him. "*I* could see Francesca for who she truly is."

The signora made a *hmphing* sort of noise. "And I suppose you are why your brother refused my invitation tonight?"

Aristide laughed, and it was only a *tinge* bitter. "Signora, were you trying to cause trouble with your invitations? For shame."

She looked almost amused, but then she waved them away in her usual way of dismissal. Another group of people arriving for her to poke at.

"Did you really need to mention Vale?" Francesca whispered at him as they walked toward their table. "That little story will end up in print somewhere before the night is even through. We don't have to make *him* look bad to make us look good."

"Let him twist in the wind for once. He's done it plenty to me." Aristide plucked two flutes of champagne from a passing tray, handed her one.

"It seems to me you've done plenty to each other. Without ever once *talking* it through," Francesca added, lifting the glass to her mouth and taking a sip.

He gave her a sharp look. "You do not know anything about my brother and me."

A touchy subject. Her entire life she'd spent tiptoeing around touchy subjects, but something about Aristide made her want to *touch* everything. It didn't matter she knew she shouldn't put a fork in an electrical outlet—there was a desire to do so that was impossible to ignore.

"You'd be surprised what I know, having spent some time with both of you and watching how the two of you react to one another while your detestable father plucks the puppet strings."

"You are *my* wife, Francesca. I believe that means you no longer get to take Vale's side on anything."

"It does not mean that, but even if it did, I'm not taking his side. Or yours." She reached out and put her hand on his shoulder, wanting to comfort even as she wanted to poke. "I'm saying I think it'd behoove you both to talk. I know if I had a sibling to discuss my terrible—"

It was as if even *thinking* about mentioning her terrible childhood, the perpetrator of it appeared.

"Francesca," her father greeted, his dark, hard gaze landing on the drink in her hand disapprovingly. "It seems you have weathered the events of the week quite well." He did not say this kindly, even though he'd turned his gaze to Aristide and plastered that smile that fooled everyone on his face.

Francesca swallowed, her arm falling off Aristide's shoulder. She had to fight the slight tremor that went through her. The abject *fear*, even knowing she was safe here in a crowd of people.

But not just *here*. She was free now, all the time, and still she felt pinned to the spot. Like one wrong move would be a disaster. Her throat clogged and her entire being iced straight through.

She had thought once she was free of her father, dealing with him would not feel this way. So much *fear* still pounding through her, even though she *was* free.

But Aristide's hand over hers was one point of warmth in all this cold and she focused on that so she could find her voice.

"Allow me to introduce my husband, Aristide Bonaparte." She knew her smile wasn't right. It was too tight, too brittle. But she managed to curve her mouth as she gestured to Aristide next to her.

Bertini held out his hand for Aristide to shake. "I think we have quite a lot to talk about, young man."

"Do we?" Aristide countered. He looked at the outstretched hand and very clearly and purposefully did not shake it. "I don't think we have anything to discuss at all, Signor Campo. In fact, I think it best for all involved if I never see you again." Aristide said this all with an easy smile, so easy and friendly it took Francesca a good beat or two to realize what he'd just said.

She should say something. Admonish him. They were in public. They should all pretend. But she could only stare up at him in wonder.

"I beg your pardon," Bertini replied, clearly needing the same time Francesca had to understand what was happening.

Aristide leaned down, close to her father, but still with that pleasant smile on his face. "If I ever see you within eyeshot of my wife, you will regret it. If you need the threat specified and in writing, I'll be sure to deliver it first thing in the morning."

Bertini's eyes narrowed. "You signed the marriage contract. You have paid me my fee. You do not get to—"

"I think you'll find I *get to* do whatever I want, seeing as I paid your fee. And I won't feel the need to destroy you, as long as I never see you in her orbit or mine again. Understood?"

Francesca watched as her father's face mottled red. She felt the familiar ice of terror, and even Aristide's hand in hers could not feel like a warm spot. The only thing keeping her upright and from scrambling away was knowing she was not going home with her father tonight. He could not hurt her.

Because she suddenly had this…protector. She did not understand where it came from. Surely Aristide didn't know the full…extent of her father's control from the few things she'd said. She had always been careful to keep it from everyone.

She'd let Aristide in on how controlling he could be, but surely he didn't understand…

Aristide pulled her away from her father. If anyone had been paying attention—and no doubt, some had—there was no missing the fact that *something* had occurred. Though Aristide had kept that pleasant smile on his face for the whole strange interaction, so many of the gossips would have a difficulty deciding what the issue was.

Francesca realized her teeth were chattering. What a silly reaction to *nothing*. Aristide led her to a little corner, somewhat hidden and shaded by some ridiculously overlarge plant. She leaned against the wall, trying to get a hold of herself.

Aristide took the champagne flute away from her, then took both her hands in between his. He rubbed warmth into them. This same man who'd been angry with her not an hour ago.

It was all just *too* much. So she focused on the current issue.

"You probably shouldn't have refused to shake his hand," she managed weakly. Even though she was glad of it.

"I will not abide bullies, Francesca." He rubbed her hands between his, somewhat absently as he tracked Bertini's movements throughout the large ballroom from their little corner. All the way to the exit. Like her father was leaving.

Because of what Aristide had said. Done. She found herself managing easier breaths, but she couldn't stop staring at the man who'd just…stepped in and *done* something.

After a while, Aristide's gaze came to land on her. She

wasn't sure what she'd expected—frustration, confusion, maybe even pity. But all she saw was a considering kind of searching in his gaze.

At first, she thought he'd say nothing and they could move on from this as though it had never happened. But after a few ticking minutes, as though he were waiting for her to get ahold of herself again, he spoke.

"My father could not care about anyone beyond himself enough to lift an actual physical finger to them. He much prefers mind games for his brand of cruelty, and that can cause fear, I suppose. But I have never felt the kind of fear I saw in your eyes when your father said your name."

She wanted to *cry*. Had anyone been even the slightest bit concerned that she was afraid of her own father in her entire life? She didn't think so. Granted, she'd learned early on to hide it lest the punishment be worse, but still. This was…too overwhelming.

"I will not abide it." He said this softly, but like a vow. More serious than even the ones they had given each other on their wedding night.

She managed to blink back the moisture in her eyes. "Thank you," she said thickly, but with feeling because… Never. Never had someone said anything like that to her. And this man might be her husband whom she was still trying to get to know. They might be friendly and have chemistry, but he was essentially…a stranger. Who wanted to keep her at arm's length. He certainly didn't owe her much.

He grunted, clearly uncomfortable with her raw gratitude. She wasn't exactly comfortable with it either, but she was still shaky enough she couldn't build back her defenses.

She really thought she would have been cured by freedom. It was lowering and frustrating to realize she wasn't. And something akin to joy to know someone would step in anyway.

"Would you like to leave?" he asked her gently. This man who said no one had ever called him *kind*. Who had been so irritated with her choice of dress, and the fact she'd had the gall to say she wouldn't mind being mussed by *him* that he'd called her a senseless virgin. Who was now…standing guard of her like some sort of shining knight.

He made no sense, but she wasn't sure she made any sense either. She sucked in a deep breath and tried to settle all the things shifting around inside of her.

She managed to shake her head. "No, it's better to stay until we can make an early exit look less about my father and more about…"

"Not being able to keep our hands off each other?"

"Yes. Precisely." She gave a sharp nod and pushed herself off the wall. "We will dance and convince everyone we're madly in love."

Even if the word *love* tasted like ash in her mouth.

Aristide held Francesca gently in his arms as they moved to a slow, classical waltz. In direct contrast to last night, when she had felt like a strong, dangerous threat, tonight she felt…fragile.

He did not *do* fragile, because it made him feel like this. Unwieldy and wrong. *Not* in charge of his own fate, because the fate of the victim was more important.

And this all took him by such surprise, even knowing he hadn't liked her tales of her controlling father. He'd known he wouldn't *like* Bertini Campo, but then he'd seen her reaction to her father.

All her commentary, her even looks, all her *strength*, it had crumbled under the gaze of *one* man. Her own father. And he had seen *true* fear there in her eyes.

And for a second, he'd seen himself as a boy. Not with his father, because Milo Bonaparte had been a strange figure in his life. A complete nonentity for twelve years, and then a sudden target, but even as a young man reeling from his new place in the world, he had always known Milo's barbs—even the ones aimed at Aristide—were meant for Valentino.

And so his *crumble* had come at the hands of his own brother, his best friend, who'd called him a liar at the lowest point he could remember. Who had promised they would *never* really be brothers. All because it didn't fit in with his neat version of what the world was.

That moment might have changed his life, but there'd been an honesty in it. *Finally.* Valentino had chosen who he really wanted to be, and so Aristide had chosen the same. And maybe, *maybe*, Francesca wasn't far off. They hadn't talked since that moment. Not really. Perhaps there was more to it all, what with the fact they'd been *boys*, not men.

But Aristide was hardly going to throw himself at the brick wall of Valentino. He'd already spent too much time throwing himself at the brick wall of his mother.

Brick walls were hard and painful, and he saw no reason to indulge. He was not after his own destruction, or the destruction of anything else.

Still, he did *not* abide bullies, not because of his brother, of that moment Valentino had turned on him. It was the way his father used that moment of contention between brothers from then on out. Like a weapon against both of them. No, Aristide could not stomach those who wielded their power like a weapon—be it physically or with schemes—because that was the purview of his father. And he'd always counted his father one of the worst monsters he could imagine.

But a man who would inspire that kind of fear in his own daughter was far worse than cruel, distant fathers and soul friends turned blood enemies.

All of Francesca's talk about being free now seemed… serious. Not the frivolous talk of a girl who'd had a slightly overbearing upbringing. But a woman who had escaped *abuse*. On her own terms, even if he'd stepped in and altered them a little.

She was *changed* to him now, and he did not know how to move forward. It was unfair, like being thrust back in time, to thirteen and lost and everyone he'd thought he could lean on crumbling under the weight of secrets come to light.

"You should probably not look as though you want to burn the place down while we dance," Francesca murmured in his ear.

She was back to herself. Stiff-spined and determined. It rearranged everything inside of him, in new, uncomfortable ways he didn't want. He felt *clumsy*, when he had known how to turn a woman about a ballroom almost as if he'd been born with the inherent talent.

He looked down at her and had to wonder if that crumbling he'd seen in her had simply been a mirage. Maybe he'd overreacted. "Did he lay a hand on you, Francesca?"

She inhaled sharply. "I'd rather not discuss him at the moment."

"I know nothing of what a good father should be, but I certainly know one shouldn't lay a hand to his daughter."

She was stiff in his arms now, and he thought back to all her discussions of the kind of *image* they should portray. So he drew her closer, to hide that stiffness. Certainly not to comfort her.

"Your father *never* laid a hand on you?" she returned, looking up at him with challenge and irritation in her eyes. She had not wanted him to press the issue, but he found he could not drop it. Not for a better time.

He held her gaze. Maybe someone would see it as *loving*. He was only going for the truth. "No. He had his own weapons, but his hands were not one of them."

She let out a shaky exhale, even as she kept that stubborn chin lifted. "I did not think seeing him would affect me, as I am no longer under his control. Unfortunately, that was not the case." She straightened those shoulders, gave him that boardroom-businesswoman look that had no bearing when discussing *abuse*. "But I will get better at it."

The fact she thought *she* should be better at it, when her father was the monster, twisted through him. He had seen the abuses of power and words and threats and control, not physical ones, and yet it all felt the same in the moment.

He had never once been able to convince his mother she was a victim, that she needed to escape. The fact Francesca had designed her own escape, even if he'd upended her plans a bit, awed him.

"We will not be anywhere he is, ever again. I will ensure it." Perhaps he said it more forcefully than necessary. Perhaps his grip on her was tighter than it needed to be as they swayed in time with the other dancers.

But this was one thing he would ensure, no matter what. As a matter of...well, those lines he drew for himself. He was not *virtuous*, but he would not let people suffer at the hands of those more powerful.

She studied him then, a hint of vulnerability in the cast of her mouth. "I am not weak," she said softly but with a resolute determination that twisted painfully inside of him.

Painfully enough, he was surprised to hear his own words emerge as gently as they did. "No, *angioletta*, that is never the word I would use to describe you."

She was still studying him, brows drawn together. "I do not understand you, Aristide," she said, almost on a whisper. And no doubt the lookers on would see a woman whispering sweet nothings to her husband.

So he lowered his mouth to her ear, being careful not to inhale the scent of her too deeply. "Let us not concern ourselves with *understanding* one another. Instead, we shall offer each other that which we need. A new reputation for me. Freedom for you."

When he straightened, her gaze was steady. There was no more hint of vulnerability. There was that same look in her eye she'd had last night.

"I think you should kiss me," she said, pressing closer to him. Sending twin reactions through him. The need to hold her tighter, press her closer. The need to stiffen and set her aside.

But she kept talking as she rested her forehead against his cheek while they swayed their way into another song. "There is a camera right there. It's the perfect photo op."

CHAPTER SEVEN

FRANCESCA'S HEART BEAT loudly in her ears. She was on shaky ground. Touched at the way he'd handled her father, confused by the seemingly disparate reactions he had to her. No one ever in her life had acted the role of protector. She'd never asked anyone to.

Yet he'd stepped in like it was his sworn duty—when she would have...crumbled. Not forever, but briefly. Apparently, freedom didn't *cure* the scars left behind.

And that was part of the shaky ground—that she wasn't as *cured* as she might have liked to be. That someone had seen that in her. But then that someone had stepped in to...help.

As she had told Aristide, she was not weak. She hadn't allowed herself to be for some time. She had come to a determined conclusion as a teenager, sporting a painful bruise that had swollen her eye so badly she hadn't even been able to hide it with makeup, that the only way she escaped abuse altogether was to make that escape happen *herself*. No one was coming to save her.

And so she had saved herself. Carefully and methodically over *years*.

She figured this was the key to success in all things.

But Aristide seemed to want to...protect her in some

way, and it felt like perhaps in this phase of her life weakness wasn't so bad. Because in her moment of weakness, there could be someone who stepped in and took care of it.

Just as she would take care of his. His reputation.

She *did* suggest the kiss because she'd seen the photographer, because she was determined to succeed *for* him, even more so after this evening, but even in this moment she knew she'd also suggested it because she wanted to feel his mouth on hers.

She did not understand him or her reaction to him, but she wanted to.

In a world of things beyond her control, figuring people out was the one thing she'd learned how to hone. How to use. She would figure out a way to use it on him, so everything worked out.

Everything.

He inclined his head down toward her. His dark eyes were inscrutable. Something...*something* glittered behind that careful mask, but she could not read it or reach it, even as he brought his mouth to hers.

She held his gaze, though her eyes wanted to flutter closed. Because watching him as he kissed her was a revelation. When she'd closed her eyes in the chapel, she'd gotten lost in the sensation, let it overtake her. There had been a humming wonder in that, but it had also sort of... happened *to* her.

Now she wasn't just aware of his mouth on hers, but of where they were. That there were eyes on them, that a camera was likely taking their picture. She could feel the points of heat that were his palms on her lower back, the soft swipe of his lip against hers—a friction that frazzled through her even as his dark, dark gaze kept her pinned to the spot. She could feel the strength of his muscles under her own palm, watch his eyes darken there before her, feel his heart beat against hers.

It lasted no more than a few moments. Brief and full of yearning—at least from her. When he pulled back—not just his mouth, but his entire body—she could not call what she'd felt in him a *tremor* exactly, but it had been some sort of reaction. Elemental, maybe.

They affected each other, and *this* was like a hit of some kind of drug. She wanted to keep finding the more expansive high.

He did not release her, but the remainder of the dance was kept at enough distance their bodies barely brushed. The entire time, she studied him, trying to understand how her body could simply…alight, when that kiss had been nothing special, and for a photo op only.

She did not believe in love, at least not for someone like her. But she knew passion existed. She'd seen it starkly in the difference between the way Vale had looked at her and at the Princess everyone was so sure he really loved.

Maybe he'd never acted on that passion in his gaze, maybe he had. She'd never considered it much of her business. But she knew it was *there*. And as she hadn't felt it for him, she'd never been particularly jealous of it. It was more an obstacle to overcome so their union worked in her favor.

Now it was somehow the swirling center of her and Aristide—the man who was supposed to give in to any passion that came his way. But he kept her at this strange, irritable distance any time that passion seemed possible.

Once the song ended, he ushered her off the dance

floor and spent the rest of the night whisking them from one conversation to the other. He laughed, he chatted. He introduced her to people, and she introduced him to some. On the outside, they appeared a perfectly happy newlywed couple, she knew.

But she also sensed something simmering beneath the surface. One of those *moods* she was going to have to get to the bottom of so she could navigate. So she could work things out.

The moment they were alone in the back of his car together, his mask fell. That lazy smile, that sparkle in his eyes, all gone. He made sure there was a distance between them in the car—not just physical, but as though his internal life was as far away from her as possible.

Francesca knew how to read a Do Not Disturb sign someone put out. She had always heeded those. Poking into people's dark spaces was risky. Francesca was not one to take a risk, because you needed a bedrock of safety from which to take risks from, and she'd never had that.

After tonight, Aristide felt like that safety. Because she'd seen him angry, and he hadn't hurt anyone. Because he seemed so viciously and vehemently against the idea of a father raising a hand to his daughter.

He could scoff at the idea of kindness, but he'd shown her his ability for it, over and over again. So, she risked. She scooted closer to him. "Is something amiss?"

He looked over at her, not outright scowling but with something *accusatory* in that expression of his. "What would be amiss?"

"I don't know. That's why I'm asking."

"All in all, I think tonight was a grand success. A good

kicking-off point." He smiled. Thinly. "And many more events to go yet to reach that end goal."

She supposed if he wanted to talk business, she could oblige. She had some thoughts on the events he'd planned thus far. "We will need to add some charitable outings, I think. To lend credence to your change. It should be something personal to you. So when people see the photo op, it feels *personal* and not like an image cleansing."

"I don't particularly like using charity to help my personal gain."

"Don't be ridiculous." She waved this strange bit of morality away. "Everyone does it, and it's not just personal gain. Whatever face time you give a charity helps that charity with publicity, which often translates into more donations. It's only…slimy if you treat money like a cure, I think."

"I have *been* the charity, Francesca. No recipient of it wants the spotlight on them. I will not be party to it."

He said that the same way he'd said he would not abide bullies. All cold, determined certainty.

She studied him. This was *not* the image he'd presented everyone for *years*. These strange pillars of *nobility* that had suddenly come out tonight. "It amazes me that someone who has clearly spent *years* crafting an image pretends he doesn't know how to do it. You are *nothing* like the reputation you've made for yourself."

"Ah, that is where you're wrong." He flashed that playboy's grin that was meant to make any woman blush. She was not *any* woman, but she certainly felt a heat creep up her cheeks, a warmth spiral out from deep inside of her.

She thought of the way his hands had felt on her when they'd danced, their bodies brushing, his mouth barely touching hers for the cameras. If all that felt as good as it did, what might *more* feel like?

She scooted closer once more and that grin of his fell. His expression clearly read *stay back*. She frowned herself, because…he made *no* sense.

But the car stopped before she could try to puzzle it out, the door opened and Aristide slid out of the car like it was an *escape*. Francesca had never thought she might *throw* herself at someone quite so unmistakably and be rejected—obviously she'd never do it if all the signs weren't there.

But Aristide continued to be some strange mixed signal she couldn't sort through. It was frustrating. She *always* figured people out. She always got to the bottom of them and dealt accordingly.

She hurried after him. "Aristide," she said. She didn't have to tell him why her voice was all admonishment. He straightened, turned, offered his arm.

Because they were still in public, naturally. She took it and smiled up at him in the warm but dim light of the hotel's courtyard. He did *not* smile back. He walked with her though, if stiffly, her arm tucked into his.

In the lobby she leaned against him a little, enjoying leaning on someone bigger and stronger than she was. Besides, people were watching. She *felt* their eyes, saw the way they huddled with each other and *whispered*.

Once they got to their rooms, the door closed behind them, Aristide extricated himself from her grip. "Good night, Francesca."

"Let's have a nightcap."

"No, thank you."

She wanted to stomp her foot in frustration, but she

kept her voice mild and her smile in place. "While to-night was mostly a success, I do think we need to work a little on our body language when we're mingling. You seemed to always keep me at arm's length when we were talking to people after we danced."

She moved over to him, took his arm and looped it around her shoulders. She looked up at him with a smile, angled her body so it brushed his as provocatively as she knew how. "We should stand more like this, I should think. Though not quite so...*buddy*. Perhaps you should put your hand—"

He abruptly removed his arm from her shoulders before she could guide his hand *exactly* where she wanted it. "I do not think I need instruction on where to put my hands."

She looked up at him, studying that angry look in his face that made no sense. Then she shrugged as if it mattered not at all to her. "It's only practice."

"I think we've had enough practice," he said gruffly. But she saw the way his eyes tracked over her. Anger and frustration, sure, but he wasn't unaffected by her. He wasn't *uninterested* in her. He was just holding himself back.

The only reason that made sense to her was if the fact she was inexperienced made him uncomfortable for some reason, but that was foolish. So she did not back off. "Then let us do more than *practice*."

He stepped away from her completely, scowling. "That's enough, Francesca." The kind of fatherly scold she'd usually expect to be paired with a slap.

But Aristide was not her father, so there was that. But the fact he could remind her of those nights made her angry enough to forget her usual carefulness. She never came out and said anything that might offend, never asked anything of people that she didn't think they'd go along with. She figured it out herself. *Always*.

But he was making that incredibly difficult, so she wanted to yell at him, and her only defense against that feeling was to demand the truth.

"I do not understand this. You act as though you're attracted to me, but you seem to be…angry about it. Everything I know about you tells me you're not someone who gets *angry* about partaking in some chemistry. So explain to me why… Why I am *so*…repugnant?" She never would have imagined demanding an answer to such a ridiculous question. She didn't know why Aristide brought it out in her, but she could hardly take it back now.

Especially when he just *stood* there, so still and detached she couldn't help but think of his brother. They presented themselves as opposites, but she saw threads of men who were the same, even if she didn't understand how or why. Probably that father of theirs. If Milo poked at Aristide the same way she'd watched him poke at Vale, then no doubt they'd both built *some* of the same defenses.

"I apologize if you were somehow misguided about what this was, Francesca," he said firmly. Stiffly. "I will not, under any circumstances, mix business with pleasure."

And she understood it then. The line he had to draw. Not about *her*.

A line between himself and his father. Her heart ached for what he must have seen, knowing his mother worked for a man like that. Loved a man like that. Who would treat them both so poorly.

Maybe not with his fists, but Francesca knew full well that abuse took many shapes and sizes. She crossed to Aristide, even as he stared at her approach icily. Because she could understand this new strange pillar of nobility inside of him, but it was out of place here.

"I don't see this as business, Aristide. No money is being exchanged between us. You have no more power over me than I have over you." She held out her hands as if to demonstrate a balanced scale. "We are simply two people helping each other out. I do not know why it would be a *mix* of anything." She moved her hands to press against his chest, because surely he would have to see this line he drew just wasn't necessary.

She wondered how a man could look that cold and feel that warm. Carefully, he put his hands over hers— but pulled them off him and released them so they fell at her sides.

"That is because you do not *know*. Playing the virginal temptress doesn't suit you, Francesca."

The barb landed as he'd meant, and maybe she should have left it at that. She would have, not all that long ago, but freedom had changed her. His protection had changed her perception of *safety*.

"You can throw my innocence in my face all you like, but it is only there because I have not had the opportunity to shed myself of it. I would *think* marriage would be the place one could do so, regardless of the feelings, or lack thereof, involved in the marriage."

His expression was cool, but his eyes were not. "Were you planning on *shedding* yourself for my brother when you were going to marry him?"

She supposed it was a fair enough question, though

it really had nothing to do with anything at all. Because her marriage—to whomever the groom ended up being— was only about securing her freedom. Not about love or chemistry or futures.

But she had always assumed at some point she would share a bed with her husband—passion or not. She wanted children, and that was how they were made. So, yes, she supposed in some distant future she'd had the vague idea she might have to share a bed with Vale.

She had never spent any time fantasizing about it. It had been a to-do item on the checklist of her life, at most. Shoved to the bottom so she did not have to really think about it.

With Aristide, it all felt different, but she supposed *feelings* didn't matter. The truth was simple enough. "Do you want an honest answer to that question, Aristide?"

"I think you should examine why you would be willing to fling yourself at either brother as though we're interchangeable parts and what right you have to be miffed you might not get your way in the matter."

"You act as if intimating that I'm mercenary is an insult. I was not marrying your brother for *love*, any more than I married you for *chemistry*. We know what we are, Aristide. And I don't think I should have to say it, have to explain myself, but if you need to hear it, so be it. I did not feel attraction like this for your brother. I did not get lost in his mouth on mine, or dream about what it might be like to feel his hands on me. *That* is all you. All *us*."

His eyes had flared, and his breath seemed to be just a *tad* more labored. His gaze was hot, and for a moment she thought he might relent. Might step for her, put that angry mouth on hers. There was the faintest movement, like he was going to step toward her.

Then he gave his head a shake and turned on a heel. "Go to bed, Francesca," he said, low and serious. "There will be another party tomorrow."

And left her there, throbbing and frustrated, and more sad than she wanted to be.

But this was not something to be…sad over. He was wrong. She would simply have to prove to him that he was wrong, and then… Then they could figure out the rest.

Aristide's body throbbed. It was *painful*, this want she stirred up inside of him.

He had never had cause to refuse an advance before, and the strangest part was he could not recall ever wanting so badly to take a woman up on one. He tended to prefer to do the advancing because he didn't like games. He liked to be forthright. He liked everything to be clear, so there was no confusion, no hurt.

Francesca was no *angel*, because she did not seem to understand subtle for the life of her, and it burned through him like some brand-new desire he'd never tasted.

That and the fact she had clearly stated something he shouldn't care about, but did nonetheless. That she did not feel the same desire for his brother that she did for him. When it didn't matter in the least what she felt for Vale one way or another. Because he wouldn't be acting on it.

But he liked what she said about wanting *his* hands on her all the same.

Still, this arrangement between them was too…complicated and confusing. And he knew that was the start of all hurt, all manipulation, all betrayal. The mixing of external goals and internal wants.

People thought him a libertine, but he had rules for *everything*. They just weren't rules like Valentino had for himself. They weren't about being *perfect*, about controlling everything within an inch of its life, or about how others saw him. Aristide knew how to bend. You did not have your entire life upended at thirteen and not know.

But there were lines he didn't cross so there were no victims left in his wake. There were chances he didn't take, knowing where anything with his heart, his expectations, his *hopes* led. This he took more seriously than *anything*.

He would protect Francesca. Give her whatever freedoms she wanted. He would even let her take charge of rehabilitating his image—because she seemed to enjoy the planning of it, and because she was good at it.

But he would not cross the line that would ever make her his victim. Or him the victim of what he felt for her.

No matter how much he wanted her.

CHAPTER EIGHT

FRANCESCA WOKE UP the next morning with plans upon plans. Some of them were very honorable. Arrange a few charitable excursions for her and Aristide in between the events he had planned throughout the glittering cities of Europe.

They could forgo the photo op since he was so against it, but they still needed to do the charitable activities and make sure the stories got around. See? She could compromise. On that anyway.

Some of her plans were of a more...*questionable* nature, she supposed. And did *not* involve compromise.

Because she was going to seduce her own husband when she knew very little about seduction. When he thought it was "mixing business with pleasure" and that was very bad.

Which was just so ludicrous. Their *business* was marriage, and making it look like they were in love so everyone thought Aristide a changed man.

It made absolutely no sense to keep their hands off each other when they both clearly wanted to know what it would be like, and it would only *aid* in their ruse.

When he had quite obviously had an alarming number of women in his bed before this moment. What was one more? Was he really going to have the only woman he *didn't* sleep with be his wife?

She understood his reticence, when his mother essentially worked for his father, even after having a son and all these years later. What a disturbing situation.

But she had *met* Milo Bonaparte, and Aristide was nothing like him.

Which made her realize, somewhat belatedly, that the woman who had served her and Vale tea with Milo when they announced their engagement had likely...been Aristide's mother.

She'd thought about that as they traveled from Rome to Milan, and there for a few days she played the role of a picture-perfect wife always looking adoringly at her husband. They appeared arm in arm, they danced, they charmed. And Francesca did not push. She let him put that distance between them, as if they were nothing more than *coworkers* while she watched him. *Learned* him.

She had not pressed him for any more kissing photo ops. She had dressed more on the side of that old modesty, as if that might lend Aristide some aura of sainthood.

It had not worked, and the stories about them had cooled. More interested in the fate of Vale and his princess—which no one could quite agree on.

"A picnic?" Aristide looked up at her from where he was reading a newspaper in a language she hadn't known he was fluent in. Because he liked to hide that part of himself. That he was smart. That he worked hard.

That at least she understood. His attempt to be the antithesis of his brother so it wasn't competition. She wondered if that was because he was afraid he'd lose, or if he did not *want* to be in competition with Vale.

While Vale's feelings on Aristide had always been centered in anger, Francesca had to surmise Aristide's stemmed from hurt. An interesting contrast.

But that was neither here nor there. She held the picnic basket she had put together herself. "We've done all the glittering parties. All the glamour. I think now is the time for someone to look at us in a…quieter moment. What better place than Lake Como?"

"We have a dinner to attend tonight."

"Yes. We do. Don't we want to prove to people we spend every waking moment together?"

He sighed, a bit heavily for someone this was all benefitting. *She* didn't care which reputation he wanted to trot out. As far as she was concerned, a good reputation never did anything for her. No more than a bad one would have.

But he got out of the chair and took her to the picnic place she'd chosen. She marched ahead, the scene already formed in her head.

She would lay out the picnic, they would talk, eat, flirt—hopefully. The photographer she'd tipped off via her assistant would come, snap a few candid photographs, and then leave.

She found her spot and spread out the pretty blanket and then set the basket in the middle. It was *beautiful*, and the pictures would be absolutely idyllic.

Then she looked back at the man who would complete the picture. He was dressed casually, as was she, and as she'd instructed. And still, the stiff posture, the suspicious expression made it seem like he was standing at the head of a meeting table rather than a cozy picnic with his new bride.

She smiled brightly at him and took him by the arm

and tugged him into a sitting position on the blanket. She pulled the food out of the basket, handed him his share of things. There was nothing too fancy, both because she'd done it herself and by design. She wanted it to look rustic and homey to the outside world, as much as to Aristide she wanted it to look like…she'd put some heart into it.

Because Aristide might be determined there were lines and separations and realities and fictions, but Francesca wanted to try out what it would feel like for everything to be a reality.

She settled herself next to him, so their shoulders were pressed together and they could both lean back against the tree shading them, though sunlight dappled through like little stars.

The only way she knew how to make things happen for the better was to plan them out. To march forward, step by step, until the goal was reached.

And somehow her goal had become her husband.

She looked up at him. He was not *scowling* exactly, but he was looking straight ahead. It wouldn't do for a picture. *Or* for what she wanted.

There was one thing she knew got through that little wall he put up. She wasn't *proud* of using her trauma to get through it, to get to him, but right now she was determined to use any and all tools at her disposal.

Aristide knew he was too stiff. Her proximity did that to him more and more. Because she became more and more casual with it. A touch, a brush, her body next to his.

She acted *all* the time as if this were somehow *real*. She made this all feel *real*, when they weren't doing anything different than that honeymoon week. She baked him things, told him about the books she was reading, insisted he be there while she swam.

But something had shifted. From a simple kind of enjoyment to...understanding.

He knew her father had harmed her. She knew that Valentino had been the one to turn his back on Aristide. He thought he could see under almost all her masks now, though she trotted them out less and less.

He was terrified she could see under his—as he trotted them out more and more.

But worst of all, she seemed to enjoy his company, as no one he could recall ever had. Not just his charm, or his money, or his physical appeal. Not just...as part of their deal, but actually *seek it out*. She seemed to *enjoy* just being together.

Like they were friends.

Like they were more.

Sitting there in a pretty little sundress that she'd somehow made up to look casual. He supposed it was modest, but any millimeter of olive skin exposed made him want to see more. Made him desperate to touch, to taste, when he could never remember an ensemble any woman had ever worn to entice him having the same effect.

"I've never had company on a picnic before," she announced, out of the blue and with a kind of cheerfulness the words didn't match.

She was forever announcing these sad little tidbits of her life that made it feel like she'd turned his heart into a pincushion.

"You had *solitary* picnics?" he returned, hoping he was misunderstanding.

"There was a little place on my father's estate where

no one could find me. I didn't go there often because I'd usually be punished upon return. But if I knew my father would be gone for a while, I would smuggle out little snacks and go there and pretend I was having a picnic in some beautiful park somewhere." She gestured at the beauty around them. As though she'd made her dream come true.

"Francesca. How *did* you turn out?" Because he had figured his way out of the slings and arrows of manipulation and meanness and rejection, but her childhood made what he'd always viewed as great trauma seem like a *joke*.

She looked down at her sandwich—one she'd no doubt made, as it wasn't neat or tidy like anyone he paid to feed them would have accomplished. "I decided to," she said, her voice small but firm.

"You are impressive, *mio angioletta*." She never balked at that name anymore. She *beamed* when he called her that. As she did now. Which meant he should stop, and yet...

He kept meaning to separate himself more and more from her, but watching her bloom in this new life of theirs was irresistible. Her palpable joy. Her confidence and determination. And what was the harm in watching if he knew what the lines were?

But every day she brought him closer to dangerous ground. Something bigger and bigger swelling inside of him. And he *knew* it could not take root or it would be a disaster for both of them.

He knew what it was to think so highly of someone. To feel those flickers of enjoyment and affinity and *need*. He had been very careful not to let these things into his life again, but she was changing everything.

He knew where that led. There was nothing he had to offer anyone that didn't cause harm. He had learned this at a young age and it had been reinforced later, so he'd grown into an adult, who made sure not to form attachments. It had been *years* since he'd felt this way.

And he couldn't escape it, because he'd married her. Because he could hardly turn her loose to fend for herself, and he still wanted the reputation she was crafting for him.

She looked up from her sandwich, offered him a smile, but her gaze dropped to his mouth.

Need slammed through him. No. Not need. *Want*. Because you could resist a want. You did not hurt people over a want. A want was a *choice*. And he did not have to choose her.

He told himself this. Over and over. Even as she seemed to make it harder to breathe. Harder to exist anywhere without putting his hands on her. His mouth on her.

"The photographer is here," she whispered, her eyes now searching his. Like looking for an answer.

He knew better than to think he was anyone's answer.

"Excellent," he replied, but he didn't move. Didn't look for where the photographer might be discreetly stationed. He couldn't give a damn about a photographer when she was this close, her eyes that dark, and everything about her simply *beautiful*.

To kiss her would be to give in. Cross a line. When he didn't cross those lines. He *didn't*.

But she tilted her mouth toward his, and she must be magnetic. The pull of her was too much. Something had happened in their time together, and she had *upended* something inside of him so none of the gravity that used to hold him center existed.

There was only her, and then the taste of her. Her mouth on his, gentle and sweet. Her arms sliding around his neck, melting into him. As though she was his. Some great karmic gift when he'd done nothing to deserve it. Her.

She was soft, safe and so damn strong it should humble anyone who came into her orbit. She set some hideous, needy, uncontrollable wildfire inside of him, and then soothed it with the brush of her hand over his hair.

It shuddered through him, and only the knowledge someone watched, someone took *photographs* had him easing back.

She fluttered her eyes open and looked so pleased with herself, and he wanted to be pleased too, but it soured in his gut as her arms slid off his shoulders and went back to her food.

He couldn't force himself to do the same. Lines kept getting crossed. Emotions kept swirling out of control. Something too close to *need* was taking hold when he knew it to be the enemy right along with expectation. Hope. Love.

But he didn't know what to do about it.

CHAPTER NINE

ARISTIDE WAS VERY cold on the way home, so Francesca gave him space once more. A few days of careful, modest, hands-off *wifing*. She didn't let herself think her plan was backfiring. If anything, it was working.

Just slower and with more fits and starts than she liked. But each time she reached out she got a little closer to the core of him.

He'd called her *impressive* and kissed her. She could live off that for a very long time. Here in this freedom she had now. She could reach out for and plan for whatever she wished.

Finally.

When they arrived in Nice, they didn't head to a hotel, but to one of Aristide's properties. He had another in London where they were headed in a few more weeks, but Francesca thought France was the perfect place to wage her own war, so to speak.

She gave him a day to settle in. To slowly warm back up to her again—because he always did. She supposed that was what kept her going. He was not *uninterested*. He did not actually dislike her or find her repugnant.

He simply had the wrong thoughts about what it would mean if they found a way to make this real. She would show him the truth, though. Because it would be…a dis-service to herself not to seek all that she wished now that she had the freedom she worked so hard for.

She wasn't afraid of hard work. In fact, she felt more settled with a goal, a plan.

So she would finally, *finally* seduce her husband.

The next afternoon, she invited him to sit out at the pool with her. For all the ways he kept her at arm's length, she knew he liked to watch her swim. She liked to imagine him weaving great fantasies about them, that he then applauded himself for not acting on.

It sounded like something he would do. Because she was slowly understanding her husband. Not everything he kept locked, deep and secret, but the way he moved through the world. The way he kept his true self locked under a careful mask.

She, on the other hand, had begun to get acquainted with her true self. She'd made them dinner last night—and had only slightly overcooked the salmon. She still did her swims, and she was reading through her books with great gusto. And in between all that, she planned their events, their image. Aristide's rehabilitation.

It was amazing to feel this free, this much *herself*. She wanted to offer the same to him.

So she would make it harder on him to hide away. To resist her. Because he wanted her.

She was sure of it.

And they both deserved the freedom to act on that.

So she did *not* dress in her swimsuit. Not even the *very* brief bikini she'd bought on a whim back in Milan. No. She simply put the swim cover over her completely naked body and walked out of her suite of rooms.

Her heart hammered. If *this* did not get through to him…

Well. It had to. And when it did, she would finally know what lay on the other side of all this…unrest. And then…

For a moment she was rendered motionless by the idea that once she repaired his reputation, once she convinced him to act on this attraction between them, there would be no other end goal.

She'd have her freedom. She'd have made her payment, so to speak, to Aristide. She'd know what it felt like to have her desire met.

Then what?

She shook away that thought. It hardly mattered. There were always challenges to meet. No doubt new ones would crop up. Why borrow trouble?

She marched on through the beautiful house, all open and airy with lots of color and light. She liked his taste. It wasn't *all* ridiculous; he seemed to save most of that for the island and there was no secret why. Still, he did not choose a staid, uptight kind of dwelling, and it always brightened her mood. So many windows, and with the house tucked back into the hills, beautiful views always spread out in front of her.

She made her way to the backyard, where the pool stretched out toward the edge of their hill, so she could swim out and look out over the bay below.

She stepped out into the bright sunshiny afternoon, warm and summery still. She would have preferred a swim in the Baie des Anges, because she loved the waves and the surf, but the lack of privacy did not suit her goals. Nor did the name.

She was not anyone's angel, even if she got a little secret thrill every time he called her that, but she did not need to remind Aristide of yet another reason he seemed so determined to keep his hands off her.

Aristide was already here, stationed under a bright blue umbrella as he typed away on his laptop.

She rarely saw him work. He liked to tuck it away like a secret. She was fascinated by the way he did that because she recognized it so easily. Keep yourself hidden from anyone who might be inclined to look too close. Carefully keep yourself *safe*.

She was going to prove to him he would be safe with her. *Always*.

"You know, I'm not even sure I really know what you do," she said by way of greeting, meandering her way by his seat in the shade, making sure to keep herself and the very brief swim cover-up in the sunlight.

His eyes followed her, as they always did. "I hardly know myself."

Which was a flat-out lie. One of these days she'd get the truth out of him. There. Another goal after she achieved this one.

Buoyed by this, she came to stand at the chair next to him. She could have drawn it out more. She could have talked herself out of it, but she had gotten through life by making calculated, determined choices, and never second-guessing herself.

Because hesitation, second-guessing, uncertainty... those so often ended in a blow. Literally. Better to be bold and true and certain.

So, without much fanfare, she lifted the cover-up off her body, just as she would have if she'd been wearing a swimsuit underneath. But she wasn't. Instead, she had briskly revealed herself to him. Entirely naked.

Her throat threatened to close then and there, but she carefully placed the cover-up over the back of the empty chair, trying to pretend this wasn't out of the ordinary. It was just doing one of those things she'd always wanted to do. Her heart hammered, and her nerves threatened to make her limbs shake, but she would not give in to it.

"I think you forgot something," Aristide growled.

She shrugged, very cognizant of the way the move made her breasts lift and fall. The way his gaze followed the move. "I told you I always wanted to skinny-dip."

"I believe you made certain to tell me you wished to do it *alone*." She knew he was trying for censure, but his eyes drank her in like a dying man desperate for water as she walked away from him and toward the stairs into the pool.

"I changed my mind. You can feel free to join me." She stepped onto the first stair. "The water is a bit cold, but it'll warm." And she didn't hurry. Didn't jump in. Even as her nerves hummed. She took each step slowly. One at a time. The cold water meeting the warmth of her skin like some kind of glorious torture.

And his gaze on her. Hot and heavy. She couldn't hold his gaze and manage this, so she turned slightly away from him, moving out toward the edge of the pool that would allow her a view down into the bay.

Water closed over her hips, her navel, her breasts. She hissed in a breath as her nipples tightened against the cold. Going from air to water its own cool, shocking caress.

What would it feel like if *he* touched her in all these places the water skimmed over her?

No. Not *if.* When. *When* he touched her. When he stoked these fires she did not quite understand inside of herself.

Because *he* understood, that much was clear. And he *wanted* to. Once he got over whatever warped impulses held him back.

With that determined, she ignored him for a while. She focused on herself. The way the water felt against *her* body. The way desire seemed to twine inside her, deeper and deeper, so that every stroke, every sink to the bottom and resurfacing felt like someone touching her.

But there was only one touch she wanted. She arched out of the water, letting her hair drip back before she blinked her eyes open to find him.

But he had not made a move to join her. He remained in his seat, fully clothed. Though his hand was now closed in a fist. He watched her, all tension and fury.

She only wished she could understand that fury. Why it should make him *mad* to want her, when she considered it a lovely little surprise. A boon, really. Who wouldn't want to *want* their spouse?

She blew out a bit of a frustrated breath. *Him* apparently. Because he still sat exactly where he was. Maybe he hadn't left yet, but he hadn't even made one little move.

She didn't pout, mostly because the impulse was foreign to her. Why feel sorry for herself when there were things to be done about the situation? Like, for instance, not hiding in the water.

She swam the length of the pool, back to the stairs, then walked right back out. She tried not to shiver as wet skin met air. Without looking at him, she went over to one of the lounge chairs and arranged herself, heart beating, body throbbing, starting to worry she would have to come up with yet another plan to make him break. She lay on her back, eyes closed against the bright sun above. The air settled over her, warming her slowly. She waited.

He would break. He *did* want her.

Finally, she heard a shuffle. She opened her eyes to look at him. He stood slowly, carefully, almost as if it hurt to move. Then he walked over to her, looked down at her.

So close, but not close enough. Not *touching*. Even as her breath sawed in and out, even as her skin *prickled* as the air and his gaze colluded to feel like very universes brushed against her.

He settled himself on the lounge next to her. Seated, not prone, but out of reach.

"I will not touch you, *angioletta*," he said darkly, and she wasn't sure whether him calling her *angel* was an insult or a praise. She found she didn't care because she liked it on his tongue either way.

"But you may touch yourself."

Francesca was the most haunting thing he'd ever seen in his entire life. All burnished gold and determined vulnerability. Dark hair and dark desires in her dark eyes.

It took every last ounce of strength to keep his hands on his knees. To not reach out and haul her to him.

Particularly when her entire body jolted at his words, as if they landed in her like electricity. Her eyes wide, her fingers flexed once almost reflexively as a pretty little blush stained her cheeks.

And then spread lower.

A siren. A curse. She'd lead him to his death and would it even matter? What could matter beyond this? It wasn't a crossed line. Not yet. A blurred one, perhaps, but he could blur it.

God, he had to blur it or he'd simply *die*.

"Go on, then," he said with a nod. "Give yourself the pleasure you seek."

Her eyelids fluttered a little, and she shifted once, with uncertainty. But she did not scoff, and she did not get up, and she did not tell him to go to hell.

There in the bright afternoon sunshine, she lifted her hand. Somehow he knew she'd be brave enough, that she wouldn't back down. All spine and resolve, his wife. Her fingers brushed over her breast, her own tightened nipple.

He felt the touch echo within him even though he had nothing to do with it. And still he stayed seated where he was, even as he could imagine what it would feel like to put his mouth where her fingers trailed.

Down soft skin, across goose bumps and into the glorious space between her thighs. Her touch was timid. Halting now.

"Do not be afraid, Francesca. Be brave. If it were my mouth instead of your fingers, I would not hesitate to taste you. Long and deep."

Her breath shuddered out and he felt that shudder within himself. His body was hot, impenetrable iron. All tension and nothing but the hard, painful beat of wanting her.

She stroked herself, her eyes going hazy, her movements becoming erratic. And still she didn't close those eyes, look away from him, stop. She held him there, in her siren's gaze, a party to this even though he didn't touch her.

Wouldn't.

Couldn't.

She began to writhe, there against her own hand, the most erotic, beautiful thing he'd ever seen.

"Aristide." She said his name on a rasp, her gaze blurred with desire. The need to be the one who set her over that edge roared through him like a shrieking storm and still he held himself still and away.

"Let yourself go, *angioletta*. Now."

She made a keening sound, low and shattering. His whole body shook in response as her climax spread over her body. She was gasping for air, pink all over, and still she didn't look away. She didn't seem any less desperate. "Aristide, let me touch you. Touch *me*."

He would not. He *could* not.

But she pushed herself into a sitting position. "*Please*, Aristide."

And it turned out, she had the key to undo him after all. Because her *please* upended him. Didn't just blur every line he'd set for himself, but erased them all.

And when she said it again, eyes big and liquid, reaching out for him, he let her find purchase.

CHAPTER TEN

FRANCESCA FELT MADE of sunshine. Heat and liquid and summer, swirling around inside a body that surely wasn't hers anymore.

She wanted it to be *his*.

There was a beat of a moment where she thought he'd set her aside yet again, but the *please* seemed to sweep through him like magic. When she reached out, he caught her, and then swiftly brought his mouth to hers.

And *plundered*. She was caught there against the cotton of his T-shirt, the hard, unforgiving landscape of his chest. All while his mouth took hers with no mercy, no give.

She didn't want any. She wanted the harsh demand of it all. The *certainty*. The way his hands moved over her as if they had a route in mind. As if he knew *everything* about her. The way his rough palm over her abdomen made her arch toward him. The way his mouth on her neck made her want to make sounds she was sure she'd never made before. Some strange kind of purring to encourage him to keep at it.

Every kiss, every nibble, every slide of his hand was some new universe opened up to her. Sparkling and vast. But giving more only opened up the need for more. She pulled his shirt over his head, following whatever impulse took hold of her.

Like scraping her nails lightly up the large, muscular expanse of his back. When he growled against her throat, she laughed with abandoned joy.

Until he touched her, where she had touched herself. For him. The memory and the reality crashing through her, dragging her up that delicious, twisting tension in need of release. But just as she thought she might find it, as she strained toward him trying to find it, he took his hand away.

And it was his turn to laugh. Then he dragged that laugh down the center of her, his mouth a delicious tangle of new sensation until he settled himself between her legs and tasted her long and deep. Just as he'd said.

She hadn't known. She hadn't dreamed. All her life she had been tethered to earth, but Aristide cut those ties and let her fly. He didn't stop this time. His mouth explored her most intimate places until she crashed apart, with a throbbing, echoing *joy*.

As he moved back over her, she saw the flash of that detachment in his eyes. Like he might pull away. Like he might *stop*. She couldn't bear the thought. Not when they'd come so far. Not when it could be so much.

And she had found the key to this. If she felt him pull away, try to find that distance he was so good at employing, she only had to say one thing.

"Aristide, please." She didn't mind asking. Begging. Whatever it took. Because touching herself in front of him had certainly been a revelation in what passion could be found with only his eyes on her.

But she wanted his touch. She wanted him. She *needed*

to know what more there could be. She reached for the pants he still wore, and he didn't stop her. He let her unbutton and unzip. To push them out of her way so she could feel more than the outline of his delicious hardness.

She touched him reverently, because it was a delicious thrill. To be this close to a man who could be so remote. To feel the most intimate parts of *him*, and know he was hard for *her*.

It was a gift to be so consumed with whatever pulsed through her that it didn't matter if she was naked or he was. All that mattered was that they found their way together.

"Please," she whispered again, meeting his gaze, one arm looped around his neck, one hand stroking the long, hard length of him. "Show me."

He muttered something dark that she didn't quite catch as he moved, pulling his pants off, so that he was as naked as she. All bronze skin and harsh lines. There was no laziness here in this body, no matter how he could affect the mask of it. He was all energy, all strength.

And for the moment, all hers.

He arranged her on the lounge, covered her body with his. His muscles tensed, his gaze fierce, and then him, there, slowly moving inside of her. Too much. It was all too much, and he was too much. She wanted to sob, but somehow in a good way. As if all releases could be good.

It didn't seem as though it were possible she could accommodate him, but slowly, inexorably, she opened, softened, accepted. Until he was so deep inside of her, she had no idea how she could ever exist again, empty and without him.

"So beautiful, so perfect," he murmured as she strug-

gled to breathe, to process, to *still*. She had to move, she
had to pant, she had to…

"So impatient," he said, with dark amusement in his
tone. "When you have found such pleasure already. Luckily, greed suits me."

He moved inside of her like this was all they were and
ever would be. Bound, fused. As if this was always where
her life had been leading. Right to this point. Right to
him. She'd escaped not to save herself, but to find him.

"Mio angioletta," he murmured there against her skin.
Deep inside of her.

She hadn't wanted to be an angel, but she would be
anything if he considered her *his*. To protect. To cherish.
To make love to, just like this.

Stars seemed to explode around her. Bigger, somehow,
when she would have said she'd already achieved every
pinnacle of pleasure there could ever be. She shook, she
sobbed, and when he pressed deep one last time, she
gripped him hard and held him to her as he pulsed out
his own release.

For a moment, they were still, shaking in each other's
arms. She needed to catch her breath, her racing thoughts.
Come back to herself. But before she could, he swept her
up into his arms. And carried her, back into the house,
through too many rooms to count into a giant bedroom
that must be his. Because she got the sense of color and
brightness, but she could not drag her gaze from his.

He placed her on his bed, looking fierce and haunted.
She shook her head because she didn't want him haunted
or hunted. She wanted him to feel what she felt.

Freedom. She got to her knees on the mattress, reached
out and traced his face with her fingers. He stood stiffly,

but not *unmoved*. No, he was trying *not* to be moved. Because his eyes didn't leave hers, and there were too many emotions in those dark depths.

But the one she recognized was fear. She had been afraid and brave all at the same too many times in her life not to recognize it.

She would find a way to reward him, for both. For this. For *them*.

It was like being worshipped. Pleasure, yes, so big it threatened to split Aristide's chest in two. But pain, because what a responsibility. To be that which this woman worshipped. Her fingertips followed every bone, every angle, ever line of his face. Slowly, gently, reverently.

And kept going. Down the cords of his neck. The ridge of muscle across his chest. Light, exploratory. Combing wildfires he did not know how to put out. Did not *want* to, if it meant she was the one setting them against every inch of his skin.

When her hand closed around where he was once again hard and wanting, he gripped her wrist. To stop her.

Surely.

But she shook her head, looking up at him with big, wide eyes luminous in the fading light of day.

"Let me. Let me show *you*," she whispered, and then said that word that made every vow he'd ever given himself and only himself crumble to nothing but dust.

If she begged him, he could not resist.

And then she followed every touch with her mouth. Soft and precious. Praise and veneration no one man could possibly deserve.

Until he was shaking. Until the need was too much to

hold himself apart. He took her wrists again, this time to move her so that she was underneath him. He spread her soft, silky thighs wide and settled himself there.

"Say it again." He'd meant it as a command, but it sounded more like a raspy plea.

He found he didn't care when her mouth curved, a sultry smile tinged with sweetness that came from some secret part of her she'd not yet shown him.

And now it was here. Something she had found because she was strong and brave and wonderful, but something he'd helped her find. Helped her create.

"*Please*, Aristide," she said, somehow knowing exactly what he wanted, somehow sounding stronger and more powerful than any woman begging rightly should. But this was Francesca. His angel. Sent to save him or perhaps he would drag them both to hell.

It didn't matter in this moment. As long as he was inside her again. Where he fit. Where he belonged. Where he took his time, moving her close and closer still, but never over that edge she wanted again.

So she writhed there underneath him. Begging and perfect.

He placed his hand on her chest, fingers spread wide, the wave of possession so big and deep he wasn't sure how any man could bear it.

Then she moved against him, all her own. An arch up against him, and a roll back down And the sound of perfect pleasure that escaped her mouth was art.

"Go on, then," he said, watching her eyes, for that flare of everything that echoed inside of him. "Find it yourself."

She did not jerk at that as she had outside. She did not

even pause. She arched against him again. And he leveraged over her, while she moved, set the pace, and raced toward her own staggering release.

She sobbed out his name as the sun set outside. As he lost himself and gripped her hips, thrusting inside of her once more. In a fever of body to body and gasping breaths and a climax so big and bright he thought perhaps the world had collapsed around them.

Since he could not hold himself up, he rolled to the side, and she fell with him. Somehow, fitting just as if she belonged tucked up next to him.

They both breathed heavily and said nothing as darkness engulfed the room. He listened as her breath went from ragged to even, as her clenched hand relaxed. Until she slept there, tucked in beside him, her head on his shoulders and her soft, thick hair seeming everywhere.

Aristide lay as the passion and energy of release slowly drained out of him, as his own breathing slowed. As everything warm and good was replaced not with exhaustion, or contentment, or anything but a terrible, beating panic.

He had not been careful.

He had lost himself. Lines crossed. Complications created. All because she was a siren he hadn't been able to resist. And normally, he would not curse himself for a lack of resistance, but he knew she was...not understanding the situation.

Francesca thought this could be something. He saw it in her careful tending of him. The careful little battles she'd waged. Giving him space when he grew too cold, then pushing him again.

She thought maybe someday they could be domestic

and happy. That chemistry could be love. That surrender could be strength. She had *planned* this, as she planned everything so carefully, so successfully.

But he had no doubt that instead of whatever dreams she was weaving, it would end with her crumbling in his clumsy, brutal hands. Everything that had to do with *love* always did. Trying to save his mother, telling Valentino the truth. Everything he'd tried to do in the wake of the terrible secret of his parentage had only ever ended in hurting.

She had now put herself in a place that allowed him to hurt her, and he could not forgive her for this. He had been *clear* what he wanted, what he needed, and she had instead gone after what she wanted with little concern to what he did.

And if they were to have a child because he had not *thought* beyond her *please*…

That had not been part of the deal. It had not been discussed, planned. It should not be *allowed*.

Something had to be done. Something more than a line drawn in the sand because he was weak and she was determined.

Sometimes, destroying the pretty thing before it bloomed was the only possible answer. And enemies had to be slaughtered before they could do the slaughtering.

Because he was nothing to be worshipped. He was nothing but a mere mortal.

What a pity.

CHAPTER ELEVEN

FRANCESCA WASN'T COGNIZANT of falling asleep, but she must have at some point as she woke sometime later to a rumpled, empty and unfamiliar bed. She pushed herself up a little, heart tripping over itself as she worried that Aristide had disappeared, but there he was.

Relief washed through her. He hadn't run away. He hadn't set her aside. His back was to her, looking out the window at a pearly dawn. But he was here. That had to be good.

Right?

She lay back in the bed, stretched out, enjoying the way her naked body felt on the soft sheets, used and slightly achy and his. Mmm. She was hungry. Surely they could eat something up here, and then, as it was a new day, see to pleasuring each other all over again.

And to think he'd been so against it in the beginning. So certain this would be a bad idea, and it had been *glorious* instead.

"See, that wasn't so terrible, now, was it?" she offered by way of good morning.

He turned then, but she saw none of that heat in his gaze. There was only a bleakness that made everything inside of her go cold. Frozen, inside out.

"Did you get what you wanted, Francesca? Are you happy now?" He asked these questions not in accusation, but with a cold finality that shivered through her.

"I…" Instinctively, she pulled the sheet up higher as if to shield herself from that desolate look on his face and the ice of his words. "What?"

"I told you I did not cross lines. You understood why. So you crossed it for me. How good of you."

"Aristide." She was so shocked, so *appalled* at the way he characterized it she didn't have words beyond his name.

"If, God forbid, last night results in a pregnancy, we will deal with it rationally."

A pregnancy. He said it with such frigid disdain she couldn't catch her breath. It was like whiplash. Like an unexpected punch.

And she knew those too well. She hadn't expected one to come from him. Her initial response was to wince away, to hide under the covers, to *disappear*.

How *dare* he remind her of that old response. How *dare* he turn last night into something…cold. She pulled the sheet around her but got to her knees on the bed. "And what is *rationally* to you?"

"We will create another contract to discuss the details. Hopefully, it does not come to that."

Hopefully. Honestly, in this strange twist of events, she didn't know what *to* hope for, but… Maybe it wasn't the right time to introduce a child into the world, but she wasn't *opposed* to having children. "I do…want children someday."

"And it has become very clear to me that it only matters what *you* want."

Everything he said was so unfair. So off-base. And it hurt so deeply she was surprised she didn't just...crumble. But there was something about how well acquainted she was with the way everything was always twisted against her, she found anger swirled inside of her instead of defeat or retreat.

"What *you* want could matter if you would tell me. If you would be honest with me. If you wouldn't lash out with these accusations. If you had a *conversation* instead of always watching me from a distance. I have *tried* to figure out what you want."

"Ah, yes. I have watched you. Maneuvering me carefully. Exactly where you wanted me. Congratulations. You won."

He made it sound like such a loss she wanted to cry. Tears threatened and only a force of will built in the tragedy of her childhood kept those tears from falling over. "I thought we both won."

"Should you ever pull another stunt like that, we will immediately divorce. Reputations and contracts be damned. Mark my words."

"A stunt?" She laughed, because it was so breathlessly cruel, she couldn't seem to find anything else but a shocked kind of humor to it all. "I did not realize I forced your hand. I did not realize I had such *power*— me the *senseless* virgin."

"You begged me."

"And I suppose you've never said no before, so it must be my fault you couldn't muster it last night? *Multiple* times."

His expression was ice. Everything about it *hurt*. Because he made it sound like she'd *hurt* him, and she'd...

She'd been so happy. So free. So sure last night could be the start of something *beautiful*. All her freedom a culmination of joy she—*they*—rightly deserved.

And he'd turned it into something ugly, mean and selfish. Tears threatened, but she blinked them away, still clutching the sheet to her chest.

Last night *had* been beautiful. This was… This was him being afraid of that. Afraid of this thing that bloomed between them. Because it wasn't just sex. It was *more*. Maybe that hurt him because he didn't want it to be more, but it wasn't fair to treat her this way.

"You turn your hurt into anger, like a weapon," she said. "And you hurt the wrong people. Because you're afraid what might happen if you don't."

"Ah, and what is this bogeyman I'm so afraid of?"

"That someone might care about you." *I care about you*. He had handed her a new world, just by listening, by watching. He had given her what she wanted. He had protected her.

And now he was ripping it away like she'd somehow… tricked him into it.

Because she had hoped that accusation might get through to him, might visibly land, but it didn't. He moved closer, eyes blazing with a fury that made her want to wince away.

"And do you know what I think *you're* afraid of? Letting anyone else have some semblance of control. You want to maneuver everything and everyone so *you* get everything *you* want and damn the consequences. Well, *cara*, I will not be your consequence. I will not be maneuvered by the likes of you."

It hit close enough to the bone that her anger wilted.

Because she *had* maneuvered him. She *had* focused on what *she* wanted. She had ensured she got it.

And somehow that had ruined everything.

Aristide spent the morning working. It was not easy to concentrate, but he did it. There were things that needed to be done around his ridiculous social calendar.

They had a charity event this afternoon, followed by a dinner.

He wouldn't force Francesca to attend any of these events. Not immediately. They could skip a few things and blame those newlywed sparks. And if it turned out she was pregnant...they could miss a few more.

He did not let himself dwell on that possibility. Dwell on why it had not once occurred to him last night to do what he *always* did and protect himself.

Because once again, it had to be her fault. She'd started everything, begged him, been...utterly perfect.

He had not wanted to be haunted by the taste of her, the feel of her, the echoes of how she sounded when he tumbled her over that blissful edge. But they were there and he couldn't seem to eradicate them.

More than once he'd found himself on his feet, as if he was going to go hunt her down. But then he'd ask himself for *what*? To follow the contemptible footsteps of Milo Bonaparte to pick at everyone, bit by bit, until there was only bitterness or servitude?

It seemed to be the only kinds of relationships his blood knew how to have. And now he'd even spread that bitterness to his wife of convenience. Impressive, really.

Fifteen minutes before they would need to leave for the animal shelter Francesca appeared, dressed and made up appropriately. He'd expected defiance, that spark of combativeness he seemed to bring out in her.

She kept her eyes downcast, her answers short.

Everything about her was…different. This was not defiance. It was defeat.

But it was better now. Now, before anything could grow. Now, before she fancied herself in love with him or vice versa. They would weather this little speed bump and go back to the *business* relationship they were meant to have.

She said absolutely nothing on the drive over to the shelter. Her gaze stayed out the window, but the minute they arrived and he helped her out of the car, she was all warmth and smiling.

At the employees and volunteers, of course. Not at him. They were given a tour of the facility, and after Francesca so adeptly and politely declined to have their pictures taken even though she'd been the one to tell him everyone used charity, they were led into an outdoor area where dogs raced around, playing with each other, with volunteers, more dogs lazing about in the sun panting happily.

"We try to keep them as comfortable as possible while we wait to find the best homes for them," the manager said. "Your generous donation is going to be such a boon for us."

"We're so glad," Francesca said. And she was all cheer and kindness, but he saw a kind of *tightness* around her mouth. A little chink in the armor she'd put around herself.

It made him want to reach out and touch her, offer his strength, but he stood stiffly by her side, hands carefully to himself.

"One of the first things we bonded over was always wanting a pet and never having one growing up," Francesca was telling the manager. "But we're having trouble deciding on what would be better for our lifestyle. I'm thinking a cat would be easier with all the traveling we do, but Aristide just loves dogs."

She said all this with a cheerful smile, a slightly conspiratorial tone, as she leaned toward the woman who ran the shelter.

A flat-out lie told so effectively. Aristide wondered if he'd stepped into an alternate reality altogether, where this was all simply the truth. She was his and that was their past and they would have a *pet* together once they figured what would suit.

But not only had they never discussed his not having a pet, he clearly remembered her saying *she* wanted a dog.

"Something big and ridiculous. The more hair, the less brains, the better."

He stared at her, but she ignored him, talking with the woman about cat and dog breeds and the like. Aristide watched the animals around them, was distracted by one that was insistently barking—at an overturned bowl. None of the volunteers were paying the large dog any mind as if this was a common occurrence.

Aristide walked over to the creature, then waved to his wife.

"Come, Francesca. Take a look at this one."

With that fake smile plastered on her face, she walked over to him, smiled somewhat more genuinely at the dog.

"The exact kind of dog I always wanted," he told her with a meaningful glance, because for some reason he wanted to prove that he'd been listening when he should prove that they meant nothing to each other.

She looked at him as if he'd stabbed her clean through. Her smile faltered, but she knelt down to pet the dog. Who, momentarily distracted from the bowl, wagged its tail and used its giant, disgusting tongue to lick her face.

Francesca reached out and fixed the bowl, so it was now right side up. "There now. No more fussing," she said with kind admonishment as she rubbed her hands over its long fur.

But the dog reached forward with a paw, upended the bowl, and then started barking again.

Aristide frowned. "Definitely more hair than brains," he muttered.

And when he looked from the dog to Francesca, he noted she'd pressed her face into the dog's side. Her shoulders shook. Once.

She was crying into the dog's fur.

He had done that to her, and he had to accept that *she* was not the poison in this scenario.

He was.

CHAPTER TWELVE

FRANCESCA PLAYED THE perfect bride for the next few weeks. Sort of. She knew she was more bleak and bland than she should be, but she couldn't quite pull herself out of the little fog of depression. Still, she refused to allow him to cancel any events, though he offered most nights, somewhat stiffly.

No. They would do everything they'd committed to. She would do her *job*. If there was one thing she'd always done, it had been that.

Even with the cold, icy distance between them. Even with her heart shattered—of her own doing. Because he had been clear, and she'd crossed his lines for her own gain. She couldn't even hate him because she felt like too terrible a person to deserve the sweet anger that came with hate or blame.

They went to their dinners and balls and smiled and chatted and put on a good show. The stories in the press were even beginning to sway toward the story they portrayed. Just this morning she'd seen an article on one of those silly gossip sites titled "Could this Angel Really Have Tamed this Devil?"

But she did not feel like the angel she was supposed to be. She felt like a husk. In her darkest moments, she pitied herself enough to think she'd traded one prison for another, but then she reminded herself no matter how much her heart hurt, she was safe here.

She could not *hate* Aristide if she was safe. If *she* had been the problem that had pushed them away from easy companionship and blistering chemistry to this horrible glacial experience.

She could only hate herself. Which somehow made it easy to put on the role of Francesca Bonaparte. Make up stories about who she and Aristide were, because there was no hope there'd ever really be a *them*. So she might as well make up a fake version for the nights they had to spend together.

Because in the light of day, he didn't eat meals with her anymore, and she didn't go near a swimming pool or ocean. She didn't bake or read.

They all felt like luxuries she didn't deserve.

Before they were to fly to London, Aristide approached her as she choked down her breakfast. It was no doubt delicious, but it tasted like nothing to her. She wouldn't have eaten at all, but there was still the possibility…

She tried not to think about how she might be pregnant. Tried not to look for signs. Tried to ignore it altogether.

And still there was a little flame of hope inside of her she couldn't quite extinguish. Just like the sight of him still made her heart flutter when she knew he would only ever approach with pain.

"We are taking a little break and returning home," he informed her stiffly and from a distance. "My mother insists on an introduction, and it doesn't do to let something irritate her enough to complain to my father."

Francesca nodded. It was only a small change of events.

They'd had a few things organized in London, but a trip home would be an easy enough reason to change plans.

She tried very hard not to think about how easy it was to consider the castle *home*.

"Very well."

There was the slightest hesitation, like he might say something else, but in the end he only turned away and left her there on the patio. Alone.

Exactly how you belong.

She knew this couldn't go on. All this self-pitying nonsense. She'd survived worse than being rejected. Maybe there was something to that. She'd never really had the time to sit around and feel sorry for herself before. Never got to just *marinate* in her feelings of hurt and inadequacy and mistakes.

So, now she'd done so. She needed to go back to finding her own personal strength in the midst of feeling bad about herself or her situation.

She returned to her room and packed, kindly begging off any of Aristide's staff who tried to take over the task. She needed things to do. Things that didn't involve Aristide. Or thinking about… She frowned a little at the twinge in her stomach. A twinge that usually accompanied…

She inhaled sharply, then steadied herself before going into the bathroom.

Well, problem solved. There was no baby.

She blinked a few times, surprised to find tears already falling. When it would have been a disaster to be pregnant. When it would have caused so many terrible complications.

"This is good," she whispered to herself. "An answer.

Now you can stop being such a fool and get on with your life." She wiped at her face, but the tears kept falling. She did not know what to *do* with this reaction. She hadn't even lost anything. Just some fantasy possibility that had been nothing but a fairy tale.

And fairy tales were not for people like her. Survival was all she wanted. All she'd fight for. The rest was a joke.

She washed her face, finished her packing, and she met Aristide at the car that would drive them to the airport.

He studied her with that old intensity, and she pretended she didn't notice. Didn't feel it. *Business* partners didn't care how the other was feeling. Because there were *lines*.

She had never expected the lines to feel suffocating. That her freedom would feel like just another version of prison. A nicer one, all in all, but one that kept her from truly being herself once again.

Once on the plane, she pretended to lose herself in a book, though not one single word penetrated the fog she could not seem to fight. She didn't have to fake a nap on the ride from airport to island, because she was emotionally wrung out and exhausted.

When the car rolled to a stop, she awoke to find his eyes on her. She pretended not to notice, though she allowed him to help her out of the car as he always did.

The sun was setting behind the castle, and the soft sound of surf and the salty scent of it infiltrated that little fog. It felt *good* to be back. Maybe that little week they'd had here was just an illusion, but it had been an enjoyable illusion.

Something about being back at his castle, that she

just…loved. Its ridiculous weathervanes and crazy sculptures. The tremulous sea in the background. It made her want to smile. It made her feel like she was *home*.

But it wasn't hers and neither was he and there was no baby to bind them, and she had to find some way to be *glad* about that.

So she'd tell him. Flat out. She removed her hand from his, met his gaze with hers, there on the walkway up to the castle.

"You will be happy to know, I'm not pregnant." A lump sat in her throat, threatening to choke her. It would have been terrible timing for a child, and still she wanted to grieve the fact that she was empty. Straight through.

He said nothing to this. Stood ramrod straight and so far away and she had known he wouldn't comfort her— he made it very clear he didn't want a child. But she still wished for some kind of warmth.

And then she heard…a bark. Aristide looked over his shoulder, and there bounded a dog out of the side door, followed by a scurrying staff member with a leash dangling from their hand.

"I bought you a present," he said gruffly, not reacting to what she'd said at all.

The dog from the charity event in Nice, at that. *More hair than brains.* She wanted to launch herself at the adorable giant ball of fur, but she understood far too well what this was.

Some sort of…buy-off. A distraction. Just another wall between them, but built using her soft feelings and wants.

She ignored the dog, looked her husband in the eye. "I hate you," she said, then turned on a heel and walked into the castle. Where she would lock herself in her room.

And if that was childish and unacceptable and all other things she'd never allowed herself to be before, well, then it was about time.

Aristide was glad to feel anger and frustration, because it was a nice change of pace from guilt and pain.

He had done something kind and she *hated* him? What sense did that make? He certainly didn't want a dog who escaped leashes and barked incessantly at upended bowls. He'd seen it as a peace offering.

I hate you.

He could not wrap his mind around it in any way, shape or form. Particularly as he stared down at the hairy beast Luca was attempting to get a leash on.

Surely she was relieved about there being no pregnancy despite their carelessness. She should be thrilled. He was. Surely he'd feel thrilled if he wasn't so confused by *her* behavior.

And *surely* her behavior didn't make any damn sense.

"Uh, what should I do with it, sir?"

Aristide grimaced at the dog but held out his hand for the leash. "I'll handle him. Thank you." Luca scurried away as if he was terrified he'd be stuck with the animal if he didn't beat a hasty retreat.

"You are *supposed* to be for Francesca," he muttered at the dog, then felt foolish for talking to a *dog*. "Come," he ordered, and began to walk toward the castle.

But the dog plopped its butt down and refused to move. Aristide frowned, tugging at the leash, but the dog didn't budge.

"Come," he repeated, through clenched teeth. He

pulled on the leash once more and the dog did *nothing* but sit there and pant at him.

"Fine, then you can run away and see how you like fending for yourself." He nearly dropped the leash, but... Francesca might hate him now, but she'd certainly hate him even more if that fool dog ran off and got itself killed.

And what does it matter if the woman who crossed all your lines and only cares what she wants hates you?

He tried to hold on to that personal narrative, but she'd gotten too many of her own hits in that night.

"What you want could matter if you would tell me. If you would be honest with me. If you wouldn't lash out with these accusations. If you had a conversation instead of always watching me from a distance. I have tried to figure out what you want."

And she had said that so earnestly, with such naked shock and hurt on her face that even all these days later, he hadn't mustered up a way to fight it.

He didn't want her to know what he wanted. He didn't want to have *conversations.* He wanted a wife who served a purpose. Not one who became...something to him. He had made a life out of *risks*—in business, in his personal life—but Francesca had swept in and made every risk feel like...life-and-death.

Aristide scowled at the dog, whose tail wagged happily. He gave one last tug before he was determined to give up. "Would you *please*..." It was as if *please* was the magic word—reminding him of too magical a night he'd turned into a disaster—that got the dog moving. It leaped up and began to run forward toward the castle. So quickly and with such force that it nearly jerked the leash out of Aristide's hand.

He managed to hold on and jog after the dog, but of course when he tried to finagle the dog inside, it only balked—and barked incessantly at the elaborate statue of a dragon that guarded this side door.

Aristide tried to use *please* again, though it rankled. Even more so when it didn't work this time. Eventually, he grabbed the dog—though it was large and heavy—and picked it up and carried it inside.

By the time he was all the way inside, and put the dog down on the ground, he was mussed and sweaty and so angry he believed he might actually storm up to her room and toss that dog in there so *she* could deal with what he'd assumed was a very *thoughtful* gift that she apparently hated him for.

Grumbling as he tried to coax the dog toward the stairs, he heard voices from the front foyer.

His mother's voice.

"You have wasted my entire evening away," he muttered at the dog. Well, they were inside now. He dropped the leash. If the dog made a mess, *Francesca* could deal with it. And now he didn't have time to fetch her for dinner.

Not that he was certain she would come.

He strode to the foyer where Vera was ushering Ginevra inside.

"Mother," he greeted stiffly, running a hand through his hair when she looked at it quizzically. No doubt a mess thanks to that monster.

Which had happily followed him and now sat obediently at his feet, like it had been doing what he ordered all evening.

Ginevra's eyes lit up and she dropped to her knees

without so much as a hello to him. "A dog." She sighed as though she were in heaven, ruffling her hands over the dog's immense body as it pranced over to her. "It is my one regret, that your father is so against pets in his home. I'd love a dog or a cat or something to need me."

One regret. In this horrible life she'd chosen, the lack of a *pet* was her *one* regret.

"You could move out." Because why should she—who had kept it for over thirty years, more than half her life—consider it *his* home where she could not be allowed what *she* wanted? Why did she settle for so little when she could have everything?

She waved this away. As she always did. She got back to her feet then looked around. "Where is your wife? Have you already scared her off?"

Aristide tried to resist a scowl, but it was impossible. As though it was *only a matter of time* before he scared her off. When Francesca had created this strange little mess they found themselves in. Because *he* had been clear.

She had pushed.

"She…is not feeling well. She will join us if she…improves." After all, Francesca lied easily and at every turn for their audiences, so why couldn't he?

"She didn't seem easily scared when I met her, but that was when she was planning to marry your brother, of course. All these stories about love whizzing about have your father in a tizzy, but I think it's sweet."

But Aristide could only focus on the first part of what she'd said. "You've met Francesca."

"Of course. When Vale brought her over to introduce her to your father."

She'd *waited* on them. He didn't know why that felt like some kind of blow. Why hadn't Francesca mentioned it? Had she not realized the woman pouring tea was his mother? Had she realized and not wanted to bring it up because she knew how he'd feel about that?

He hated to admit it, but the latter seemed far more plausible. Francesca knew the players in any room she entered. She was brilliant that way.

"I was a bit concerned you were doing this just to start trouble with your brother, but I saw a picture of you two. Some picnic. You looked happy." She reached forward, touched his cheek. "It has been a long time since I've seen you happy, and you do not look it today. So, why don't we sit down to dinner and you can tell me how you've messed it up already."

She'd taken him by the arm and was leading him toward the dining room. She didn't often venture over to his side of the island where his father was *not* welcome and refused to come anyway. Aristide had to assume the only reason she had this evening was because of his *wife*.

Who apparently hated him.

"She is…unhappy with me, I suppose. But it is hardly a mess and certainly nothing I can't handle," he insisted, pulling out a chair for her at the table.

She settled into it and waited until he took his seat. Then she leveled him with one of her motherly glares.

"You must tell her how much you need her."

"I beg your pardon." Was he that transparent?

"You are too independent. You never let anyone know you need them. What's a woman to do if she can't be needed?"

Not transparent, no. Just… "A woman could be her

own person," Aristide suggested through clenched teeth. All he'd wanted for his mother was that, and she never taken any opportunity he'd given her.

Ginevra rolled her eyes. "I know you have no use for me, but you must have some use for your wife, and she must know it. If she knew it, she would meet your mother. Not hide in her room."

No use. There had been so many "uses" he'd had for his mother, but someone *else* had always come first. "I needed you," he said.

She laughed, and he wished he'd kept his mouth shut.

"You made very clear you did not. Even Valentino was a better student in my kitchens than you were. He listened. You resented."

"He had his own mother."

"And so do you."

He liked to blame his father, but maybe *this* was why his mother rarely trekked out this way. They had the same circular conversations *every* time. And still he couldn't help himself, because he couldn't understand her. "I have… I have tried to give you everything."

"No, you have tried to give me what *you* want for me. But I don't want a house alone somewhere. I want to be with your father. He needs me. What would I do if I was not taking care of him? Certainly not take care of *you*. You wouldn't allow it."

"Why can't you simply take care of *yourself*? Or no one at all and just enjoy your life?"

She looked at him as if the question didn't even make sense. "What would there be to enjoy?"

Aristide shook his head. Perhaps he could just never understand her. Or Milo. Or Valentino. Or his own damn wife. Perhaps he was so alien he could not make sense of any of the people in his orbit.

Of course, there'd been a time when he'd thought he understood Francesca. Before they'd slept together. No. Before he'd told her it would not happen again. Before he'd told her…

"You love her, don't you?"

He hated the gentle, *knowing* way his mother said that. Because the way she loved his father disturbed him and he wanted nothing to do with it. "Love is a parasite," he returned, but that only made him think of Francesca.

He did not want her to need him. He did not want to need her. He did not like the version of love his mother explained to him. But there was *something* sharp and painful inside of him when it came to Francesca. Maybe his own version of a parasite.

His mother smiled indulgently. "That's not an answer to my question, Aristide."

CHAPTER THIRTEEN

FRANCESCA REFUSED TO leave her suite for three days. Even when she was tempted. Tempted to see if the dog was still around. Tempted to go for a swim. Tempted to ask Aristide why they were *here* if he wasn't making her go to some dinner or function, if he wasn't insisting she meet his mother again—because she'd been all set to refuse everything he'd asked, and then he'd gone and not asked for anything.

She focused on wallowing. Sleeping, eating whatever she wanted, drinking however much she wanted, and barely leaving her bed. She was bored and restless by day two, so she'd tried to read.

When she'd arrived at the great love confession in her book, so sweet it made her cry great wracking sobs, she'd ripped out every single page of the confession and tossed them into the fireplace, watching each lying word burn.

It had made her feel better for about five seconds.

Burning fiction didn't solve her reality.

And that was the realization she'd come to finally, which had her showering, getting dressed, and leaving her room. She'd had the sulk she'd never been allowed growing up, but that didn't change the reality.

She had to face it and determine what she wanted to

do about it. She might have her freedom, but she was not completely devoid of *responsibility.*

She was so *angry* at Aristide, for so many reasons, but she had also made a mistake. He had not been wrong about her. In her taste of freedom, she had thought only of what she wanted. She had maneuvered him into what *she* wanted, because that was how she was used to surviving.

This wasn't survival anymore. It was just life. So she owed Aristide an apology. Regardless of whether he owed her one too. Regardless of whether he would offer it. An apology would not solve or change anything. That morning after back in Nice had…broken something inside of her that she did not think she could ever repair.

But perhaps they could find some common ground. A space to create two separate lives for most of the year. After all, it seemed like they'd mostly fooled the press. Maybe Aristide wasn't yet viewed as a paragon of virtue, but that would take time. As long as they stayed married and he stayed out of trouble, it should be an eventuality that came sooner rather than later.

That had been the plan anyway. Not chemistry. Not sex. Not love—that fairy tale, that *parasite* as Aristide had called it. And it was all those things, surely, if it made her feel like *this.*

She decided to take a walk on the beach to plan out what she would say to him, but the moment she stepped onto the sand she saw him in the distance. His back was to her, but he stood there on the beach, shirtless, dark swim trunks low on his hips. His hair was wet.

In front of him was the dog he'd allegedly bought her as a present.

"Stay," he ordered the dog. "Please."

At the *please* the dog went from a sitting position to a lying one. Aristide slowly began to back away from the dog—whose tail wagged harder and harder. The dog began to whimper, but it stayed.

At a certain point, Aristide stopped walking away from the dog. He turned a little, though she didn't think he'd seen her yet, but she could see his profile. A smile curved his lips. Something sharp and painful settled in her heart. A longing so deep her eyes filled with tears.

"Come," he ordered the dog and the dog leaped to its feet and bounded for him. He knelt in the sand and caught the dog's happy approach, running large hands over the dog and praising it for being a good boy.

Francesca stood frozen, watching the whole tableau play out. And she realized then and there what the real problem was. Because she had spent lifetimes convincing herself of fictions to get through the day. Finding dreams to reach for so she didn't get mired in the realities of her present.

But this was no fiction or dream. It was simply what she felt. Somewhere along the way, she'd fallen in love with him. Not just lust, not just interest, but actual love. That was the terrible choking feeling that kept taking up residence in her lungs.

That first week, he'd given her something no one ever had. And that had opened something inside of her. Not just a chance to look and enjoy her own wants and desires, but a chance to see herself as a free adult human being.

And in doing so, she'd seen him as an adult human being. Who was kind, and messed up, yes, but strong and solid and noble, whether he believed it about himself or not.

So she'd fallen in love with him—foolish, parasite—it didn't matter. That was the feeling in her chest, and it would always be there. Causing her pain.

Because she knew, even if he ever fell in love in return, he would only view it as the enemy. As the *parasite*. There were no happy endings for her. There never had been.

But she could find a *good* ending nonetheless. A solid one. She would find it, even in the midst of this swirling realization, because she would not find herself in another prison. She would make the best of her reality. Always.

He turned suddenly, as if he'd sensed her there. But he must have heard something or seen her out of the corner of his eye.

For long, ticking seconds they only stared at each other. Across the expanse of a beach. She wanted to run to him. She wanted to run away. And she did neither.

Eventually, he walked to her, the dog staying put as if he'd given it an order to stay. When he finally approached, he surveyed her outfit. Casual pants, sneakers and a T-shirt.

"You are not dressed to swim," he observed.

Francesca looked out at the waves lapping against the beach. "No, I don't feel much like swimming." All those things she'd found joy in felt tainted now. Maybe that feeling would fade, but for now she had no interest in throwing herself into the waves. Because it felt like that was something *he'd* given to her.

Kindness, then cruelty. The swims, the cooking lessons, the dog whimpering off in the distance clearly wanting the go-ahead to run to them. She could not make sense of him. "Why are you so…determined to give me things I want? When it is quite clear you don't want *me*." She had to account for the heat in his gaze. "At least, you don't *want* to want me."

He was very quiet for a while, but she didn't move. Didn't take the question back. When he spoke, his voice was low.

"I needed a certain kind of wife. And wives being people aren't simply tools that one can use and discard in a closet."

"Hmm." There was that kindness again, but it wasn't about *her*, was it? "So, it is a kind of payment." Which felt…depressing. That he'd offered her things, that he'd listened and made her feel heard, only as some kind of payment.

His eyebrows drew together. "I suppose." But she could tell the way he agreed reluctantly that he didn't *actually* agree.

It didn't matter. She had things to say, and although she wasn't as prepared as she'd liked to be to say them, she needed to get it done. She met his gaze, chin raised, as if she was going to battle.

Because it felt like she was.

"I'd like to stay here while you go to London. We can pare back our outings at this point, I believe. You can focus on business. It is the natural progression of a marriage. Perhaps I'll find some sort of charitable endeavor to focus on so it seems as if I have work too. Should a large event come up, I will of course attend. If we need to be seen together, we will."

He did not say anything. He studied her with a faintly

puzzled frown. So she kept talking. She needed to get it all out.

"And I would like to apologize."

The puzzled frown turned into an all-out confused scowl. "For what?"

"I should not have…pushed. *Maneuvered* you, as you said. We do not have to be at odds anymore. You were right. I will keep my distance and this will go back to what it was meant to be. A business deal. Your reputation. My freedom. Two separate, safe, content entities working together on occasion."

She forced her mouth to curve pleasantly, even though she felt positively dead inside. "So, I will leave you to your morning." She marched past him, toward the dog. "And I'll collect my present. Come," she instructed to the dog, who immediately raced up to her, then pranced about her feet as she walked resolutely down the beach.

She didn't have a destination in mind. She'd just keep marching until the threat of tears was gone.

The dog, naturally, followed her command without a second of concern for him and with none of the disobedience it had shown Aristide the past few days. Only making *some* progress today.

Well, he supposed the obedience was because of him. She could thank him later.

When? When she doesn't go to London with you?

And he was left standing on the beach as though a bomb had just detonated in his chest while her and the dog's form got smaller and smaller.

When, really, this was ideal. Time apart would be good for them. No doubt with some space they could get back to how it had been in the beginning, as she'd suggested. An easy kind of…friendship wasn't the right word. She'd said business deal, but he didn't love that phrase either.

Well, it didn't matter what they called it. Everything was back on clear, even ground where they belonged.

But she didn't come to lunch or dinner that night, even though he'd sent a staff member to fetch her. They'd returned, looking uncomfortable, with news that Francesca preferred to eat in her room as the dog would no doubt misbehave in the dining room.

The following day, he'd hoped he might catch her for a walk on the beach—she'd taken over the care of the dog, so certainly he'd have to run into her outside at some point.

But he never did.

Knowing she was here had been one thing when he'd thought she was angry with him. He was used to anger. To being shut out because he had disappointed or hurt someone. Everything he'd done during those first three days they'd been here had been *at* that anger. Take care of her idiot dog, work as though he was not upset or preoccupied, dine with his mother and such. He'd done it to prove her anger had no sway over him.

And he'd felt all of thirteen, existing in the icy silences of Valentino's determination that there was nothing more between them now that they shared a terrible father.

But now he knew she wasn't angry, or at least said she wasn't, and he didn't know what to do with the tired way she'd come to him with a truce of sorts. How she'd *apologized*. How he was supposed to feel as settled as though they were on the same page, when it seemed she was still avoiding him.

Well, he did not have to be avoided in his own home. He did not have to use his staff as *messengers*. He stood, forgetting his half-eaten dinner and strode across the castle to her suite of rooms. He knocked on her main door—with probably more force than necessary—and warned himself to get his strange, confusing, tempestuous feelings under control.

He would not take them out on her. That was not who he was. And he didn't *need* her. To be his dinner companion. To *need* to be his. *Need* had no place here.

This clawing feeling inside of him wasn't any of the things his mother had talked about. No. They were just needing this settled, when clearly if she was avoiding him, *she* was not settled.

Francesca opened her suite door, a careful look on her face. He thought she was trying to look placid, but he saw the trepidation and suspicion in her dark gaze.

She had opened the door wide, but she still held on to it, like it might be needed to shut it in his face. The dog was curled up by the unnecessary fire in the hearth.

Everything about the scene was cozy, down to what she wore. Despite the fact fall was on the way, it still felt like summer, but she was dressed in soft, fuzzy material meant for lounging. She looked so…soft. Infinitely touchable.

He shoved his hands in his pockets. *He* was the one who'd drawn that line, had he not? "I came to tell you I am going to London in the morning," he said stiffly.

She smiled, with absolutely no warmth. "Excellent. I hope you have a wonderful trip."

"I'd like you to join me at the end of the week to attend a fundraiser."

She nodded, still gripping the door. "Naturally."

That should be it. Their staff would handle the arrangements and he would see her again in London at the end of the week.

"Have you ever been to the National Gallery?" he asked.

"Well, no."

"We can go together the following day." They should do more than events, after all. Keep the stories about them.

"For a photo op?" she asked, carefully.

Yes, that was what he'd been thinking. He should nod and agree. But something about the scene in front of him had him...wanting to be a part of it. "It does not have to be."

"Then I would not want to intrude on your schedule." She smiled blandly at him. Like she had in those first moments he'd stolen her away from Vale. She'd held her own but kept herself carefully under wraps. "I'm sure I can handle a visit on my own."

"It does not suit our image if you're wandering about the museum without my company."

She nodded thoughtfully at that. "Well, perhaps another time, then."

Because she'd rather not go than be with him at all. After...making amends. After apologizing to him. She made no earthly sense. And it should make him angry. He was angry.

That was the twisting, clawing feeling inside of him. Anger, not panic. Control, not loss.

"Was there anything else?" she asked, sounding vaguely curious when he could see exactly what she wanted in her eyes. She wanted him to leave.

Leave.

"Breakfast. We will eat a meal together before I go." He did not dress it up as a question, because it was an order.

She looked back at her *dog*, lolling in front of the fire like some kind of boneless creature with fur. "Liborio is still learning his table manners." She returned her gaze to him with that fake mask of a smile. "Perhaps when you return."

It was not a real excuse. The dog didn't *need* to eat with them. And he could have pointed that out. Might have, if there was not some hint of vulnerability underneath that mask she'd once worn so well.

But he could see under it now. He could see *her* now.

"Is that disastrous dog really deserving of such a name?"

For a moment, just the smallest, quickest moment, he saw the flash of temper in her eyes. One he would have welcomed in the here and now, because it was more like… before. When they had enjoyed each other's company. Before everything had been complicated by crossing *lines*— just like he'd known everything would be.

Without answering his question, she stepped back, and didn't meet his gaze. "Good night, Aristide."

And she closed the door. Gently. But in his face all the same.

CHAPTER FOURTEEN

WITH ARISTIDE GONE to London, Francesca put herself
to work. Mostly on training Liborio, who was indeed a
bit of a disaster. But a wonderful one. He gave her a purpose and company. She didn't feel quite so lonely with
Liborio in tow.

Mostly.

But she refused to think about what the castle felt like
without Aristide's presence in it. Empty and like all the
color was muted. She focused on a list of to-dos she curated for herself instead.

She went through Aristide's charitable endeavors. The
ones he kept quiet. Looking for an idea of how she might
spend her now ample free time. She had always managed
her father's life, but Aristide had a staff in place for that.
Perhaps she should take over some of it, but right now she
still felt too raw to insert herself into his plans.

No, she'd find something for herself. Perhaps she could
throw her own version of a fundraiser here for one of the
organizations he'd donated to. Before she could really dig
into a plan, though, she was interrupted by a staff member entering the room.

"Signora Bonaparte. There is a phone call for you."

She blinked once at Luca. She was almost used to

being called Bonaparte now, but it was the idea that someone was calling the house to talk to her that made her feel…out of place. She couldn't think of a single person who would do so rather than call her mobile.

Except…perhaps Aristide. The way her heart leaped at the thought was downright *depressing*. And still, she reached for the phone with a terrible bubble of hope in her throat that she didn't want.

She didn't want him or love or hope. She wanted her old certainty back. Her old purpose back. Somehow, Aristide had taken that away from her and she didn't know what to *do*.

Blowing out an irritated breath, she held the phone to her ear. "Hello?"

"Buon giorno, Francesca. This is Ginevra. Aristide's mother."

"Oh." She tried to find something to say to that, but she didn't know why Aristide's mother would be calling her when Francesca hadn't even shown up to the dinner they'd had a few nights ago.

"I thought perhaps if you weren't busy this afternoon, you could come to tea. I have an open afternoon and would love to get to know you."

Again, the only thing Francesca could think to say was, "Oh."

"And bring your dog, if you'd like."

She looked down at Liborio, who was on his back, wriggling around, as if trying to reach some itch. "I…" She didn't want to go over there. Maybe she should claim illness again.

"See you at two, then," Ginevra said cheerfully, and then the line went dead.

Ending any possibility of refusing. Francesca stared at the phone in her hand for some time before it penetrated that she needed to hang up the phone. Probably fix her makeup a bit. Find Liborio's leash. If they left now, they could walk over to the main Bonaparte estate and arrive on time.

So, that was what she did. Hoping the walk would settle her some, give her some ideas on how to talk to Ginevra. Regardless of her feelings for Aristide, she was married to him for the long haul. She wanted to be…well, not his friend. That hurt too much. But a separate partner, and that certainly meant being on his mother's good side would be a positive.

She set out across the island, chastising the eager dog for pulling on his leash. Summer's heat had lifted, and though when it was sunny it could still be quite warm, fall was making its way onto the island.

When she arrived at the titular Bonaparte residence, she did not feel any affinity for the classically beautiful and historic estate. It felt…cold. A defiant slap of man against the wild, instead of Aristide's artistic, wild partnership with it.

Which was neither here nor there. She picked her way up the yard to the main entrance. The door was wide open, and a woman stood there. Liborio immediately started yipping happily but Francesca kept a firm grip on the leash.

She needed *something* to grip on to. She plastered an old, polite smile on her face as she approached Aristide's mother. "Good afternoon…" She trailed off because she realized the woman wouldn't have the last name Bonaparte, so she did not know how to address her.

But the woman smiled all the same. "It is good to see you again, Francesca. Please, don't hesitate to call me Ginevra." She looked warmly from Francesca to Liborio's wriggling body.

"I heard Aristide was in London and you'd stayed behind. Perhaps I should have waited for him to return, but it seemed like the perfect time to meet my daughter-in-law without my son to color the meeting." She knelt down to meet Liborio's incessant barks. "And to see this one again." She scrubbed her hands over his fur. "He is a prize."

"Aristide...picked him out."

Ginevra leaned back on her heels, looked up at Francesca speculatively. "Fascinating." Then she straightened. "Well, come. Follow me inside. Milo is on the mainland, and a woman can only polish the sconces so many times, even in a house such as this. So it seemed the perfect day for an elaborate tea and some company."

"I can tie Liborio outside if—"

"Nonsense. Bring him in. Liborio. What a clever name."

Francesca followed her inside. A grand foyer, an even grander main room. All dark woods and what must be ancient art and furniture, very well-tended but...dark. Stuffy. Overbearing. Until they moved into a small room off the kitchen. A sort of breakfast nook. Bright and colorful. Whimsical enough to remind her of Aristide.

He had spoken of his mother's love for his father in terrible terms like *parasite*. Vale, if he'd deigned to speak about his father—never his mother—had been much the same. And it made no sense to Francesca either, that all this light and color would stay amid all that dark.

"Sit. Sit. Nothing formal." Ginevra smiled, pointing at a table already piled high with tiny sandwiches and cakes and a pretty, floral teapot.

Francesca took a seat, quietly ordered Liborio to sit— which he thankfully did, panting up at the two women happily.

"I was sorry to have missed you the other evening," Francesca said as Ginevra poured. "I wasn't feeling quite up to it."

"You and Aristide were having a fight. I wouldn't want to sit at a dinner with anyone either in that situation."

Francesca opened her mouth to argue, even if it would have been a lie, but she saw a knowing kind of look on Ginevra's face. Had Aristide *told* his mother they were fighting?

"I couldn't get the whole truth out of him, of course," Ginevra continued with an easy wave of the hand. Everything about her was so...*effortless*. "He hasn't told me a whole truth since he was thirteen."

Thirteen. Yes, she supposed a lot of Aristide had changed at that moment. Finding out his real father, somehow gaining and losing a brother in one fell swoop.

"Though this time it wasn't so much that he didn't want to tell me what was wrong, it was more he could not seem to figure out what he did wrong."

"He didn't do anything wrong." Francesca looked down at her hands. How awkward this all was.

"Ah, I do not wish to make you uncomfortable, if you don't want to discuss it. I just know how...contained Aristide can be. And how isolated this island can be. I wanted you to know, you can view me as a friend. And I happen to be a friend who...well, I don't know that I *understand* my son, but I see him better than most. So many don't see the real him because he can put on a show. Like his father."

Ginevra was about the only person Francesca thought she'd seen smile when mentioning the feared Milo Bonaparte.

"Having met…all of you now, I think Aristide takes after you more than Mr. Bonaparte."

Ginevra cocked her head and studied her as she piled two plates high with all manner of treats. She put one in front of Francesca, and one in front of herself, then tossed a little piece of biscuit to Liborio.

"I doubt he would agree with you, but I am glad to hear it. I've always thought so myself, but Aristide is good at… masks." Ginevra took a hefty bite of a sandwich, then chewed thoughtfully. Her gaze seemed to flit about the pretty room, the dog, but then zeroed in on Francesca.

"And so are you. You're not quite like how I remember you when you were with Vale."

Francesca didn't know what to say. Ginevra didn't say it scathingly or accusingly, but it was still…touchy. She had jumped from marrying one brother to another. In one day.

"Vale was never mine, of course, but I cared for both boys. As best I could. I'm not holding moving from one to another against you. I know how easy it is for people to look at a situation and judge it. *I* am a judgment-free zone."

Francesca did not know this woman well enough to tell her the truth. That it was hard to be judged when she had been willing to marry either brother for those mercenary reasons that seemed so far away now, even though just over a month ago she'd still been under her father's thumb.

She should be happy, really, that her problems now were not being worried about life and limb. Just the state of her foolish heart.

"You know, dining with my son earlier this week reminded me of when he was younger. When he and Vale had their falling out. He is very good at *reacting*, but not always so good at understanding."

Francesca didn't laugh exactly, but it verbalized what she felt about trying to get through to Aristide. He had all his lines, all his ideas, and in his mind everything had to follow. If it didn't, he didn't find out why. He simply... shut it down.

"But I suppose that is our relationship. A lack of understanding. He does not understand why I stay. What being needed means to me. We don't understand each other, I suppose, since he has made certain to build a life where no one needs him, and he is not needed anywhere. That makes *me* sad, but perhaps it makes him happy." Ginevra reached across the table and took Francesca's hands. "I would so like it if you could make him happy."

Francesca looked into the woman's warm, dark eyes. "By...needing him?"

Ginevra nodded.

But it landed in Francesca all wrong. It wasn't *need* she felt. Need was not...a choice. Need made it sound like an addiction, a cure to a disease. This horrible feeling inside of her that ate her up wasn't need, because she could live without it. She would happily live without it.

It wasn't that she *needed* him. It was that she wanted him. To do nice things for her, while she took care of him. She wanted some semblance of…connecting. She did not want to be stuck in a mausoleum, waiting on him, all to feel needed.

No, she understood Aristide's position on his mother, because she knew Milo. She wouldn't judge Ginevra. Perhaps there was something in the odious man that worked for her, but Francesca could not call it love.

It reminded her too much of her father's control. A man who would continue to treat the woman he'd fathered a child with as an *employee*. Who allowed her to have no say, no visibility in his life. This was not a man in love.

"I don't need Aristide, and he doesn't need me," Francesca said gently, hoping to explain it in a way that might make sense to Ginevra. "I think…we have made great mistakes with each other on a personal level, but we can be… Well, our relationship won't be about love or need. It's more a…partnership."

Ginevra studied her for a long while, still holding Francesca's hands. "Forgiveness of mistakes is a choice."

Francesca didn't doubt it, but she could not continue to forgive someone for the same thing for thirty years. She couldn't hide herself hoping for a crumb or a morsel of need. No, this was not the life she wanted for herself, regardless of Aristide.

"I think…love might be too." She thought about the *before*, when she'd been falling in love with Aristide. Perhaps she could have stopped it, but she hadn't because loving him opened up a lifetime of wonderful possibilities.

For him, it wasn't that he did not have some feeling for her, it was that he did not like the possibilities her love offered.

So, they had chosen. And that was that.

She changed the subject to dogs, to the weather, to the decor in this room. They had a lovely little tea and spoke of superficial topics from that point on. Still, it was nice. It didn't feel like a performance so much as the layers to a possible friendship. Sometimes serious, sometimes not.

When she got up, she allowed Ginevra to hug her. And when she said, "Thank you," she meant it.

Ginevra pulled back, held Francesca by the elbows. "I always dreamed of a daughter. It would be my great pleasure if this could become a weekly occurrence for us. Regardless of love and Aristide and Milo, I would like to be friends with you, Francesca." She smiled.

A lump clogged Francesca's throat. To think she could be friends with someone at all, let alone when they didn't agree, felt like…an epiphany. "I'd like that." She looked down at Liborio's happy panting. "He would too."

"Excellent. We will consider it a date."

Aristide paced the main room in his modern London apartment. He'd purchased it as a direct contrast to Valentino's staid, upstanding home here. He had wanted to highlight those differences, always. It had felt like *proving* something.

But he realized starkly in this moment as he waited for Francesca, tied up over Francesca, *desperate and aching* over that woman, that every petty little thing he'd done in the past twenty years *at* his brother had only been this.

Trying to get his attention. Because he didn't have the words, didn't know how to tell Valentino what he wanted—a brother, a relationship, some reparation now that he had almost fully eradicated Milo from his life.

So, unlike his castle back on the island that he had

built *mostly* for himself, and only a *little* at Valentino and Milo, this ugly, empty, monstrosity of an apartment brought him no joy.

He wanted to turn his anger at this to Francesca. How would he have realized these gestures were so pathetic and empty if she hadn't accused him of hiding his wants?

So all this pain, this upheaval, this *emptiness* was her fault and she wasn't *here*.

She had agreed to come, and they would need to leave for the event soon. So not only was she at fault for the roiling disarray inside of him, but she was *late*. It stoked his temper even higher.

Surely it was *temper*, not fear. What did he have to be afraid of?

He heard voices in the foyer, and then Francesca *finally* appeared. She smiled at him, that bland, heiress smile from *before*. She was already dressed for the fundraising event. A simple black dress, not going too far toward staid matron, but not quite the sparkly purple contraption that still haunted his dreams.

"Are you ready to go?" she asked by way of greeting.

"No dog in tow?" he asked, and he knew it sounded like a growl, like an accusation. He did not know what to do to stop it. Because *she* was the only one who ever stripped away his control.

She was the problem.

"Your mother was kind enough to offer to watch him. She's quite fond of him."

"My mother."

"Yes. We had tea yesterday. I quite like her." The fake smile warmed a degree. "I think you take after her more than you'd like to admit."

She said this like a compliment when it was the *worst* thing that she could have said to him. Was this awful, roiling thing inside of him what his mother felt for Milo? Was this the *need* she spoke of that made her put a terrible, horrible man above all else?

But Francesca isn't terrible. He didn't know where that voice in his head came from. He could only stare at her, terrified she had ruined him irreparably.

"What have you done to me?" he demanded, at his wits' end. Because he did not recognize this version of himself. The kind that couldn't let go. He had always set people aside. Built an armor that kept *out* anyone who wanted in.

He did not *need*. He was not a glutton for punishment. He did not demand to be in the orbit of people who didn't want him.

Because no one does.

His chest felt tight. He wanted to believe that very clear message life had taught him, but she kept being here, kept…hurting him by simply existing. And he did not know how to permanently set her aside. He kept *wanting* her.

And it felt so uncomfortably like the *need* his mother spoke of, he wanted to rip this apartment down to the studs with his two bare hands.

Her eyebrows had gone up and she studied him with that detached way she had with *other* people. She wasn't supposed to have it with him. Why could *she* control this?

"I don't understand what you mean," she said, carefully enunciating each word.

But neither did he. He didn't understand *any* of this.

Except he wanted his hands on her. He wanted to forget

his lines ever existed. He wanted to watch her swim and take her to bed and bring her a million gifts so she would smile at him like she had when he'd tasted her first cake.

"What you want could matter if you would tell me," she had said to him. Naked in his bed. Hurt, from the words and accusations he'd hurled at her.

But how did he tell her what he wanted? When that seemed to ensure he would never, ever have it?

"If we plan it out, we could have a child," he said, and he *heard* his own desperation, the beat of panic at offering such a ridiculous thing. But this would work... It would have to work. She'd been so upset about not being pregnant, and even if she should have been relieved, she hadn't been. She wanted a child and... And...and...

Much like with the dog, this did not have the desired effect. She did not look happy or excited. She didn't even look detached anymore. She looked furious.

"Oh, could we?"

And sounded more so.

"I am trying to give you what you want," he ground out, wondering why she had to make that so damn difficult. Why he couldn't make her respond the way she was *supposed* to.

She shook her head. "No. I don't know what you're trying to do, but throwing *gifts* at me as if I'm supposed to be constantly grateful to you is... It has to stop. Now, we should go or we will be late and people will talk."

"I do not want to go."

She rolled her eyes at him. "Ah. What would *you* like to do then, Aristide? Or can you find the words to say even that?"

"I want..." Something was crashing inside of him,

crumbling into nothing but dust. His very bones perhaps. What did he want? Not this. Not this crushing. Not this *need* that would destroy him and her.

He wasn't sure he could *breathe*. Something in her expression changed like she could see that. Some of her anger softened. "Perhaps I was wrong," she said quietly. "I assumed you kept what you want hidden, but maybe you truly don't even know what you want."

I want you. I want you. I want you.

But he couldn't say that. If he did... If he did...

"I find that sad, but I am slowly realizing what *I* want in the wake of all this, and it isn't...what we're doing. It isn't misery and shouting matches and...whatever this is."

"What are you saying?"

"We should take some time apart. Really apart. If people begin to talk, we'll come up with a story. But I think we need some time away for the dust to settle."

"No."

"Aristide."

She sounded so *tired*, so *resigned*. When she was the one who'd upended *his* life. "You did this."

She shook her head. "No. No. I'm not doing this." She whirled around, ready to march out of the room no doubt, but he grabbed her arm.

And found absolutely no words when she glared at him.

"How about this, Aristide. Maybe *this* will get through to you." She sucked in a breath and let it out and continued with words that made absolutely no sense. "I love you."

It was like being lanced clean through. A sharp, unbearable pain. He thought perhaps he'd even stumbled back, but he wasn't sure he could feel his body.

"And I know you do not want that. *I* don't even want it. But I cannot seem to make it go away. So being near you hurts. And I will not put myself through any *hurt* just because..." She waved a hand at him. "I want... more. I rather enjoy—or at least enjoyed—your company. Perhaps I pushed too hard too fast at that first taste of freedom, but I like working together. I like you. What I want is not a child or a dog plopped down in the absence of feeling. I don't want *needs* overriding choice. I want a life."

Life. Every time he'd hoped for *life*—a brother, a father, a mother who put him above the man who *needed* her, he had been rebuffed. So he had built a life that demanded nothing of him. Because that was all he was meant for. "I cannot give that to you, Francesca."

"I didn't ask you to. I told you what I wanted. You have given me much, Aristide, but I never asked any of it *from* you. You saw it, decided to give it. All on your own."

"I don't know what you're talking about." Because that made it sound like...he'd done it on purpose when it was just...

She laughed. Bitterly. "No. Baking lessons and ridiculous dogs were certainly not *your* choices. You go out of your way to make everyone in your path happy."

If only that were true. But he could not think of a single person in his path who was *happy*. "You don't seem happy."

"No, but that is *me*, Aristide. I am not happy because no amount of *things* you throw at me can change the fact that I want more. Like I said. A *life*."

He did not mean to say the words in his head. He'd meant to keep them to himself. "I don't have that in me."

For a moment, when he caught just a flash on her face of some kind of sympathy, he thought it might be all right. She'd feel sorry for him enough to *stop* this. Or to fix it, somehow. She with her plans and her strength, she could fix it.

But it was only a flash.

"Do you not have it in you, or are you afraid that it will be difficult? That you will make mistakes? That we will fight and feel things that hurt?" She shook her head, and tears were filling her eyes but they didn't fall. "Aristide, we are not our parents. We are not simply *pain* dressed up in skin. We get to decide these things. What we want. What we love. What we stand for. But you are afraid to open your eyes."

And she said that with such dismissiveness, more words he didn't mean to say poured out. "I am *afraid* that I will destroy you."

Like I destroy all relationships.

He never meant to. They just all crumbled in his hands.

"Because once upon a time your brother could not handle the truth?" she demanded, somehow seeing through him when he barely saw through himself. "A truth neither of you have ever once addressed in nearly twenty years. Because you do not understand your mother and she does not understand you? What other relationship have you ever attempted?"

He wanted to find some way to stop her. Stop *this*, but she just kept talking. Each word a sharp stab of pain. Of truth.

"None, is the answer, Aristide. Something painful happened to you at thirteen, and you shut yourself off from all other painful things. Because you had the *luxury* to do so. Well, I never had that choice, so I guess I never learned how to deal with them like an adult." She shook her head. "Maybe love itself is not a choice, but doing something about it is, and we have made our choices."

She kept saying *love*, like it did nothing but backfire. Disappoint. *Hurt*.

"Actually, I take that back. *I* have made my choice. Per usual, you have let all the choices of others fall on your shoulders so you can disengage and blame someone else. If you want me, Aristide, if you love me, you will have to *choose*. I cannot do it for you, and even if I could, I wouldn't. Give the hosts my apologies. I cannot be near you right now. I cannot…*do this* with you anymore."

And as quickly as she'd arrived, she left, and somehow, he felt worse.

Worst of all, for the first time in his life, he had no one to blame but himself.

Which meant, he was the only one who could fix this. The only one who could…lay himself bare. Say what he wanted. Like she had done.

And trust that his angel, his life, his *love* was strong enough to handle it.

CHAPTER FIFTEEN

FRANCESCA DID NOT know where to go. She only knew that she *had* to go.

"If we plan it out, we could have a child."

How could he hurt her so much without even meaning to? Because for all his faults, she knew there had been something genuine in that offer. Not about having a child but giving her something he thought would make her happy. He hadn't meant for it to hurt.

And she wanted it so badly, it nearly cut her in two. But she couldn't stand the idea of sobbing in front of him right now. She needed to make this stand. They could not keep hurting each other if he was not willing to *grow*. To be brave.

She had not been to Aristide's London apartment before, and she did not know her way around. She should march back out the front door, but one of the staff members had taken her things and put them somewhere. She at least needed her purse so she needed to find…someone to tell her where to go.

But the apartment seemed deserted, and every room she stuck her head into offered little help, until she came across the strangest thing. A wall of glass, and on the other side of it…a pool.

So surprised by this, she went for the door. When she stepped inside, the air hit her, heavy and warm, like an embrace. Big potted plants were clustered in different corners of the room so that it was a bit like a tropical oasis. The pool was not large, but it was blue and flashed invitingly under the overhead lights.

She moved forward until she was standing at the edge of the pool. Somehow swimming had become the first beacon of her freedom. This wasn't the ocean, but…she just needed to do something. Act.

Feel.

She jumped in. It was foolish. Worse even than skinny-dipping as she was probably ruining her clothes. What would she do when she emerged? She had no towel, no change of clothes.

But she had found her joy in the water. In throwing herself into the waves that first week of freedom. She had felt baptized and sure and made new, and she needed *something* to make her feel that again. Even if it was the most nonsensical thing she'd ever done.

Falling in love is the most nonsensical thing you've ever done, some harsh voice in her head whispered.

And fair enough. It was certainly why she was here. When she should have known better. Should have some-how predicted he would make the most insulting, hurtful offer he could muster.

"If we plan it out, we could have a child."

Like it was a bargaining chip. A *bribe*. Only she couldn't decide what he wanted from her. Not love. Not a true wife. So *what*?

He thought she'd *done* something to him, but he'd rejected her. Set her aside. Made it very clear his lines were all he wanted. And he couldn't *love*.

What rot.

She let herself submerge under the water completely. Ruining her makeup, no doubt. Her careful updo. Ruining *everything*.

She welcomed it. Never in her life had she been allowed to ruin anything without consequences, and so this was just another freedom. She resurfaced once her lungs couldn't hold any longer, making sure her hair was swept off her face as she stood again. If she was crying, she couldn't tell because she was now wet straight through.

But the ragged breath that came out of her sure sounded like a sob that echoed around the room. But after that echo there was…another sound. She looked over at the entrance to the room.

Aristide.

Looking like some sort of avenging god as he strode across the tile to the stairs into the pool. Her breath caught in her throat, even though she did not want to fight with him any longer. She didn't want *this* any longer. She wanted…

Oh, if only she knew what she wanted that didn't involve *him*.

He didn't *stop* his approach. He didn't demand she get out of the pool like Francesca expected. He walked right into the water. Suit and all. Right toward her. Strong, impatient strides like the water was nothing. "I do not like who I am when you are away," he bit out like an accusation. "I do not like who I am when we are fighting. I do not like the idea I have…hurt you."

She wanted to swim away but found herself rooted to the spot by his hot gaze and angry mouth and the fact he had not left her. He had…come after her. Like there

could be change, growth. Like maybe… But his words…
My God, the man was dense.

"The *idea*? You *did* hurt me. You hurt me on purpose."

He shook his head, moving closer still. "On purpose
would mean I did anything *to* hurt you, but all I keep trying to do is to *save* you." He held out his hands, palms
up. "Don't you *see*?"

But his hands were empty, and even though he looked
anguished, she very much did *not* see. She knew she
should turn away. Knew she shouldn't let him do whatever this was.

But she loved him, for good or for ill, and she did not
know how to turn her back on this love even if it would
save her from more hurt.

Maybe, just maybe, the hurt was worth it if love was
the end result.

"I do not know how to hold the people I love without…
sending them away. Without them sending *me* away," he
said, each word a pained confession from deep within.

Love. Her heart leaped, even though it had no business
doing so. "Do you think I would?" she managed through
a voice little more than croak.

"You already have!" he all but shouted, his voice echoing
with pain in the small room as water lapped around them.

"Because I didn't thank you for your pity dog or take you
up on the offer for a pity child?" she demanded, wounded
that he could possibly claim these things were him trying.

"It isn't pity," he growled.

"Then what is it?" she returned, wondering why she
was letting this conversation happen. Why they were
standing in a *pool*, for Heaven's sake.

"Penance!" he roared, loud and painful, like an admonition that had been wrenched out of him with great force and pain.

And she had no idea what to say to that, how to wrap her mind around such a thing. "Aristide. For *what*?"

"I have tried. To make it up to anyone. I tried to be as good as Valentino and I could not be—my father wouldn't let me be. I was…a tool to hurt his *real* son, at best. I have tried to get her to leave, to find her *own* life. But I could not convince her." He didn't need to say who. Francesca knew he meant his mother.

And she had known his parents pained him, but perhaps she had not fully understood the scars they'd left. Because he was very careful not to let that show. And could she blame him? Hadn't she hidden her father's abuse from *everyone*?

Everyone except him.

"As for Valentino…" he said roughly.

But he never finished his sentence. Never seemed to find the words to verbalize what he felt about his brother. Francesca couldn't help but wonder if it was because there was still some hope there. That half of his anguish was the continued hope that the family who had hurt him might change.

But while he waited, hoped, he had fashioned his life in the shadow of what they'd done to him—purposefully or not—and she understood that too well to keep her heart hardened to him.

She reached out and took his outstretched hands, still both of them standing in this warm pool with their dinner clothes on. "You cannot judge yourself on other people's choices, Aristide. Do you not think I hear my father's voice in my head sometimes? That I am worthless? That I deserve whatever hurts come my way?"

He made a noise of protest as he gripped her hands, but she continued on.

"Of course I do. Of course I feel that sometimes, but I refuse to let the harm he caused me define me or my life."

"Francesca."

But he said nothing else. Just her name as if it was pain, as he held her hands tightly in this pool. She wanted to laugh. She wanted to cry. But what they needed, she knew, was an answer.

An end, some little voice whispered at her. And maybe she would have listened to it just a few moments ago, but being reminded that *sometimes* the voice in her head was not her own, not about her best interests, she shoved it aside.

"Come. Let us…go have a rational conversation. Somewhere dry."

Aristide helped her out of the pool. He could not fathom how they had come to such a ridiculous situation. Soaked and fully dressed. It was out of control and solved nothing. How could this solve anything?

Except here she was. Touching him. Letting him dry her off. He moved the towel over her hair, her shoulders, while she watched him with those careful dark eyes.

He hated that she was careful with him. Hated when she put on that mask. And yet when she'd dropped it, that night all these weeks ago now, he'd hurt her. On purpose, he supposed, even if he'd been thinking more of saving himself than hurting her.

He had hurt her.

To save himself.

And that…cut him to shreds. On top of all the other things swirling inside of him, because even now, looking a bit like a wet poodle, she made him feel all of these things he had so carefully eradicated from his life. She made him *face* them, all because…

All because he loved her. Beyond any kind of reason he could find. That thing he'd been so careful to avoid. Love and need and the inevitable end of the things he cared for.

But the things she said…like ends were not inevitable. The things she'd been through and could still come out on the other side believing… She was good and whole and worthy. She was, of course. So good, his angel.

She couldn't really believe… Not when she was this driving force.

She had been trying to understand him, get to the bottom of what he wanted. And she wasn't perfect. She hadn't always used good means, but she was *trying*.

What had he done? As she'd accused him, just thrown things at her that might make her happy in the hopes he would not be called upon to do so.

He blotted her face with the towel, then dropped it and let his hands cup her skin. Damp and soft. Warm and his. Oh, how he wanted her to be his. But…

"Francesca, *mio angioletta*, I am afraid that everything I feel will hurt you."

She studied him with those serious, dark eyes. A study that spoke of great contemplation. She was weighing his words, and it hurt that she did not have an immediate response, and yet this consideration made him think that whatever she said would be true and important and deep. Not just a knee-jerk reaction.

"Maybe your feelings will hurt me, but…as you said, this is not a hurt that is *meant*, that is done *at* each other. Life…hurts. Cruelty and hurt are not the same."

"Is the bar so low that not being cruel is all you expect of me?" he murmured, brushing wet strands of hair off her face.

She shook her head, her mouth almost curving. "Aristide, I have been so angry with you, so frustrated, but it wasn't until I told you *why,* directly, that anything changed. That you walked into that pool with me. Perhaps the trick is not…worrying so much about hurting one another, but being brave enough to tell each other when we are hurt, and…jump in the metaphorical pool and work it out."

"I would give you anything."

She sighed, clearly not happy with those words, but she reached out and touched her fingertips to his cheek rather than step away. "I do not need your gifts. I need you. Not in the way your mother spoke of need. I do not think that is love, because it is one-sided. Whatever she does for your father, is one-sided. Perhaps she gets something out of it, but it isn't from *him.* I need *you.*"

He did not know how to give himself. Or maybe, he knew. However, he had never been rewarded for such a choice. But this was Francesca. Even amidst a fear born of a tempestuous childhood, he knew she was somehow the beacon of light through that.

And he would have to tell her, really admit it. Because trying to separate from her didn't work; it only made this pain worse. "I love you, and I worry that it will be the end of me. The end of you."

"Change doesn't always have to be bad, Aristide. I have changed my life for the better. Even jumping into that pool fully clothed, even fighting with you, even having my heart shattered, this is better."

He closed his eyes in pain. That so little could be better.

"And maybe it will be an end. An end of a you or a me that no longer serves us."

He scowled a bit at that. "You sound like my mother."

"I like your mother. I might not agree with her on everything, but she is… She loves you, Aristide."

"Yes." It was hard sometimes, because she had made choices that had valued his father over him. It was hard, because she was not perfect. She had deep, meaningful flaws.

But…perhaps the point was that he did not have to make the same mistakes. Perhaps the point was that the love Francesca offered him *was* love, and that meant…

Here she stood, saying she loved him. Trying to *reach* him. No one had ever done such a thing for him before, and he didn't want to trust it.

But he trusted Francesca. How could he not?

"Say it again," she said, her fingers in his hair. Her eyes large and luminous. And the warmth of her—body and soul—seeping into him. Yes, it turned out, he would risk anything for this, fight anything for this, even his own deep-seated fears.

"I love you, Francesca."

Her mouth curved, so beautiful. So perfect. His angel.

"I love you too, Aristide."

"Then we will build our life from here on out. On that love. On that promise. And I will learn how to be strong. From you. I promise you, Francesca, I am yours. Forever. If you will be mine."

"Forever," she whispered, and then pressed her mouth to his. A promise. Hope. All those things he thought were the enemy, but all they'd ever been were…

His for the taking. Just like her.

EPILOGUE

THEY RETURNED TO the island and spent the next few weeks determining how they would build this life they would share. As husband and wife. As two people who loved one another. They laid out what they wanted, and they didn't always agree, but Francesca was glad for it.

Because neither of them balked at that first fight after they'd said their *I love you*s. Oh, they'd gone to their separate corners, no doubt. Francesca had ranted to the dog while she'd taken him out on a walk. Aristides had disappeared into his gym.

And when they'd both returned home, sweaty and out of breath, they'd met there in the middle of the castle and just begun…laughing.

She knew not all arguments would be resolved so easily, so cheerfully, but some would be. It was the *life* she was after.

Just like befriending Ginevra, planning a charitable fundraising event on the island, and extending an invitation to Valentino to attend.

There'd been no response to that, but Francesca was determined, and everyone knew what happened when Francesca *determined* something.

She was gratified when Aristide stopped trying to talk

her out of it, and instead made a suggestion of his own. As they were lying in bed one night. After the *very* hard work of perhaps starting their very own family.

"We are slated to go to an event in London in a few weeks. I will head to the Diamond Club. Make certain to run into Valentino there. Offer an olive branch."

"What kind of olive branch?"

"We'll think of something."

She pressed a kiss to his beautiful shoulder. "I like the sound of *we*."

In a smooth move, he easily rolled her on top of him and grinned up at her. "A we forever, *mio angioletta*."

And nothing was better than *forever*.

When they returned to London, with the express intent of making the first step of an inroad with his brother, it was with happy news. A child on the way. Not a deal, a bribe, or unplanned. A choice. Born of love.

"He may not be ready yet," Francesca said firmly as Aristide readied himself for a visit to the Diamond Club. "But you are opening a door."

They had discussed it at length, so he nodded, even if he was not sure he was ready for this. But not only would he do anything to make his wife happy, he wanted to *try* to fix what he and Valentino had broken as young men.

She gave him a squeeze at the door and he slid his hand down her abdomen as he couldn't seem to stop himself from doing multiple times a day, marveling that a child would grow there. Their child. A mix of them both and a hope for a future.

"And I will be here, even if it remains closed. Always." She rose to her toes and brushed a kiss across his mouth.

He smiled at her, his angel, and bid her goodbye so that he could make his way to the club. Much like he had in the past, he had ways of knowing when Vale was there. How and when to show up to irritate his brother.

But that wasn't the goal tonight. He would try very hard for that not to be the end result either.

He had thought little of the Diamond Club since Francesca had swept into his life—because as much as he'd been the one to steal her—she had been the one to change everything. But it remained unchanged as ever.

The clubhouse itself was on a discreet and quiet street. Like his brother, Aristide kept a suite there. The staff was almost supernaturally excellent, capable of anticipating every whim almost before it was formed.

And so, it was easy enough to find the room where his brother sat, scowling with a drink in hand. Aristide got himself a drink before he carefully made his way over to the seat on the other side of Valentino.

When Valentino looked over, he scowled. "I do not recall inviting you to sit," Valentino said after a baleful moment. "But then, you have never needed an invitation to intrude upon me, have you?"

Aristide didn't *sigh*, though it was a hard-won thing. He had learned that sometimes…relationships took work. Time. He could not expect to undo twenty years in one moment.

Even if he could wish it. "Surely you must exhaust yourself with all of these slings and arrows, brother. Besides, it is all very boring. If you must insult me, is it too much to ask that you come up with something new?"

"If I had wanted conversation, I would have addressed my mirror," Valentino replied coldly. "That would have provided me with far more opportunity for reflection and honest interchange than whatever games it is you think you will be playing with me tonight."

They stared at each other, all of that history between them.

"I thought you should know," Aristide said after a moment, choosing each word carefully since he could just about tell that tonight would not be the night he got through to his brother. And still, he wanted to tell him. And still, he wanted to extend this olive branch in the hopes someday it would be planted and bear fruit. "It is early days, but Francesca and I are expecting a child."

Valentino stared back at him. "Why are you telling me this?"

"I appreciate your congratulations." Aristide shook his head, almost tempted to laugh. "In the past, you have had a tendency to assume the worst, so I thought you should know. My wife and I are having a baby. It is not an assault on you, or your position as heir—whatever that means with a father such as ours. I merely thought you should hear it from me."

Valentino didn't move, except to perhaps clench his glass tighter. "It is funny, is it not, that you have anointed yourself the messenger of all of these things. That despite the reception you must expect from me, you consider it your duty to fill me in. What does that say about you, I wonder?"

"Perhaps nothing," Aristide said quietly. "But then, I am the one who trusted you to remain my friend no matter what happened. You are the one who broke that trust." Not an accusation. Just the truth of what hurt. Like Francesca had taught him.

"Your mother taught me to cook and clean as a child," Valentino said instead, abruptly. "Do you remember?"

Aristide did not understand the change of direction, but he was willing to follow it.

Olive branch, he reminded himself.

"Of course I remember. I was there."

"Why?" Valentino asked, as if he was demanding to know the whys of why life existed. "Why did she do such a thing? Was it…did she get some amusement from this?"

Aristide still did not quite know how to characterize his mother. He had seen more of her in the past few weeks than he had in the past few years, as she and Francesca always had their heads together. And he had seen her in a new light, in the way she was with Francesca, offering his wife a mother she'd never had the chance to have.

It had reminded him of all the ways his mother had been good, even if there had been quite a few mistakes she'd made that hurt him deeply. She was not perfect.

Like the rest of them, she was learning as she went.

Which meant she was no one's enemy either. "Cooking and cleaning is how my mother loves, Valentino," Aristide said, trying to be gentle. "It is how she shows her love. Not quite the villain in your story, I think. Just a woman in love. For her sins."

Valentino stood abruptly. "I commend you on your ill-gotten marriage and all the many moral lessons it will teach an impressionable child," he said. And then, "As it happens, I have also married. And I'm also expecting a child."

It hurt. Not because he wasn't happy for his brother, but because Valentino said it like an accusation. Like they were still at odds and in competition, when it should be…

Aristide saw what a future *could* be. Them growing their families together, in hope and in love.

Valentino seemed to have neither at the moment, and so he wasn't ready yet. Aristide offered a wry smile. "But of course you are."

Valentino nodded. "May the cycle continue," he said, then turned on a dime and stalked away.

Aristide had finished his drink, contemplating the exchange. Still not sure why it did not hurt quite the way he'd expected. It was only when he recounted the evening to Francesca that it dawned on him.

"He was not himself. Not cool. Not calm. Not collected. I recognize the hunted look of a man not quite sure what to do with good."

"An excellent sign, then. He'll come around."

And she was right. Because Valentino did come around. With his pregnant wife, the bright and dazzling Princess Carliz, and it was clear Valentino had indeed been hunted that night. By love.

Amends were not immediate. The building of a relationship with his brother was careful, but they had both been changed by love. So it came that they found careful ways to rebuild a friendship that had been broken by young hurting hearts.

And when Milo refused to acknowledge Aristide's son as any kind of heir to the Bonaparte name—as if it would hurl that wedge back between Valentino and himself—they hadn't let him win.

It helped that Aristide was very rich on his own, of course, but neither he nor Valentino had any use for the legacy of meanness and cruelty that they had been brought up in.

It wasn't very long before Milo died, ingloriously, that Aristide and Francesca finally convinced Ginevra to move to their castle. At first, to help with their growing family.

Then, once Milo was indeed gone to hell where he belonged, and Vale suggested they turn the old Bonaparte estate into an orphanage, his mother moved there to work with the children. Francesca also lent much time to the establishment, as did their children over the years.

The Bonaparte brothers filled their island with the sound of children, of joy, of life. Something Milo would have *hated*.

But Aristide almost never thought of his own father anymore. Like Francesca had said all that time ago.

They were not their parents and they were not their pain. They got to choose.

And he had chosen his beautiful wife, his children, his brother, and love over all else.

* * * * *

COMING SOON!

We really hope you enjoyed reading this book.
If you're looking for more romance
be sure to head to the shops when
new books are available on

Thursday 15th
August

To see which titles are coming soon, please visit

millsandboon.co.uk/nextmonth

MILLS & BOON®

Coming next month

GREEK PREGNANCY CLAUSE
Maya Blake

'You have thirty seconds. Then I walk out,' Ares warned in a soft, dangerous murmur.

Odessa believed him. After all, hadn't he done that once, this man who was a world removed from the younger version she'd known. Or was he?

Hadn't he possessed this overwhelming presence even back then, only caged it better?

Now the full force of it bore down on her, Odessa was at once wary of and drawn to it, like a hapless moth dancing towards a destroying flame.

She watched, mesmerized despite herself as his folded arms slowly dropped, his large, masculine hands drawing attention to his lean hips, the dangerously evocative image he made simply by...*being*.

At what felt like the last second, she took a deep breath and took the boldest leap. 'Before my father's memorial is over, Vincenzo Bartorelli will announce our engagement.' Acid flooded her mouth at the very thought. 'I would rather jump naked into Mount Etna than marry him. So, I'd...I'd like you to say that I'm marrying you instead. And in return...' *Dio*, was she really doing this? 'And in return I'll give you whatever you want.'

Continue reading
GREEK PREGNANCY CLAUSE
Maya Blake

Available next month
millsandboon.co.uk

FOUR BRAND NEW STORIES FROM
MILLS & BOON MODERN

The same great stories you love,
a stylish new look!

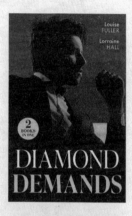

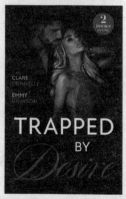

OUT NOW

MILLS & BOON

LET'S TALK

Romance

For exclusive extracts, competitions and special offers, find us online:

f MillsandBoon

X @MillsandBoon

◎ @MillsandBoonUK

♪ @MillsandBoonUK

Get in touch on 01413 063 232

For all the latest titles coming soon, visit
millsandboon.co.uk/nextmonth

Afterglow Books is a trend-led, trope-filled list of books with diverse, authentic and relatable characters, a wide array of voices and representations, plus real world trials and tribulations. Featuring all the tropes you could possibly want (think small-town settings, fake relationships, grumpy vs sunshine, enemies to lovers) and all with a generous dose of spice in every story.

♪ @millsandboonuk
⊙ @millsandboonuk
afterglowbooks.co.uk

#AfterglowBooks

For all the latest book news, exclusive content and giveaways scan the QR code below to sign up to the Afterglow newsletter: